Born in Liverpool, S.E. Moorhead has told stories since childhood and uses writing as bubblegum for her over-active brain – to keep it out of trouble. Fascinated by meaning, motivation and mystery, she studied Theology at university.

Over the last twenty-five years, apart from teaching in secondary school, S.E. Moorhead has attained a black belt in kickboxing, worked as a chaplain, established a Justice and Peace youth group, and written articles for newspapers and magazines about her work in education and religion.

She still lives in her beloved hometown with her husband Seán and two sons.

WITNESS X

S.E. Moorhead

TRAPEZE

An Hachette UK company

1 3 5 7 9 10 8 6 4 2

A CIP catalogue record for this book is
available from the British Library.

ISBN (Mass Market Paperback) 978 1409 18033 3
ISBN (eBook) 978 1 4091 80340

Typeset by Born Group

Printed and bound in Great Britain by Clays Ltd, Elcograf S.p.A.

MIX
Paper from
responsible sources
FSC® C104740

www.orionbooks.co.uk

There are things known and there are things unknown, and in between are the doors of perception.

Aldous Huxley

Prologue

I used to think of sleep as though it was swimming in a pool.
Some nights I slept deeper than others.

Now, after seeing you beneath the water, eyes open – but blind –
I wonder if death is the same, different layers, different depths.

I can't change the past.
I can only reach out so you know how much I miss you
Whilst we are absent,
one from another.

Chapter One

THURSDAY 1 FEBRUARY 2035

5.45 p.m.

The low, booming growl of mortar fire filled Kyra's head, quickly followed by the rapid crack of gunshots. She was still sightless, but all around her she could hear bawled orders and yelps of pain. Over everything was a blanket of suffocating heat.

She jolted backwards as the visual burst into life and she saw figures in desert camouflage uniform, carrying weapons as they ran for cover, like a horrifying clip from a war movie. In front of her eyes – no, she had to remind herself it wasn't her eyes, but *his* eyes – a crumbling wall exploded into rubble. Everything became a blur of yellows, brown and khakis beneath sunlight so harsh it hurt to look.

Was this Afghanistan? Basra? Helmand, maybe? It took her back to when she was a child, playing with Emma on the carpet while her dad watched the news on the screen.

The scene suddenly switched, the desert sun setting low, a melting golden ball sinking into the horizon, the sky daubed with dazzling orange and lilac. Kyra dropped her gaze to see desert fatigues, well-worn army boots and a rifle clutched in her hands. Some instinct told her it was a 59 Minimi, even though she'd never held a gun in her life. She inspected the smattering of fair hairs catching the light, the muscles that tensed beneath the freckled skin. These weren't her hands, her arms.

They were Brownrigg's.

Night fell – hot, dusty, black. Not city black, like she was used to, where the light pollution sent out a constant glow. This darkness was an inky cloud smothering her, pitch pouring into her eyes, her ears, her mouth, so that it was difficult to breathe. Had she lost transference? But her eyes slowly adjusted and she gazed around.

Up ahead, she saw the tiny glimmering lights of oil lamps in the small square cut-out windows of mud-built, flat-roofed houses. Clusters of shrubs and grasses rose behind them and beyond those, sand and rock that she imagined stretched as far as the horizon. She made a few more observations through Brownrigg's eyes, registering and logging details, as his body swivelled round until her gaze came to rest on two soldiers, one male, one female. Brownrigg held his fist up and they stopped still.

There was no sound. Kyra tapped her VR headset. Then there was a crackling in her ear and a voice came over a radio. 'Execute.'

Brownrigg jabbed a single finger and led the others towards the houses. She could feel the grit of tiny stones beneath his boots as he crept forwards. There were three wooden doors in the small complex. Kyra watched as he directed the two soldiers to the outer ones, and he stood in front of the central one. A three-finger countdown and they disappeared into the buildings. Brownrigg entered blind, his gun pointing ahead. She could feel his heart rate rising. There was no night vision device, the only light a small torch attached to the barrel of the gun, casting a tiny beam of brightness around as he searched the property.

'Clear!' came the male soldier's voice.

'Clear!' echoed the woman.

A movement ahead caused Kyra to catch her breath. Brownrigg crept closer to examine a bundle of rags on the ground. She could feel the tension in his shoulders as he held his rifle close to his chest. The scraps of cloth at his feet appeared to squirm. She felt his body as he stepped back into stance, his finger twitching at the trigger.

A small, fragile hand appeared slowly from beneath the rags, then the fevered face of a young boy. Brownrigg immediately relaxed his body and blew out a lungful of air. He swung his rifle round on its strap, so that it rested against his shoulder blades, and knelt down.

'You okay, mate? Feeling poorly?' The boy looked blankly at him. Brownrigg reached out to feel his forehead. The child moaned and tried to move away.

'Don't worry, mate, we'll get you some help.' He sat back on his haunches and went to reach for his radio. As he did so, the boy's other hand shot out from beneath the material. He was holding a curved, rusted blade. He lashed out awkwardly at Brownrigg but it was enough to do damage.

A poker-hot sensation traced a jagged line across Kyra's throat followed by a burst of adrenaline and panic coursing through her body – through Brownrigg's body – as he jerked backwards. The child jumped up, shedding the tattered cloth, face jubilant.

Outside the house, a man shouted unrecognisable words and the boy stood up straight, alert. The crack of a rifle cut the voice dead.

The child hesitated, blade still in his hand, then spat viciously in Brownrigg's face as he lay grappling at his throat, the blood seeping wet and hot through his fingers.

Then the boy ran out of the door.

Brownrigg flailed and writhed on the ground in blind panic. He kicked out, knocking a small table that clattered to the ground, the sound of glass breaking.

Kyra gulped in air, feeling his primal fear.

She heard his colleagues shout to one another.

A single gunshot.

Then the silence of the desert.

Finally, what seemed like minutes later, the two soldiers appeared and leaned over him.

'We got both of them, sir,' one of them said. 'Hold on. Stay with me now!' His companion shouted coordinates into the radio, begging for urgent medical help.

Then everything seemed to melt into the blackness.

Kyra leaped up from the recliner she was lying on, and ripped off her headset, but her eyes were still blind in the blacked-out lab. She moved around frantically, until someone grabbed her tightly by the arms.

'Get off me!' she yelled and started kicking out.

There was a man's cry of pain, followed by a voice, loud in the darkness, 'Cosmo, lights fifty per cent.'

Immediately, the room brightened.

Disoriented for a moment, Kyra stood still. Her lab partner was holding her steady. 'You're fine, Kyra! You're in the lab. It's me, Jimmy.'

She looked around, saw the familiar machinery, the black granite worktops, her mug sitting nearby, and began to settle. This wasn't the first memory transference procedure they had done, but she didn't usually react like this.

'God, Jim, I'm sorry.'

'You've done worse.' He smiled, then let go of her, arms still outstretched for a moment, before he bent to rub his shin.

'I was scared.'

4

'I know.' He guided her back to the recliner with a gentle hand on her shoulder as she struggled to get her breath back into a calm rhythm.

'Just take it easy,' he soothed. 'It's okay, Kyra. You're okay.'

She sat down and swiped at her throat, feeling sweat and mistaking it for blood. She held trembling hands up in front of her face. Her own hands. She turned them over slowly.

Clean.

Her heart rate began to slow, but her breathing was still strained.

She tapped her fingers against her chest. Jimmy understood instantly and pulled his inhaler from the pocket of his white lab coat. Grabbing it from him, she pumped the canister and sucked at it desperately.

Moments later, Kyra could feel her airways starting to open up. Her breathing became steadier, deeper. The sweat began to cool on her body, and she reached up to feel her neck again. Jimmy watched her, concerned and confused.

He patted her back briefly. 'Not going to puke this time?'

She shook her head grimly. 'Made sure I didn't eat beforehand.'

'You're getting good at this,' he smiled. 'Try to get some water down.'

He reached for a glass on the nearby work surface and passed it to her.

She drank thirstily, grateful to have him nearby.

Jimmy checked her pulse with an electrical monitor and examined her eyes with a transilluminator. Kyra glared angrily towards Carter, her business partner and owner of the CarterTech lab.

'Look forward,' commanded Jimmy. 'Pupil reaction normal,' he said and took the empty glass from her, replacing it on the worktop.

'The army, Carter? The bloody MOD? After what we'd talked about?' she said angrily.

Carter put one finger to his lips and with his other hand pointed to CASNDRA, the large, white, doughnut-shaped machine on the other side of the lab. The bright white metal of the apparatus contrasted with the dark grey walls and black work surfaces. Lying on a white bed with his head at the centre of the aperture was Lieutenant General Brownrigg from the MOD.

Carter shrugged. 'Business is business.'

'I'm bringing him out now,' said Jimmy.

Kyra lay back for a moment. Even the ceiling was dark in the lab, painted black to hide the wires and the air vents. She supposed Carter thought it was stylish. She gave Jimmy a weary thumbs-up.

'CASNDRA, retract bed,' Jimmy said as he carried a glass of water over. There was a gentle whooshing sound as the bed moved forward, bringing Brownrigg out of the machine. He sat up slowly and took the glass.

He seemed much older than a usual serving soldier and Kyra concluded that the memory of his that she had seen had been from early in his career. He didn't speak at first but watched her with his steady fixed stare as he drank his water.

'Do you feel alright?' asked Jimmy.

Brownrigg nodded, finished his water and handed his glass back to Jimmy who said, 'The pico-stimulators and nano-receptors will pass out of your bloodstream in the next few hours. You won't feel a thing. But it's just as well to drink plenty of fluid.'

'They're the things that I couldn't see that you injected me with?' Brownrigg said. He must have seen Jimmy's face fall and said with a wry smile, 'Don't worry, son. I've been injected with all sorts in my career. Didn't know what most of it was.'

His voice was deep and smooth. He was in good shape for an older man, no paunch, his shoulder and chest muscles visible beneath his crisp pale blue shirt. He swung his legs neatly round to the side of the bed, but Jimmy raised a hand. 'Give it a minute or two so I can check you over.'

Carter leaned against the grey wall, half hidden in the shadows. He wore a midnight-blue pinstripe suit, with a handkerchief that matched his pale aqua tie. All tailor-made – not available in the shops. Many of the Chinese businessmen wore them as a symbol of the rapid rise in wealth of their country over the last decade and suits were beginning to make a comeback in London. It was another of Carter's pretensions, Kyra reflected, like the white coats he insisted she and Jimmy wore as it made them look like 'professional medics'. Even though they were technically equal partners in the company his suit made the statement that he was clearly the boss, never mind the fact that his name was above the door.

Interestingly, Carter never let her delve into his memories. Too intimate, he said.

Something to hide? she wondered.

Carter had been nervous before the transference and, if she was honest, so had she been. He'd been cagey about the client but Carter had reassured her that afterwards they would make a decision together about how to proceed. Sometimes she was grateful to him for offering her the opportunity to develop her technology, other times she wished she'd picked her money more carefully. All those promises about the tech going to the right people . . . he hadn't meant any of it.

He was headstrong, but then again, so was she.

'So then?' Carter said expectantly, nodding at Kyra.

Brownrigg locked eyes with her and she felt a connection with him. How could she not after having been in his memories?

'There was fighting, soldiers. The desert, maybe Afghanistan,' she said. 'There were three little houses. I thought they were abandoned, but then there was . . . a boy . . . just a child . . .'

Brownrigg watched her, unperturbed.

What had happened out there – had it affected him at all?

'It was a . . .' She searched for the word. 'An ambush. The boy . . . cut you.' She reached up to her neck again. 'He slashed your throat.'

No reaction.

She said the next words very quietly. 'Your colleagues shot him.'

How could an experience so awful, the killing of a young boy, whatever the circumstance, not show in his expression like a veil of grief and regret?

Carter's eyes flicked between the two of them.

Brownrigg reached to open his shirt collar and reveal a long red, ragged scar.

'An accurate account, Doctor Sullivan,' he said, his voice steady.

Carter's face lit up.

Relief, she assumed.

Kyra rubbed her brow, still feeling disoriented. Her eyes wandered onto the black granite worktop. She studied the tiny glinting silver flecks in the darkness to ground herself, wanting something solid, familiar. Her eyes moved along to her mug. *Hand over the coffee and no one gets hurt* – a present from Jimmy. Then she looked up to one of the glass walls of the lab, her own reflection visible against the dark backdrop of the corridor beyond.

She saw herself clearly, her short, choppy dark bob, her long legs bent up in front of her, her shoulders that were a little too wide. She locked eyes with Brownrigg again, feeling a guilt that didn't belong to her.

'Did they . . . did he die? The boy?' she asked, afraid of the answer.

Brownrigg didn't reply. Instead, he broke her gaze and stood up.

Carter jumped in. 'As you can see, Lieutenant General,' he said, 'Doctor Sullivan has developed quite extraordinary technology in CASNDRA.' His face was earnest, trying too hard. God, she resented him.

Brownrigg smoothed his clothes. There was something almost coy about him now. She wondered if he felt vulnerable after the transference. A scientific version of the morning-after walk of shame.

'You most certainly have,' he said to Kyra, still not looking at her. 'CASNDRA – like the Greek oracle?' He smiled, but she wasn't sure if his tone was mocking. 'Remind me, what does CASNDRA stand for again?' he asked.

'Computer Assisted Scientific Neurological Detail Recall Aid.'

'So now you've sampled the goods, so to speak,' Carter interrupted, ushering Brownrigg towards the door, 'Let's talk terms.'

'I'm fine, thanks for asking,' Kyra said. Carter scowled but kept moving.

He wasn't even going to include her in this part of the process. Irritation bloomed in her chest and she stood unsteadily, moved over to them and grabbed at Brownrigg's shirtsleeve.

'May I ask . . .' The two men paused and faced her. '. . . how will you use my technology?' The muscle in Brownrigg's arm was rock-solid under her fingers. He glanced down and she released her grip.

Carter glared at her.

Brownrigg, however, appeared unperturbed and gave a thin smile. 'Tackling terrorism.'

'How?' She wasn't going to let this drop.

He hesitated, then continued in a firm voice. 'Interrogation. We believe it could be . . . useful in getting information about terrorist cell members, even after an attack.' He waved a hand through the air. 'Their contacts and addresses, locating where the cells meet or where the weapons are coming in, that sort of thing. If we can catch a live one, then there's no reason we can't get some intel that would prevent an atrocity.'

'Interesting.' She cocked her head to one side, pretending to consider. 'But I think the human rights lobby will have something to say about invading people's brains against their will.'

Carter's face darkened.

Brownrigg smiled, clearly amused by the sudden tension in the room. He took a few steps towards her.

'Doctor Sullivan, terrorism will only get worse as the gap between the rich and the poor continues to polarise. I am sure the British public will be eternally grateful for your technology and the lives it can save.'

They stood for a moment, eyes locked. A defiance rose in Kyra.

'I'm disappointed, that's all.' Her heart was thumping as Carter glared at her, 'But no matter, at least the criminal justice system will get full permission from their clients when they use it.'

Brownrigg looked at Carter, confused. 'This isn't what we'd agreed.'

Kyra saw something pass between the two men.

'No, this is merely a misunderstanding. A lack of communication, that's all,' Carter stammered.

'This has to remain Classified,' Brownrigg said firmly, his expression serious. He pointed at Kyra and Jimmy. 'You do understand the implications if this sort of technology gets into the wrong hands? Do you realise just how powerful what you've invented is?'

Kyra didn't know whether to be flattered or outraged. Who was he to tell her what she could and couldn't do with her own invention?

'Imagine how this could be used against us if—' Brownrigg began.

'Us?' snorted Kyra.

Carter scowled at her.

'Doctor Sullivan,' Brownrigg said in a low, menacing voice. 'Your technology is going to *save* people's lives and, in order to do that, it must be kept top secret.'

'Top secret?' Kyra guffawed. She looked over at Jimmy, but his face was white. It hit then that Brownrigg was deadly serious.

'What I am trying to express to you, Doctor Sullivan, in no uncertain terms, is that this technology would be *dangerous* in the wrong people's hands. It needs to be kept confidential. We can't take the risk.'

'I invented this technology.' She was openly angry now. 'It's not for you to decide.'

'You'll be compensated,' he said coldly.

'I don't want to be compensated! I want this tech to go to people who need it! The criminal justice system—'

'Sort this,' Brownrigg commanded Carter, making a waving movement with his hand.

'Of course. It will be sorted,' Carter said obsequiously. 'Let me show you to my office and we can talk privately.'

Brownrigg moved through the doorway and Carter jabbed a finger at Kyra angrily.

Nausea suddenly overwhelmed her and she sat back down on the recliner, exhausted and disappointed.

This wasn't what she'd had in mind.

Not at all.

Chapter Two

'I'm absolutely fine,' Kyra insisted as Jimmy's fingers flitted over the virtual keyboard and he focused on the computer screen, intently reading the output from her monitors. The blue-white light highlighted his aquiline nose and reflected as tiny bright squares in his dark blue eyes. She drained the second glass of water he had brought her, to help cool her body and swallow down the bitterness of her interaction with Brownrigg.

'Just following protocol, Doctor Sullivan,' he said with a smile. Jimmy brushed his dark curly hair out of his eyes. Kyra thought he had a pleasant face and he could certainly turn on the charm. He worked mainly with bio-chips and tracking devices. He had tested one on her car and she'd teased him about being a stalker, or Q from James Bond. She'd never asked why he'd left his previous job as a GP. She didn't want to pry.

She had spent ten minutes in CASNDRA's scanner, seething, after Brownrigg and Carter had left. Now she was standing next to Jimmy looking at images of her own brain.

'All looks good to me,' he said, studying the screen. 'Your amygdala is lit up like a Christmas tree.' He faced her, curious now. 'What was it like in his memory?'

'Stressful,' she said, exhaling. 'It's a shame I don't get some sort of heads-up beforehand of what I might see.' Her hand reached up to her neck again. 'It's not every day you get your throat cut.'

'It proved the tech worked. He seemed pretty impressed.'

'I wish I'd lied now and told him I couldn't see anything,' she said, deflated.

'I'm sorry. I know it's not what you wanted.'

'Bloody Carter. He only sees the money,' she grunted.

'Watch yourself,' Jimmy said, turning back to the screen. 'You're on thin ice with him after the last row. You know what he's like.'

She ignored this and sat back down on the recliner. 'Cosmo, look up Lieutenant General Brownrigg.' A montage of photographs and articles immediately filled the wall-mounted screens in front of her – Brownrigg as a young handsome soldier, sandy hair, green eyes; then older, with medals, bravery awards, leading his men out on the field. It all appeared so noble. Nothing to do with the death of a boy. She couldn't imagine the forces would want that highlighted. Even the hypernet didn't always get to the hidden truth.

'Your heart rate is coming down. It should be lower though. It never goes up like this when you're in my head. Cosmo, lights one hundred per cent.'

She shielded her eyes against the brightness as the computer obeyed. 'Why did you call the lab computer Cosmo?'

'Name of my first dog,' he replied, looking at the screen. 'Loved that animal.'

She nodded approvingly.

Reading memories was different with Jimmy. CASNDRA

had been her innovation, she'd developed the nano- and pico- technology for it, but Jimmy had built most of the equipment using her blueprint. He had been one of the first people she'd dared to test her work on other than her lab assistant, Phil Brightman. Jimmy trusted her enough to let her rummage around in his brain. It was an intimate experience which she dealt with gently. She'd gone looking for very specific details in his memory to test the machine. It was like a game of hide and seek. Jimmy would ask her something she couldn't possibly have known, and she'd had to find the answer somewhere in his memory.

She could still remember the first time, the most thrilling of all, when they knew the tech worked. They had spent most of the day playing games, Kyra trying to discover tiny snippets of information from Jimmy. *What set my asthma off in Spain when I was thirteen?*

She'd seen it clearly, a beautiful young Spanish girl, her long dark lashes over brown eyes, Jimmy trying to talk to her in broken Spanish. The girl had suddenly reached her arms around his neck and kissed him on the lips and then ran away laughing. Jimmy had been so thrilled or panicked, maybe even both, that it had triggered a mild asthma attack. Later, when they were laughing about it in the lab, Jimmy had said he'd been so embarrassed that he hadn't told a soul.

He didn't laugh so much when Kyra told him some weeks later that she had been experiencing a tightness of her chest occasionally, usually immediately after they'd used the technology. It was then that she had begun to wonder about the less obvious side effects of CASNDRA. Was it really possible to pick up physical traits after being in someone else's memories?

Going into Jimmy's memories was like going into a friend's house to collect an important item. She knew her way around and didn't feel uncomfortable poking about or peering behind the scenes, as long as she was quick and respectful.

By contrast, travelling into Brownrigg's mind had felt like trespassing. She'd never met him before and hadn't known anything about him before she'd gone in. Who knew what she might have found inside his brain, what she might have picked up?

Jimmy grabbed a small scanner and wheeled his chair over to the recliner and passed it over her face and neck.

'He's seen some awful things. It was literally like Hell.'

Jimmy checked the reading. 'All looks good here.'

He faced the main screen and Kyra stood up and stretched.

'What time is it?' she asked.

'The time is eighteen hours four minutes,' came a disembodied electronic male voice.

'Thank you, Cosmo. CASNDRA, reset please,' Kyra commanded. There was a mechanical gliding sound as the bed moved back into position, then two beeps and a small red light on the main circular part of the machine turned green.

'Are you sure you're okay?' Jimmy asked. 'Tight chest again. Anything we should worry about?'

'No,' she shook her head. 'I'm just annoyed.'

God, if she could pick asthma up from Jimmy, what the hell might she have inherited from Brownrigg?

'Psychosomatic at worst.' She paused and then said tentatively, 'You don't think Phil Brightman's heart attack had anything to do with CASNDRA, do you?'

Helping Kyra with testing the kit in the initial stages of development had been one of Phil's main duties. He had died in his sleep, not long after a transference experiment.

16

That had been when Jimmy had stepped in, taking time out of his own work in the lab next door to Kyra's to see how the kit he had helped build worked.

'No,' Jimmy said, concentrating on the screen in front of him. 'I don't think people have psychosomatic heart attacks.'

'I suppose not,' Kyra took off her white coat and hung it on the back of the door.

'Undiagnosed heart condition. Could have seen him off at any time,' Jimmy added.

'Yes, of course. Nothing to do with CASNDRA,' she reassured herself.

He turned away from the screen to look at her. 'Have you been having any more of those dreams?'

She wished she hadn't told him if he was going to keep on making a fuss about it.

They had decided that the vivid dreams she sometimes had after transferences were residual memories, things that had somehow stuck in her brain. But they seemed bloody real in the middle of the night when she was in the dark, alone.

'No.' The corners of her mouth dipped as she shook her head, but there was tension in her jaw, and she didn't meet his eyes.

'Well, here's my prescription,' he said, scribbling on a piece of paper and handing it to her.

She knitted her eyebrows, anxious for a moment. There was one word on the piece of paper.

Coffee.

'On me,' she said, relieved for the time being.

Kyra pushed open the heavy glass door to the lab and Jimmy followed, the rubber soles of his shoes making a slight squeaking sound on the grey, matt tiles. The lights in the corridors were a series of spotlights from above which caused pools of brightness intermittently along the dark floor, and at the base of the walls there were glowing strips of light-beading which gave a kind of backgammon board pattern.

Carter had done a good job of designing this space. He was good at what he did, using money to make money. *Quality attracts quality*, he said often enough.

Many of the walls in CarterTech were glass. Kyra could often see Jimmy working in his own lab, next to hers. His tech was increasingly in demand – he inserted bio-chips under the skin for banking, handy if you left home without any money, and bio-tracking devices for children of paranoid parents, or errant husbands as he sometimes joked. More recently, he had developed a tech that allowed him to implant nano-mobile communication devices under the skin – bio-phones he nicknamed them – but Kyra wasn't too sure she liked the idea of being ever-available.

The coffee machine was in the waiting area, or the 'foyer' as Carter liked to call it. He had placed large canvases of what Kyra supposed he considered 'arty' paintings around the room – images of various parts of the human body in gaudy colours in thick lines of paint; a blue hand, an orange back, a green face. There was a ceramic sculpture of the human brain on a pedestal on the reception desk, the phrenological areas marked out in black lines and glossy lettering. Kyra hated that the most.

She flashed her credit card towards the coffee machine for payment. 'Two black coffees.' She wasn't ready for a banking chip under the skin, she had decided, even though Jimmy had offered her one.

Jimmy sprawled onto one of the grey angular sofas whilst the machine took its time to dispense the coffee. As soon as one cup was full, Kyra picked it up and moved over to hand it to him.

Carter burst in from the main door. She jumped, hot coffee spilling on her hand. Jimmy sat up straight.

'Thanks for nearly fucking that up!' He stood in front of her, shoulders squared, face florid. 'I've shown Brownrigg out but, believe me, I have had to do some serious work in the last half hour to convince him to go through with this deal.'

Jimmy stood up, took his coffee from Kyra and quietly made his way back to his own lab.

'Human rights? What on earth were you thinking? Have you any idea how long it took me to set up this meeting, how important the lieutenant general is?'

Kyra turned her attention back to the coffee machine, her blood feeling like the churning hot water being spewed out from the nozzle onto the synthetic coffee granules.

'The army, Carter? Don't you think I should have known that before I went into the war zone in his head? The things I saw in there . . . You could have bloody warned me!'

'I said from the start, when we made this partnership, you're the brains, I'm the business.' He screwed up his eyes and then opened them. 'You have the ideas and I sell them. I let you do whatever you want in that lab, and I pay for all of it,' he growled. 'You have to let me do my job. You've got to trust me that I have the interests of the company at heart. I approached the MOD first because we have the tech, they have the money: it's a straight trade.'

She turned to face him. 'Yes and look how they're going to use it. We're talking about going into someone's memory without their consent, Carter! It's not a bloody police state. You can't go into someone's house without a search warrant. There's no way the government would sanction this. I wouldn't have left criminal profiling if I'd known my tech was going to be used for brain-hacking people against their will.'

'It's a necessary evil to beat the terrorists. Think of the recent anti-poverty protests, the acid attacks, the arson, the water poisonings. They're not going to go away, Kyra! The public is afraid, and where there's fear there's money! Come on, think about what you could do for your family – pay your mum's mortgage off, university fees for your niece.'

'Leave Molly out of this,' she hissed. How dare he use her niece to emotionally blackmail her. 'Brownrigg clearly seems to think this is cut and dried. In fact, he says I *can't use my own technology* because it's got to be *top secret!*' The hand holding the coffee was shaking. She put the cup down on the reception desk.

'Jesus, Kyra, for a smart woman you're being really stupid right now!' He sighed heavily. 'Don't you get it? The MOD are terrified your tech is going to get into the wrong hands and—'

'Wrong hands!' she spat.

'Brownrigg says it's good if we have it on our side, catastrophic if it's on theirs.'

'Our side?' snorted Kyra. 'All of a sudden you're interested in politics and terrorism?'

He stepped in close to her and she leaned back a little. 'Yes, if they're going to offer the sort of money that Brownrigg's suggested! We won't need to sell the tech to anyone else, we'll be flush!' His eyes always lit up when he talked about money.

'Carter, how many times do we have to fight about this before you get the message? You knew all along why I designed this tech. You knew I wanted it to go to the justice system. Imagine the accurate witness statements, helping innocent people who have been wrongly convicted and assisting families who need closure.'

His facial expression changed momentarily, becoming softer. Was he going to be swayed? But then his eyes narrowed again.

'That's pie in the sky, Kyra! You know there's no way that you could use this sort of tech-accessed witness statements in court, not for years yet. There's still work to be done before it gets to that stage. More empirical evidence to show it's one hundred per cent reliable, more testing needed. There's no way we'd get any money from the justice—'

'Jesus, Carter, it's not all about money!'

'Look, I know you're upset,' he began.

'I'm not upset, I'm furious –' she jabbed a finger towards him '– with you. And yet here you are, ready to sell it to the highest bidder *exclusively*,' she said, picking up her cup and turning back to face him. 'So not only will it go to brain-hacking interrogators, but I won't be able to use it for anyone else!'

'Calm down!'

'We're partners. You shouldn't have agreed to anything before speaking to me. You saw the money and thought: screw Kyra's opinion.'

'We both signed that agreement when we made this partnership. If you break the contract, then you might as well go. We don't have to work together, Kyra. If you can find someone who will fund your work and let you invent what the hell you like, then fine, you can go and work with them.'

'Is that a threat or a promise?'

'If you go against me again, you'll find out.'

She focused on the sculpture of the brain. So crass.

'It's out of my hands, Kyra. The MOD will take it from us anyway, even if we don't sell it to them. It's too powerful. Might as well make some money on it. Move on to a new project. What about the memory-loss project you told me about; that sounds like a goer.'

She didn't answer, was too busy fighting back hot tears. She didn't want him to see her cry, so she turned back and picked up her cup, sipped at the coffee and winced. She remembered when she was little and her dad used to make a pot of real coffee and the smell of it would waft around the house. Not like this man-made rubbish.

'I know you want to do what's right. Look on the bright side . . .' He paused, dropped his hands to his waist. 'Selling to the MOD will do good. You can't argue against preventing terrorism. They've really upped their game lately. You can't go shopping these days without someone setting off a device nearby because they're pissed off that someone else has more money than them, or some eco-warriors are kicking off.' He sighed, clearly burned out. 'There're other people out there who would be grateful to work here.'

She faced him, unable to hide her fury. 'What, you're going to take your ball home, Carter? You're going to sack me?' she goaded.

'Don't make this difficult for both of us. I picked you because you were the best.' He scowled at her. 'But don't mess this up. You've got to focus on the future, your future.'

'I can't believe that I was so desperate to build the tech that I would work with anyone, even you.' She leaned over and, through her teeth, said, 'If I'd have known what an arsehole you were, I wouldn't have taken your money.'

His ego wouldn't cope with that. She might as well have slapped his face. Some of her anger subsided into anxiety. Had she gone too far this time? She wasn't going to back down now.

'You're totally out of order,' Carter growled. 'I've warned you before that your behaviour was going to cost you your job if you went against me again—'

'Against you? We're partners, you arrogant—'

But he ignored her. 'You were the best we've ever had here, but your obsession and your pig-headedness mean that we can no longer sustain a working relationship.' His expression was aggrieved, betrayed. 'If you could only have stuck to the rules, toed the line. But this . . .' He shook his head. 'Such a shame. Get your stuff. Get out.'

Moments later, Kyra stood outside the door, bag in hand, coat over her arm.

What the hell had she just done?

Chapter Three

THURSDAY 1 FEBRUARY 2035

6.56 p.m.

Driving home through the rain-washed streets of London was like moving in a vivarium, the temperature rose slightly as the tall buildings trapped the warmth. The last time Kyra had seen frost in the city had been before she lost Emma fourteen years ago. A cold February seemed to be a thing of the past. Even at this time of year, the damp and the warmth gave rise to mossy bricks and pavement-crack weeds, life forcing its way out of every crevice like sweat from pores.

Eco-auto-drives and push-bikes moved up and down the street. There were fewer cars, as public transport had been heavily invested in and was made free to workers to reduce higher living costs, but also to minimise impact on the environment. Her electric car was a luxury she was prepared to pay for, and one that her work afforded her.

Kyra parked up and walked along the high street, the stink from the drains in the gutter giving way to the delicious aromas wafting from the open door of the deli. The sky was dark, but bright salespops shone out of every shop window – short, snappy 3D commercials projected out onto the street. Sometimes they included Personalised Targeted

Adverts – PTAs triggered by identity smartcards in bags and pockets. A pair of brown leather ankle boots, her favourite brand, presented themselves right in front of her, mid-air, and spun around slowly so that she could see them from all angles. This time yesterday she might have been tempted, but right now all she could think about was how angry she was with Carter. She'd have to wait until she got a new job before another shopping spree.

Bloody Carter! Just when everything had seemed to be going her way. She had her life the way she wanted, didn't she? She could afford her own place, a nice car, decent wine – the little luxuries. Even Molly, her niece, seemed quite settled lately. Kyra thought about the last time Molly had run off – after the argument about college. Now that she was nearly eighteen she might start to act more maturely, find some balance. There were other screens stationed intermittently down the street, so cheap they were everywhere these days, on walls, or standing upright from the pavement at the bus stops. They displayed mainly adverts or newspops – short news videos. The one currently showing was about the recent crime wave associated with the Chinese drug Lè. Along with the influx of Chinese trade and brain-power came the inevitable dark side too; the sex workers and the highly addictive Lè.

Kyra rummaged in her bag for her purse as she walked along, swerving stationary viewers who were staring at screens. It was one of life's little irritations when trying to get around town. *Did you enjoy your last holiday to France, Kyra? Have you thought about travelling further afield? Leave all your problems behind for a little while . . .* suggested one screen. From the corner of her eye Kyra noticed a man moving in time with her down the street. She turned around to look. He was wearing an army uniform. When he saw her turn around, he stopped to look in a shop window. Outside the pharmacy, a scanner turned in her direction and a salespop asked her if she was stressed and suggested she should try Vitamix Energy Boost. She swatted it away like an annoying insect and went into the convenience shop next door and bought two bottles of wine. It was only British Sauvignon Blanc, grown somewhere along the Thames Estuary, but expensive enough. She might as well whilst there was still money in her pocket and it would take the sting out of Carter's betrayal, for tonight anyhow.

She put the bottles in her bag and went back out into the street. Tomorrow she would think about a new job. She would relax and take it easy tonight. God, what if she ended up in one of those awful genetic research labs? For a brief moment, she thought back to her time with the police. Yes, the pay had been amazing, and her work in the profiling department had been fascinating, but she didn't have the guts for it anymore. It had all been so uncertain, guesswork – educated, possibly; informed, definitely – but guesswork nonetheless.

She pushed the idea out of her mind and made her way back to the car, the two bottles chinking together softly in her bag. She checked her Commswatch to see if there were any messages from her mum or Molly. Instead there was one from Jimmy:

You okay?

She ignored it, unwilling to think about what had happened, and moved further down the street. She reached the car and, out of the corner of her eye, noticed the soldier again, hanging back a little, and her blood boiled.

She pulled her Commset out of her bag, deliberately using it and not her hidden earpiece. 'Dial Carter.'

26

The line connected but switched straight to answer machine.

'It's Kyra. Look, you can tell your mate Brownrigg,' she said loudly, 'that I'm no threat to national security, so he can call his spies off.'

She turned to face the soldier, hoping to embarrass him, but he was gone. She looked up and down the street. He was nowhere to be seen.

She threw her Commset back into her bag, furious that Carter had put her in such a position. She reached the car and put her hand out for the handle, only to stop halfway as the nearby screen attracted her attention with a newspops:

URGENT – HAVE YOU SEEN THIS MAN?

Kyra froze and caught her breath. Her guts immediately knotted into a small, tight ball, her ribcage became a hive of bees buzzing in the space where her heart should have been. She recoiled from the image, stepping back into the path of a big woman who pushed her roughly aside and called her a vulgar name.

Kyra's mouth dried as she gaped at a face she hadn't seen for fourteen years, a face she had prayed never to see again – the soulless dark brown eyes, set beneath heavy brows, the face puffy and angry, lips pressed together in a thin, cruel line.

Police have launched a nationwide manhunt for an escaped criminal – David Lomax.

How could the newsreader sound so calm? Did she know what sort of man this was? The people passing by were getting on with their everyday lives, no hint or suggestion of fear or distress.

Lomax, 58, nicknamed the Mizpah Murderer, was convicted of the death of six women fourteen years ago. This afternoon he managed to evade police when granted permission to attend his mother's funeral at City Necroplex. Despite an intensive effort, Lomax has not been apprehended. Police have warned the public not to approach him but to contact them immediately if . . .

This was the man convicted for the death of six women, one of whom had been her beautiful, funny, rebellious sister Emma. Her heart ached, a grief she kept so well hidden suddenly rearing.

She had worked on Lomax's case and it had almost destroyed her. She had been the psychologist who had built a profile and made suggestions to the police, but it hadn't been enough. She should have been able to find something definite that would have led the police to the killer before he took his next victim. Before he had taken Emma.

The image of the names and dates scratched into the back of her notebook as the case progressed came to her mind. Two women each February for three years in a row.

2019 – Unknown woman and Skylar Lowndry

2020 – Madelyn Cooper and Jennifer Bosanquet

2021 – Emma Sullivan and Amelia Brigham

It had been an unusual case, an unusual modus operandi. The first woman each year – described by the police as Type A – Unknown, Madelyn and Emma – had been mutilated and dumped in a horrible place. Then, within a week, another woman – Type B – Skylar, Jennifer and Amelia had been abducted and killed, but left whole and posed in water. Each of the Type B victims wore a necklace

– a Mizpah pendant which had given rise to the killer's moniker in the press.

After Emma's death, Kyra had eventually pulled her life together again. When she had helped to get her mum and Molly through the worst, she had left her old life behind; her job with the police, her apartment, her relationship, tried shedding her grief along with everything else, and gone to work in the department of Neuro-psychopathy at the university. It had kept her busy, given her a focus other than sorrow and regret. Her work in the safe place behind the white walls of her lab became almost a mission, trying to locate the problem in the criminal brain, and in some cases, even, to some degree, fix it. It had been whilst she was trying to work in this particular area that she had designed CASNDRA. Then Carter had made her an offer and she had moved to CarterTech.

An image of Lomax's first victim came up on the screen – a woman, but only a pencil sketch, there had been no identity and therefore no family to provide a photograph of her alive. Kyra remembered the empty chapel at the Necroplex. The grey pencil lines made the woman look transparent, a ghost, as though she had hardly ever existed in real life.

The next photograph showed Madelyn Cooper in her school uniform, fifteen years old, thin, mousey hair, watery blue eyes and a reluctant smile. Kyra had advised Tom – the detective in charge of the case – to show this image, as opposed to any other, probably the last one of Madelyn before her hectic lifestyle took over. The public would be more inclined to help if they could see the person behind the dishevelled mess that she had become in the last two years of her life.

Kyra moved rapidly to another screen at a nearby bus stop, not wanting to be in the presence of others when the inevitable appeared. And then there she was, Emma, never to age, long dark, shiny hair, in a crimson dress, taken from a social media posting of a night out, the arms of friends still visible around her shoulders on the periphery of the image.

Kyra cried out in the street, unable to repress the swell of anguish as she was immediately taken back to the moment that they had found Emma's body; Tom restraining her as she screamed and wrestled against him to get to her sister's body.

She had resented him for it at the time, even though she later understood why.

And suddenly she was back in the nightmare.

She ran back to the car, the image of her sister still on the screen, looking after her with judgement. If only her last words to Emma had been kinder. She placed her hand on the palm-reader lock, the door clicked open and she threw herself in, shut the door and put her forehead onto the steering wheel, her hands gripping the rubber, feeling as though the world outside was spinning.

Her first instinct was to ring Tom. He would know what was going on. He would reassure her, wouldn't he, that they were going to catch Lomax, that he wouldn't be waiting somewhere in the shadows to do to another woman what he had done to Emma?

She immediately hated herself for looking to him. Tom had been so much more to her than just the senior investigating officer. That had been another thing that the Mizpah Murderer had taken from her.

But as the sweat cooled on her brow she remembered the relief that she had felt; cutting ties with the police all those years ago and cutting ties with Tom. What choice had she had but to walk away? She had needed to draw a line under that time of her life and, sadly, that had meant Tom too. How could they have stayed together, enjoyed any happiness at all, in the face of all that grief, that guilt?

Lomax was out!

A rising bile burned her throat. She opened the car door and vomited into the gutter.

An elderly couple walking past moved away in disgust.

Kyra spat the bitterness from her mouth and sat back up in the driver seat, pulling the door shut. 'Doors locked,' she said, not feeling the usual satisfaction at the click when the car complied. 'Search hypernet, contact number Tom Morgan, detective,' she commanded and, seconds later, a number appeared on her Commset watch.

She took a deep breath. This was opening up old wounds.

But she needed to know.

'Dial.'

A brief beep and then, 'Tom Morgan.'

She cleared her throat and steeled herself.

'It's Kyra.'

A pause on the other end.

'Kyra. Hi. I wondered if I might hear from you. Are you alright?'

She was tongue-tied for a moment, not sure how to start.

'Look, I should have called you,' Tom began, filling the awkward silence. 'I was hoping to have better news by the time I called.'

'You mean he's still out?'

'Yes, I'm afraid so.'

The hive in her chest started buzzing again, the bees travelling through her bloodstream, into her limbs, making them feel weak.

'Tom, he killed Emma,' she said. Her voice sounded small and far away.

As if he didn't know. As if he hadn't been the one holding her back so she didn't have to see the destruction.

'We're going to find him, Kyra.'

The words brought back bitter memories. So much had changed in the last fourteen years but hearing Tom's voice somehow brought the two points of time together.

'He followed me back then . . . the box outside my house . . . who else would have left that?' Over a decade ago, but she still remembered the pretty box, the satin ribbon, her heart-stopping fear as she opened it . . .

. . . her relief when she had found it was empty.

But it had been a warning.

She peered out at the people moving along the street past her car. Was he out there, watching her, hidden in the shadows?

'He doesn't know where you live. You've moved since then, haven't you?'

'Yes.' How could she have stayed at her old place with those memories surrounding her like ghosts?

'I've got your number now. I've got to go. It's intense here.' He paused. 'I'll call you as soon as I hear anything.'

As the call ended, it occurred to her that she had moved, but her mother had lived in the same house since before Kyra was born. If the killer had followed Kyra to her apartment back then, might he have also followed her to her mother's house? Might he know where to find them?

'Call Mum,' Kyra commanded. Through the Commset at her ear, she could hear her mother's staggered breath down the line.

She already knew.

'You okay, Mum?'

'Yes.'

'Don't let Molly know yet.' Kyra put her thumb to the

ignition and the engine fired up. 'I'll be there as soon as I can.'

She pulled away from the pavement, knowing her only passenger on the drive would be the awful memories of what the Mizpah Murderer had done.

Chapter Four

FIFTEEN YEARS AGO

Life extinct.

Two drones buzzed overhead, illuminated by the blue police car lights that flashed aggressively in the dark. The peripatetic medical officer, or peri-med as they were known, sat in the ambulance, he had pulled over to let Kyra in through the narrow gates. As she drove past, his face was briefly lit up by his mini-screen, presumably receiving another emergency call. The windscreen appeared smeared, making his face look smudged. He gave her a brief nod as she drove through the gates.

There was no need for an ambulance now.

As she parked up, she could see Tom and the team working at the far end of the concourse. Her boot heels clattered across the concrete as she made her way over towards the steep dunes of plastic and metal scraps, mid-way through being sorted and crushed into bales. The nearby machines had been disabled by the human managers in central control and now stood like huge metal skeletons casting angular shadows across the forecourt.

The Organic Waste Recycling and Energy Recovery Centre was usually run by automated systems. It was a large factory-like complex built around a concourse, the roofs covered in solar panels and ecological green thatch, thriving even though it was a cold winter. At the centre of the site sat eight swimming pool-sized vats of soil and sand where the smell was strongest. The frothy scum on top glittered with a layer of silver frost.

There was a platoon of police here; a number of uniformed officers controlling the gate, a crime scene photographer, and a few detectives. Nearby, the Crime Scene Investigation team had set up lamps which cut shards of light into the late evening gloom. The CSIs dipped in and out of the surrounding darkness looking like ghosts in their white overalls.

Kyra could see Doctor Helen Wilson, the medical examiner, at the heart of the action in front of her. Tom, illuminated by the lamps, rested on his haunches over where Kyra assumed the body lay. They had worked together this time last year, in 2019, when the first two victims of the Mizpah Murderer had been found. She assumed he wanted her opinion as to whether or not this was the same killer.

Drawing closer, bracing herself against more than the cold February breeze, Kyra could see what he was looking at. All that studying at university – the Psychiatry and Neuropsychopathy, the theory, even the photographs, couldn't have prepared her for the desecrated bundle that lay at her feet. At first glance, it appeared as though the woman had curled up to sleep in a foetal position, her back to them, the buttons of her spine visible through her thin, pale skin.

Helen turned to greet Kyra, putting her gloved hands on her ample hips as she stood up straight. Tom gave a gruff hello, eyes still on the corpse. He'd asked for Kyra specifically. Did he want her opinion? The least he could do was to look at her.

From this proximity, Kyra caught the reek of death. She brought her mind into focus, looking for patterns, anything to help her build on her profile notes. As she stepped closer she could see that the head had been wrapped tightly in silver duct tape, mousey hair sprouting from the top. She was naked, apart from a black biodegradable bin liner which had been wrapped around her waist and lower torso. A fine sheen of frost swirled in fern-shaped patterns across the black plastic shroud, like lace, glistening in the artificial light. Her knees were bent and her tiny feet crossed at the ankle, the soles heartbreakingly dirty like a child's called in from play.

The shell-pink painted toenails gave Kyra a pang of sorrow.

She forced her eyes to look further. The woman had her arms raised in front of her like a boxer. Part of the bin liner had been torn away – by a fox perhaps? She shuddered. A long winding tattoo of a snake began at the woman's shoulder, curled around her bicep, past her elbows and down to her wrist – where the snake abruptly ended, decapitated. No serpent eyes or baring of fangs. Nothing but bloody stumps.

The woman's hands had been amputated at the wrists.

Kyra gagged, stomach roiling, and she tore her gaze away. She took deep breaths, waiting for her body to calm. But she was compelled to look again. White shards of bone jutted out from blood that had turned black and viscous like tar.

Turning to Helen, Kyra asked, 'Do we know cause of death yet?'

Helen leaned over the body and pointed a purple plastic-gloved finger. 'Likely it was asphyxiation and, if it's anything like last year, she would have been dosed up first with a strong opiate. Should show up on the toxicology report.'

Kyra tapped her chest with a finger. 'Is it the same as last time?'

Helen brushed back a lock of auburn hair from her forehead with the back of her hand. 'See for yourself.'

Kyra leaned over the corpse, forcing her eyes to look at the ribcage to where Helen indicated. There was a gaping hole between the small white breasts which was ringed with dried, blackened blood and greying skin.

Kyra retched.

Some things could never be unseen.

Helen didn't look at her, but said, 'You feeling okay?'

Kyra grunted, her hand over her mouth.

'Sternum's been removed but put back into the body after the heart was taken out.'

Helen probed the chest cavity with her fingers. 'We'll know more once I've completed the autopsy.'

Kyra swallowed hard.

Tom asked, 'Hands removed post mortem?'

Helen picked up the lower arm, brought it close to her face and studied the stump, the jagged bone protruding from the brown mess of dried blood.

Kyra saw Tom wince.

'No, looks like prior to death judging by coagulation. If he had wanted to remove evidence that might have been caught under the fingernails, it would have been easier to do after death. Could be torture.'

'Or to make her more powerless,' suggested Kyra. Her anger rose as she imagined the small woman trying to defend herself.

'She died elsewhere and then she was dumped here. There would have been a lot of blood otherwise.'

'He chooses small women,' Kyra said. 'I don't think he's a big man. He wants the upper hand physically – wants to make sure he can control them. The plastic wrapped around the torso . . . I don't think this is a sexually motivated murder. In fact, he's covered her up, deliberately.'

Tom regarded her.

'This looks exactly like the woman we found last February, the unknown woman, the prostitute we found at the sewage treatment works.' She took a step back, away from the body. 'Same time of year, same type of injuries, similar deposition site. It's him.'

'Looks that way,' Tom agreed.

'The peri-med was the first on the scene, but it was obvious that she was already dead.' Tom looked at her, his eyes glittering amongst the shadows. 'We don't know who called it in.'

This is what Kyra was trained for, to profile criminals so that they could be caught, and then studied; she could scan the perpetrator's brain and analyse his psychology to try to find the root cause of this behaviour. The focus was so much on prevention these days, and how could they prevent, if they didn't understand?

A rapid burst of flashes shattered the darkness temporarily. The CSI photographer was already packing her equipment away in a case.

'Bloody journalists!' Tom barked at two nearby officers and pointed in the direction of a man who had somehow managed to get into the compound.

Kyra took off her coat and held it over the body, trying to shield it, until the intruder was rugby-tackled to the ground and finally manhandled away. The last thing the victim's family needed was to see an image of the gruesome damage that had been inflicted on her that could show up any time on the hypernet.

'We're ready to move her now, sir,' Tony Rowson, the crime scene manager, informed Tom. Kyra put her coat back on. Rowson's large, angular frame pushed against the shoulders of his overall as he stretched to unzip a body bag on a gurney. Four of the team moved around the body, like pall-bearers. There was a hushed, reverential moment of stillness before Rowson counted down and they lifted her.

She seemed so small as they laid her out on the white polyethylene bag. Kyra estimated a little over a metre and a half.

'They haven't found the hands?' she asked Tom.

'Not yet.'

The poor family – having to bury their loved one, knowing that parts of her were still missing.

Or else they would find the rest of her, but that would mean . . .

The snap as Helen pulled off one of her gloves brought Kyra back. 'Estimated time of death?'

'Judging by body temperature, and lividity, I'd say two days. Probably died sometime on Thursday night.'

'It's a pattern,' Kyra said.

Tom bobbed his head, tight-lipped.

'And that means only one thing,' she said, not even wanting to say the words.

He looked at her, his eyes merely shadows in the darkness, and finished the sentence for her.

'That another woman will be dead within the week.'

Chapter Five

It was dark when Kyra drove up to her mother's house along the wide, curved road between the green lawns and mature trees that had already begun to thrive, even though it was only February. The 1930s semi-detached houses were mainly owned by retirees. They were considered unaffordable to the young, and enviable for their amount of space. The majority of workers, even those with families, had moved into apartments exactly like her own in the ever-expanding city, which had gradually oozed into the suburbs.

'Is Molly in her room?' Kyra asked, as she burst through the front door and into the living room. Her mother stood frozen in the centre of the floor, a blue-checked tea towel clenched in her hands, staring at David Lomax's image, which filled the screen. Her face was pale and strained. Kyra moved over to her, and she turned her head slightly towards her daughter and nodded but her eyes were still glued to the news.

Emma's face appeared briefly on the screen – her public status in death reduced to that of being one of Lomax's victims – a news item.

Her mother let out a moan and Kyra saw her eyes, light brown like Emma's, were glassy with unshed tears. Underneath the shock, Kyra knew there were fourteen years of pain and anger that simmered, that took energy and courage to contain. Her mother was petite, as Emma had been, but somehow her grief made her seem smaller.

'He was allowed out to go to his mother's funeral. Emma won't get to go to mine.' Her head dropped for a moment.

Kyra didn't reply but swallowed hard.

'Instead, I had to go to the funeral of my own child. Because of him.'

'I'm going to stay here tonight,' Kyra said, putting her arm briefly around her mother's shoulders. 'I'll speak to Molly first and then I'll come and look after you.' Kyra took one last look at the screen, remembering Emma at seven years old lying on the carpet watching cartoons.

Her mum nodded sadly and reluctantly. Kyra turned away. She could see the dent in the door where Emma, at fourteen, had thrown a cup at her when they argued over a jumper.

At twenty-one Emma was dead.

Her baby sister, seven years younger than her, would have been thirty-five now had she lived. Kyra could see her dad, sitting in his armchair, lowering his newspaper in shock as Emma told him that she was pregnant at just seventeen, his face falling, probably afraid at what his daughter's future held.

He could never have possibly imagined.

A swelling rise of guilt that she usually kept so well contained overwhelmed her.

If only she had known what she knew now, she would never have let those have been the last words she had said to her sister before she had left the cafe. She would have apologised, said she was wrong, she hadn't meant it. She would have pulled at her sister's sleeves, offered little Molly another cake – *any cake you want, sweetheart* – so that they'd stay.

Walking through the hall and up the stairs, Kyra followed a trail of photographs; her mum and dad – a young married couple, new parents, older then – her and Emma growing up, Kyra in her graduation gown, and then Molly making the transition from a rosy-faced baby to a beautiful young woman.

There was no reply when she knocked so she pushed the door open. Molly lay on the bed, facing away from her, not moving, hidden by her lilac bedcover.

Kyra had once shared this bedroom with Emma and even though her mother had redecorated in pastels, with white furniture and a double bed, the ghosts were always present, like a bittersweet aroma that lingered: their old twin beds, the late-night conversations, Dad telling them off for giggling in the dark.

She sat on the bed and tentatively put her hand on her niece's back.

'Molly, love, I need to tell—'

'I know. I saw the newspops,' came her muffled reply.

Had she been crying?

'Do you want to talk?'

'No.'

Kyra wanted to comfort her, but there was no point in pushing it. It had to be in Molly's time and in Molly's way. Sometimes she was childlike and needy, at other times she held herself back, self-contained. Kyra would just have to bide her time.

'I'll be next door. Anytime during the night, come and get me . . . if you need me . . .'

Kyra sat comforting her mother for some time before retiring to the box room where she kept some of the things she needed when she slept over, the room that her dad had painted in shades of cream and pale yellow once he had come around to the idea of being a grandfather, the room that Molly had never slept in. By the time Molly had been born, Emma had already moved out into what her dad had referred to as a 'communist cesspit' with a bunch of other eco-warriors and the boyfriend she claimed was Molly's father, but whom they never met.

For all the conflict, her father had died not long after Emma, broken-hearted.

As Kyra cleansed her face in the mirror she remembered the wine in the footwell of her car. Would it help to have a few glasses, get the thoughts of Lomax out of her mind before sleep? She decided against it. She was exhausted and not long after she had climbed into bed, the border between wakefulness and sleep had been crossed, and she had slipped into her dreams.

She saw blue flashing lights, felt her arms wrapped around three-year-old Molly, pale and motionless, clinging a little too hard, eyes fixed on the place where she had last seen her mother.

The scene began to change, the surrounding buildings shrinking and turning into shades of beige and brown, the Tarmac and concrete disappearing to be replaced by sand. Kyra gazed at Molly, still holding her tightly, as the child began to vaporise into a cloud that was made up of her colours – her brown hair, her black coat, her golden eyes, her pale skin – all in streaked smudges that rose into the air as her niece disappeared in front of her like smoke from a votive candle, and her arms were left empty.

The clouds of colour swarmed above her for a moment and then dropped lower and began changing form. They swirled before finally solidifying into the shapes of three soldiers, one ahead of the others, their guns pointing forwards. They stopped dead as the leader raised his fist. Kyra immediately recognised him as Brownrigg. He jabbed a finger and they continued to move again.

The temperature rose rapidly. Kyra opened her eyes, lying on her bed, on her side, one hand under the pillow. The hairs on the back of her neck stood up as she heard a noise behind her, a soft shuffling, the creak of a floorboard.

Heart pounding, she slowly lifted her head and turned to face the shapes of the three soldiers moving slowly, deliberately, across her bedroom floor. Even in the darkness the muzzles of their guns were visible – pointing towards her. The smell of sweat and desert dust filled her nose and mouth.

Closing her eyes, she held her breath momentarily, not daring to move a muscle.

It was a dream, wasn't it? A residual memory?

She waited a few seconds, heart beating loudly in her ears, and then reopened her eyes, breathless.

She was alone.

1.07 a.m.

My agitation always quietens after the first one dies.

It rids something in me – anger, resentment, fear? It's taken me hours to come down from the rush – the release is so intense.

But now I need to clear my mind. I need to prepare myself for the next part.

The second one is always so different, not messy and cathartic, but a sacrament almost.

This one will belong solely to you, Elise.

I made a promise to you that, even though I couldn't be there, I wouldn't leave you on your own in the darkness, that I would send someone to look after you.

I will keep sending them until one day when I will be there myself and we will never be apart, one from another, again.

The next part is always more difficult.

I have to prepare. I am still too dirty, too soiled. I am glad that you are not here, so that you cannot see what I have become, that you have not become corrupted like me. You will always remain pure, unsullied, innocent.

There is work to be done, the procedure to be followed.

Everything needs to be just right.

I make my way slowly through the house, turning the mirrors to the wall, moving photographs, closing doors and locking them.

My hands reek of the other one, the one I left at the dump. I can still smell her sticky blood on my hands, even though there is not a mark on them.

I go into the kitchen and pull the bleach from the cupboard under the sink.

I unscrew the lid and pour the thick yellow liquid over my fingers and palms, then I swap the bottle for the scrubbing brush and scour until my hands are red raw.

It's not enough.

I pull a packet of salt from the cupboard above the cooker, tear it open with my teeth and pour it over my hands, rubbing them together, grinding in the grains until they burn and I can feel tears stinging my eyes.

'Elise! Elise!' I cry over and over again.

I can never be clean enough.

I'll run a bath, that's what I will do. I will fill it as high as it will go and submerge myself completely. Then, when the water is still, I will lie beneath its glassy surface and open my eyes, to see what you saw, to feel what you felt, and maybe, somehow, you will know that I am ready to send you another angel.

Chapter Six

FOURTEEN YEARS AGO

The armoured police response van doors flew open and six men in riot gear and helmets and holding snub-nosed semi-automatic machine guns leaped out and charged around to the back of the row of shops. Four more men had been stationed at the front, crouched ready to pounce. The sun was still an hour or so from rising. The freezing rain fell in sheets, bouncing off the Kevlar and running in rivulets down the waterproof material of the officers' uniforms.

Tom went to the bottom of the rusty metal steps that led to the flats above the shops. Next to him, Pete Donovan, the head of Armed Response, a silver-grey flat top, fierce ice-blue eyes, and a weather-beaten face that gave nothing away, stood waiting for everyone to be in place. A split second of stillness and then his hand-signal, prompting his officers to move swiftly and quietly up the steps.

The doorframe splintered as the lock shattered against the battering ram. There was an excited surge forward, gruff shouts of 'Police!' as the team diverged into the four rooms of the tiny, dank flat. Tom casually followed in their wake, hands in his coat pocket. How could he be so calm? Kyra followed him up the steps, her heart hammering furiously.

There was more shouting: 'Here! Here!'

They'd found their quarry.

They had finally caught the Mizpah Murderer, the monster who might know where her sister was.

Roused by the brutal alarm of the officers' shouts, Lomax was cuffed and contained. Donovan ordered the officers to stand down and they moved away from the hub of action, job done. There was a lull as the adrenaline fizzled out. Kyra followed Tom into the dark bedroom. Two armed officers stood in the far corners, hands on their weapons, muzzles trained on their target. Tom indicated the curtains and one of the officers ripped them open.

David Lomax was a few years older than Tom, but not as in good shape. He looked shorter from this angle, but he was much broader, his belly bulging out from between his greying vest and boxer shorts. He sat on a grimy sheet, the duvet in a twist on the floor, his hands cuffed behind his back. His brown hair stuck to his pallid face. The room reeked of sweat.

'What the fuck?' he growled, as Tom stood in front of him, eyeing him calmly.

'David Lomax?

'Who else?' scowled the man. 'Who the fuck are you, and who's this bitch?' he eyeballed Kyra and she had to force herself to stand her ground.

She wanted to scream, 'Did you take my sister?' but she had been warned by Tom. Her training had taught her that Lomax was the sort of criminal who would enjoy her pain, taunt her about where her sister was, if he knew. The police weren't sure. Emma didn't exactly fit the pattern. Had it been the Mizpah Murderer who had dragged her into his car two weeks ago? What had Kyra expected when she had climbed those metal stairs? That Emma would be there, locked in a room, distressed and exhausted, but still alive?

They knew his pattern now, the first victim each year killed at midnight on a Thursday in February, the second woman would be killed at midnight on the following Wednesday. This was the third year of his cycle. They had already found Amelia Brigham – a Type B victim, a young social worker, in the underground reservoir near China Bank a few days ago. If Lomax had taken Emma, Kyra knew she would already be dead. He would have fulfilled his pattern. It was just that they hadn't found her body yet.

The thought of her sister lying somewhere, desecrated, broke her.

She shouldn't even be here – this was personal. Any officer who was in any way connected with a case could be immediately taken off, as protocol. Tom had been furious when she'd shown up – he'd warned her not to come when he called her to tell her that they were arresting Lomax. But when he had seen her at the bottom of the steps by the flat he hadn't told her to go home. Because she was the only psychologist attached to the case? Or because of his feelings for her?

Tom spoke calmly. 'David Lomax, I'm arresting you on suspicion of murder. You do not have to say anything, but it may harm your defence if you do not mention, when questioned, something which you later rely on in court. Anything you do say may be given in evidence.'

'I ain't done nothing,' snarled Lomax, wrenching his cuffs. Then his body stilled. 'Murder?' he repeated, as though he didn't really understand the word. Kyra studied his face as he tried to make sense of the charge. She had to restrain herself from begging for the information.

He would enjoy that.

'Arresting me?' This incensed him. He fought to get up. 'What the fuck is this? Get these things off me!'

One of the armed police flung him back down on the bed. 'Shut it!'

He struggled to sit up again, spittle flying from his mouth.

'You have a temper on you, Lomax,' Tom said pleasantly.

One of the armed police came back in. 'Sir, the search team are outside.'

'Send them in,' Tom said, keeping his eyes focused on Lomax.

Why wasn't Tom asking about Emma?

Tom sat down on a small set of drawers near the bed so he was almost level with the sweating man in front of him. He spoke in a quiet, gentle voice, in control.

'A few days ago a woman, Rachael Molloy, came to speak to us,' Tom said. 'She told us that you beat her.'

'Never heard of her,' Lomax said, looking out of the window. Was he trying to mirror Tom's calmness?

'Only, she says you do know her. She says you've been to buy her services a number of times. "Regular" was the word she used.'

'It's not illegal.'

'It is if you don't use the designated sex industry houses.'

'If the stupid bitch wants to let me fuck her for a few quid, who's getting hurt?'

'Obviously she is, judging by her injuries,' Tom said.

Kyra's blood was boiling now. *Get on with it, Tom! Ask him about Emma.*

Lomax laughed slowly, mockingly. 'Is that what this is about? Me roughing up a whore?' He looked around at the other police officers in the room, smiling. 'This is bullshit.' He scowled again. 'Whores get beaten up all the time. Haven't you got any proper crimes to deal with?'

'As I said, I'm arresting you on suspicion of murder.' Tom put his hands in his pockets.

'Don't know nothing about a murder. It weren't me. Rachael's old man probably done her in when she got home 'cause he found out how she makes her money.' He grinned, showing his brown, tombstone-like teeth.

'Ah, but Rachael's still very much alive,' said Tom. 'Which means she'll be able to testify against you.'

'She won't do that,' he sneered. 'If she knows what's good for her. How long do you think I'd get for beating up a whore? Six months, max? I know where she lives. It won't even get to court.'

It was Tom's turn to smile now. Kyra watched as he waited until Lomax's face fell.

'How can you arrest me for murder when she's still alive?' There was an edge of concern in his voice. 'What the fuck is this about?'

'Kyra, can you tell the search team to make a start? We won't be here much longer.'

Why was he sending her out? Was he going to ask if Emma was still alive?

If Lomax wasn't going to talk, maybe the search team would uncover a clue as to where her sister was.

'Tom, please . . . ask him.'

Lomax studied her, curious.

'Search team,' Tom commanded, eyes locked on Lomax, and she huffed and left the room.

She gave the thumbs-up and a steady stream of officers in white overalls, blue plastic over their shoes, invaded the flat and began to tear it apart, lifting greasy cushions and emptying chaotic cupboards. They used handheld metal detectors and X-ray cameras on the furniture, walls and floor. She was surprised at the state of the place. She had told the investigating team that he would be a highly organised killer and they were invariably meticulous. That would be another reason for them to scoff at her.

She stood in the hall, but leaned on the bedroom door-post, watching Lomax and listening to Tom. 'We took samples from Rachael Molloy, Lomax. She said you bit her. We took DNA from the bitemark, and other parts of her body.' Tom left that one hanging for a moment. 'Problem is, you see,' he said, leaning towards Lomax, 'The DNA that was found on Rachael's body is already on our database.'

'Then it ain't mine. I've never had my DNA taken. So, it ain't fucking me.' His expression was one of weariness.

'No, that DNA was found on two bodies. Two women who turned up dead,' Tom said flatly, watching for his reaction.

The word 'dead' made Kyra's stomach clench.

Lomax's eyes, bloodshot and bulging slightly, fixed on her. 'It ain't me, I'm telling you. You got the wrong man. I like fighting and fucking. I've never killed no one.'

'You mean you've never been caught,' Kyra said.

'That Rachael bitch is lying!' Lomax burst out, but there were beads of sweat on his brow and a nervous tic had started up in the corner of his eye. What was he afraid of – being caught, or being blamed for something he hadn't done?

'We have CCTV showing you meeting Rachael on the night. Your face is very clear on the footage,' Tom added.

Lomax sighed heavily.

'We'll show it to you when you get to the station, after we've taken a sample of your DNA to match up with the sample from Rachael.'

Kyra was starting to feel light-headed. The small flat was full of people moving around noisily, lifting and carrying things out down the steps to the vans below. The smell of damp and the cloying heat of the radiators made her feel smothered. Being so close to Lomax was making her blood itch.

Where's my sister, you evil bastard?

'But we've got you now, Lomax.' Tom's voice was so low he was almost whispering. 'We're going to take you down to the station, take a bio sample, and we're going to prove you committed those murders. You'll never see the light of day again.' Tom stared him out for a few moments. 'But you can make things easier on yourself – tell us where Emma Sullivan is.'

Lomax 's eyes narrowed. 'Who?'

'Emma Sullivan, the woman you abducted two weeks ago on Lawson Street.'

The room seemed to shrink, everyone else seemed to disappear, the only sound Kyra's heart beating so loudly she thought her chest might burst.

After what felt like minutes, Lomax snarled, 'I told you, I ain't done nothing.'

All of a sudden, all the noises, movements, people, smells, came crashing in on Kyra. She rushed towards Lomax with her fists flailing. 'Where is she, you bastard?'

'Get her out!' Tom shouted. One of the officers grabbed her around the waist and pulled her into the hall before blocking the entrance to the bedroom. She stamped her foot in frustration. The hallway was so small that she had to squeeze back against the wall to let other officers past as they fetched and bagged items. She watched as a mini-screen, wrapped in a transparent bag, was carried out of the flat and down the steps to the van. Would there be any evidence that her sister had been there?

She heard Tom say, 'Cover him up.' Then he came out, followed by Lomax who was wearing joggers and sports sandals, a jacket thrown over his shoulders, an officer in front, and one behind him. As he moved past her, she could see that he was much bigger than he had seemed on the bed. He suddenly lunged towards her and she cowered, but he stopped short and swore in her face.

Furious with herself for showing fear, she stood up straight and put her hands on her hips. Two of the guards grappled with him, and he struggled against them as they made their way to the front door in a tangled trio. Tom was ahead, about to make his way down the steps when someone in the living room cried out, 'Sir!'

One of the female CSIs, white hood pulled over her hair, only her dark brown eyes visible above her face mask, came out of the living room. She was on the other side of Lomax and the officers, and the lack of space meant she couldn't get close to Tom. Instead, she stretched out, almost touching Lomax's chest with her blue-gloved hand, a silver chain with a pendant dangling from her index finger.

It was a half-heart of a Mizpah pendant.

That was it, the last piece of the jigsaw.

Tom's eyes lit up.

'Found it down the back of the sofa, sir.'

'Good work. Bag and tag it.' He locked gaze with Lomax for a moment and smiled contentedly.

Kyra studied Lomax's face, watching his confusion, as he examined the necklace without recognition, until the penny finally dropped.

A cold, prickling sensation swam in Kyra's stomach. And she resented the wisp of doubt that was creeping into her mind. It all seemed so straightforward, so why was she beginning to doubt it?

Lomax momentarily locked eyes with her, his expression horrified.

'No,' he shook his head. 'No!' he shouted louder, eyes wide, panicked now. 'It weren't me! It weren't me! You think I'm some fucking psycho who butchers women?' He began to jerk around, agitated, struggling against his handcuffs. The officers grabbed his thickset arms and tried to restrain him, but he fought against them.

Kyra moved out of the front door for safety.

'It weren't me! I ain't going down for this! There's been a mistake! Rachael fucking stitched me up! I ain't going to prison!' Lomax yelled, lashing out with his feet into the scrum of officers.

A few of the neighbours had come out to see what the police vans were for. Kyra moved down to the bottom of the steps. Even from this perspective, she could see Lomax charging like an enraged bull into the officer in front of him and then kick out at his knees, one of which bent at a weird angle and the copper went down yelping in pain. Then he headbutted the other officer who slumped to the floor, face a bloody mess.

The icy rain was coming down in sheets as Kyra ran over to one of the vans and banged on the door to get some back-up. She turned back to angry shouts, as Lomax, hands still cuffed behind his back, bulldozed Tom at the top of the steps. The back doors of the van opened and two of the officers jumped out and followed Kyra's eyeline. Tom, taller than Lomax, but not as well built, was pushing against him, trying to stop his escape. Lomax had lost his jacket, and his vest had been torn away; his chest was drenched. The two men struggled for a few moments at the top of the stairs before Lomax gave one final push with his shoulder, hands still cuffed behind his back. Tom tried to grab the railing, but it was slick with rain and he went toppling down the metal stairs until he hit the concrete at the bottom and lay motionless.

Lomax charged down after him, Kyra wasn't sure if he was going to run, or attack Tom again, but as soon as he reached the bottom, five coppers were on top of him and he lay sprawled out, taking vicious punches. He looked up amidst the beating and saw Kyra staring at him.

'I'm going to kill you, you fucking bitch!' he yelled.

Kyra, shaking and legs weak, collapsed on the ground next to Tom as the blood from his head mingled with the pool of rainwater in which he lay.

Chapter Seven

FRIDAY 2 FEBRUARY 2035

7.32 a.m.

The bus judders to a halt, the rumbling heat moving through my body bringing a surge of nausea. I adjust my expression to copy the one of bored indifference that I often observe on the other passengers, even though my heart is beating ten to the dozen with anticipation. The others probably think I'm off to work, but most people don't even see me, except some of the mothers with little ones. They draw away from me, almost as if they sense there is something to be feared but can't exactly put their finger on it.

Instinct.

The moment she steps on board, all my anxiety disappears, replaced by a lightness of being. She swipes her Commswatch on the pad by the driver and then moves down the aisle. I lower my eyes, watching her in my peripheral vision. She usually sits in the middle of the bus, to the left if there is a free seat. It took me a few trips to get her pattern. But today she moves up close, her pale, delicate fingers catching the pole nearby to steady herself as the bus pulls off, so close, then she sits down right in front of me.

From the moment I saw her I knew this one was the perfect offering.

Yes, this one will diminish the darkness, the loneliness, the fear.

I lean my head against the window and half close my eyes, adrenaline and joy moving through my body. I breathe in her scent, light and playful, roses and jasmine. She wears her gleaming fair hair in a loose bun, a long, pale tendril of it spilling over the collar of her coat. My fingers twitch as I resist the urge to reach out and touch it.

She reaches up and rubs the back of her neck and I take some pleasure in thinking she might be able to feel me watching her.

I came across her weeks ago – unexpectedly. Sometimes I go to her workplace and hide in plain sight. On one occasion, she smiled in my direction, but I knew she wasn't really registering me.

I want so much for her to see me, but not yet.

Not until the time is right.

7.45 a.m.

It was always a watershed moment, finally getting home and shutting her own front door behind her. Kyra had crept out before Molly and her mum had awoken, not wanting the difficult discussion about why she wasn't going to work.

It was cool and dark in the flat. She usually adjusted the lights and temperature remotely via her Commset before she left work. There was no point in using a timer. She had a quiet life – no partner to eat meals with, no kids needing picking up from after-school club, no cat to be fed – she had toyed with the idea, so that there was another living being in the flat, but had decided it was too much of a cliché.

Part of her liked the fact that everything was exactly where she had left it, how she had left it; the windows slightly open, her own breakfast dishes still in the sink, the toilet lid closed. There were never any surprises or anyone else demanding things that her exhaustion couldn't deliver. When Molly came over to stay, one night always seemed like enough. How much mess and noise could one teenager cause? Molly slept on the pull-out sofa. Having her own room would be too much of an invitation.

The symmetrical block of compact apartments was identical to the other blocks along the street and probably fairly similar inside too. She suspected they all had the

59

same small black built-in, easy-clean kitchenette and the open-plan living area, which was big enough for a sofa and small table and chairs. Kyra had tried to individualise her flat with a few personal items on the shelf unit, including a photograph of her dad and Emma, a tiny crackled china vase with a shamrock design that had been her grandmother's, and a handful of non-digital books that she couldn't let go of.

She made a coffee and went to the fridge to replace the milk. On closing the door, she read the digital smart message on the front:

replenish salad boxes, eggs; low on milk; butter past use-by date 2 days; remember to take daily Nutri-Pod.

'Screen on,' she commanded as she moved back into the living area and slumped across the sofa. An exercise programme burst onto the screen, shown regularly before the news updates on the hour to try to encourage the fight against obesity.

Between worrying about her mum and Molly, and wondering about Lomax, sleep had evaded her the previous night. And those dreams about the soldiers . . . they were probably projections of her brain after the Brownrigg transference, but she might mention them to Jimmy. Shit – she still hadn't replied to his text. She'd call him tomorrow, when she wasn't so fed up. She took her Commset off her wrist, took her earpiece out and put them on the table nearby.

'Kyra Sullivan – jobs search.' The screen immediately switched from programmes to hypernet search. She had saved her data from before she had met Carter but she hadn't expected to be using it so soon. She scrolled down the results, but there was nothing exciting or unexpected

– genetics lab, research lab, child mental health psychologist, neurology clinic. None of them seemed as interesting as her last job, none appeared to allow for much creativity or independence, certainly none of them were paying as much money as Carter had given her.

With a feeling of dread, knowing what she might see, she said, 'News channel.'

She immediately recognised the face of one of the first victims of the Mizpah Murderer: Skylar Lowndry, the first Type B victim, killed in 2019. Kyra wasn't surprised the news had chosen this particular image. Skylar's slightly lopsided smile on an otherwise perfect face gave her a look of heart-rending vulnerability. Why was it that the death of a beautiful young person always seemed more tragic? Wouldn't that have been what she would have advised when working with the police? Get the most attractive photographs of the deceased, the most relatable, the most sympathy-inducing, to trigger people to help catch the monster.

Kyra remembered when they had found Skylar, her white dress fanned out in the water, blonde hair radiating, open eyes like pale marbles under the glassy surface, the silver Mizpah pendant around her neck. It had reminded her of a painting she had seen in the Tate – *Ophelia*.

It was an image that would never leave her.

The pond had frozen over solid, making it impossible initially to remove her body or examine her. The surface of the water had been like glass, Skylar's face breaking through as though a mask had been laid on top of the ice, the rest of her body visible but untouchable. Kyra shook at the memory of Skylar's pale blue lips, the tips of her eyelashes covered in tiny icy beads, her small black pupils unseeing, the tops of her fingers poking out from the ice as her hands had floated, palm-up.

And resting on her chest, a box, brightly coloured, shocking pink, tied with an orange satin ribbon . . .

It had been the contents of the box that had linked the two deaths, proving the two women were killed by the same man, establishing the pattern.

On her thirtieth birthday, in the midst of the investigation, her mother and Molly had bought Kyra a special gift, one they knew she would appreciate, and presented it to her in a box with a bow. She could still see the confusion on their faces, the shock when she dropped the box and ran to the bathroom to vomit.

How could she have explained to them what had been in the last box like this that she had seen?

Kyra's Commset rang, vibrating against the wooden surface of the small table on which it lay, snapping her out of her thoughts. Her mother's face appeared on the small screen, her expression distraught, giving Kyra a stab of anxiety.

'Mum? What's wrong?'

'Molly's gone!' A gasp from her mother as though she was shocked by her own words.

'Again?' Kyra flopped back onto the sofa and put her hand to her forehead.

She got it, Molly was upset, but she couldn't have picked a worse time to do one of her disappearing acts.

'When?' She focused back on her mother's face.

'I went in to wake her this morning and her bed was empty. I'm so worried . . . and with him out, and—'

'Mum! Mum! Take a moment.' The thought of her niece being out and about when Lomax was free made her stomach cold with fear.

Kyra watched as her mother wiped her eyes with a tissue.

'Try not to worry, Mum. She'll come back, she always does. You know what she's like. She'll be home before you know it. She's bound to have been distressed with you know . . .'

But her words belied her own anxiety and guilt. She should have checked on Molly before she left, but she had listened for at least half an hour through the bedroom wall as the poor girl had cried herself to sleep in the night and she hadn't wanted to disturb her.

Molly was beautiful, smart and headstrong, but incredibly fragile. Who wouldn't be in her situation – seeing her mother abducted, never having known her father, and then her beloved grandfather passing away. So much loss in her short life.

But still. Why cause more trouble?

'I've tried her Commset a million times, but nothing,' her mum said.

Why the hell didn't I get one of Jimmy's bloody tracking chips? Then she would have known exactly where Molly was, could have gone straight there and given her a piece of her mind. But Molly would never have agreed to a chip. She was nearly eighteen; the legislature banned chipping children without their consent over the age of twelve.

'She's had a shock. She just needs some time to think. She'll call us soon. I'm sure of it.' Kyra paused. 'I'm sorry. I should do more. She should stay with me for a while, give you a break.'

Her mother's eyes were rimmed with pink, her cheeks red from crying.

'That wouldn't work,' her mum sniffed. 'Molly needs someone who's around all the time. You're always at work. And you have no patience.'

Kyra ignored this. 'She might have left for college early.' It was unlikely, knowing Molly. 'I don't really know what we can do right now except try to ring her again. She'll come home when she's hungry or tired. Try not to lose it with her, okay? She probably needs to calm down, have a bit of head space. When she's back I'll come over and talk to her. There's no point in you two clashing horns again. It will only make things more difficult for you.'

Some psychologist I am! I should have anticipated that Molly would have had a reaction to her mother's killer being back out on the streets. She might have only been little when her mum died, but it never goes away.

But, on reflection, she knew it was her own guilt that was blinding her. *If it wasn't for me, Molly would still have her mother.*

She pushed the thought away.

'She'll calm down once the police have got him back in custody.' Kyra couldn't bear to say his name.

'She'll be back by Tuesday for Emma's anniversary, won't she?'

'Of course she will, Mum.' Kyra tried to sound as confident as possible. Reassurance was what was needed.

'Fourteen years.' She watched her mum on the screen shaking her head. 'Right then.' She took a deep breath. 'I'll call you as soon as I hear anything.'

'Okay, Mum, speak later.'

As her Commset screen blacked out, Kyra lay back on the sofa.

Her mind drifted back to the pretty gift box that had lain on the chest of Skylar Lowndry – the shocking pink cardboard, the orange satin ribbon pulled and placed in an evidence bag, the tension as the lid was lifted . . .

And, inside, a pair of severed hands holding a real human heart.

Chapter Eight

7.58 a.m.

He's waiting for her at the bus stop near the hospital, almost pulls her from the step in his eagerness, wraps himself around her. He's handsome, older than her. I wonder for a moment if I've made a mistake, but then I see her face in profile, a reluctance, a wariness. She leans away from him slightly.

An old man in between us is struggling to alight. I reach out my arm to guide him; he takes it gratefully, his wrinkly face smooths momentarily with a smile, reflecting my own, well-practised one.

I move towards the hospital in the slipstream of people but duck out to stand close to the couple as he corrals her outside the entrance, his face earnest. He has a few admiring looks from women passing by. It might be the uniform he wears, they probably think he's a doctor.

I study my mini-screen, raising my head intermittently, pretending I am waiting for someone so that I can listen. I shift my feet slightly, I've found that if I stand too still people notice something's not quite right.

As they talk I swipe through the photographs I have collected of her; yoga at the Well-Being centre, in the gym, going to the Farmer's Arms with her friends, working at the hospital.

I have been this close to her twice before; once in a queue in a shop, and once when I was handing out anti-poverty leaflets

65

in the street. I stole them from a protestor so that I could get close to her. That time, I got to look in her eyes. I've even sat in the waiting room, another faceless patient, but she didn't seem to notice that my name was never called.

This is the closest I have been to them when they have been together.

'Have you thought more about my offer, Isabel?' he asks, moving his face in front of hers whenever she looks away so she can't avoid his gaze.

Isabel.

Such a beautiful name.

'Please say you'll move in with me,' he whines.

I've heard her speak before but, every time, it gets me in the guts, like a beautiful piece of music that moves me.

'I need to concentrate on my exams first, Andrew. Let's talk about it then.' She nods as if to verify her words, or maybe to appease him.

He takes her hands and holds them in his own, together in front of her, as though he is praying, and I am reminded of a statue at the children's home of the Virgin Mary, her pale hair and blue eyes not unlike Isabel's.

On the ring finger of his left hand there is a white indentation, a history in pigmentation, a warning.

'Don't go out tonight, stay in with me. We'll get some food, wine, have a cosy night in.'

'I promised the girls I'd go out with them.' She pulls her hands away from his and loosens the collar of her coat as she talks. 'Can't we meet in the canteen when you've finished your first shift?'

You are not worthy of her, Andrew.

'Give them a miss tonight – I need you more than they do! Anyway, the Farmer's Arms is a dump! Wouldn't you rather be with me?'

That is all the information I need.

Tonight is the night.

66

Kyra's Commset rang off just as she stepped out of the shower.

The screen was still bright when she picked it up, hoping to see Molly's number.

TOM MORGAN.

Her heart rate rose as she commanded a return call, audio only. Holding her towel tightly around her, she placed her Commset on her ear, rivulets from her short, slicked-back hair running down her back.

He answered immediately.

'We found a body, early this morning at the Scrambles. It looks like she died last night.' He sighed. 'I'm sorry if this brings back difficult memories, but I want you to hear this from me. The heart and the hands . . . they're gone.'

A wave of horrific recognition rolled over her. She opened her mouth, but it took a moment for the words to come. Feeling as though she had been punched in the stomach, she reeled back and sat down on the edge of the sofa.

And so it had begun.

His ritual – two murders, six days apart.

'Was she a Type-A?'

This was how the police had referred to the first women found each year, the ones who had been butchered and dumped. It had probably been the kindest way to refer to them, as they had been women down on their luck, pariahs according to the press: a prostitute in 2019; Madelyn, a drug addict, in 2020; and then Emma.

Kyra had struggled to understand the link between the other women and Emma. She had been no saint, but she had been no pariah either. Yes, she had lived an unconventional life, residing in a squat, having a baby young, but she had fought for the environment; that had been her passion. Maybe that was it – she had been arrested a few times for eco-protests. But that wasn't the same as prostitution and drug-taking, was it? What had the killer known about Emma that made him take her? As a profiler it was her job to know these things, to understand the pattern, but she had failed. Maybe Tom had been right, she had been too close to the case; she hadn't been able to see beyond her love for Emma.

'Yes, she was Type A,' Tom answered eventually.

'But you can't find him? Why not? Can't you use his bio-tracker?' she said finally. It was obvious, wasn't it? All criminals had bio-trackers injected before they even left court.

'It was an old one. Lomax has been locked up for fourteen years. He must have found a way to block the signal. The body was found down at the Scrambles, there're plenty of the criminal fraternity down there who would be willing to help Lomax with the tech.'

Kyra knew of the Scrambles from her time working with the police. The Croxley Estate, as was its official title, was a ghost town of tiny abandoned houses, part-government owned, created as affordable housing for public sector workers. It had been built at the turn of the century on a landfill site on the Thames which was later discovered to be hazardous, uninhabitable. Junkies and drifters were its main residents now, and those with nowhere else to call home. There was a feeling of collective tiredness, a malaise, as though the toxicity had poisoned their spirits. It didn't surprise her that there was an illegal dump out there, the detritus of humanity mixed with the detritus of everyday life.

'He might be hiding down there,' Tom said. 'I can't see anyone grassing him up. We've sent an armed team in, but we don't want another riot on our hands. They hate us as it is.'

Us?

So, she was officially back with the police.

'What are you going to do now, wait until next Wednesday night to see if he follows the same pattern?' She couldn't help the bitterness in her tone.

'We're going to do everything we can to catch him before that happens.'

Once the call was over, Kyra dried and dressed in a jumper and jeans. In the living room she put the news channel on and images from the Scrambles appeared. The reporter at the scene was saying: *'There are rumours she may be the latest victim of the serial murderer known as the Mizpah Murderer. David Lomax, jailed for the killings fourteen years ago, recently escaped during his mother's funeral and is presently at large. Police have not yet made any statement as to whether or not Lomax is responsible, nor have they given the identity of the woman whose remains were found on a refuse dump here in the derelict Croxley Housing estate which is known locally as the Scrambles . . .'*

Kyra let her mind wander over thoughts that she had locked away for so long. There were some things that didn't make sense – why had he picked Emma? What did Lomax's expression mean when he saw the Mizpah pendant? Why were the two types of victims so disparate? If she could only find the clue that would help her crack the code and get to the truth of the matter. Didn't she owe it to her sister, to the families of the other victims? And if she could understand why the killer did those things, wouldn't she be able to prevent someone else from dying?

Kyra suddenly imagined herself using CASNDRA with Lomax, lying near the sleeping beast in a darkened lab, excavating the untapped depths of his depravity.

The thought made her shudder.

Would she find the answers to all the painful questions that had tormented her for so long if she looked into his mind? Could she bear to?

It wasn't possible anyway. They didn't know where Lomax was. She would have to use a more conventional method of finding answers.

Today was Friday. He had killed last night. She had until midnight on Wednesday before he killed his next victim.

She lifted her laptop from on top of the shelving unit and sat at the small table. With a sense of trepidation, she brought up the psychological evaluation report files from the original case which she had hidden away for fourteen years, prepared to hunt for a clue as to where he might be hiding now.

With a deep breath, she typed in the password MIZPAH.

9.09 a.m.

I can smell her perfume standing here, the roses and the jasmine, and I feel so close to her. I have taken off my shoes, left them at the bottom of the stairs as a worshipper might when they enter a temple barefoot, wanting to feel the carpet she stands on beneath my skin.

I walked back from the hospital to give myself some time to think. Her father left early for work. It's only the two of them.

Elise was only a child when she died, but I wonder if she would have had a bedroom like this when she reached Isabel's age – a bridge between girlhood and womanhood played out between the childhood bed and the dressing table full of make-up, the soft toys on top of the wardrobe and the seductive clothes inside, the pink floral wallpaper and the spiked heels.

I open a drawer and touch some of Isabel's clothes, lift them and put them next to my face, they are soft and fragrant. I run my fingers across her mirror, thinking of what she sees when she looks into the glass. I pull back her bedclothes and touch the cotton sheet beneath.

The feeling of being so close to her, in her space, overwhelms me.

But then I think of my Elise, all the things she never got to do, to be. There was no perfume for Elise, no growing up and exploring her life as a woman . . . and before I know it, great sobs are choking me. I am on my haunches, broken, in the middle of the bedroom floor.

Finally, when I am spent, I rise up.

I pick up a glass angel paperweight that sits on the dresser amongst the bottles and tubes of make-up. It is crude and colourless, the head no more than a spherical blob, the body wide at the base, two tiny wings denoting its status melded to its featureless bulk.

I decide it is a sign that Isabel is the next angel I should send to Elise to protect her.

She was always afraid of the dark.

Chapter Nine

FRIDAY 2 FEBRUARY 2035

2.15 p.m.

A young female officer, who had introduced herself as DC Alex Finn, had shown Kyra in to Tom's office ten minutes earlier. She had stood over Kyra, watching her suspiciously as the computer read her ID card, and her name, address and occupation came up on the screen. She had been pleasant and polite enough but had scrutinised Kyra when she had rejected her offer of coffee. How could she drink anything now? Her guts were churning thinking about the files she had spent all morning poring over, knowing what she was about to get herself involved in.

A can of worms.

Kyra gazed through the glass wall that overlooked the main core of the station – the Hub, as it was known – and could see fair-haired Alex moving cat-like through the group of other officers who were getting on with their work. The Hub had changed a great deal since Kyra had last been there. The room was not the confusion of computers, sockets, wires, filing cabinets and in-trays that it had been. Now it was stripped back, minimalist, decorated in pale and mid-grey tones which gave a calm, serious atmosphere. Gone were the laptops, replaced by large motion-and-voice-activated computer screens placed almost continuously around the walls of the office, like windows onto the world of crime. There were no radios, telephones or even mobiles visible now that discreet Commsets were the standard.

The door to Tom's office opened and suddenly he was there, his familiar scent of woody notes and spice – cedar and amber? After all this time, he still wore the same aftershave. It immediately took her back to late nights at the station, the horrific crime photographs, the determination – the desperation.

He came up close and she wasn't sure if he was going to shake her by the hand, but he pulled her to him for a brief embrace. 'Good to see you.'

She was embarrassed and pleased at the same time. Being so close to him brought back happier memories, too. She hadn't exactly been fair to him when she had left. Was this his forgiveness?

Standing back, they studied each other, assessing the changes. He appeared well; older, still attractive. She could see the kindness in his deep-set grey eyes, although they were more haunted than the last time they had met. The silver had travelled in his hair from the temples and now there was a peppering of grey throughout. Time had passed, but the scar on his temple was still visible.

She wondered what changes Tom saw in her. No doubt she had put a little weight on, she wasn't in her twenties anymore, but being above-average height she thought she got away with it. There would be more lines around her light brown eyes, no doubt. Her dark hair was shorter than it had ever been.

'There's only fifteen minutes to afternoon briefing, so this will have to be quick,' he said, not unpleasantly, sitting down and pointing towards a chair on the other side of his grey desk which housed an integral screen, a stack of paper files next to it.

She saw him tracing her eyeline. 'Old habits. I prefer something I can hold.'

She sat down, uncertain of how he was going to react to her theory.

'You good?' he asked, and it was as if she had only seen him yesterday, as though they were sitting in the squad car, about to go out on a job.

'I'm good. I thought you'd be finished up by now, enjoying your retirement,' she said. Fifty-five was the usual age. 'I can't imagine you gardening, somehow.'

'Neither can I. I've got six months to go.'

'You'd better take up a hobby. I bet your wife won't want you under her feet all day.'

'I'm still on my own.'

She was taken aback and began to feel self-conscious standing in front of him, her body remembering. She didn't want to think about how her life could have been different, what she had left behind, what might have been. It was too painful. She had shut that part of herself down a long time ago. But she felt a loss.

'What about you?'

'Look at the pair of us, no partners, no kids. Married to our jobs.' She couldn't bear to think about CarterTech right now. She took a deep breath. 'Tom, I think there's something sinister with the Lomax case.'

'Such as?' he asked steadily, his expression flinty.

'I'm not one hundred per cent sure that Lomax did it.'

He pursed his lips, his eyes narrowed. She knew him so well.

'Look, I know it sounds . . . incredulous, but just hear me out.' She held her hands out in front of her as if bracing herself against his response. 'I know, it was a traumatic arrest, and you were hurt . . .' She kept her eyes locked onto his, so she didn't look at his scar. 'And then the other DI took over the case while you were in hospital . . .'

'Where's this going?' His voice was flat. 'We haven't even re-arrested him yet, but you're saying . . . what are you saying?'

'This morning, after you called and told me about the body, I went back into Lomax's files to find out where he might be hiding, see if there was anyone he might have contacted . . . anyone who might help him hole up—'

'We're on it, Kyra.' He glanced away, obviously irritated.

'I know, I know, but I found something that might suggest he didn't do it after all.'

Tom rubbed his eyes. 'Kyra, I don't need this now. I'm in the middle of a major manhunt, the DCI is on my back, the press on our heels—'

'Please, Tom.'

He sat back in his chair, staring at her, his expression unreadable.

'Look,' she began, aware of the wobble in her voice, 'there were doubts about Lomax, if he was the real killer.'

He sat forward now and pointed at her. 'No, you had doubts, Kyra. The evidence spoke for itself.'

'Yes, but I was thinking about his arrest. I saw his face, Tom, when he saw that Mizpah necklace that we found in his flat and he genuinely didn't recognise it.'

'You were the only person who saw his reaction. I can't put any weight on—'

'I know,' she interrupted, 'but I've been over the records, the interview I did with Lomax . . . before . . .' She stumbled on her words.

'Before we found Emma,' he finished for her.

76

That painful, brief window of time when she hoped Emma might have still been found alive.

'Kyra,' he said, his voice lowered, 'You shouldn't even have been allowed to interview him. I should have sent you home.'

'Yes, but we didn't know for sure at that point what had happened to her.'

Tom put his head in his hands, his elbows on the desk. She stood uneasily.

Finally his eyes met hers again.

'It's not your fault. It was all against my better judgement. I was in charge and I had . . .' Was he blushing? '. . . feelings for you, and I should have been more professional.' He cleared his throat. 'I shouldn't have let you. You were too fragile. You weren't thinking straight. There's no way that you could have made a professional judgement with what you were going through. Christ, if the DCI had known you were so close to the victim—'

She cut him off. 'Today I read the case files of the other psychologist, Dr Marie Taylor, the one who took over the case after me. Lomax told her that he didn't do it and at the first available opportunity he would get out and find the person that did. He's been waiting all this time to get revenge on the person who set him up.'

'He was manipulating you and Marie. Don't you see? That's what these people do. You of all people should know that.'

'Marie's one of the best we have. There's no way he'd pull the wool over her eyes. If you think that Lomax is some smooth-talking sociopath, Tom, then you're very much mistaken. He's not that sophisticated. During his interviews he was angry and he lost control. Even the screw at the prison reported him ranting about getting revenge

77

on whoever got him banged up.' She could tell by his face that she wasn't getting through to him. 'I heard him too, but I didn't want to believe it because I wanted someone to be punished. I didn't realise back then that's not the same thing as justice. Don't make the same mistake that I did.'

His eyes searched her face, as if trying to make sense of what she was saying.

She couldn't bear his expression and turned away, back to the window over the Hub. She watched as more officers came in and stood staring at the screens, talking to the computers, and to each other, in a constant relay of information – CCTV, photographs, diagrams and information popped up around them as though they were visible thought bubbles. One or two officers held their hands out, swiping and enlarging, even at a distance, to make the information more accessible.

Two of the images showed live webcam footage at the crime scene, police tape flapping in the breeze as a police officer stood guard.

'Look at the evidence. This latest body,' his voice was calmer now, 'it has all the hallmarks of Lomax's signature. See for yourself.' He looked up to the three large screens on his office walls to the left of his desk and said, 'Case 370928, Carmichael, Caylee. The computer swiftly complied and the centre screen displayed the image of a petite woman with long brown hair, brown eyes and fine features. The other two screens in the harrowing triptych showed a map of the body deposition site and a crime scene photograph of Caylee's body, discarded in black plastic, head wrapped in silver duct tape, hardly distinguishable from the refuse surrounding her. Her image filled the screen – her pure white skin, her arms ending in bony stumps, the coagulated blood capping the wrists where the hands should have been.

The photograph had been taken from above and showed Caylee's body lying on its side, the cavity of her missing heart hidden by broken bottles and what appeared to be a smashed screen.

Tom pointed up at the screen. 'Naked apart from bio-deg plastic, no sign of sexual assault, duct tape around head, the hands and the heart gone. No blood at the site, so mutilation has been carried out elsewhere and she's been dumped here just like Madelyn and—' he stopped. 'Like all the Type A victims.'

Kyra couldn't stop a little gasp escaping her lips.

He turned to look at her.

'I'm sorry,' he said, and then softer, 'but this is the work of the same man. It's too similar. All the hallmarks. I don't know if I should be showing you this. You're not with the police now.' He shrugged in resignation, 'but you know all this anyway.'

Her regular nightmares held testimony to this, her sister crying through the silver duct tape, begging her for help.

When she didn't reply, he stood up and came over to her. 'I'm trying to reassure you.' His voice was gentle as he leaned over her. She wanted to curl up in his arms, listen to his heartbeat, like the old times, forget all this horror.

'But all this . . . it made you ill back then. It forced you to give up everything, leave your job, us . . .'

She bristled.

'Lomax did it,' he continued, 'and that's all there is to it. I'm sorry to say this, but your judgement is clouded because of what happened to Emma. Lomax convinced you that he didn't do it. That's what psychopaths do. They mess with people's heads. They are so credulous. It's nothing to be ashamed of, falling for it . . . we'll never be able to know the truth of what is in such a mind as his . . .'

Never be able to know the truth . . . what's in his mind . . .
Her thoughts briefly flipped back to CASNDRA.

Kyra stood up straight and moved towards the door. 'Regardless of whether he is guilty or not,' she said in a cool tone, 'Lomax is still a risk to me and my family.' She turned around to face him. 'Either he's guilty and he killed my sister and he knows that I was on the team that arrested him or,' she paused, 'he isn't guilty and he knows I had doubts and I didn't stand up for him.'

'What do you want me to say?' Tom asked.

I want you to say you believe me! I want you to say you'll find the truth and stop the doubts and torment. I want to know my sister got justice!

Instead, she stood at the threshold of the door and said, 'If the real killer is out there, there will be another murder in the next few days – he won't be able to help himself, the pattern has to be fulfilled. It's what he has to do. We'll soon know if Lomax is the killer or not, because another woman will die.'

And with that, she let the door close on Tom Morgan.

Chapter Ten

FRIDAY 2 FEBRUARY

6.45 p.m.

ISABEL

She frowns at her reflection in the mirror. Why can't she be as tall as Liv or curvy like Ruby? She dresses quickly, having set out her clothes before her shower on her bedroom chair – a soft pale pink shirt, black skirt, faux-leather boots. It's only a drink in the pub with the girls, but she takes her time at the dresser over her make-up. Andrew doesn't like it when she wears too much make-up and she isn't allowed to wear any at all in the hospital – Health and Safety, apparently – so she makes the most of it in the evenings.

She's going to have to revise over the weekend so she decides she won't drink to excess. She thinks back over her tiring day – Bio-Mechanical Surgery Management at 8.30am, followed by another lecture at 10.30 a.m. in Psychology of Patient Care. Then ward rounds in the afternoon. Meeting Andrew for lunch in the canteen. It was cloying sometimes, working together, even if he was out and about in the ambulance most of the day. She wishes he wasn't so full-on sometimes.

Her dad will be back from work soon. He'll be tired from his shift at the power station. Good money but long hours – longer than hers. His tea is in the oven – his favourite, steak pie and she's made mash too. Since she can remember it's only been the two of them, but they're happy. How can she leave Dad living here on his own? But Andrew is pressing her for an answer.

'Offer' was the word he had used – more like ultimatum. Andrew would expect her to take over where his still-not-ex-wife had left off. She's not even sure if she loves him. She feels too young for that sort of commitment. If she agrees to moving in with him, it will mean the end of her Friday nights with her friends and what else, besides? Work together, live together, would it be too much? There would be no chance of her going on holiday in the summer with the girls then. They're her best friends – she needs them.

Her dad would be mad if he knew how old Andrew is. Although if he finds out Andrew is divorced, well, nearly divorced, he'll be furious. Not good enough, he would say. What about her gran – what will she say?

She looks around for her Commswatch and remembers she left it on her dresser before her shower. It lies next to her gran's ancient fob watch, a present for her twenty-first birthday just two months ago. What would she have done without her gran after her mum had gone? With no siblings it's a small family, intense sometimes, only her and her dad, as much as she loves him. That's another reason she needs the girls. They are her family too.

She straps the watch onto her wrist, and the black shiny square face lights up as soon as it feels her pulse. She'll be meeting the girls in just over an hour. She places her Commset in her ear and puts her mini-screen in her bag with a few bits of make-up. Lipgloss, a foundation compact. Almost immediately a message pings on her Commswatch, alongside a few photographs from the pub from last Friday night – Liv, her eyes crossed and tongue out, and one of Ruby pulling a duck face.

Looking forward to tonight!

And another one of her and Ruby chatting to a group of lads they used to go to school with. She deletes it, just in case.

She picks up the fob watch and puts it to her ear to hear its faint mechanical heartbeat, feeling its comforting tick against her cheek. 'It never loses a second,' her gran had said. She'd worn it on the wards in the 1960s and 70s when she'd made her rounds as a young nurse. 'I'm so proud of you,' she'd told Isabel, her eyes gleaming. 'Another nurse in the family.' Her dad had rolled his eyes, but then he'd smiled.

She thinks about Gran, with the watch pinned to her skirted uniform throughout her working day. These days they wear zip-up anti-bacs and there is no need for the three reasons her gran had given her for wearing a watch; recording patients' vitals, giving medicine at the correct intervals and recording accurate times of treatments on documentation. All of these details are taken care of electronically now by scanning devices.

She puts the fob back in pride of place next to her little glass angel. It was her mother's, one of the few things she had left behind, probably by mistake. Isabel can't part with it. She notices that there is something wrapped around the neck of the angel . . . a small silver pendant.

She doesn't recognise it.

She unwinds the chain from the angel's neck and looks closer – it is a half of a heart with words inscribed – the Lord between while one from – *what does it mean? What does the other half of the message say? It must be from Dad, an odd sort of present, she thinks, if she can't understand what it means. She doesn't want to hurt his feelings and so she puts it around her neck and then looks at herself in the mirror.*

'In my day,' her gran had said, 'unless you were a nurse,

watches were only for telling the time, for counting down to the next time we were off shift and could have some fun.'

At least the weekend is here. There is always something to look forward to, she tells herself. Soon she'll be out with the girls.

She can't wait.

7.15 p.m.

'I'm only going to the pub, Dad.' Her smile radiates love, concern, gentleness, all the things I have seen shine from her in the last few weeks, all the things I need for Elise.

He stands at the door in his black and yellow power station overalls. I am so close that, from my vantage point, I can almost see the letters on the insignia on his chest. His shoulders slope, one hand on the doorframe.

'Stay safe. Home by twelve. I can pick you up if you like.'

For a moment, I think my plans are in tatters and I feel a mixture of irritation and anxiety.

'Dad, you've had a long day,' her voice is high-pitched, teasing. It breaks my heart. You need a good sleep. Your dinner's in the oven, your favourite. Go on!' She points him back indoors, and they both smile.

I feel my adrenaline rush.

This is it.

From the shadows, I watch as Isabel moves off down the road, her father waving at the door. This will be the last time he ever sees his daughter alive.

He turns to go back inside but stops and looks around. He stands there for two minutes or so. I wonder can he sense me out there, waiting, watching.

I can't risk being seen now. I feel a rising heat – I need to move and move fast if I am going to get her by the bus stop.

Why doesn't he just go in?

Eventually, he shakes his head and turns around, closes the door behind him.

But by the time I get to the bus stop she has already gone.

I stand for a moment in the street, recalibrating.

I stay calm, not letting the anger escape. I'm going to need it to guide me. I keep it inside, letting it implode within me, turning the energy back into the driving force that will propel me.

I go to my vehicle, parked nearby. I start the engine, knowing exactly where she's going.

I adapt.

That is what I have always had to do.

It's what I am built for.

Chapter Eleven

FRIDAY 2 FEBRUARY

10.36 p.m.

Kyra marched straight up to Molly's room when she arrived at her mother's house, prompted by a phone call that her niece had returned. Her frustration was brimming, exacerbated by a fruitless search through the case files on the Mizpah Murderer.

'Kyra,' her mother called after her, 'don't be too tough on her.'

She stood outside Molly's door for a moment and took a deep breath.

How was she supposed to comfort someone whose mother's killer, or alleged killer at least, had escaped from prison?

The streetlight seeped through the long, pale lilac curtains in a gentle glow. All the doors on the two double wardrobes hung open, clothes spilling out. Old teddies sat on a top shelf and stared idly at the multitude of printed-out photographs of Molly and her friends in a collage on the wall opposite.

'You're back.' Kyra sat tentatively next to her on the double bed and flicked on a small lamp. Molly winced against the light.

Without her make-up she looked so young.

'Where've you been, Mols?' Kyra sounded disappointed although she had meant to go for sympathetic.

'With friends.' Molly did not look at her.

An old-fashioned framed photograph sat at the side of the bed, next to the lamp, which showed Emma, the same age as her daughter was now, looking adoringly at Molly, a toddler with chocolate smeared on her face staring right at the camera, dark curls like her mother, huge golden-brown eyes.

'Molly, you have to let us know where you are going, try not to worry your nan—'

'I can't help it if I'm upset! I'm fed up with you two always telling me what to do. I'm nearly eighteen!'

'I know, I know . . . but you can't run away whenever you feel like it! We've been worried about you.'

'I'm practically an adult and all I get is Molly do this, Molly do that!' She pummelled a pillow.

'What would Grandad say about this sort of behaviour?' Kyra asked gently, trying to reason with her. 'About running off and upsetting Nan?'

'Nothing! Grandad's dead! Like Mum!'

Molly flung herself back down on the bed and started to howl, like a toddler.

Kyra sat and stroked her long dark hair as she sobbed. Molly didn't push her away. Instead, they stayed like that, until she had cried herself out and lay with her face half smothered by the lilac pillow, her eyes swollen and sleepy.

'No one gets it,' she murmured.

'Gets what, love?'

'What it's like to have a mum who was murdered. My mates, they're lovely to me when I talk about it, but they don't get it.'

How could they?

Kyra smiled at her. 'I used to stroke your mum's hair like this when she was little and couldn't sleep. I used to put her to bed every night, when your nan was working late. She always insisted I got into her small bed which was a squash for the both of us. Sometimes we even put a sheet over the top and pretended we were camping.'

Molly gave a teary smile. 'You used to do that with me!'

'That's right. Your mum loved stories and I would read to her until she was tired, and then I would lie next to her in bed and stroke her hair as she drifted off, like I used to do with you too. That's my favourite memory of your mum.'

Molly's face fell again. 'Ky, I don't even remember her. I don't remember what her voice was like or what she smelled of or . . . anything. I only know her face because of the photos. I keep thinking I have real memories of her, but then I realise that I only saw a photograph and my mind is pretending that I remember the real thing. It's like she never existed . . .' Her voice was snuffly. 'There's a big hole in my life.' She put her hand on her stomach. 'Here. Or it feels like . . . I don't know . . . a heaviness squashing me down all the time.' Her eyes closed. 'And he . . . him . . . that bastard! He's out and free and doing it again! I wish he could be punished, the way I feel punished . . . all my life nearly . . . such a big part of me is missing.' She began to sob again.

How could Kyra explain to Molly that it was partly her own fault – Kyra's fault – that Emma had been out in the street when she had been taken? That she could have, should have, prevented her mum running out of that cafe if she had only thought about what she was going to say before she said it, if she hadn't said cruel things. Then this lovely girl, the daughter Kyra never had, wouldn't be suffering like this.

Guilt washed over her.

After a while, Molly settled and then her face became like a little girl's again. Moody Molly, Huggy Molly, Tidy Molly, Headstrong Molly, Untidy Molly – there were a whole load of Mollies at the moment.

'What was she like, Kyra? Tell me again.'

'She was very independent. She wanted to save the planet,' Kyra said with a sad smile. 'She always stuck to her guns. Headstrong, like you. Terrible dress sense, she clashed those colours!'

Molly's eyebrows were raised as she took in every word. 'And she lived in a commune?'

'That's a posh word for it. It was more like a squat really. I went there a couple of times – they had batik sheets with elephants on the walls and mattresses on the floor for beds. They didn't even have electricity or running water . . . buckets for toilets, that kind of thing.' She saw Molly's face. 'But they made the best of it. It was kind of . . . cool, I suppose. She was a free spirit.'

Free spirit, as though it was a good thing. She had to be loyal to Emma's memory, show her good side, her passion, her determination for the environment. There was no point in sullying Molly's ideal. 'When she was sixteen and supposed to be doing her exams she ran away and took part in a protest outside the Houses of Parliament about what was happening to the environment.'

'Was Grandad annoyed?'

'Yes,' Kyra said seriously, then smiling, 'but Nan and I were secretly proud of her. She was brave, your mum.'

'I looked her up on the hypernet. She was arrested once, wasn't she?'

So Molly did know about that side of Emma.

'Once or twice.' Kyra smiled. 'The government were trying to play down the eco-threat at first. They didn't want people panicking.'

'And they didn't want to stop making money from dodgy deals that affected the environment.'

'Correct.' Wow, it could have been Emma sitting there right in front of her. An immense surge of love flowed through Kyra that somehow seemed to heal the difficult day she'd had. 'They tried to hush it up, give the protestors a bad name, but then it all came out that Emma and people like her were right. But I've told you all this before!'

'I know, I just like hearing it.' Molly snuggled down. At least she seemed calmer now, less upset.

'Did she never tell you who my dad was? Do you think I could ever find out?' Molly didn't make eye contact.

She could ask all she liked, but Kyra only knew his first name, Trent. Once Molly was born, Emma had never spoken of him again.

'The most important thing is that your mum loved you, from the moment she found out she was having you.' She remembered a tiny Molly in a see-through hospital cot, her sister's tired face and radiant smile.

'She loved me, didn't she?'

'Of course she did. Always.'

Molly suddenly sat up and wrapped her arms around Kyra. 'I love you, Ky.'

'I love you too, Mols.'

Molly lay back down. Kyra flicked off the bedside lamp casting the room back into semi-darkness and sat stroking Molly's hair until she was sure her niece was fast asleep. On her way out, she caught her own reflection in the mirror. Her skin was dry and taut, her eyes more dull than usual. From this angle shadows pooled around the base of her throat and Kyra reached up to check it wasn't blood. God, she needed some sleep. Something in the corner of the room caught her eye. She swung round, thinking there was someone standing there.

But it was only a heap of clothes on a chair.

Untidy like Emma too.

She went back down to the kitchen, her mother sat at the table, a milky film across the top of her long-cold tea. 'Shouldn't you be in bed by now?'

'I won't be able to sleep,' her mum replied.

'That poor kid, she's grieving for a mother she never really knew,' Kyra sighed, overwhelmed by a terrible sadness. She walked over to her mum, put her arms around her and kissed her gently on the forehead. 'At least we have our memories, Mum.'

'What can we do to make things better for her?'

'It's grief. There's not much we can do, except be there to pick up the pieces.' Kyra's heart ached for her niece. 'Whatever we do, there'll always be a mum-shaped hole in her life.'

Kyra's Commset rang. Her mother glanced at her anxiously as she answered it.

TOM MORGAN.

'What's happened?' she asked Tom, keeping her voice steady for her mother's sake.

'Nothing . . . nothing bad. I wanted to tell you myself, we've got him.'

The tension that she had felt since she had found he had escaped suddenly broke and she let out a gasp. 'Oh, thank God!'

She raised her eyebrows and nodded at her mum. 'They got him.' She pointed to her earpiece. 'It's my friend – she's watching the news,' she lied.

Someone was talking to Tom in the background. She waited until the muffled conversation stopped.

'Look, I've got to go,' he said. 'Don't worry. They've just arrested him. He's in custody.'

'Where was he?'

'Some hovel down at the Scrambles.'

The muscles in her stomach relaxed a little.

Then something occurred to her. Why would Lomax hide right by where the body had been found? It didn't make sense. It was another doubt, along with the case files and Lomax's protests.

'Are you sure—' she began.

But his tone went cold. 'We've got him, Kyra. Trust me. No one else is going to die now. It's over.'

And the line went dead.

Chapter Twelve

SATURDAY 3 FEBRUARY

9.01 a.m.

Kyra was lying in bed half-asleep when her Commswatch lit up on the bedside table next to her. The tiny wrist screen showed Tom's face via the camera at her front door.

She jumped up and pulled on her jeans and a sweater. A quick look in the mirror to smooth her hair and wipe away any residue of make-up and she let him in. He stood in the living room, shifting from one foot to the other.

'I'm sorry to call by so early. I hope you don't mind.'

She could smell his scent, mingled with the leather of his old messenger bag slung across his body.

'How did you know where I live?'

'Your ID reading when you came into the station. It's on the records. I hope you don't mind.'

Of course, when Alex had scanned her. She shrugged and showed him to the small wooden table. He pulled a chair out and sat down, leaving on his navy coat but taking his bag from his shoulder.

She made her way over to the small kitchenette, painfully aware of him watching her.

'Coffee? It's only synthetic, I'm afraid.'

He nodded and she spooned it into two mugs and poured water from the thermal tap.

She sat back down and passed him the coffee as he tugged at his earlobe. She could always tell when he was preoccupied.

'A personal visit? Is there something I need to know?' Her anxiety was reflecting his serious expression. 'You have got him, haven't you? He hasn't hurt anyone else, has he? I mean, we weren't too late?'

The 'we' again.

'No . . . no, he hasn't hurt anyone.'

She exhaled but when he continued to look pensive, she asked, 'So, what is it?'

'I need your help.' He paused and sipped his coffee, which was clearly too hot. He winced. 'We removed Lomax's bio-tracker and analysed it. It was still working. He had tried to remove it but failed. In the end, his only option was to use a blocker. Anyway, we could see the routes he has taken over the last two days.' He tugged at his earlobe again. 'Lomax wasn't anywhere near where the body was found. In fact, he wasn't anywhere near that part of the Scrambles.'

Kyra took a moment for this to sink in. She thought back to her doubts the previous night. Killers didn't usually hide so close to the deposition site.

'So, you're saying?'

'I'm saying that either Lomax had an accomplice, someone who dumped the body for him . . . or he didn't do it.'

A creeping coldness enveloped her.

'Tom, yesterday I told you there was something weird going on and now you're telling me what? That I was right?'

'We can't jump to conclusions.'

She folded her arms across her chest. 'I don't see why you're telling *me*—'

'We want to interview Lomax, to get to the truth of the matter.'

She shrugged again. Why should she make things easy for him?

'What's that got to do with me?'

She reached out, took her coffee mug with both hands and looked at him over the rim, taking a sip. She put the mug back down on the table slowly.

'I want you to interview him.' His eyes bored into her. 'Analyse him, find out whether he's telling the truth.'

Her chest became a beehive again, her stomach prickling with tiny stings.

'You're joking, right?' How could he ask this of her? After everything that had happened? After the fact that she had told him what a threat Lomax was to her?

He shook his head, unblinking. 'You've done it before.'

'Yesterday you thought I was a crackpot, and today you want me to do your dirty work? What's your DCI going to say? Surely she won't let me on the case, too involved?'

'There's no way she'd let anyone on the case if they were this close. I've told her you're a freelance consultant profiler and that you worked on the original case – she doesn't know the connection. You'll be paid.'

'So just throw money at me and I'll do whatever—'

'Look, I know how difficult this must be for you—'

'Do you?' she asked, eyebrows raised.

'And I wouldn't put you in this position if I really didn't have to. I wouldn't want you to be upset. Whatever happened between us in the past, you're still my friend.'

She remembered him holding her back when they found Emma's body, his strong arms around her, preventing her from seeing her beloved sister broken and dead.

He wasn't holding her back anymore.

'Please, think about it. Who would be better than you to talk to him? You were there on the original Mizpah Murder case, someone who got the whole picture. Someone who understands how he works.'

She pushed her coffee mug away. 'Tom, I'm not a criminal profiler anymore. I'm not sure I can—'

'Please, Kyra.' He reached out to touch her hand, but she withdrew it.

'Jesus, Tom! Yesterday you practically threw me out of your office because I said I doubted he even did it! And now you're asking me to, what? Sit in a room with a man who might, or might not, have butchered my sister? Or who is at the least furious with me because I didn't stand up for him when he knew that I had my doubts? Do you know what he might do to me?'

'There's no one else on the team now who was on the original case. You were there; you saw it all, and you were the only person who questioned the conviction.'

Yes, and look where that had got her – ridiculed by the whole of the department back then, rejected by Tom just yesterday. It had been another reason she had left that life behind.

'You were never one hundred per cent convinced. I couldn't understand why as the evidence seemed clear-cut. But now . . . with the findings today, there might be some substance to your doubts.'

She sat in silence, watching him.

'But maybe . . .' He leaned forward, elbows on the table, and made a steeple of his fingers, 'Maybe you saw something that I didn't. I wanted the case to be over, boxed off and the evidence seemed so strong – Lomax had a violent history, witnesses placed him near the scene of the crime, his DNA on some of the bodies—'

'It seemed like he did it,' she agreed finally.

But still, she had checked the news every February for years afterwards.

Just in case.

They sat in uneasy silence for a while.

'Why did you call me? I don't see what I can do,' she protested. 'I left all that behind, Tom. The case, my sister . . . the other things.' She saw a hint of recognition in his eyes. 'It was overwhelming. I'm not sure I want to be reminded of all that.'

He ran his fingers along the edge of the table and then their eyes met. She could see the desperation.

'I need someone to help me find the truth.'

The truth. He knew that would tantalise her. He knew that was what drove her.

But she knew him too. She knew there was more to it than that.

'You're not telling me everything.' She was afraid of what was coming.

Tom leaned forward. 'Please, Kyra, I need to get to the bottom of this and Lomax says he'll only talk to you.' He sat forward. 'No one else.'

So this was Lomax's request.

Kyra felt her chest tightening, the blood rushing to her head, her saliva honey-thick. Images flashed before her: the grimy flat, the metal stairs, a Mizpah necklace, Tom lying on the ground, the blood.

'No way, Tom.' Her breathing became ragged. 'I don't work with the police now. I'm a neuropsychologist. I look at people's brains to see if I can fix them, make them better. I'm right at the end of the queue when it comes to talking to criminals, and whatever you say about Lomax being wrongly convicted, whether or not he's a serial killer, he's still a vicious, violent bastard. Look what he did to you!'

Tom stood up, and she was surprised at a sudden feeling that she didn't want him to go. He checked his Commswatch. It must have been on silent as she hadn't heard anything.

'I have to take this. I'll right be outside.' He reached into his bag and took out a police-issue mini-screen. 'I am sorry.' He looked genuinely remorseful, but then his face hardened. 'I have no other option.'

He placed the mini-screen on the table, his eyes imploring. 'I can't let him get away, Kyra. I need to wrap this one up, especially before I call it a day with the job.' He spoke into his Commset, 'Detective Inspector Morgan . . .' as he walked out of the door.

Kyra could hear the buzz of his deep voice in the hallway, but not make out any of the words he was saying. Despite her protestations, her mind was already turning over the details, still fresh even after fourteen years. Her brain warned her not to look, screamed for her not to get involved but, automatically, her finger reached out and started swiping at the screen.

The need to know was so strong, irresistible.

Images of an autopsy room, the horizontal shiny white tiles and dark grout that reminded her of the swimming baths when she was young, pulling on Emma's armbands.

Her head started spinning.

Caylee Carmichael . . . female Caucasian . . . 160cms . . . aged twenty-four . . . identified via dental records . . . and . . .

Next there was a photograph of the body at the deposition site.

. . . distinctive features – scar on right shoulder, mole behind left ear, tiger tattoo on left thigh . . .

She swiped to the next photograph – the tattoo – the slightly blurred blue of old ink, the tiger's claws drawn to look as though they had dug into the skin, three inscribed scratches.

Appendix and Caesarean scars . . .

Her stomach roller-coastered at the thought.

She swiped again – Caylee's face unwrapped, expressionless, a bluish tinge to the eyelids and lips. Her porcelain skin was marked with striations from the tight banding of the duct tape which had been cut off by the scalpel and lay at the side of her head. Kyra could see clumps of dark hair stuck to it.

How dare Tom pollute her sanctuary by bringing these abhorrent images to her home – to the table she ate at! She would never be able to sit here again without thinking of these pictures.

But her heart went out to Caylee. That poor woman. The caesarean scar.

Why should she put herself through this? She didn't owe Tom anything, did she?

A few minutes later, Tom came back into the room. Kyra would not look at him. Seeing the autopsy report and the photographs had opened some long-hidden wound inside her. The swarm of bees in her blood raged through her body, her nerves buzzing, reaching the very ends of her fingertips.

Tom glanced at the mini-screen. Was he going to leave it there until she agreed to do what he wanted?

He stood by the doorway for a moment, watching her. Did he expect her to give him an answer now? Her mind was a mess of memories and emotions and those bloody images. She couldn't have spoken even if she'd wanted to.

He picked up his bag. 'I have to go.' He paused. 'Have a think, call me later?'

The door closed quietly behind him.

This was the case – the one that never left you, the one that kept you awake at nights, roamed about in your mind at your lowest points, that would haunt you in retirement.

Was Lomax the Mizpah Murderer? Had they got the wrong man? Had she got justice for Emma? Would she find out anything about her sister's last moments – the thing that haunted her most of all?

Maybe this was the way to exorcise the ghosts.

Panicked by her own decision, but determined to see it through, she braced herself and ran out after him.

'Tom!' she yelped, leaning over the banister, her voice reverberating around the communal stairwell.

He stopped mid-step and stared up at her, his mouth set in a hard line.

'I want to help.' Her heart threshed.

She couldn't take it back now.

He sighed heavily and then gave a brief smile. 'Thank you. I know what this means to you. I'll drive. We can talk on the way.'

A micro-expression flitted across his features. What was that, fear? Concern for her? She brushed it aside. She was here now, ready to face these ghosts and lay them to rest.

Once and for all.

Chapter Thirteen

SATURDAY 3 FEBRUARY

9.35 a.m.

ISABEL

Pain explodes in her skull, forcing her awake. She peels open her eyes, but the darkness is thick and unrelenting. Lifting her arms to rub her face, her muscles feel weak and heavy. She is in a deep dream and cannot rouse herself. Where is she? Where has she been? She blinks and widens her eyes, but she is still blind.

What time is it? How much did she drink last night? She had only meant to have a few. She should be studying today. How can she do that with a hangover? She reaches out a hand for her Commset, to put the light on, but instead of finding her bedside drawers her knuckles hit something hard and resistant.

Feeling a growing panic rising and desperately trying to find some light, she raises her head, but it makes contact with something above her and a metallic hollow rumble terrifies her.

She lies still for a moment, listening to her own heart as it slowly beats out time, feeling doped, wondering if she'd been spiked at the pub. Where is she? Tentatively, she raises her arms above her head. She doesn't have to reach far to find ice-cold metal, smooth beneath her fingertips; it stretches as far above her body as she can feel. In fearful clarity, she recognises that she is surrounded, enclosed by unrelenting steel.

She can hear screaming, bouncing off the metal casing, and it's only when her throat burns that she realises the howling sound is coming from her own mouth.

Suddenly there is movement nearby and the clanging, banging sounds terrify her. She struggles harder to move her body, but her muscles will not respond.

The door of the metal box is thrown open and brightness floods in, scorching her eyes. She thought she would be relieved when she finally saw the light.

Instead, there is no escape from it and she is completely vulnerable in her blindness.

There is someone there with her.

Her slight body trembles as the metal tray is pulled out, the vibrations of the wheels rattle through her bones. The thin sheets and the cold make her feel even more vulnerable; laid out on the table, she reaches down, not understanding why she can't move her legs, and feels thick straps across her waist and the lower half of her body. She raises her hands weakly in a futile attempt to shield herself.

An antiseptic smell fills her nostrils, as a shape blocks the light and her fear peaks. Her ears still ring with her own terrified screams. Her pupils, flooded with light, are useless, but she half-closes her eyes and tries desperately to focus, to see something to help her understand. When she looks behind her, she sees the receptacle she has been held in – so familiar to her at the hospital – a mortuary fridge.

And she thinks: I'm going to die.

'Right, I'll introduce you to the rest of the team,' Tom said, leading Kyra into the Hub.

Things had changed at the station — the security pad was long gone, but she could still recite the door code by heart even after fourteen years. She watched as Tom approached the door to the Hub and it opened automatically via a Behaviour ID reader that scrutinised his movements. She was impressed; they had still used iris scanners in the lab. Since the crime wave associated with Chinese Lè and the terrorist attacks over the last ten years, the government had finally heeded the warnings and put money into the system.

Tom ambled in, held up his hand and everyone in the room immediately stopped what they were doing. There was an uncomfortable shuffling at the stranger in their midst. Only Alex, who had shown her in yesterday, gave her a small nod, but then eyed her suspiciously like the others. Alex stood next to Tom, her arms folded across her armoured vest, so thin and lightweight that they could be worn most of the time. She wore her fair hair in a plait over her shoulder which gave her a girlish look. Kyra noted she must be nearly twenty years younger than her. Young enough to have been her daughter. The thought gave her a jolt.

'First things first.' Tom's eyes swept round the room at the people who had gathered. 'Be aware of the Amber threat at the Hallgate factory near the docks. The press have recently outed them for flaunting emission regulations and there have been a few rumblings of an eco-terror threat. It doesn't affect our work but be aware.'

He took a deep breath. 'Now, on to the Lomax situation.' He inclined his head towards Kyra. 'This is Doctor Kyra Sullivan, a behavioural psychologist who worked on the original case. I thought it would be helpful to invite Kyra onto the investigation due to her extensive knowledge of the case. Please treat her as one of the team.'

She felt Alex's scrutiny, her eyes running up and down her civilian outfit of jeans and sky blue jumper. Was it obvious how out of her depth she was – a victim's sister pretending her interest was professional, just because she was the only one that Lomax would talk to? What would Alex make of that if she knew?

Behind Tom a computer was noting and recording everything he was saying, his words appearing on a screen. There were over twenty officers in the room, many of them uniformed, men and women of different ages and ranks. Most of them stood, but some leaned against the angled stools that sat in front of chest-height sloping desks on one side of the room. They were mainly empty as the body-cams and constant computer auto-logging meant there was less need for paperwork and writing. Kyra remembered the advertising campaign when she was last there: *Let the computers log and report, we're fighting crime!*

'Right,' Tom said, his eye twitching slightly, 'as you know, we've got a body – Caylee Carmichael, who was reported missing yesterday morning. Caylee lived with her sister Chloe who saw her last when she left for work on Thursday morning. She told Chloe she was doing a double shift at the Gainsborough factory on Fairfield Road and that she'd be back after midnight. She failed to return home. As we all know, Lomax was out on our ground at the time of the killing. It would be obvious to make the assumption that Lomax was responsible for Caylee's death due to the striking similarities. However, this particular murder is proving to be more complex.'

One of the officers, a sandy-haired man, locked his eyes on Kyra, his jaw going up and down as he chewed gum, and she was relieved when he finally looked away. She studied him out of the corner of her eye; his pale eyelashes, his belly pushing at his shirt buttons, his cynical expression.

'Lomax's bio-tracker has pointed to the fact that this case might not be as straightforward as it first appeared.' Tom pulled up a tracker-map on one of the screens behind him. It clearly showed the area around the Scrambles overlaid with a red dotted line. 'He appears to have made his way into the estate and into one of the houses,' Tom said, pointing towards the screen, 'and then looped back and out again. He said he spent the night here.' He indicated a red x on the map. 'In one of the local prostitute's houses.'

'Has she corroborated that?' asked a tall, dark-skinned officer. He was softly spoken for such a big man. A gentle giant, Kyra thought.

'Yes, Will,' Tom told him.

'Not exactly a reliable alibi,' said the sandy-haired man.

'Possibly not, Harry, but when we brought her in for interview, she said that he was with her all night when Caylee was murdered.'

'I'm surprised she spoke up,' Alex said. 'Won't she be charged with harbouring a criminal?'

'She's got bigger problems than that,' Will said. 'Do you know what happens to grasses at the Scrambles?'

Kyra had a brief memory of a young man hanging from a lamppost, a scrawled sign around his neck.

She flicked at her fringe with her hand to swat away the thought and turned her attention back to the screen again.

'Yes, but imagine what Lomax would do to her if she didn't give him an alibi?' said Harry.

'He's in the nick,' said Will, shrugging, his brown eyes scanning the room and catching Kyra's briefly. 'There's not much he can do to her now.'

'The tracker chip shows he didn't go anywhere near the rubbish dump at the body deposition site,' Tom said, pointing to the screen to the red x where Caylee's body had been found. 'We need to sort this mess out and find out what's going on.'

'It doesn't mean he didn't do it,' said Harry, still chewing. 'The chip might have been faulty.'

'I've had it checked.' Tom answered him directly. 'Although Lomax had it blocked so the prison couldn't find him, the tracker itself was untouched. He'd had a go at trying to remove it, but it was embedded quite deep into the thigh and he couldn't get to it. He made a right mess trying to get it out. We had one of our doctors remove it and then it was sent to the lab. It's an older version but it was accurate. He didn't go near where she was found.'

The bio-tracker made Kyra think about Jimmy.

Damn, she still hadn't called him back.

'Right, you've all read the brief on the original murders so I'm not going to go through the whole thing, but let's look at the evidence that convicted him.' Tom turned back to the main screens on the walls. 'Prisoner 573804 David Lomax,' he commanded. A photograph came up, repeated over and over around the room. Kyra had to force herself not to look away, aware of the officers' scrutiny.

Tom waved a hand at the nearest image in a sweeping motion and the face immediately appeared to come out of the screen and become larger. Tom turned his finger in a circle and the 3D image did a complete rotation of Lomax's head so that he could be seen from all angles.

'Life, full-term sentence, no possibility of parole. The court were convinced. It took us three years to make an arrest – less than three hours for the jury to convict. We had difficulty finding the killer because we didn't have his bio-matter on database to make a match. However, it was an attack on a prostitute in April 2021 that led us to Lomax. When his bio-matter was uploaded after that assault, a match came up with DNA that was found on two of the Mizpah victims.'

'Pretty convincing evidence,' said Harry.

'Yes. It is,' Tom replied. 'Lomax's record points to violence against women. There were numerous complaints of domestic violence against this man, but these accusations were always withdrawn when we tried to take them further, the victims no doubt coerced by Lomax himself. There was an arrest for violent disorder back in 2015, but his sample wasn't loaded to the bio-database, probably because it was unusable, but the case was never followed up.'

'Domestic violence doesn't lead to serial murder, though,' said Alex, arms still folded, eyes on the screen.

'Kyra?' Tom pointed at her and immediately her throat tightened. She stepped forward.

'No, that's true,' she said, her voice shaky. She cleared her throat. 'But frequently killers indulge in different types of criminal behaviour before they escalate to murder. No one becomes a serial killer overnight. There will have been indicators – possibly cruelty, petty crime, theft, sexual offending.' She sensed members of the team working out whether or not they rated her, Harry still chewing, Alex's face inscrutable.

She straightened her back. 'So, yes, it is possible. However, Lomax doesn't show many of the psychopathic traits one would expect in such a case as this.' Harry was fiddling with the buttons on his shirt. 'I assessed him, briefly, after his arrest,' Kyra said quietly.

Alex raised her eyebrows. Was she impressed or surprised? Harry looked up.

'In my professional opinion,' Kyra continued, 'Lomax, although a violent criminal, is not a psychopath. He wasn't calm under pressure; in fact, he was quite the opposite. He was very angry, claiming he'd been stitched up. He lacked charm and didn't appear to be smart enough to be manipulative. Lomax uses brute force to get what he wants. He did not fulfil a serial killer profile in a number of ways.'

'That could be how he was manipulating you,' suggested Alex. 'He hid his psycho-ness from you by pretending to be normal.'

Harry smirked, but it had been a serious comment.

Kyra liked her.

Everyone turned back to Tom when he began to speak again.

'Looking at the original conviction, it was sound. We even had witnesses and CCTV that placed Lomax near one of the dump sites. Only near, however, not at. Maybe there were presumptions, but the jury were convinced by the DNA.'

The team studied the screens. Harry broke the silence. 'What's the point in wasting time and resources when it's clear from the evidence in the original crimes that Lomax did it?'

There was a murmur of agreement around the room. Tom appeared weary but squared his shoulders.

'There are still some questions that need answering,' he said. 'To start with, Lomax has always protested his innocence. Nothing unusual about that. He has an alibi which, although shaky, is corroborated by the tracker. Obviously we know now that he wasn't at the body dep site. However, Caylee was found like the others: black plastic, duct tape, heart and hands removed.' He rubbed his forehead. 'There's no way Lomax could have gotten the items he used or got rid of the body without help.'

'Yeah, you can't exactly buy those things in the local shop without drawing attention to yourself,' said Harry.

'He certainly wouldn't be able to get his hands on a sternal saw,' said Alex.

'Unless he had them stored somewhere?' suggested Will.

'It's always a possibility', Tom said, '. . . but back in the day we tore apart all the properties he owned.'

'And with no real friends or associates . . . no visitors that we can trace yet . . . he was an angry, nasty man who seems to have had a history of pissing people off and being an alpha – those sorts of people don't tend to have close friends,' Alex added.

When Kyra nodded in agreement, she saw the corners of Alex's mouth twitch.

Tom said, 'When the SOCOs cleaned him down, they had found no evidence of Caylee on him. He hadn't got any scratches, or blood, no injuries from someone who was defending herself. According to the lab, he hadn't appeared to have washed since he had left prison, so I think we should have found some evidence on his body but there was none.'

'Are you saying he didn't do it?' asked Harry, confused.

'I'm saying that there's something clearly not right and we need to explore all avenues. We need to get down to it. Kyra and I are going to visit Caylee's sister to inform her of Caylee's death and see if there are any leads.'

'Do you want me to come?' asked Alex.

'No, we're good.' Tom didn't look at her.

Alex gave Kyra a hard stare. 'But she's not even police.' Alex sounded more disappointed than annoyed.

Just as they had been starting to see eye to eye.

Tom ignored her.

'Right, when I get back, I want a list of Lomax's associates, visitors, enemies, the works.'

Kyra followed him to the door. She turned around briefly to say goodbye, but everyone was focused on their jobs, except Alex who watched as she left the Hub with the boss.

Chapter Fourteen

SATURDAY 3 FEBRUARY

10.27 a.m.

Chloe Carmichael looked much as Kyra had imagined her sister, Caylee, to have been in life. She was small, with dark hair and a hint of a tattoo visible below the neckline of her top which gave an edge to her prettiness. But now, her face was grotesque with grief.

'I knew it! Oh my God, I knew it!' she cried out. She dropped the computer controller she'd been holding when she had answered the door to Tom and Kyra and collapsed on to the sofa. The screen in front was showing an anti-anxiety interactive programme. These were prescribed free by the healthcare profession, dished out with medication. Kyra picked up the controller and placed it on a stack of programmes and read some of the titles – *Parenting Skills, Addiction Fight, Teach Yourself Management, Mindfulness* . . .

'I knew it!' Chloe sobbed again. Then, turning to Tom, she wailed, 'You lot said you'd find her!'

'We're so sorry.' Kyra sat down next to her and tentatively put a hand on Chloe's back. She felt more frail than she appeared. 'Would you like us to call someone to come to stay with you?'

'Oh God, oh God,' Chloe wept, grabbing at her hair, her shoulders shaking with sobs.

Opposite the sofa on which Kyra and Chloe sat was a small kitchen area, with shiny white cupboards, fashionable some twenty years ago, and an overflowing rubbish bin. The smell of fried food hovered thick in the air. There were toys strewn across the floor making a trail to a basket that was half-full in the corner. Tom hovered, near the open door, through which Kyra could see another screen, switched on – a child's programme with the sound turned down – a double mattress on the floor, the bedcover in a knot.

Chloe turned to her, mascara streaking her face.

'I knew something had happened to her. I knew it.' Her voice broke. 'Caylee speaks to Riley every night if she's not here. She didn't call on Thursday. She always calls before he goes to bed. I know she was busy, but she never misses a phone call. Never.'

At that moment, a little dark-haired boy, dressed in navy overalls and trainers, ran into the room. 'Biscuit?' he asked, his hand in front of him making a grabbing sign like a duck's beak.

Chloe reached out and grabbed him to her roughly, sobbing into his hair. He seemed bemused by her distress and asked for a biscuit again. Kyra was grateful that he was oblivious to the significance of the moment.

Chloe pulled away from him, held him at arm's length and sniffed loudly. She gave a crooked smile and said, 'Yes, we'll get you a biscuit.' He grinned, satisfied, but then put a chubby forefinger on her cheek, which was wet with tears. His expression turned to one of concern.

'Aunty Chloe sad?'

'Yes, Aunty Chloe sad.'

He turned to Kyra and Tom, as if suddenly realising they were in the room and said, 'Aunty Chloe sad cos Mummy gone.' He held his hands outstretched like little starfish. He shook his head and his eyes opened wide with surprise as he repeated the word 'Gone'.

Kyra's heart broke for him. She remembered Molly, at a similar age, crying for her mother. Unlike Molly, this boy hadn't seen his mother taken, but one day he would grow up and find out the horrific circumstances of her death. Chloe was sitting staring into space now, her mouth open, her face red and wet, lost in her grief.

'Come on, let's get you a biscuit,' Kyra said, standing up and taking the little boy's hand, 'and we'll get Aunty Chloe a cup of tea.' He seemed happy to go with her. Chloe nodded gratefully.

'Are you going to show me where the biscuits are?' asked Kyra. Riley pulled her over to the battered fridge and pointed up. As he did so, his sleeve drew back and Kyra could see a deep purple mark on his arm, covered with transparent clinical wrap.

Tom turned to Chloe. 'We need to ask you some questions.'

She glanced anxiously at the little boy.

'My friend, Sophie, lives next door. She'll take Riley.'

'I'll go and get her,' Tom said and left the house.

Riley's eyes lit up as Kyra brought the box of chocolate-coated animal shapes towards him.

'What's your favourite animal?' she asked.

'Monkey!' the two little duck-beak hands were going again, his arm hidden under his sleeve.

Kyra peeked into the box, put her fingers in pretending to be scared. 'Ow!' she pulled her hand out quickly and Riley's expression was one of concern. 'A lion bit me!' she smiled. 'I'm not brave enough, you'd better get one!'

Riley giggled as she put the box on the counter and watched carefully as he reached up, standing on his toes, and the chubby arm shot out again.

The mark appeared to be a burn – a severe one.

'Ooh, that looks sore,' Kyra said.

Riley blinked at her.

'Poor you.'

Chloe jumped in.

'It was an accident. He's fine,' she said quickly.

'When did he do that?' Kyra asked, curious.

'The hospital checked him over,' she snarled.

'I'm sorry, I wasn't . . .'

She stood up and moved over to them. 'What you going to do, call the bloody Child Welfare Department on me?' She scooped Riley up roughly. He didn't seem fazed and began eating his biscuit. 'I'm not losing him as well.'

At that moment a woman burst in. Motherly but fierce-looking with a cloud of unruly curly bleach-blonde hair, she enveloped Chloe and Riley in her arms. Chloe crumpled against her and wailed. 'Soph! Soph! She's dead!'

Kyra turned away to let them have some privacy, also trying to shield herself from the painful recall of telling her parents that her sister was dead, a brief flash of her mother collapsing, her father trying to catch her before she hit the floor, the animal howl of grief.

Tom stood by the door. Kyra flicked the kettle on and opened the cupboard to look for cups. In a chipped mug she saw a glass pipe, a spoon and a lighter. Chloe's or Caylee's?

Riley's future seemed even more grim. The Child Welfare Department would be all over this now after Caylee's toxicology report.

Kyra couldn't let herself go down any further today; instead she would let this push her on, give her fire in her belly to fight for justice for Riley's mother. What else could she do?

In the cupboard there was also a small mirror and a tube of lip gloss. As she pulled a cup out, the mirror slipped slightly and she caught sight of her face, but then realised it wasn't her face at all, but Emma staring back at her. She gasped and the mirror fell flat. When she picked it up with shaking hands, it was her own reflection that peered back. She looked around, hairs on the back of her neck standing.

'I'm right next door,' Sophie was saying, Riley in her arms. 'I'll look after the little prince here.' She smiled down at the boy. 'Any trouble,' she glared at Tom and Kyra, 'just shout and I'll hear you.'

When Sophie and Riley left, Kyra sat back down next to Chloe. 'Do you think you could manage to answer a few questions?' she ventured.

'I'll try.' Her face was a mess with tears, and much of the mascara had come off, leaving dark circles beneath her eyes.

Kyra said, 'You told us Caylee was working at the factory on that particular night.' She watched Chloe's face carefully. 'But the manager says she wasn't due in until Friday.'

What was that she could see in Chloe's face? Kyra wasn't sure – feigned surprise, irritation? Whatever it was, she was going to have to work to get to the truth.

'She told me she was working until midnight, but Riley came into my bed at 6 a.m. asking where she was.'

'He's a lovely little boy,' Kyra smiled. She could feel Tom observing from the doorway.

Chloe eyed her suspiciously.

'Have they been staying here for a while?'

Her voice was nasal now, her chest still heaved. 'She never has much money, too short on the rent so she lost her last place.'

'There were traces of Chinese Lè in her system, amongst other things in the toxicology report,' Tom said.

Kyra glanced at him, irritated.

'How do you know he didn't put that in her?' Chloe snarled.

'You're saying she was short of money. She could have needed money for drugs,' Tom said. 'Might she have turned to prostitution to get that money?'

'No!' barked Chloe.

'We're not judging. We need the facts so we can catch the man that did this to her. ' Kyra tried to sound reassuring.

Chloe sniffed, pulled out a baby wipe from a packet sitting on the sofa arm and wiped her face.

'Her life is . . .' Chloe looked as though she was struggling to find the word, '. . . messy at times, but she loves that boy.'

'When you say messy . . .?' Kyra asked gently.

'No one's perfect,' she said defensively.

'Try to give us as much information as you can,' Tom said.

Kyra's eyes flicked to the cupboard and Chloe's shoulders fell. She stood up and paced the room anxiously before saying, 'She uses a bit of Chinese Lè. Only occasionally. Never around Riley. She needs money for that.'

'That might be helpful, thank you. You don't know her dealer?'

'I don't want anything to do with the stuff!' Chloe snapped, her voice high-pitched.

'I know it's hard but we need to find who did this. Can you think of anyone who would want to hurt Chloe?' asked Kyra. 'Anyone else who she didn't get on with? Someone who she might have come into contact with that could have done this?'

Chloe quietened a little and then shook her head. 'No. She's a normal girl who likes to have fun . . . doesn't have a lot of money . . . struggles at times, like we all do, but she's got a good heart. She loves her boy . . . loved him.' There was a brief look of horror on her face as she registered the past tense. She made her way over to Tom.

She grabbed hold of the collar of his coat with her thin hands, pleading, 'Get him. Get him, for Caylee. For Riley.'

But Tom didn't reply.

What would happen to this little boy with the burn on his arm now his mother was dead? Would his aunt be able to keep him? Could she cope?

How much would it mean to Kyra herself, her mother, Molly, to know for sure that they had caught Emma's real killer? Would it start the healing process?

Riley was without his mother now.

There was nothing she could do for Emma.

But Kyra wanted to find the bastard who had done this and help to put him away for a long, long time.

Chapter Fifteen

SATURDAY 3 FEBRUARY 2035

12.43 p.m.

'It could be a copycat,' suggested Alex. Tom was pacing the Hub as the rest of the team focused on the screens around the room, trying to figure out the puzzle. Kyra was impressed with the digital timeline board Alex had produced that ran across the short wall nearest the door and displayed names, dates and locations, including maps of industrial estates and wasteland areas where some of the bodies had been found. There were photographs of the crime scenes and images of the victims, alive and dead.

'Could be,' said Tom. 'Although the press knew the hands were missing, it was never made known that the heart was also taken. We managed to keep that one out of the news, so it's not in the public arena. That means that if the killer is a copycat, it would have to be someone who knows the exact details so they could replicate them.' Tom put his hand to his brow. 'I need a whiteboard.'

Old school, thought Kyra. She wondered what the team made of that.

Kyra saw Harry shake his head. One of the younger uniformed officers disappeared and returned a few moments later with a tripod whiteboard and pen. He set it up in front of Tom.

'Thanks, Gabe,' Tom said as he wrote on the board in small, tight capitals COPYCAT? and drew a rectangle around it. Kyra remembered back in the day, the pages of his distinctive angular handwriting, his need to think it out between pen and paper.

'If details weren't made public, then it can't be a randomer,' said Alex. She hadn't looked at Kyra since she returned from Chloe's with Tom. 'Could Lomax have spoken about the details to a cell mate who re-enacted them once he was released?' Kyra could see the glint of eagerness in the other woman's eyes and felt a flush of approval. She remembered a time when she'd been just as eager – a time when a case meant a puzzle to be solved, the hints and clues that pointed to the truth. Now, she envied Alex's fearlessness, her naivety.

Will spoke. 'He's been in solitary confinement for much of his sentence due to violent outbursts, but he has had two long-term cell-mates, one who died of cancer in 2029 and one who's still in the nick.'

'Thanks, Will, so it can't have been either of them who killed Caylee. Have we got a list of visitors?'

Will continued, 'There was his mother, she visited him regularly every week before she became ill last July. There was his lawyer. We've already established that Lomax wasn't the most popular person and that's all that we've found so far. We're trying to find any visitors he had before he was moved to Rockwell.'

'It looks more likely to have been an accomplice,' suggested Alex after a few moments of speculation. 'I mean, if Lomax's DNA was on some of the bodies, but he didn't kill Caylee, then it doesn't necessarily mean he didn't do it. It might mean that he had a partner in crime.'

'It would make sense of how Caylee was killed in the same way, but Lomax wasn't at body dep site,' said Will.

Harry asked, 'Yeah, but why would an accomplice suddenly start killing people again after fourteen years? Wouldn't he have killed in the interim?'

Tom turned to Kyra. 'What's your perspective?'

'If Lomax did have a partner in the Mizpah Murders, it's possible he's killed again in the interim, but his MO would be different without Lomax, therefore we might not have registered it. On the other hand, some killers can remain dormant for years, living off the images of their previous kills,' she continued, feeling more confident as the officers appeared to be listening closely. 'There's always a trigger, for instance the break-up of a relationship, someone close to the killer died, or maybe even a woman humiliated him in some way.

'However, there's always the chance that he might have been in prison or abroad. He might have even settled down, started a family and believed that he could maintain a normal existence, happy to let Lomax take the heat for the original crimes but then found he needs to kill again.' She gave a half-shrug. 'So, yes, it's possible it's an accomplice.'

But her gut was telling her different and she couldn't hold back. She glanced at Tom and added, 'But I think it would be a much more likely scenario that someone is trying to frame Lomax.'

He shot her a glance.

'Yes, but they would have to know that Lomax was out of prison,' Alex said.

'No,' said Harry looking at Kyra and shaking his head. 'Lomax killed because he was out of prison.'

Kyra shook her head. 'You're looking at it the wrong way. Our murderer has killed *precisely because he knew Lomax was out.*'

'What type of person would wait fourteen years to frame someone?' asked Will.

'Someone who wanted revenge,' said Alex.

Kyra and Alex locked eyes.

Tom broke their attention. 'We'll have to wait for DNA results to see what is on the body, but it is possible that if someone wants to frame Lomax then they could place stolen bio-matter on the body to make it seem as though it was him.'

Kyra watched Alex's face as she processed this.

'If Lomax was framed for this murder, he'll be able to appeal against his conviction for the previous murders.' The team watched Tom silently. 'Presented with this latest body,' he said slowly, his face grave, 'we have to face the fact that, yes, it's possible the wrong man has been convicted, and I take some of the responsibility for that.'

Tom wrote 'FRAMED' on the board, reluctantly.

If Lomax was wrongly convicted, then Kyra could understand why he would be so frustrated in prison. If he was innocent, and someone was trying to punish him, then they were succeeding.

'But how did they get Lomax's bio-matter?' asked Alex. 'For the original crimes, I mean?'

'That's what we need to find out,' Tom said, rubbing his face. 'We're going to have to reopen the original case and prepare for a shitstorm when the press realises there's more to it than meets the eye. We need to search records for anyone who has been in prison for any similar offences that fit the timeline. Will, as soon as you find any other visitors, if there are any, I want to hear straightaway.'

Will nodded.

'Harry and Alex, I want you to start going through the original case files, fresh eyes and all that.' Kyra could see him swallow hard. 'I spoke to the governor at Rockwell. I have an appointment with Lomax later today and I can ask him about some of these ideas. I'm taking Kyra with me to interview him, see if he can think of anyone who might have framed him and why. Whatever the circumstances, this needs to be sorted and solved.'

Kyra felt her stomach drop. Was there no one else they could interview to get to the truth of the matter? She looked back up at the digital timeline; the maps, the photographs, the notes. Under 'witnesses' there was too much white space – one name only, Ray Clarke. He was a homeless alcoholic who claimed he knew something about Jennifer Bosanquet's abduction, but his confused ramblings had only served to waste time.

There might as well have been no witnesses at all.

She couldn't avoid thinking about Lomax anymore.

She was going to have to meet him.

Face to face.

1.17 p.m.

ISABEL

'Don't struggle.' She freezes at the sinister whisper.

She feels her arms being strapped to the bindings at her waist.

Then a moment of silence.

Suddenly, a strong, dry hand that smells of bleach grabs her face. She struggles against it, trying to move her head, afraid she will be suffocated.

The grasp tightens and the air supply to her nostrils is cut off by fingers gripping her nose, the palm pushing down on her forehead, as though her head is in a vice. The lack of oxygen immediately sharpens her focus and she looks up.

She can't make sense of his face – there seems to be a translucent shine to it, the eyes behind cut-out circles, one a strange pale blue, the bone structure hidden by a semi-transparent film. She finally realises he is wearing a mask.

'If you struggle, it will hurt more.'

Her chest is juddering for air now, her brain panicking in response to the lack of oxygen, and she opens her mouth. He forces the end of a tube into her throat and presses down on her so she can't resist. She gags as the plastic tube is pushed further, choking her as he keeps forcing it down, scraping her oesophagus, all while her mind is screaming NO! NO!

Once the tube is in place, he releases her nose and she stops struggling, snorting in the oxygen, taking in terrified snippets of precious air. Her eyes wide and terrified, she watches unable to move as he attaches a funnel to the tube and holds it above her. He pours a liquid into it using a yellowing plastic jug, which stupidly makes her think of the one in the kitchen at home. She eyes it, horrified, as the liquid slowly trickles down the tube right in front of her eyes, into her body.

The second it hits her stomach it begins to burn, but she can't even cry out. After a few moments, when the jug is empty, he pulls the tube out slowly, and then all she can manage is a whimper, her throat already raw from screaming.

He presses a dry finger over her lips, crushing them. 'Shhhh! It won't be long now.'

She waits with him, seconds stretching out into torturous despair. Her father's face comes to her mind. How will he cope without her? She doesn't even know where she is. The horrifying thought passes through her mind: how will they even find my body?

A painful spasm grabs her guts. Her intestines coil and uncoil, and spikes of agony shoot through her body. She retches hard and, as she does so, he loosens the straps holding her wrist, and then the waist, leaving only her legs still buckled.

Her body convulses, curling with the growing pain in her stomach. A grinding ache starts somewhere at the back of her neck where her spine crunches into her skull as he comes up behind her and forces her up into a sitting position.

'There, there, won't be long,' he soothed. 'You do want to be pure, don't you?'

The rumbling, growling pain in her stomach suddenly produces violent vomiting. It pours out of her, splattering across her thinly covered lap as he holds her beneath her arms so that she is upright and it splashes on the trolley and all over her legs. It keeps coming, wave after wave of yellow bile, until she feels completely spent, sweating, her heart pounding and her mouth bitter.

Collapsing backwards, she slumps against him, exhausted. He slowly lies her back down on the trolley and, for a brief moment, there is respite, until the spasms begin again, this time lower down, in her guts. The pressure continues to build, and then her bowels evacuate, the foetid, acrid smell making her want to vomit again, but her stomach is empty.

She lies still, sweat cooling on her face, shocked that she is lying in her own mess, and all the while he stands by watching with his odd mismatched eyes, the rest of his face hidden behind the creepy shiny plastic. Her intestines spasm and twitch one last time and then, as quickly as it had started, it is done.

He brings a syringe close to her and she is too weak to even lift her hands in protest. There is a sharp jab and then she feels the liquid spreading through her bloodstream, relaxing the muscles as it travels through her body, taking the edge off the fear and pain. She watches in a disembodied, mesmerised way as he starts to undress. He folds his clothes slowly and carefully and places them on a chair. Nearby, she can see the mortuary fridge and even with the drugs, she feels herself shiver.

What more is he going to do to her?

He removes his simple white T-shirt. From where she is he appears fairly short but strong, and dark hairs cover tight muscles in his arms and chest.

A single tear runs from her eye.

As the concoction he had given her reaches her brain, she hears singing, beautiful, unearthly harmonies. She looks up to the glowing lights floating above her and is entranced by the prisms and rainbows. She hardly notices as he takes a sponge which he dips into a bucket of hot water and he begins to wash her down, slowly, gently, throwing away the sponge as it becomes soiled and using a new one to dip back into the hot, clean water. He clears up her mess thoroughly and carefully, then he turns his attention to drying her and dressing her, as a child might dress a doll. He struggles against the deadweight of her body as he puts a white garment on her, then covers her with a clean sheet and pushes the trolley back into the mortuary fridge.

This time she welcomes the darkness.

Chapter Sixteen

SATURDAY 3 FEBRUARY 2035

2.43 p.m.

Two inmates in coarse grey cotton sweats, not unlike the colour of the sky above them, downed their gardening tools and gawped at Kyra. She pulled her coat tighter around her and hung back so that she was walking behind Tom. She had endured a thorough security check at the hands of the over-eager female prison guard before she had left the main entrance block, but the men's eyes made her feel more violated still.

'Men, resume your work,' barked Governor Bennett, louder, in Kyra's opinion, than should come from such a petite woman in her expensive navy suit. Both men immediately turned back to their gardening, eyes down. They worked in a large allotment, bars running three metres high all around them, and even across the top, forming a cage. On either side of the cage was an armed guard. There were a few hovering drones patrolling the high perimeter wall. Were they weaponised? She tried not to look up at the observation tower which loomed over them menacingly. Rockwell Prison was a grim, terrifying place, however much the governor seemed proud of it.

'Our inmates tend small winter crops at this time of year: potatoes, sweet potatoes, sprouts, cabbages, turnips, carrots and onions, all of which are sold and the money reinvested in Rockwell.' Kyra could hear the pride in her voice. 'We believe giving our inmates plants to care for gives them a sense of responsibility and achievement. It all helps in their reformation.'

This didn't surprise Kyra. With a huge emphasis on recycling and rehabilitation in society, convicted criminals were seen by some in government departments as commodities to be re-educated and, if they couldn't be fixed, to be re-purposed and at least live useful and productive lives behind bars.

'How does Lomax take to the gardening?' Kyra asked, hardly imagining he could nurture anything.

'We call it agriculture, not gardening,' the governor corrected. 'Lomax does not have the status for agriculture. He remains in the A Wing on the far side, the most serious offenders are housed there. There is no agriculture in A Wing.' She marched along the path, commenting to Kyra and Tom as they moved through the prison complex. She was arrogant considering Lomax had escaped under her watch. Was she trying to brazen it out?

'We bought the land from the education authority; with the continuing fall in the national birth rate, the school wasn't needed.' A heavy metal security door was opened by an armed guard and the governor led them into a highly fortified building, the corridors painted pale grey, the floor buffed to a gleam. The guards inside bobbed their heads towards her as she swept past. 'It looks as though society has less schoolchildren and more prisoners these days.' Governor Bennett gave an odd giggle and Tom's eyes flicked to Kyra. 'We knocked the whole thing down and rebuilt for our purposes, but the tennis courts are still there. We don't use them of course. We did, however, manage to retain plenty of the books from the library. Many of the prisoners had never even seen a book in its non-digital form.'

The governor had already used the word 'empathy' three times since she had met them at the main entrance, but Kyra suspected there was also a granite-strong disciplinarian underneath judging from her rigid back and disdainful glances at some of the inmates. There was certainly a hint of narcissism about her as she showed off her miniature kingdom.

'It's not exactly what I'd expected,' Tom said, looking up at a poster – *Everyone can be reformed at Rockwell.*

'Yes, we're very proud of what we have achieved here. My office is full of certificates and awards. Here at Rockwell we have always led the way since the full privatisation of the Prison Service.'

'Have you ever had a prisoner escape before?' asked Kyra steadily, irked by the fact their host had taken Tom's comment as a compliment.

The governor stopped still and turned to Kyra, her eyes challenging.

'Whatever happens under my roof is my responsibility. Prisoner Lomax escaped whilst under the watch of Tartarus Security. Believe me,' the governor spoke quietly, pulling herself up to her full diminutive height, 'there will be questions asked, and contracts broken over this fiasco.'

She turned swiftly on her heels until they reached a guard standing by a sign that read REFECTORY.

'Good afternoon, Danielsson.'

Danielsson regarded her from beneath his cap with his sky-blue eyes. He seemed younger than Kyra, but his skin was rough and lined. His face was closed, giving nothing away, a mask of loyalty. He towered over the governor and stooped as she spoke.

'Ma'am,' he replied.

'You've reminded the prisoner about his manners, to prepare him for his visitors?'

'Yes, ma'am.'

The governor turned to Tom. 'I have to warn you, Lomax recently lost his latest appeal against his conviction. He is not in the best mood. I'm going to leave you to it, Detective Inspector, Doctor Sullivan,' she said with a nod of her head. 'You'll get more out of Lomax without me there but do let me know how it goes.' She gave an odd, dry little smile. Kyra imagined she hated not being in control.

'Could I request that Officer Danielsson might wait outside, Governor?' Kyra asked.

Danielsson's blue eyes slid to the governor, awaiting direction.

'I know it isn't protocol, but I am sure you can bend the rules a little in such a case?' Kyra asked, hoping to appeal to her ego.

The governor glanced at Danielsson and gave a slight nod. 'If there's any sign of anything . . . untoward, Danielsson here will be in like a shot.'

She stood still for a moment and Tom said, 'Thank you, Governor Bennett.'

Then she turned on her heels and marched away.

Lomax sat with his back to them at one of the long tables. The wide windows opposite were made of opaque armoured plastic, the metal food bar in front of it cleared at this time of day, but the air was still musty with the smell of mass-produced meals.

He didn't turn around when they approached him but sat hunched over the table top. Even from this angle Kyra could see that he had bulked up in the prison gym, his deltoids and triceps straining against his grey sweat top, his neck muscles thick and powerful. She thought about the last time she had seen him, the damage he had done. Was it such a good idea to leave Danielsson outside after all? Was Lomax cuffed? When they got closer, Lomax turned his head slightly but waited until they came around to face him. He focused his dark eyes on Tom.

'I didn't expect to see you walking, Tommy, after your little accident last time we met.' He bared his tombstone teeth, one or two now missing, but then his face fell. 'What the fuck do you want?'

If Tom felt anything about the last time they had met he didn't show it.

'Hello, Lomax,' Tom said pleasantly. 'How are they treating you here? I heard the food's okay.'

Lomax took his time looking Kyra up and down and then his eyes finally settled on hers. She couldn't decide if his expression was one of lust or disgust. Her stomach turned to water, but she was determined not to show fear. She threw her leg over the bench and sat down nearly opposite him. Tom remained standing.

Lomax reached his hand up to scratch his face and Kyra flinched, but the sound of chains reassured her he was secured. She could see there were manacles around his thick wrists attached with the chains through a metal loop on the rim of table. His arms, though, seemed huge to her, the swell of his biceps covered in veins that looked like rivulets running down a mountainside.

'Miss Sullivan,' Lomax leered.

'Doctor,' Kyra parried.

'Doctor Sullivan,' Lomax mocked. 'Long time no see.'

Through the window, she could see Danielsson's profile.

'I haven't got time to mess about, Lomax,' Tom said flatly. 'We're here because we want some more information about the murders you've been convicted of.'

Lomax took his time looking Tom over. 'Did your accident leave you brain-damaged? It must have done if you think I'm gonna talk willingly to you lot.'

Tom blinked slowly.

Lomax suddenly slammed his fist on the table in front of him. Kyra jumped. He leaned forward, face serious now. 'I always said you stitched me up. When are you going to get me out of this shithole?'

Tom put his hands in his pockets but didn't reply.

Kyra could see that the length of the chains meant he couldn't reach her, but even sitting so close to him, she could feel anger and violence radiating from him. She kept her hands hidden so Lomax couldn't see them shaking.

'What do you want, bitch?'

'Lomax—' Tom began, threat in his voice.

'I've got this, Tom.' Kyra tried to sound as confident as possible.

'Watch your manners, Lomax—' Tom said.

'Tom!' Kyra turned sharply to look at him. 'I said I've got this.'

'She's a feisty one, Tommy. Not sure you're man enough for her,' Lomax mocked.

Tom moved away over to the door, hands in pockets still, looking down at the floor. Kyra knew he would be taking every word in.

She put both hands flat on the table in front of her and locked eyes with Lomax, who crossed his arms and leaned back a little. 'So then, *Doctor* Sullivan. What's all this about? You missed me?' he sneered.

'Apparently *you* wanted to talk to *me*.' She leaned back and crossed her arms, mirroring him.

'Thought we could chat about old times.' He licked his lips. 'Don't get much of a chance to see a pretty woman round here. The female guards are all dogs.'

She ignored this. 'If you've got nothing to say that's fine, but I want to talk to you. Your DNA was found on some of the bodies in the Mizpah Murders. The court considered it was an open-and-shut case.'

Lomax's smiled faded. 'Circumstantial.' He looked away, bored.

'Possibly. But something's come up, which might cast some doubt on your conviction.'

Lomax uncrossed his arms and leaned over the table towards her now. She resisted moving backwards.

'Another body has turned up, a woman, same type of victim, same MO, looks very similar to the crimes that you were convicted of, while you were out. Looks like you've been bad again.' She searched his face for minute reactions before his eyes narrowed and he growled slowly.

'Someone is fucking stitching me up.'

She leaned into him now, drawing on all her courage to face him.

'It might *appear* that someone else committed those murders,' she said quietly. 'Your tracker . . .' she indicated his leg with a slight nod, 'says you weren't near the body deposition site.'

Lomax threw his arms wide and roared, 'I told everyone I was innocent!' His face was triumphant.

Danielsson's rugged face appeared at the window of the door. Tom put his thumbs up and the guard took a long look at Lomax and disappeared again.

'I told you I never done it, Tommy Boy!' he grinned maniacally. He slapped his hands together and the chains on his wrists jangled. 'It looks like you fucked up. I'm an innocent man. I'll be out of here before you can say "miscarriage of justice". Tick tock, Tommy.'

'Take it easy,' Kyra began steadily. 'It's not as simple as that, Lomax, but maybe we can help each other out. Two bodies have your DNA is all over them, makes it look like you did it. So you need to think hard who might have put that DNA on there because, at the moment, it's a toss-up between you being framed or you having an accomplice. The latter doesn't get you out of here. But if you can help us find whoever it is who might want you banged up for some reason . . .'

'You should have helped me fourteen years ago. You were the only one who thought I never done it . . . and what did you do?' he spat furiously.

'I had my doubts, but—'

'Fuck all – that's what you did to help me back then.' He moved toward her. 'You knew I was innocent and you didn't do nothing about it. You should have fought harder for me, bitch. I've been here in Disneyland for fourteen . . . fucking . . . years . . . Who do you think I blame the most?' He gritted his teeth and let out a low growl.

Kyra's breath quickened, the bees were stirring again. 'If you didn't do it—'

'I never,' he jumped in.

'Well then.' She tried to make her voice sound as steady as possible. 'We want to catch whoever did. So, here's how we can help each other – you help us to find out who did it, and we'll help you to get out of here. We'll speak up for you in court. Hold our hands up, say we made a mistake.'

She watched Lomax mull this over for a moment. Was she getting to him?

'And how are you going to make up for all the years I spent in here?'

She ignored this again. 'Can you think of anyone who would have framed you?' she asked.

'Like a copper, you mean?' he snarled, looking over at Tom.

Tom had said that only someone who knew the intimate details of the case could have replicated it. Could it have been a police officer?

'Can you think of anyone who would want to get you locked up?'

'Lots of people.' His voice had lost all levity now. His face had darkened.

'What about someone who could get hold of your DNA to plant on the bodies? Your hair, blood, that sort of thing?'

'Anyone who came into contact with me, I suppose. Some fucker from here might have done it when they got out.'

'We're going to look into that and look at your visitors. Did you ever tell anyone in prison about the details of the crime, a detail that no one else knew about?'

His eyes narrowed. 'How could I have if I never did it?'

'Of course not.' He was too smart for her to be able to trip him up. But there was something in his eyes. What was that?

She didn't speak for a moment, giving him time and space to let an idea or a memory come to the fore. She had watched Tom do it so often in an interview, giving them *enough rope to hang themselves with* he said sometimes. But this time it was different. Could Lomax give them the key to who was doing these terrible things?

A heat rose in Kyra. If the real killer was still out there, and he was going to follow the pattern, then they only had four days to catch him before he did it again. Another young innocent woman would die horribly.

From the corner of her eye, she saw Tom twitch.

Lomax was thinking; his pupils darting around, was he going to give them a lead?

She held her breath.

He opened his mouth to speak.

'Considering your DNA was on the bodies . . .' Tom said from the other side of the room.

Lomax snapped his head round to face Tom.

Bloody hell, Tom! Kyra was furious, the moment had gone. Lomax had wanted to talk to her, hadn't he? Not Tom.

'I'll get out anyway. I don't need you,' Lomax said.

'Don't you want to know who framed you?' asked Tom. 'Don't you want us to find the man who put you in here for the last fourteen years, possibly even for the rest of your life?'

'I think I'm looking at him already.' Lomax's nostrils flared.

After a moment, he turned back to Kyra. 'Nah,' he said finally. 'I don't need your help. I'm going to find out who done this myself. We've got business, me and him, and you lot can stay out of it.'

'If you're thinking about taking the law into your own hands, Lomax, then I strongly advise you . . .' Tom began.

'You strongly advise me!' laughed Lomax, but then his face fell. He stood up, as far as he could with his hands restrained, and leaned over the table towards Tom, the veins in his thick neck popping. 'I got life for a crime I didn't commit, because you're a bent copper,' he spat. 'When I get out of here, Tommy boy, I'm gonna come and find you and I'm gonna finish off the job I started on the steps back at my place. And, this time, you won't be getting back up again. It's gonna be tick tock for you then, Tommy.'

A shiver ran down Kyra's spine. Tom rubbed his temple near the scar then locked eyes with Lomax, but it was Lomax who finally looked away.

'Okay,' said Tom finally, 'you take your chances in the court. Don't say I didn't offer to make things right.' He banged on the canteen door and Danielsson's face appeared. There was a heavy mechanical clunk as the door opened.

Kyra stood up. 'Never mind, Lomax. We could have helped each other out. We don't need you. We'll figure this out ourselves.' She tried to look unconcerned, even though that was the last thing she felt.

'Fuck you,' Lomax spat at her. 'And fuck you,' he said to Tom. 'You two better watch yourselves. I'll be out of here before you know it. And guess who I'll be paying a visit to?'

As the guard at the exit locked the final gate behind them and they made their way back to Tom's car, Kyra mind turned back to CASNDRA. Could she use her technology on Lomax? Would she be able to cope going into a mind such as his, to face what she might see, *experience*? Even the thought of it terrified her. There would be consequences – how could there not be – going into a mind like Lomax's? Even the idea of being in the same room as him threaded fear into her blood.

No.

There was no way she could do it.

Not without losing her mind.

Chapter Seventeen

SATURDAY 3 FEBRUARY 2035

5.13 p.m.

'Sewage treatment works, recycling centre, rubbish tip, illegal dump.'

Kyra was talking to herself more than anyone else as she studied at the screens in the Hub. *The unknown woman, Skylar, Jennifer, Madelyn, Emma, Amelia,* and the new addition, *Caylee.* The pictures stabbed at Kyra's heart; Jennifer cuddling a pet cat, Madelyn smiling in front of a Christmas tree, Caylee at a party, others less jarring, but still showing life taken too early – Amelia, a passport photo, serious; Jennifer, a high school photograph; Skylar, a graduation picture.

Kyra didn't look at her sister's photograph – she knew it by heart from the wall at her mother's house, from the newspops. Emma's expression was vague, impersonal. It wasn't a smile exactly, and therefore Emma's dimples weren't visible. It took the sting out, somehow. But she couldn't look because every time she saw it the last words she said to her sister rang in her ears, *You're a terrible mother!*

'I'm trying to find a connection,' Kyra said when Alex came closer. 'He treats the Type A victim with such contempt, and yet the Type B victim, there's almost a reverence,' she continued. 'Her body is intact, no mutilation. There's no injuries prior to death or afterwards. She's killed by an injection of a high dose of morphine. She won't have felt a thing, like going to sleep. She's posed in a beautiful place. Two very different approaches to the victims. Why take the heart and hands from one and leave them with the other victim?' Kyra shook her head. Then she asked Alex, 'What's missing here, something that is usually seen in a serial killer's work?'

'No sexual assault,' Alex answered immediately. Will and Harry had been discussing a document nearby, and Harry looked up at them with interest, chewing gum as usual.

'Exactly. There's rage, anger, resentment, for the first victim, but nothing sexual.'

'The white dress – it could be a symbol of purity?' suggested Alex.

Harry had moved closer; the smacking of his lips as he chewed irritated Kyra.

'These women represent a non-sexual relationship to him,' surmised Kyra. 'His mother, maybe?'

'Bloody psychologists and their mothers,' Harry said.

Alex gave him a hard stare.

'The Type B victims were found in water, why?'

'To wash away evidence?' Alex suggested. If she was still annoyed that Tom had taken Kyra instead of her to speak to Chloe and Lomax, then she didn't show it.

'Possibly, but then why leave the first set of victims with so much evidence on them?' Kyra scanned the screens again. 'What other patterns do you see, Alex?'

She watched as the young officer's eyes scanned the screens. 'The second victims – they're all young women, blonde, all physically fairly small, mainly living at home with parents, one was a church youth worker, one was a trainee social worker, one was a primary school teacher, they seem to be just ordinary young women.' Alex's eyes narrowed.

'So we can assume if, when, he takes a second victim then she will follow the pattern – under twenty-five, Caucasian, fair-haired, a "nice" girl who will be in a caring profession or office work,' said Kyra.

Alex pointed to the other screen. 'The Type A vics, however, it's not as clear what the pattern is. Divorced, single, married, on the game, an eco-campaigner, a factory worker – we can't see to find anything to link them, beyond them all being female and Caucasian. They're not from the same area, they don't seem to know each other, they have different hair colours . . .' She faced Kyra. 'I can't see a pattern.'

'Neither can I. Not yet.'

Relief on Alex's face. 'And you seem to really know the case.'

Was that a compliment or an insult?

'Unless he considers them somehow . . . immoral,' said Alex looking at the screen. 'The first woman was a prostitute, Madelyn had a drug problem. Maybe Emma Sullivan was on the game or an illegal activity, something to make him think she was somehow . . . impure.'

Kyra's body reacted to the comment before her brain could override her feelings. Alex had seen her facial expression, she was sure of it.

'They were all people, they all deserved better than this,' Kyra began, her voice a little higher-pitched than usual.

Alex's eyebrows twitched slightly as she scanned Kyra's face. She opened her mouth to speak, but Harry barged in between them and she closed it again. Kyra's heart was pounding. Did Alex suspect she knew more than she was letting on?

'What do you think the Mizpah pendant means?' asked Alex, finally. Kyra was relieved she had changed the subject. 'When I first heard it, I thought it was MISPER – as in slang for Missing Person. I mean, I know it's a love or friendship token, very popular in Victorian times. But what does it mean *to him?*'

'Mizpah coin,' Kyra commanded and up on the screen appeared various images: pendants, some silver, some gold, some heart-shaped, but most circular, all split in two halves by a zigzag. When joined together they read MIZPAH *The Lord watch between me and thee whilst we are absent one from another.*

'Each of the three of the B Type victims found in water was wearing one half of a Mizpah. We haven't been able to trace the pendants' origins as they are mainly sold second-hand so they could be from the hypernet, flea markets, antique fairs, or he could have had them for years,' Alex added.

'Many serial killers take an item from a kill, a trophy. In this case the killer leaves something behind,' Kyra said. '*Mizpah* is Hebrew meaning "watch tower". It was used to mark an agreement between two people with God as witness. It represents an emotional bond between two people who are separated.'

'I wonder what sort of agreement?' mused Alex.

'We're not sure what significance this has, but it will have some meaning for him.' Kyra was sure of it. 'If we could figure out what that might be it could lead to some answers. In the past, theories have been that the killer might have lost someone very close to him, or else he can't find the sort of relationship he wants.'

'So where is the other half of the pendant?' asked Alex.

Kyra felt a blooming admiration.

Alex turned back to the timeline and said, 'Will, anything on a vehicle yet?'

'One of our big problems is lack of CCTV footage,' Will replied. 'In a city this size, with the amount of surveillance we have, you'd think by now we'd have a vehicle registration at least to go on, but nothing. This fella's a ghost. In and out, nothing to be seen. Even the recycling plant security drones captured nothing.'

'So how is he placing the bodies?' asked Harry.

'Somehow, he's hiding in plain sight,' Kyra said.

'I think Lomax did it and now he's in the nick this is all over, no one else will get hurt,' said Harry.

As if to contradict that, Tom came through the door.

'Right, everyone, listen up. We've got a MISPER. Isabel Marsden, aged twenty-two, student nurse, lives at home with her dad who has reported her missing. She went out with friends last night to a local pub, he assumed she was in bed this morning when he left for work and when he came home he realised that she was gone.'

Kyra's hive-chest tightened making it harder to take in oxygen.

'The friends she was out with have come in to talk to us. They're in the interview rooms now.'

The women on the board, *Jennifer, Madelyn, Amelia, Skylar, Emma* . . . their names never left Kyra, but her brain repeated them over and over at times, like a mantra.

She had to do something, to stop these women crying out to her in her dreams at night, to finally lay Emma to rest, to help herself heal from the guilt. It didn't matter how afraid she might be, what Carter might say, what the MOD might do. Kyra knew she had to take action. It was the only way to put the police on the right track and get justice for the women, for their families. She just had to get Lomax to agree to it.

ISABEL

Time doesn't exist in the silence of the mortuary fridge. She has no idea how long she has lain there, accompanied only by her own terrified thoughts, which kaleidoscope around her in the sensory deprivation.

Worse than the darkness and the unknowing, is the utter torment of listening, making every second endless, straining to hear any movement outside her metal sarcophagus, to tell her if her captor is returning.

Finally, the light comes again. He pulls out the tray. His hands are sheathed in blue gloves, like the ones she wears in the hospital. She feels like a rare butterfly pinned in a museum drawer. His face is hidden still behind the mask. She wonders if that is a good sign. Maybe it means he doesn't want her to be able to identify him. Maybe that means he won't kill her.

After her cleansing last time, she is incredibly thirsty. Her tongue is dry, her mouth sticky, bitter. He unbuckles her straps and sits her up. He holds a bottle in front of her – it looks like water – and hands it to her. She pauses, momentarily – what if he has put more drugs or even poison in it? But she is so parched she gulps the water down until it is all gone.

He takes the bottle from her grasp and puts a plastic food tray in front of her, the type a child might use, with bright pictures of zoo animals hiding under the food. Chicken nuggets, baked beans, apple slices, a tube of yoghurt with a cartoon character strawberry on the front. She is hesitant at first, and then, the overwhelming smell, the growling of her stomach – when was the last time she ate? – overwhelms her and she shovels it into her mouth with her hands. From less than a metre away he stands watching, motionless, his mismatched blue eyes unblinking behind the mask.

'You always loved the chicken bites,' he says.

She stops halfway through a mouthful, regards him, and then begins chewing again, slowly.

'I miss you, Elise.'

Why is his voice trembling? Why is he calling her Elise?

She knows he is staring but she focuses on the food. If he is feeding her, then he might want her to live. When she finishes, he takes the tray and turns to place it to one side.

She wipes her hands on her white shroud and the tomato sauce from the beans smears across the cotton like blood seeping through a bandage.

He turns back, holding a muslin cloth, and sees what she has done.

His eyes narrow, and she grows afraid again.

'Look what you did, Elise!' he hisses. 'He'll beat you for that. He will, if he sees you, you'll be in for it.' He becomes distressed, wringing the muslin cloth between his hands. 'What will we do? What will we do?' he cries, his alarm inflaming her own fears. What the hell is he talking about? She feels her heart kick into overdrive, the food feels like concrete in her stomach.

'He'll be back soon,' he whispers. 'Then we're in for it.' His odd eyes widen behind the plastic. Is he afraid? 'Let me think. Let me think.'

He straps her arms back down and ties the muslin cloth around her arm like a tourniquet. He turns around to a metal tray behind him and brings back a syringe. A globule of liquid drips from the tip before he jabs it in her arm. When the barrel is empty he takes it out. He turns away again, briefly, and when he faces her again he holds a scalpel.

The drug immobilises her almost immediately. What has he given her? She tries to think of the medications that she has learned about in the hospital, but she can't concentrate. She stares helplessly at the sharp metal blade. He moves closer to her, pointing the scalpel at her chest, then her belly, then up to her neck. Isabel thinks she is screaming, but there is no sound at all, except the high-pitched zipping sound as the scalpel slits her garment from the neck to the hem. He cuts down the arms and somehow pulls the cloth from underneath her, leaving her naked, exposed.

But he averts his eyes, not even looking at her face.

Then he leaves her alone, shutting the door behind him.

Her body feels heavy, a prison for her petrified mind. The room is cold and, without any covering, she feels the temperature drop. Is she shaking? In her peripheral vision, to her left, she recognises the metal tray like the ones in surgery, the flat grey lines of terrifying steel instruments laid out in preparation. The drug doesn't take the edge off her fear of what they could do to her body. She listens to the gurgling in her stomach as the water and food digest, wondering why he has fed her if he is going to kill her, trying to read into every little thing he says or does to make sense of what is happening, what might be about to happen.

In front of her, near the door, there is an ancient rusted red generator chugging away. Cobwebs hang from the ceiling above her. To her right, high up, a frosted-glass window lets in a dull light. Is it a garage, an outhouse?

Her fingers twitch with minuscule movements, her eyeballs flick back to the instruments, the agony of being able to see them but not to reach.

He is in total control.

She is going to die.

Chapter Eighteen

SATURDAY 3 FEBRUARY 2035

5.27 p.m.

Will stood with one arm bent up to his mouth, tapping his lips with his index finger. He was a big man and the observation room was small. Kyra could feel the heat from his body as he focused on the screen.

Liv Brown looked much younger than her twenty years as she sat in the harsh light of one of the more pleasant interview rooms at the station. She wore no make-up, her blonde fringe sat over her blue eyes which were wide with dismay as she sat biting her fingernails on the low sofa. Alex wore her hair loose, she'd removed her body armour and had borrowed a pink cardigan from one of the cleaners, making herself look less of a cop than Kyra had seen.

'What have I missed?' whispered Kyra, although she knew they wouldn't be able to hear her in the interview room.

'Three friends, Isabel, Liv,' Will pointed to the screen, 'and another girl, Ruby, met at the Farmers' Arms, eight o'clock. She says nothing was out of the ordinary, no one giving them any hassle. She says the other girl, Ruby, ended up getting really drunk and she felt sick so they went outside. There was a man lying on the floor, looked like he was injured and the girls rowed because Isabel wanted to help the man, but Liv thought they should be looking after their friend. She was meant to meet Isabel at the gym this morning. When Isabel didn't turn up, Liv thought she was still annoyed with her. When Isabel's dad called her this afternoon after he came home from work, asking where Isabel was, then she realised something was wrong.'

'I see.'

'Can you tell me anything else about the man in the street?' Alex asked Liv. 'Was he unconscious?'

'He wasn't moving. He had blood on his head.' She wrapped her arms around herself as though feeling a chill.

'Had you seen him inside the pub that evening?' asked Alex.

Liv frowned. 'I don't think so. I thought he'd drunk too much and fallen or had a fight. He was flat out, face down.'

Kyra whispered, 'What if he was only pretending to be injured, made himself look vulnerable, so he could trick her? He could have waited until they were alone and then attacked her.' There were cases in the past that she had studied, killers pretending to be injured, wearing casts, on crutches, arm in a sling, looking as though they needed help, as though they were weak and defenceless.

Predatory.

But Will kept his eyes on the screen.

'And what happened during the argument with Isabel?'

'Issy – Isabel – she's a nurse, a student – she had a look at him and said she was going to call for a peri-med. Ruby was out of it. She kept crying that she wanted to go home and then she vomited. Issy stayed with the man and I took Ruby to hers. We didn't even know the man.'

'You left Isabel? Alone – with the man?' Alex's voice was neutral.

The corners of Liv's mouth turned down. 'Issy said if I was going to be like that then I should go.' Her eyes flicked up to Alex and down again. 'She said she was going to ring

Andrew. He was on shift and she would meet him at the hospital. I took Ruby home and she threw up again at her house so I stayed to clean up. I walked past the pub on my way home, but Isabel wasn't there.'

'Was the man with the head injury still there?' asked Alex.
'No.'

'Going back to Andrew. Who's that?'

'Her boyfriend. He works at the hospital, he might be a peri-med, or he might just drive the ambulance, I'm not sure.'

Tom had already said that no calls had been made from Isabel's Commset. It had been found on the ground next to the main door of the pub.

'I don't really know him. They've only been seeing each other for a couple of months.'

'What's his full name?'

'Andrew Harper.' Kyra jumped as Will spoke into his Commset. 'Harry, check out a name for me, Andrew Harper, works at the Royal University Hospital, peri-med or ambulance driver.'

'We spoke to Isabel's dad but didn't say anything about a boyfriend,' Alex said.

Liv's eyes grew wide. She bit her lip and then said, 'He doesn't know.'

'Any reason for that?'

Liv shrugged. 'I'm not sure.'

Alex made another note. 'What was their relationship like from your perspective?'

'I don't really know. I think she preferred to keep her love life and her friends separate.' She scrunched the tissue up in her fist.

'What do you mean by that?' Kyra noticed Alex looking away again. Less intense for Liv?

'That she'd see us on a Friday, and him the rest of the time.' She paused for a moment and then said, 'Now I think about it, he was a bit . . . controlling really.'

'Go on,' Alex said, looking away again, giving her space to think, Kyra thought.

'Ruby and I agreed that doesn't sound like Issy at all. She used to see us all over the weekend.'

'Did anything else change? Would he stop her going certain places or wearing certain clothes?'

Liv shook her head. 'Not that she said.'

'Andrew never threatened her or anything?'

Tom came into the observation room at this point. He nodded at them and Will nodded back.

Liv pondered this before answering. 'Not threatened . . . exactly.'

'What do you mean?'

'I think he put a lot of pressure on her, I mean, reading between the lines.'

'Pressure to do what?'

'To do things his way.'

'Can you think of anything else that might be relevant?'

'I think he wanted her to move in with him. Issy didn't seem keen, and, I mean, we haven't even met him yet, but I don't really know any more than that.'

Alex stood up. 'Thanks, Liv. We'll be in touch if there's anything else we need to know. Or if you think of something, please contact us.'

Liv dropped her eyes for a moment. When she lifted them again, she said, 'Am I a terrible friend? I should have stayed with her, shouldn't I?'

Alex put a hand on her shoulder. 'You had a lot to deal with. You had to look after Ruby.' After a moment, she removed her hand. 'Did Ruby see any of this?'

Liv took a tissue from her bag and wiped her face. 'She wasn't in any fit state to see anything. She says she doesn't remember much after ten o'clock.'

Liv stood up too, pulled her coat around her and folded her arms across her chest, head down. Alex led her to the door but, as she put her hand on the handle, Liv said,

'Wait, there is something, stupid really, but it was odd. Isabel was wearing a necklace. I've never seen it before and when I asked her if Andrew had bought it for her, she said something weird . . .'

Kyra watched as Alex stood still for a moment and then turned around slowly.

'She said she'd just found it in her bedroom and she thought her dad had left it there. But it looked as though it was broken . . . Why would her dad do that?'

In the observation room, Kyra, Tom and Will moved closer to the screen.

'What did it look like?' Alex asked slowly.

'Like a half of a heart, with writing on it.'

The door opens again. He moves towards her, unties the bindings and picks her up easily, fireman's-lift style. Her head hangs over his back. She can feel his shoulders underneath her ribcage, his arm across the back of her legs. He doesn't feel like a big man, but he is strong. Her eyeballs swivel as she fights the drug. Her sight rests on the metal surgical tray – on an instrument with a serrated edge.

Her eyes begin glazing over, her breathing slows as he carries her naked body up the stairs to the ground floor, her cheek banging rhythmically against his back. In the hallway, she catches glimpses of a white plastic front door, blinds closed against the fading daylight, a candle burning, the sickly smell of vanilla. Then he takes her up another flight of stairs, the banister a shiny white gloss. In her haze she sees photograph frames with no images and smashed mirrors, all but a few silver mosaics remaining where the glass once reflected.

The light in the bathroom hurts her eyes. He manoeuvres to enable him to lean over the bath and half-lower, half drop, her into the water, the sound of splashing ringing in her ears. The freezing cold water steals her breath. Her muscles clench up painfully, gooseflesh crawling, burning with cold. He holds her head with one hand as he leans her body backwards into the deep water, the tap still running.

'Please, please . . .' she whispers, pleading, as he lets go of her.

She doesn't have the power to keep her face above the water, her body is so heavy with the drugs, so weak from her ordeal.

'Please don't let me drown,' she tries to say, but no words come. Her lips, already turning blue, are shaping the words silently, her tears mingling with the bathwater as she slips beneath the surface.

5.42 p.m.

'It's him,' Tom said as soon as the team was back in the Hub. 'It's our man. Isabel was wearing a Mizpah. It's the right time of year and it's his style; a clean, quick abduction. She fits the pattern for the Type B victim: a student nurse, 152cm, lives at home. In the past, there's been speculation that the killer is posing as a minicab driver, because in many of the cases, there does not seem to have been a struggle, so it would seem the vics don't initially realise they're in trouble, no real reason to raise the alarm. That could have been how he took her.'

The team took a collective breath.

·'Will, call around the hospitals see if anyone was brought in with a head injury on Friday night or if any ambulances were dispatched to the Farmer's Arms. We need to find that man to eliminate him from the enquiry and to find out if he saw anything, which, judging by the sound of it, is unlikely. Of course, Isabel might have taken him to hospital another way. We know she didn't use a cab, but she might have accepted a lift from another driver. We also need to speak to people at the hospital, friends and colleagues, see if anyone saw her that night. As Liv said, she was at Ruby's for quite a long time, longer than she expected, which means there's a window of about an hour, 10.45 to 11.45 p.m. Harry, when you speak to the regulars later, ask if anyone saw her outside, maybe gave her a lift. Talking of which, Kyra, I'll take you home now. The hospital is on the way. We'll call in and get Andrew Harper's details from Human Resources.'

Kyra wished she'd come in her own car now, was embarrassed by the preferential treatment of getting a lift.

Tom's face was pale, his jaw clenched. The team watched him expectantly.

'If this is Lomax's handy work then obviously he took Isabel before we got him and he has hidden her somewhere. We need to find out where as soon as possible.' He glanced at Kyra. 'We could interview him again—'

'There's no point. When we arrested him, after Amelia Brigham's death, the last year he was fully active 2021, there was another victim who was missing.' Why couldn't she just say Emma's name? She could feel Alex observing her, but she focused on Tom, 'and if he was guilty then he refused to tell us where she was – either he doesn't know or he won't tell. Either way, it's pointless . . .'

Will cut in. 'But she might still be alive. If there is another killer, and he follows the pattern, then we have until Wednesday midnight. But if it was Lomax, then she might be locked up somewhere and starve to death. He's only been back in custody for a couple of days, but who knows how long he will hold out until he tells us something.'

'If he has taken her, he won't talk,' Kyra said. 'In fact, it would probably only add to his feeling of power. Many killers, even when they have been arrested with no chance of release, will remain silent on where their victims are. It's their way of being in control. Think of the high-profile cases, the ones out pretending they're trying to help the police find the bodies after so long, but really they're simply getting a kick out of the fact that they know.'

'If there is an accomplice, he might panic and kill her anyway because Lomax has been arrested,' added Alex.

There was a collective shuffle, a sense of despair until Tom commanded, 'Right, then we'd better get on. Do what we can.' Then, to Kyra, 'I'll get my things from the office.'

The team quickly moved away, and Kyra was left alone, standing in front of the timeline, the murdered women looking down on her, urging her on.

What was she going to do, let Isabel starve to death?

A flush of heat gathered in her stomach and spread throughout her. She hadn't been able to save Emma, but there was no way she was going to let another woman die. Yes, she was afraid of Lomax, terrified of going into his mind. Yes, there were risks, to her own health even, and she had no idea what the MOD would do to her if they found out she was using the kit.

But first things first, she would have to persuade Tom that this was going to work, she was going to have to talk Lomax into going through with it and she had to get access to the lab.

And there was only one person who could help her do that.

Chapter Nineteen

SATURDAY 3 FEBRUARY 2035

9.30 p.m.

Jimmy was already at the bar when Kyra arrived. It was a quirky 90s place, blasting out tracks that she vaguely remembered her mother singing when she was a child: Oasis and Nirvana.

'What's with the last-minute drink? I thought you weren't talking to me,' Jimmy asked.

'I'm sorry. I meant to message you. I've just been busy.'

He raised his eyebrows.

'Really, I'm sorry. I didn't want to face up to the fact I lost my job . . .'

'You mean you expected a lecture?'

She ignored this. 'And I've got myself involved in a situation and I need your advice.'

'My advice?' He grimaced. 'What do you mean got yourself involved?'

She caught the bartender's eye, pointed to Jimmy's drink and motioned for two more.

'Sorry, Jim, did you have plans tonight?'

He was looking up at a nearby screen which was playing a soundless re-run of *Friends*.

'No, I was going to stay in and mess about on my

computer, one of those virtual holidays. I fancy having a look at somewhere in China.'

The bartender delivered the drinks which they took to one of the tables in a quieter corner and sat down.

'So, then?' Jimmy sat forwards elbows on the table.

Kyra swilled the drink around in her glass, wondering where to start. 'You know I used to be with the police force? I've been in touch with a copper I used to work with.'

'Okay.' Jimmy pulled a bemused expression.

'We were on a case together, the Mizpah Murders. It was . . . harrowing. It was one of the reasons I left working with the police. It looks like the criminal is active again.'

His face fell. 'I saw it on the news.'

She took a drink. It was sharp and sweet; Sunny D, heavy on the vodka, exactly what she needed to have this conversation. She took a large gulp and a warmth spread in her stomach that travelled into her blood, quelling the anxious bees in her chest.

'They think the latest victim was killed by the same guy. Tom, the copper, he wants me on the team as an advisor.'

'They want you on that case? Bloody hell.' Jimmy sat back. 'But didn't he kill . . . sorry.' He shook his head. 'How do you feel about that?'

How did she feel? Afraid, confused, frustrated?

'This case . . . it . . . stayed with me all these years. When we arrested Lomax, that's the man in prison, the one who was convicted, there was this one moment when . . . I thought there was a possibility he didn't do it. I mean he's a brute, violent, nasty but there's something not right.'

'I'm sure the police did all they can, I mean it was their responsibility, not yours.'

'I know, but I just can't let it go.' She took a drink and watched as he processed this.

158

'If it was such a horrible case and made you want to leave, then why would you want to get involved again?' he said finally.

'I want to know for sure who killed my sister. What if Lomax didn't and her killer is still out there?' She lifted her glass to her mouth to hide the pain she was sure would show on her face.

After a few moments, Jimmy said, 'They think it's the same man?'

She threw her hands up, despairing. 'I don't think so. The police aren't sure. It could be but . . .' She put her glass down and locked eyes with him. 'There's always a second victim. Another woman has gone missing. She was wearing a Mizpah necklace. She could still be alive, trapped somewhere. Whether Lomax did it or not, she's going to die in the next few days if we don't find her.' She took a deep breath. 'I want to use CASNDRA.'

He scanned her face.

'Why . . . I mean . . . what for?' Was that horror in his expression?

She sat up straight, prepared to fight for it. 'I need to know for sure who killed these women, and I need to find Isabel before it's too late.'

'I don't . . .' he began.

'I need to know, Jim,' she said, her voice quiet but determined.

He took a drink and his eyes travelled up to the screen again, but she could tell he wasn't watching it. An old song Emma used to love came on, 'Smells Like Teen Spirit'. It brought back memories of her sister dancing to it in the squat, the smell of joss sticks, the lights softened with chiffon scarves over the lampshades, little Molly asleep in a makeshift cot fashioned from a drawer.

'How are you planning to use the tech? You can't exactly go into the minds of the victims, they're all dead.' He briefly closed his eyes and shook his head. 'God, I'm sorry.'

She waved a hand to dismiss it.

'What about using the tech to go into the witnesses' minds, you'd be able to get such accurate testimony.' Then his shoulders fell. 'No, the legal system would never let that sort of testimony in court, not for years yet. There'd have to be thorough testing, safeguards, all the rest.' He thought for a moment. 'Unless you kept their identity hidden, like a witness X.' He sat up straight again. 'You could do that, you'd have to use CASNDRA to get the information and then get the witness to say what you had seen in their memory in court—'

'Jim . . . Jim . . .'

He fell silent.

'There are no witnesses.' She thought back briefly to Ray Clarke.

He knitted his brow. 'So, if it's not a victim or a witness . . .'

Kyra clammed up as a pair of women made their way past, cackling with laughter.

'I want to go into Lomax's memories and establish, once and for all, whether he's guilty, see if he knows where Isabel is, see if he killed Emma.'

He took a moment for this to sink in. 'You're joking, right?' He was clearly horrified.

She shook her head.

'I know you always wanted to use this tech for criminal justice but isn't this a bit extreme – going into the mind of a killer?' He leaned over the table, agitated. 'Kyra, I wasn't happy about the transference with that soldier, Brownrigg, and look what happened – when you came out of transference, you thought you'd had your throat cut! What the hell is going to happen if you go into Lomax's mind?'

She eyed him defiantly. 'I'll find the truth, that's what will happen. I'll know for sure who killed my sister.'

'And what if he did?' Jimmy slammed his glass down on the table. 'What if he killed your sister . . . Imagine what you will see! How that would affect you?' He put his head in his hands and peered at her through his fingers.

'Jimmy, the dreams I have, the things I see sometimes, and the symptoms . . . We knew this was a side effect of transference, but that's all they are; phantoms. There's no real danger. It's worth it if—'

'Look what happened to poor Phil,' he said, putting his hands back on the table.

Jimmy was usually so laidback and went along with her plans. Why was he being so difficult?

'We've been through this! The hospital said he had an undetected condition before he even went into transference and that was what caused his heart attack. I've had my health checks.' She reached out and put her hand on his. 'Come on, Jim, you monitor me all the time!'

He pulled his hand away. 'I don't mean that. What if the things you see make you ill? Phil Brightman – he already had an underlying problem. What if this technology exacerbates other underlying conditions that we don't know about? Not physical ones? What about mental health issues too? How do we know that you won't get Post Traumatic Stress Disorder from seeing bad stuff in some psycho's head? Lots of witnesses to crime get PTSD and that's exactly what you're going to be – a witness to some horrible, evil crimes. You'll be seeing it first hand as well . . . through the eyes of the person who did the killing . . .' He seemed lost for words for a moment.

'I don't even think he did it. The others think he might have an accomplice.'

'Then you might see his accomplice kill your sister! It's not about who did it, but what you might see in there.'

She slumped back in her chair. 'It's what I want. And I can't do it without your help. There's no way Carter will let me back into the lab.'

Jimmy groaned and closed his eyes for a moment. 'Oh, Kyra.'

They sat in an uneasy silence.

'You know Carter will go mad if he finds out about this. You've already lost your job. I might lose mine.'

'It's my kit,' Kyra urged. 'And another woman might lose her life!'

He sighed. 'It doesn't matter what I say, does it?'

She shook her head, then took a shaky breath. 'It's almost like I need to *be* Lomax, even if it is only for a short time. But if it means getting to the truth—'

'You're not only my colleague, well, ex-colleague, you're my friend. I'm not happy about this, but I wouldn't let you go through it on your own. You've had a lot of grief in your life. If CASNDRA does exacerbate underlying conditions, then . . .' He paused and shook his head. '. . . please be careful.'

And, very briefly, Kyra shivered.

It made my blood boil to think of him, out in the world, with a freedom that he doesn't deserve. But I turned it to my advantage. At the Scrambles I was so close to him throughout until he slept and then I completed my work. He went with one whore, I killed another.

He even spoke to me briefly, made physical contact.

But he wouldn't know me now, unless he saw the scar he left me with. I was careful to hide beneath a hood. The scar reminds me of the damage he can do. The child in me is still afraid but I calm him by telling him that Lomax cannot hurt me now.

He can't hurt Elise anymore.

If only I could have protected her then. She was so young, but I was only a child myself.

But I will do what I can for her now.

He would never give me a second thought, a second glance. He probably doesn't even know that I am alive. He will have no idea that sometimes I sit outside the prison, just to feel the thrill of knowing he is trapped in there wondering who did the deeds he is accused of. He taught us the meaning of suffering and now I'm teaching him what it feels like to suffer.

One day I will tell him it was me, when my plan is accomplished.

It's time I ate, so I go to the fridge and open the door, but the light hurts my eyes. I reach for a pizza without looking at the two packages wrapped in cellophane on the meat shelf. I close the door and turn to switch the oven on.

Elise should have been a beautiful woman now, like the woman downstairs in the box. It pains me to keep her like this. I want to take her out and admire her light, but she doesn't belong to me. Not like the other one did.

The thought spoils my appetite and I put the pizza in the bin and switch the oven off.

I need Elise to know that I am thinking of her constantly, that I will do whatever it takes to keep the darkness away, to protect her, wherever she is.

Chapter Twenty

9.17 a.m.

Kyra had spent the previous night wrestling with disturbing dreams of being trapped in the CarterTech lab with Lomax. When she had been awake, she had been trying to predict Tom's reaction to her suggestion, and the consequences of her actions, but she was determined to go through with her plan of a memory transference. She just had to wait for her opportunity to persuade Tom, to explain the tech to him and get him on her side so that he would be able to get permission from the governor, and help her to persuade Lomax. God, it seemed like an impossible task already.

She stood in front of the digital boards, nursing a mug of coffee. Isabel's photograph and details only served to show the parallels between her and the other previous Type B victims – 152cm, blonde and blue-eyed, student nurse.

She fit the profile.

Kyra's eyes travelled across the board, following the notes, her head aching with concentration. Underneath an image of a pub with an archaic, shield-shaped hanging sign it read: *FARMER'S ARMS – Marlborough Street – Isabel last seen here 10.45 p.m. approx.*

No CCTV outside – landlord has delivered internal closed circuit to be examined.

CAB FIRMS pick up at the Farmers Arms – but no one matching Isabel's description and no one giving her name.

BOYFRIEND – ANDREW HARPER – INTERVIEW 11 A.M. TODAY

HEAD INJURY MAN ???

LOMAX ASSOCIATES? None so far, no criminal/gang links, no known adversaries

PRISON VISITORS – mother, lawyer

WITNESSES – Ray Clarke ???

And then a single name that she didn't recognise

Martin Coombes

Alex joined her. 'We've got CCTV from inside the pub. We're running it through facial-recognition software now. Landlord says what happens outside isn't his business. Lots of the regulars know Isabel, no one saw anything out of the ordinary.'

'What's the family situation?' Kyra asked.

'Mum upped and left fifteen years ago, no siblings. Mr Marsden works long hours, saw her off at the door night before last, said she seemed happy and relaxed. She was looking forward to seeing her friends. He says she's a good girl, studies hard in her nursing course, sensible head on her shoulders. He says she never stays out without telling him. Family Liaison are at the house. Search turned up nothing.'

'Who's Martin Coombes?'

'Will managed to trace one visitor, from the time Lomax was held on remand,' Alex explained, 'before he was sentenced and ended up at Rockwell. Coombes was an apprentice mechanic at Lomax's garage on Gresham Road between 2004 and 2006. We can't find anything on the police system to suggest he was in any way dodgy, but we

166

are trying to trace him so that we can collect a bio-sample to rule him out. But Lomax's DNA has been confirmed on Caylee's body,' Alex said with a shrug.

'He's been framed. Gut instinct,' Kyra explained without looking at her.

'I'm not convinced,' said Alex, her eyes on the board. 'Some poor cow will die soon if we don't get this sorted.'

The words hit Kyra like a blow to the stomach. She tried not to react but the exhaustion, the stress of trying to get Tom on board, the implication that Emma had been only some 'poor cow' all came crashing together. Her throat started to close up, her chest tightening, her breaths shortening. She rummaged in her pocket for the inhaler which she kept close at all times now. She took two puffs. Tears began springing from her eyes. She tried to turn away before Alex saw what state she was in and, when she could no longer hold it together, she escaped from the Hub to the toilet.

Locking a cubicle door behind her, she lowered the toilet seat and sat down. The inhaler allowed her airways to open enough to let the wailing escape.

When she heard the door, she choked back her distress and put her hand to her mouth to stifle a sob.

'It's me, Alex.'

Kyra could see the shadow in the gap beneath the cubicle door.

Would she go away if she didn't reply?

Alex knocked gently on the door. 'You alright?'

The kindness in her voice added to Kyra's feeling of misery.

'Let me in.'

She wasn't going to go. Kyra leaned forward, unlocked the door and it swung open slowly.

Alex opened her mouth and closed it again. She smoothed her hair back and tried again. 'Did I say something wrong?'

Kyra glanced over to the wide mirror above the sinks in front of her. She could see Alex's plait hanging down her back, her hand on the cubicle door. One of the taps was running, the thin trickling turning into a gurgle as it disappeared down the plughole.

She bit her lip. What would Alex think of her if she told her the truth? Would she march right out of the bathroom and tell the DCI, get her kicked off the case, get Tom into trouble? Or would it help to tell Alex? Would she see Kyra for who she really was, then, not someone who wanted to take her place in the boss's estimations, but someone who was trying to find justice, on a personal level?

It was a gamble. 'He killed my sister.' She took a staggered breath. 'Emma.' Saying the words out loud felt like a bereavement all over again. But it also steeled her, as though out of the haze of sorrow and sleeplessness there was a goal in the distance, giving her meaning, direction.

Alex's face fell. She pointed a thumb towards the door. 'The girl from the board?'

'Yes.'

She bent down on her haunches and blew out heavily. Her eyes settled on Kyra's.

'There's me, thinking you were some smart-arse consultant.' She briefly rubbed Kyra's hand. Her fingers were cold. It felt odd but comforting. 'I am so sorry.'

Kyra pulled tissues from the roll and wiped her face.

'Jesus, this must be so hard for you.'

Alex's words galvanised her. She didn't want to be a victim.

She wanted justice.

'I want to get him, Alex! I want to sort this mess out,' she leaned closer to her, 'for Emma, for those women.' It made her even more determined to get Tom to agree to her plan.

Was that admiration Kyra could see in her eyes?

Alex studied her for a moment, weighing her up. Kyra had done it hundreds of times herself, as a psychologist. She put her chin up, her shoulders back in defiance of her personal situation.

'Let's do it then,' Alex said, standing up. 'I'll give you a few minutes . . . wash your face and, when you're ready, I'll see you back in the Hub.' She paused at the door and turned back. 'Let's get him.' And then she left Kyra alone.

There was a shift in the atmosphere between them, a lightening of the tension. They were in this together now. Bonded in secrecy.

She took a couple of deep breaths, stood up and went over to the sink. She bent over, splashing her face with running water, feeling it cooling her skin. As she turned the tap off and stood back up, she reached over blindly for the paper towels to dry her face.

Something brushed her hand.

She opened her eyes, the water immediately running into them and blurring her vision.

Someone was standing next to her.

'Alex?'

But it was too small to be Alex.

Grabbing at the towels, she patted her face quickly. When she looked again, she saw the boy from Brownrigg's memory standing next to her, anger blazing in his eyes, his white garments covered in desert sand. He was holding the curved, rusted knife and her body froze in terror, even though her mind knew he wasn't really there. She couldn't move a muscle, even as he drew his arm backwards, ready to attack.

She felt the burn of the blade and the boy spun on his heels and ran out of the bathroom door.

As the door closed, a single gunshot rang loudly in the corridor.

Kyra looked her reflection, horrified to see blood seeping from the gash in her throat into the collar of her white shirt.

The bathroom light flickered off briefly, and when they came on again the blood disappeared.

She touched her neck. Her fingers were clean.

Christ, Kyra, pull yourself together!

She leaned over, hands either side of the sink for a few moments, breathing deeply. There was no way she was going to let the team see her like this. She waited until the panic and nausea had died down, then stood up straight and faced herself in the mirror. She pinched her cheeks to get a bit of colour, then held her head up and made her way back to the Hub.

10.23 a.m.

Martin Coombes.

I remember him so clearly.

As a child, I wished that he had been my big brother. He was probably ten years older, but with similar dark hair and blue eyes to me. He was an apprentice. He told me that was someone who learned as they went along.

I have had to learn as I go along.

Learn how to plant evidence, track my prey, hide my movements.

I wonder how different my life would have been if Martin Coombes had been my big brother? Would he have stopped that man from being so cruel to us? Would he have taken the beatings for us? Would he have been able to save Elise?

Martin Coombes was kind to me. He used to give me biscuits sometimes when that man wouldn't let me eat. He would slip me fifty-pence pieces and pound coins with a wink and put his fingers to his lips.

The bastard told the mechanics to ignore me when I came home from school, forbade them to speak to me. And they obeyed.

All besides Martin Coombes.

Our house was on the same plot of land as the garage. The bastard only stayed with my mother because of the yard, I know that now. Somewhere he could live for free, use the land for his business, use her.

It was such a lovely place, 'in the country' she used to say, even though it was only a few miles from the city. We used to play in the fields nearby. We had a vegetable patch and my mother grew roses.

Before she met him, my mother was devoted to us. She would play games with us, take us on long walks and tell us all the names of the flowers and birds. We were the centre of her world, me and Elise, before he came and cut all the roses down to build his garage.

After he was arrested, I wanted to go to the prison. I wanted to look him in the eye and tell him what I had done. What I had done for Elise. What I had done for revenge. But I knew there was no way he would have agreed to let me visit.

Why would he let his ex-girlfriend's kid visit?

I didn't think he would even have remembered my name.

So, I pretended to be Martin Coombes, the man who knew how cruel and destructive the bastard really was, the man who gave me hope that things could be different.

When I faced him in jail I felt eight years old again.

Even he thought I was Martin at first too, like the screws. The photo ID was pretty convincing and, of course, Martin's bio-chip under my skin couldn't lie. It hadn't been easy, getting that chip. I had grown to look so much like the man who had been kind to me. The bastard only recognised me because of my scar – a craftsman always recognises his own handiwork.

I had wanted to go and tell him what I had done, that it was me who followed him in the darkness, killed the women, planted the evidence to make it look like he had done it – that, after all these years, I was going to make him suffer for what he had done to me, to Elise.

But before I could say any of this, he laughed.

He told me I was a weak, worthless shite who deserved to die like my little sister.

And then I couldn't tell him what I had done. I couldn't speak at all.

I pissed myself — right in front of him.

And I ran away like a child, like the eight-year-old I had been.

I went out that night and beat a man senseless purely because he looked similar to the bastard. It took me a while to get over the humiliation but, once I had, I promised myself that I would continue to punish him, whatever it took, however long it took.

After Elise died, my mother couldn't go on. The authorities believed that man's lies and it was recorded as an accidental death, although my mother was under suspicion of neglect.

She never recovered.

When I was ten years old, my mother took her own life. And everything I had ever loved was gone. But part of me still blames her too.

It was a shame what happened to Martin Coombes; after all, he was one of the very few adults who had ever been kind to me. His last act of kindness was to give me his bio-chip.

Well, I took it.

But it was Martin who gave me the chance to get revenge. And I grabbed that chance with both hands.

Chapter Twenty-One

Tom looked exhausted as he scrolled down the screen at his desk. Reading his body language, Kyra surmised he wasn't in the right mood, but they were running out of time. Now that she had made her mind up, she didn't want to wait too long before she went through with it.

She braced herself. 'Tom.'

'Hmm?'

'I've got an idea that might help. It's totally unorthodox, and I'm not one hundred per cent certain how successful it might be, but . . .' She shifted her weight from one foot to the other.

He glanced up at her but she could tell he was distracted.

'After I left the Behavioural Science department – I don't know if you know – I went on to focus purely on Neuropathy. I changed from looking at links between criminal behaviour and psychology to looking at the possibility that there were neurological reasons for criminal behaviour; actual physical problems in the brain that could somehow be diagnosed.'

'Sick of mopping up the mess so you went into prevention instead?' he said, looking back down at his screen briefly.

He got it. She was reminded of one of the slogans from the institute where she had conducted most of her research: *If we can predict . . . we can prevent!*

'Exactly.'

She sat down on the other side of his desk and he faced her properly now.

'Is that how you ended up in CarterTech?' Was he interested or just humouring her?

'Yes, I needed the sort of money Carter had to turn the research into reality.' She wasn't exactly proud of that.

He rubbed his earlobe. She could tell he was itching to study his report, but she pressed on. 'I discovered that it is possible to retrieve memories from the brain's cortex – whole, unabridged, accurate. I developed a technology that can do this.'

He didn't react. Had he heard what she'd said?

'I want to use it on Lomax.'

She swallowed hard, wondering what he was going to make of this, to what degree she was going to have to fight her corner.

He sat back in his chair. 'Go on . . .'

'Using equipment that I've developed, it's possible to read these memories directly from another person's brain.'

'But how?'

'We inject tiny receptors and transmitters into the bloodstream of the reader and the subject and they travel to the brain. They pick up memories, like picking up radio waves, I suppose, and send them through a computer programme which translates them and relays them into a VR headset. That's a very simplistic way of describing it, but you have to believe me. I can do this and I think we should try to persuade Lomax that we should use the kit on him.'

Come on, Tom. Back me on this one. Say yes!

He took his time as if he was trying to slow down what she'd said, replay it in his head, and understand. 'You're telling me that we can look at Lomax's memories, find out if he killed Caylee or not?'

She saw a mixture of disbelief, curiosity and intrigue. Then she saw the police officer kick in.

'We could find out if he killed the original victims for certain?'

'I don't know. I mean, it's not like a video history, I can't just rewind his life and see everything, but I might see something that helps; incriminates him or suggests that he didn't do it. At least we'd know.'

'Can I do this? Can I see into his memories?' He was restrained, but she could tell he was interested. His arms twitched as he leaned forwards slightly.

There was no way she could let him do that. What if he started picking up residual memories, as Jimmy had put it, or phantoms as she called them now because they were so real it was like seeing ghosts, like the desert boy in the toilet at the Hub, and realised that the kit wasn't as ready as it should be?

'There's not enough time to train you on the equipment. If we're going to do this, if you give me your permission, then we need to do it as soon as possible so that we don't waste time barking up the wrong tree. You can trust me. I'll relay everything I see.'

'Is there any way of, I don't know, recording what you see in his mind, or projecting it so that we can use it as evidence.'

'Tom, let's get this straight, you're never going to be able to use this stuff in court. It won't be evidence you can prosecute with.' She started to panic. Couldn't they keep this to themselves? No one needed to find out, did they?

Not Carter, not the other officers, not the MOD. Why was he taking so long to agree?

She waited for a moment. Then, 'So, what do you say?'

'I'm trying to get my head around it, Kyra, that's all.'

She thought back to what Jimmy had said about a witness X. Maybe they could use the information they gleaned from the CASNDRA – the machine itself would be witness X, protected by anonymity. The MOD would never find out that way.

'The point is that I get first-hand access to Lomax's memories. I get to see where he's been, what he's been doing. We need to find Isabel, and soon.'

He nodded slightly and she took it as encouragement.

'If I see anything that leads us to believe that he did it . . .' She looked down at her hands, 'then at least we can put this to bed once and for all, knowing that we got the right man. If I can't find evidence of Lomax committing these murders, then I might be able to find new lines of enquiry – things that show us where to go next.'

She studied his face as he mulled this over and then said, 'If he killed Caylee, then Lomax won't agree to it. '

'That in itself might suggest he's guilty,' she replied. 'But if he is innocent then he will let us try, and we might see something that gives us an idea of what is going on.'

Tom reached up and rubbed his scar.

'Can we use it on him even if he won't agree to it?'

This was what she had been trying to avoid with the MOD. *Brain-hacking.* But if a woman's life was at stake . . . would she be able to overcome her dilemma?

'If it's an accomplice, he'll kill Isabel in three days' time. If it's Lomax, she'll starve to death. We have to act. Let's use the tech on Lomax. Please, trust me.'

Tom stood up. 'Right . . . I'll call the governor of

Rockwell straight away, see if we can get permission.'

Just over an hour later, Tom and Kyra sat opposite the governor and Lomax, close together in a room almost too small for four people, a desk and two chairs. The fluorescent strip light hummed constantly and flickered intermittently. The window was a yellowing opaque Plexiglass square, high up on one of the grey walls. Lomax smelled of coffee and sweat. Kyra held her breath.

'You're agreeing to this?' Lomax asked, stunned, and Governor Bennett gave a brief, insincere smile.

'What's in it for you?' Lomax asked her.

'She has her reasons,' Tom said.

'I bet she does,' Lomax sneered at Bennett. 'Don't look too good on the little lady that I was out and about, does it?' There was still the hostility, the bravado, but underneath was also frustration, or was it confusion?

'I've always run Rockwell as a centre of excellence, with cutting-edge treatments and putting my prisoners' welfare at the top of my priorities.' the governor said primly. 'This can only add to our list of firsts.'

'Trying to compensate for the fuck up of my escape, you mean,' Lomax said with a sneer.

'Watch yourself, Lomax,' the governor barked. 'Your chip shows clearly that you were down at the Scrambles during your little trip out.'

'I didn't deny it – I was only getting a bit of pussy . . .'

'I don't tolerate language of that nature!' barked the governor, but Tom cut her off.

'We need to find the real killer. I want to prove you didn't do it, Lomax.'

He eyed Tom suspiciously. 'What is it, then, some kind of lie-detector machine?' He sounded curious now.

'Sort of,' Kyra said. 'I'm going to read your memories,' she said, choosing her words carefully. 'I want to find anything that might help in our investigation.'

His expression changed back to suspicion and he turned to Tom.

'What if you see something else that incriminates me in another crime?'

'We're not interested in anything other than the Mizpah Murders.'

'Yeah, you say that now . . .' he sat back and crossed his arms, the table shifted slightly across the floor as he knocked it. 'But what if I don't *want* to let you look inside my brain?' he sneered and Kyra felt the bees in her chest beginning to mobilise.

Governor Bennett pulled rank. 'I've left documentation approving your transfer to Stoker's Keep. If you don't agree, then I'll make sure you rot there, a task I shall relish.' The gleam in her eyes verified the fact.

Lomax's face fell. 'You've got some fucking nerve, Bennett,' he spat.

She gave a wry smile. 'You won't be top dog, there, Lomax. There'll be no hot showers, privilege, screens or any of the little luxuries we provide here at Rockwell. It will be purely work and punishment, twenty-four seven. And who knows what fun the other inmates have planned for you?'

His shoulders dropped.

'Do you know the regime at Stoker's Keep, Doctor Sullivan?' the governor asked, flicking a non-existent piece of fluff from her tweed suit. 'It's notorious amongst the inmates. Not many people come out and, if they do,' she said, turning a steady eye on Lomax, 'they're a shadow of their former selves.'

'You're telling us one thing,' Kyra said, ignoring Bennett and focusing on Lomax. 'but the evidence is telling us something else. At the moment, with your DNA on the latest body . . .' she let that one hang. Lomax's eyes darkened.

'On the other hand, if we can prove that this wasn't your kill,' the word nearly stuck in her throat as she pushed away an image of Emma – she had to convince him. 'I can prove you're innocent and then we can set about looking for the person who really did this.'

Could he tell she was lying? Would he be able to look into her eyes and see that the real reason she was doing this was to find the truth, see who killed her sister? Would he know that she didn't care one jot about what happened to the brute in front of her?

Lomax leaned into her, seemed almost to be sniffing the air around her as he weighed this up.

'So, what's it going to be, Lomax?' Tom demanded.

Kyra held her breath.

'Don't look like I've got much choice, does it?' Lomax rolled his eyes.

Tom remained poker-faced.

'I thought as much,' said Governor Bennett.

Did this mean he was innocent, or did he think he could beat the tech?

'You let us read your memories,' Kyra said flatly, 'We can get you out of here.'

'Win, win, all round I'd say, Tommy boy.'

Kyra relaxed a little.

'When am I gonna use this little lie-detector of yours, doc?'

Tom looked to the governor.

'I've given my permission for Danielsson and another guard to take you to the lab this evening at nine o'clock.'

'Out and about under cover of darkness, eh?' Lomax grinned. 'You paying Danielsson double-time from your own pocket, Governor?'

She didn't answer.

'It's a shame you didn't come up with this invention of yours fourteen years ago when they banged me up in here,' he snarled at Kyra.

Tom interrupted. 'And you can keep your mouth shut about it. Or the deal's off and you're going to Stoker's Keep.'

Lomax rolled his eyes again.

'You know,' he began, looking at Tom and then back at Kyra, 'if you find out that I'm innocent and I get out . . . regardless of the fact you helped . . . you put me in here in the first place . . . so I'm still gonna come for you.'

Bennett jumped up and called in two of the guards. 'Get him out of here,' she roared and the guards pulled him off the chair and dragged him towards the door. He turned around and gave Kyra one last grisly smile.

'See you around, Doc.'

The thought suddenly occurred to Kyra:

It will be down to me if Lomax gets out or not.

And the sudden weight of responsibility was crushing.

Chapter Twenty-Two

SUNDAY 4 FEBRUARY 2035

9.08 p.m.

'Are you sure you don't want a coffee?' Tom held up his own cup. 'It's getting late – caffeine might help?'

He was only trying to distract her, Kyra knew that, with idle chat and gossip about the officers they had worked with back in the day, but she could tell he was nervous too, though for different reasons. How could he possibly understand the risk she was about to undertake?

She took a few deep breaths and said, 'I usually puke if I eat or drink anything beforehand.' She could see Jimmy in the lab; he hadn't spoken to her since he'd arrived. But at least he was here.

'What's that about? Mind-travel sickness?' asked Tom.

'Sort of.' She couldn't manage a smile. 'Do you think he'll be handcuffed?'

'I won't let him near you.'

'God knows what I'm going to see in there.'

Tom studied the sculpture of the brain on the reception desk and ran his finger over one of the lines. 'What's it like, going into someone else's head?'

'Like watching home movies. That's the only way I can describe it; flashes of different images and sometimes words come to my mind, or feelings that aren't mine overwhelm me. Unlike the movies, I sort of . . . experience things . . . I can even smell things at times.' Her stomach was churning with anxiety.

'Can you feel sensations? Does it hurt?' he asked, curious.

'No, not physically. Although once I went into Jimmy's head and he had had rather a lot to drink the night before and I caught his hangover. Believe me, I felt that!'

'Really?' Tom sounded amazed.

'Yeah, it was . . . weird.' She tried to manage a smile, but it must have looked more like a grimace. 'Not fair, really, all of the hangover, none of the beer.' She thought about the other side-effects she was suffering these days. They were getting more intense.

She heard a noise outside. Oh God, was this it?

She was glad Jimmy was there, but she wished he'd talk to her. Didn't she need her friends at a time like this? She saw CASNDRA's bed move out, the lights turn from red to green.

'I can't guarantee any useful information,' she told Tom. 'It's like I said, I don't know how much control he'll have over his memories. When I work with Jimmy I ask him to focus on something specific and that's usually what I see. I suppose to some degree it depends on what Lomax wants to show me. I'm not sure yet whether someone can withhold memories or not. We haven't tested for that.'

'No worries, just give it a go,' Tom said.

Give it a go, like it was a fairground game.

'I think the best tack to take is if you ask Lomax a few questions before we go down, try to tune him in to what we're looking for.' She paused. 'Tom, say this doesn't work, then what are we going to do next? How are we going to solve this? Is there anyone else we can use the tech on?' She thought briefly of Ray Clarke.

'You haven't even tried yet. Don't lose your bottle now.' There was an edge to his voice.

That was definitely a car outside. Her chest tightened, the buzzing began.

'Seriously, you don't have to do this, you know.' His words were steady, but she saw the desperation in his eyes.

'Of course I do!' she snapped. 'There's a young woman out there somewhere who could die, *who will die*, any day now, if I don't at least try this! It's on me!'

'You're not responsible for her,' he said slowly. 'I am.'

'Tom, no. We were all on the team together back then . . .'

There was a quiet knock on the door, and her fight-or-flight instinct kicked in. She wanted to run. She wiped her palms on her thighs.

Oh God, I actually have to be Lomax . . . see the things he did . . . or might have done.

Her fingers fumbled with the familiar lock. She was aware of Tom's eyes on her as she braced herself for Lomax to barge in, but Danielsson led the way. Out of uniform, he looked less like a guard, more like a gangster, or even a Viking, Kyra thought, now that she could see his blonde hair without his cap. He stood over 190cm, his shoulders wide and strong, much bigger than Lomax. He wore all black, an expensive leather jacket. How could a guard afford such an item? Maybe the governor had paid him off, after all.

Lomax shuffled in behind him, cuffs and links on his wrists and ankles, like an old-school criminal on a chain gang. He was followed by another guard, a small black woman, her muscles neat and taut underneath her tight-fitting dark jacket and trousers. Kyra greeted her, but she only had eyes for Lomax – eyes with yellow flecks in the brown irises. Kyra suspected they were smart lenses, with nano-cameras. Whatever she was seeing would be relayed back to the governor at the prison.

'Told you I'd see you around, Doc. Nice gaff you've got here,' Lomax said, as though he'd just arrived at a party.

Kyra stepped outside the door to check that no one had seen Lomax come in. CarterTech was halfway down a side street, affording some privacy. A black car was parked against the graffitied wall opposite with its bright sprayed slogans of *Fair play for the poor!* and *Smash the money power!*

At least they hadn't used a prison van.

Out of the corner of her eye, there was a movement.

She froze. Further down the street, she saw a black shape was slumped against a wall in the shadows. Was it a man crouching? Was Brownrigg still spying on her? What would the MOD do to her if they knew she was still using the kit? Would they tell Carter?

Her skin crawled.

She jumped as a piece of litter blew up in a mini-twister of a breeze.

Was that a face? Eyes looking at her?

No, it was only a pile of refuse bags slumped against the wall.

Get a grip!

She locked the door carefully, relieved for the time being. Jimmy came out of the lab. 'Take him through,' he commanded, pointing the direction and the guards led Lomax away. Ignoring Tom, Jimmy focused on Kyra.

Her heart was thumping furiously in her chest. The lights came on automatically as Lomax and the guards moved along the corridor towards the lab where CASNDRA shone bright white behind the glass.

'I'll go and start with a few questions and images to get Lomax into the right frame of mind,' Tom said and followed the others.

When they were alone, Kyra said to Jimmy, 'I wasn't sure you were going to come.'

'I'm your friend and I wouldn't let you walk home on your own in the dark, so there's no way I'm going to let you do something like this without me.' He raised his hands, palms facing her, his face serious. 'But I don't really agree with what you're doing here, Kyra. I mean it's bad enough breaking into the lab without telling Carter . . .'

'We're not breaking in! I'm his business partner . . . was . . . it's my kit!'

'You're already suffering nightmares and asthma and God knows what else you haven't told me . . . It could be the receptors . . . the ones we injected into you. They should have passed out by now, but there's always the chance they could still be there, causing problems in your brain.'

'Oh, Jimmy, leave it—'

'No. We need to look into it. Tom needs to know that there are problems, so that he can keep an eye on you—'

'What problems?' They turned around to see Tom standing there. 'Sorry, I forgot my coffee.' He pointed to the cup by the sculpture of the brain. 'Is there something you omitted to tell me, Kyra?'

Omitted. Police talk.

'About the asthma, and the soldier?' Jimmy sounded annoyed. 'If Kyra's going to be taking risks for you, then you should know some of the side effects.'

For you . . . was Jimmy jealous?

'Fuck's sake, Jimmy!' Kyra mouthed.

'Should we be doing this?' Tom asked.

Jimmy looked back at Kyra. 'It's your call.'

'Yes, it's my call,' she said fiercely. 'We're doing it.'

'What about a soldier?' Tom gave her that expression, one that used to be so familiar; the dog with a bone. He wasn't going to let this drop.

'We'll talk later,' she said. 'Let's get this over with.'

They moved into the lab. Jimmy made some adjustments on the screen and glanced up to see Tom staring at him. 'We used to use the computer to read the memories, but the images were far too low grade.' He passed the VR headset to Kyra and helped her attach a few electrodes directly to her temples. She didn't look at him, even though he was so close.

Jimmy went on, 'We found that the human brain could decipher the images much more accurately.'

Tom came over to look. Was he trying to smooth things over with Jimmy? She didn't need them joining forces.

'It's as though the brain is speaking a language that can't be fully interpreted by the computer, so we need a human reader. It's like if you listened to another language you might hear the words and get some of the meaning, but you would miss the nuances, and then it doesn't make enough sense. The receptors and the headset work together to provide a fuller picture.'

'Are you sure it's safe?' Tom asked Jimmy. 'I mean, you said—'

'Considering the clarity of interpretation the human brain can give, it seems to be worth the risk for the quality of information,' Kyra snapped, anxious to get on. Jimmy had already injected her with receptors. She watched as he injected Lomax with the stimulators and put the needle in the yellow sharps box. 'Did you ask him what you wanted to, Tom?'

'Yes.' He held up his mini-screen to show her, then put it into his leather bag.

Lomax lay, still cuffed, and strapped for extra security. Jimmy had sent Danielsson and the female guard back outside the lab, on the other side of the glass, where they could keep an eye on him but not overhear the details.

'Cosmo, prepare for transference,' Jimmy commanded and the bed on which Lomax was lying began moving into CASNDRA's centre.

'Welcome to the jungle, Doc!' Lomax boomed. 'Enjoy the show!'

I remembered the woman with the dark hair from all those years back. She seemed to sense me outside the door when they took him in to CarterTech. The website is a mish-mash of techno-bullshit and crass slogans: Where Imagination and Innovation come together. *They do tracking chip work. Is that why they brought him here? But I don't think it is official business as the guards weren't in uniform.*

After the girl in the ice, it became like second nature to follow people. I followed the women that I chose. I followed the police officers. I watched their confusion about the connection between the two women, until they found the box.

I saw them picking around the corpses like carrion birds, looking for clues.

All the time I was there.

I followed the psychologist. I even saw them together, alone, her and the policeman. I hid in the everyday ordinariness of life. I didn't stand too close. I didn't look too long. I always kept my distance.

Before that I had only followed the bastard – knew his every move. I knew where he was, who he was with, what he was doing. How else was I to trap him? He could never be punished for what he did to my family, but I could get him punished for something else.

I chose the victims carefully. I chose the time and place carefully. It had to be when he was around, when it could be proven by witnesses, by CCTV, that he had been there. The DNA was more tricky, but for everything else it looked as though he had done it.

I knew it would take time for him to be caught. But I was prepared to wait. I had waited for my revenge since I was a child, hadn't I? What difference would a few more years make?

But I remember her. Kyra the psychologist. I was in the cafe that night. I had been following her, some might say coincidence, some might say destiny, fate. I sat close to her – at the next table. Then a woman and a child came in. A beautiful little girl, like my Elise. I even patted her on the head as I walked past her in the cafe and she gave me a radiant smile, but the women hardly noticed me, they were so deep in conversation.

Later, when the deed had been done, and the rush had dissipated, I thought back to that little girl, how I had left her motherless.

And I cried my heart out.

Chapter Twenty-Three

SUNDAY 4 FEBRUARY 2035

9.28 p.m.

A glass flew over Kyra's head in a poorly lit, stuffy bar and splintered against a bare plaster wall. She watched as her fist, Lomax's fist, smashed into a man's face. She heard the crunch of contact and the man flew backwards, an arc of blood and saliva spraying from his mouth marking his trajectory as he fell. A cheer went up all around, animals honouring their pack leader.

She took the headset off for a moment and rubbed her face. Jimmy gave a thumbs-up sign, his face concerned. *Don't let your fear hold you back. Think of Isabel, think of Riley.* She gave the thumbs-up in reply and then, like someone about to dive into murky water, took a deep breath and replaced her headset.

She shifted on the recliner, agitated. *Come on, Kyra. You can do this!*

When she tuned in again, the blood, barstools and smell of beer had disappeared, replaced by a worn leather sofa, cracked with age, a table set for dinner, a small sprig of freesia in a tiny, clumsily made pottery vase. What was that she could smell? Chicken and herbs? In front of her she saw Lomax's hands again – one gripped a woman by her shiny black hair as she cowered in front of him on her knees, her eyes squeezed shut, waiting for the blow, her hands up in surrender. Lomax's other hand was a white-knuckled fist.

Looking through his eyes under the table, nearly invisible in the darkness, Kyra saw a young child, a boy trembling in the shadows. Then another child's face appeared from behind him, a little girl, no more than a toddler, her eyes wide with fear. The boy pushed her back down. Kyra's instincts to protect the children boiled as she watched the ugly scene unfold.

Hardcore pornography filled her mind immediately – violent jabbing, writhing bodies, cries of pain. Her stomach roiled, but then an anger rose in her. Lomax would want her to see this. He was taunting her.

Suddenly, she was standing alone on a dark road – wide, smooth black Tarmac underfoot. THE CROXLEY ESTATE was proudly emblazoned in wrought-iron fence-work above the red-brick boundary wall, silhouetted against the yellow light of the few remaining street lamps on the other side. Kyra glanced down at her body – at *his* body – the tattooed arms, the grey prison sweatpants.

In front of her lay derelict chaos, full of KEEP OUT signs: some printed onto shiny boards belonging to the council, some made by the residents themselves, a mixture of spray paint and swear words. The graffiti also indicated which sordid and illegal services could be bought where. It was easy to tell the sex-workers from the Lè addicts – the addicts ducked into the doorways to hide, but the male and female prostitutes suddenly came to life, showing off their wares like a mechanical puppet display. It was as though an architect's drawing of the ideal estate – a sunny place with people walking hand in hand in brightly coloured clothes, blossoming trees and shiny cars – had been plunged into a nightmare.

It was sickening for her to be in his body; it was as if an infection was travelling into her. Kyra could feel his powerful strides as he moved along, the weight of his being. She could sense his sexual desire, built up after so long incarcerated, his predatory instincts, as he made his way over to a stick-thin woman – frail and vulnerable – his excitement rising. The thin woman stood in the doorway, she inclined her head to the front door, beckoning.

He cut across the patch of rough earth that might have served one time as a lawn and moved towards the house. A candle glowed softly in the window, and Kyra could smell incense, patchouli and roses. Soft music travelled through the door out onto the night air, contrasting with the stark brutality of the estate.

As Lomax approached the door, Kyra heard footsteps, someone running along the pavement nearby. Lomax's body tensed. He moved his head slightly, as though he was an animal using echolocation.

The noise stopped close by and Lomax turned slowly, shoulders relaxed, chin up.

A hooded man, smaller than Lomax, stood motionless facing him. The top of the nearby street lamp dangled, his face was hidden in shadows.

'Fuck off, I was here first.' Lomax moved to go to the house but noticed that the man stayed in the same spot and Kyra felt her body, Lomax's body, stiffen.

'You wanna pay to watch, mate?' Lomax growled. She could feel the rage growing in his guts.

The man swayed slightly from foot to foot, clenching his hands into fists and then releasing. 'I'm not afraid of you!' the man shouted.

Lomax took a step forward and then began to laugh. 'You're fucking joking?'

Did he recognise the man? His voice, maybe? Was it what he said?

When the stranger didn't move away, Kyra could feel irritation in Lomax, mixed with an instinct for brutality and she knew this was a dangerous cocktail for the woman waiting in the house for him.

With a grunt, Lomax moved towards the other man. His opponent stood his ground, but Lomax grabbed him by his top and swung him with great force so the man rolled over and over on the road and finally came to a stop. He lay still for a moment and Lomax shook his head and went towards the house. As he got to the door, he looked back over his shoulder; the man was back up on his feet, coming closer. His face was grazed, his forehead bleeding down onto one eye which flickered with the drips, the blood black in the darkness. His hooded jacket was torn and hanging from one shoulder.

Kyra saw that under his top he wore a T-shirt with a familiar logo – the two snakes wrapped around a winged staff – that she had seen frequently at the hospital, on ambulances; all the doctors and nurses wore them on their uniforms. Was he a medical worker? He was no match for Lomax, that was certain. He stood, clenching and unclenching his fists again, stepping from one foot to another.

Lomax barged into him, leaning down to press his forehead against the man's. Kyra could feel the man's resistance, his skull hard on Lomax's. She tried to take in details of his face, but it was difficult as she was too close. Under the cut on his forehead, his left eye was sticky with blood.

Lomax spun quickly and caught the man on the side of the face with a ferocious punch. He fell hard and Lomax went into the house and shut the door.

As Lomax grabbed the woman roughly by the shoulders, Kyra took in every detail of her face; the sharp cheekbones, the hollow eyes, the overly plucked eyebrows and heavy make-up. She had never seen this woman before. It wasn't one of the Mizpah Murderer's victims. She knew each and every one of their faces in detail. It certainly wasn't Caylee Carmichael. It must be the prostitute who had given Lomax his alibi.

Lomax pushed her out of the way and leaned over to look out of the window.

The man was nowhere to be seen.

Where had he gone? He didn't seem to have had a vehicle. Did he live nearby? Was he known to Lomax? Kyra willed Lomax to go back outside but he was intent on the woman now.

Kyra was revolted by the feelings of sexuality that were seeping into her from Lomax; the moment the violence began, reeling with nausea and disgust, she pulled her headset off and threw it across the floor.

Immediately there was a screeching in her head, like white noise, which threatened to rip her skull apart. She grabbed her head in her hands as the noise seemed to increase in pitch, and then finally it subsided. When it fell silent, she leaned forward on the recliner and vomited, splattering the floor in front of her, startling Jimmy and Tom.

'Side effect of transference,' she told Tom, once her nausea had quelled.

Jimmy passed her some paper towels. 'You look like death warmed up. Are you okay?' He had never appeared so anxious about a transference before. Should she be worried too?

The awful pain in her brain began to lift a little and she muttered, 'Don't fuss, Jim.'

She took a few deep breaths. Her eyes had a pre-migraine halo and her mouth was dry. 'Water.' She pointed to a nearby jug and glass that Jimmy must have put there earlier.

'God, yes, sorry,' Tom said as he took a glass, filled it with water and passed it to her.

She sipped at it, wiped away the cold sweat with some of the paper towels she was holding and then sat back, trying not to vomit again. She was embarrassed; Danielsson and the other guard were stood watching everything.

Lomax was snoring now.

'Anything?' asked Tom.

She lay back on the recliner. 'He's been to The Scrambles for a prostitute,' her voice cracked. God, her head hurt. 'He beat a woman in front of her kids. He has a particularly niche taste in porn. But I didn't see any of our women. He was wearing his prison sweats, so it was the right date. He's a nasty, violent bastard, but there's nothing that said he killed any of our victims.'

'You don't think he saw Caylee or was with the body?' Tom asked more urgently.

'I didn't see anything like that, but it doesn't necessarily mean he didn't.'

'Fuck,' Tom said, scratching at his scar.

She wanted to get up but felt too woozy. 'I was hoping we'd get more than that too, Tom.'

'Sorry, I didn't mean . . .'

She knew Jimmy too well. His expression was one of: *was it worth it?*

'I should have stayed longer . . . but I . . . couldn't do it . . .'

'No, you did well to stick it out,' Jimmy reassured her. He rubbed her shoulder then pointed to her glass. 'Drink your water.'

She sipped at it again.

'There was a man watching him when he went to the woman's house,' she told Tom. His eyes narrowed.

'Go on.'

'Lomax said, "I got here first" and hit him.'

'Could you identify him?'

Somewhere in her mind, she knew she had seen a specific clue – what had that been? For the moment she couldn't recall. Was it his face? No, that had been covered in blood. Was it his T-shirt? Yes, that was it, but she couldn't pinpoint it; it was as though she was reaching into a dark cupboard to find something that was just out of grasp of her fingers. Was memory loss going to be another side effect that she would have to suffer? She wasn't going to let on to Jimmy.

'No, it was dark. I couldn't see his face.'

Jimmy pointed at her glass and she drank again.

'But they didn't seem to know each other?'

'I couldn't tell. It was very brief. But Lomax laughed when he saw him.'

'Laughed?'

She shrugged and looked over to Lomax lying at the centre of CASNDRA, a huge hulking brute, fast asleep.

'He's a nasty bastard, but I didn't see anything to say he was a killer.'

She tried to get up, but Jimmy put his hand on her shoulder. 'Take your time. Sit there until you feel better.'

'I'll drive you home,' said Tom. 'You can collect the car tomorrow.'

'No. Give me five minutes and I'll be fine,' she insisted.

Tom indicated to the guards and they came in to collect their prisoner. They woke him roughly. He shuffled off the bed and moved towards the door, urged on by the guards.

'Who did you see at the Scrambles, Lomax?' asked Tom.

'The man you hit,' Kyra added.

He grinned at her sleepily. 'I told you, I saw the woman. No one else.'

Tom glanced at Kyra. He believed her, didn't he?

'So, then, when do I get out?' Lomax asked sleepily, as the guards rearranged his bindings.

'It's going to take more than that,' Tom said. 'We didn't find out what we needed.'

If Lomax was disappointed by this, he didn't show it. 'Oh well, I had a nice sleep and woke up with a hard-on. Win-win, I say.'

Danielsson manhandled him towards the door; the female guard gave the lab a once over and then followed.

As Lomax shuffled out he gave Kyra a lecherous grin.

'See you in my dreams, Doc!' he said cheerfully and whistled down the corridor in time to the chains on his ankles jangling.

Back in her flat, behind the locked door, Lomax's last words swam around her head as Kyra fell into a fitful sleep.

See you in my dreams, Doc.

At some point in the dead of night she was disturbed by a loud thud. She opened her eyes and lay listening in the darkness. Was there someone in the flat, or was she dreaming?

She reached out for her Commset.

A shuffling sound coming from behind the bedroom door – something being dragged across the tiled floor?

The hairs on her skin shot upright; her breathing was shallow. Her mind rifled through the items in the bedroom for something that could be used as a weapon.

A man's voice. 'You stupid bitch!'

Her eyes widened in the darkness, a loud rush of blood pulsating in her ears. Her stomach clenched. *Oh God, someone was in there!* She heard a dull thud and a groan of pain. What the hell was going on?

She crept along to the door, the floor gave a loud creak and she froze. The noise in the living room stopped dead.

'I'm going to kill you!' she heard a man yell.

Oh God, Lomax has sent someone to kill me!

She moved towards the window in a panic but stopped when she heard a woman's feeble cry.

'Please, don't! Help me! Help me!'

Kyra hurried back to the door and put her ear against it. What was going on in there? Who was out there?

There was a loud crash and a bang on the other side, the tremors rumbled through her skull. She jumped away, stumbling back onto the floor, unable to suppress a cry as she fell.

'I'm sorry! I'm sorry!' she heard the woman crying. 'Please don't do this!'

Kyra pulled herself up, flung open the door and, holding up her Commset like a weapon, shouted, 'I've dialled the police! They'll be here any minute!'

But the light from her Commset illuminated an empty living room.

She moved the light around, doubting her eyes, then threw all the doors open, flicked on every switch in the flat and checked the front door was locked. Finally, she leaned back against the wall and slid to the floor, her legs weak with adrenaline.

Had she had some kind of waking dream? Was it another phantom, more vivid than ever before? These residual memories were getting stronger and were beginning to threaten her mental balance.

Whatever was happening, Kyra knew that she had to find the killer fast, or she was going to lose her mind altogether.

Chapter Twenty-Four

MONDAY 5 FEBRUARY 2035

9.45 a.m.

The memory of the stranger's T-shirt had come back to Kyra during the vivid re-living of Lomax's memories that had haunted her when she finally managed to sleep. Again, she had been late into the Hub and had to wait until she could get Tom on his own; when the discussions were over and the team had moved on to their tasks. He was walking towards the door as she approached him.

'The man I saw – the one in Lomax's memory, I remember now, he was wearing a T-shirt with a medical logo on it,' she said quietly. She brushed her fringe aside, self-conscious under Tom's scrutiny. He indicated she should follow him.

'Doesn't Andrew Harper, Isabel's boyfriend, work at the hospital?' she asked as they made their way up the stairs towards his office.

'Yes, that's where she met him. Ambulance driver. We interviewed him yesterday morning.'

'What did you make of him?' she asked.

'Isabel's friends say he's a control freak. He said they'd had a row about moving in together. He seemed harmless enough.' She followed him into his office. 'The Mizpah necklace Isabel was wearing tells us who took her.'

'And bio-testing?'

'None of his DNA on Caylee – only Lomax's.' He sat at his desk, but Kyra remained standing.

It occurred to Kyra that an ambulance was the ideal way of transporting a body. She opened her mouth but, at the same moment, Tom called up an image of Harper on the screen, taken from his interview.

'Is this the man you saw in Lomax's memory?'

Andrew Harper had auburn hair, a strong jawline and dark eyes. He was distinctive looking, almost handsome, but he didn't resemble the man at the Scrambles.

Then again, his face had been covered with blood.

'I don't think so. How tall is he?'

'183 centimetres.'

'No, no. It's not the man I saw. He was only 170, 173 at most. Any luck trying to find Martin Coombes?'

'Are you going to sit?' He indicated the chair.

She shook her head.

'No luck yet. We have CCTV images of him visiting Lomax back in the day.' His eyes travelled up to the screens. 'Martin Coombes,' he said aloud. Immediately a number of images appeared showing the young man from various angles. 'Does this look like the man?'

Kyra studied the face. He looked the right height, same sort of build as the man Lomax had hit.

'That could be him, you know. I mean . . . I'm not sure. It was dark, but . . .' She switched her attention back to Tom. 'It's very possible.'

'We haven't found Coombes yet. After his last known residence, back in 2021, it became confusing as to where he moved next. His neighbours seemed to think he had moved out of London altogether. He's been estranged from his parents for years. It's possible if this is Lomax's accomplice then he might have gone underground and be keeping a low profile. He might even be hiding with Isabel. We're working on it.'

'We're running out of time, Tom,' Kyra urged. 'Head injury man is nowhere to be seen and we can't find the only visitor Lomax has had who might fit the bill.'

'You think I don't know this?' His jaw tensed.

'I'm so sorry I couldn't have done more in the transference, found more—'

'You tried,' he said, but didn't look at her.

She looked down to the Hub. The women on the murder board called to her, names, places, dates, their eyes, staring at her, pleading for justice.

A single witness.

She took a deep breath. 'Let's go back to Ray Clarke. He's the only witness we have. I know he had . . . problems, but don't you think we should at least try to find him?'

'Come on, Kyra! Ray's memory was messed up fifteen years ago. It's not exactly going to be any clearer now, is it?'

'We might be able to find something he didn't remember,' she insisted. 'I mean, we've never tried to read the mind of someone affected by alcohol. But we could give it a go.'

Tom sighed and rubbed his forehead. 'Not much of a bloody witness, is he? A mashed-up memory of something he *thought* he saw but then he says he can't remember where he saw it.'

'How many days have we got until the next woman dies? Two? We know the killer's pattern. We need to do whatever we can. I think if the Mizpah Murderer has ever made a mistake it would have been early on, before he evolved into what he is now – an efficient, wily predator, skilled at cleaning up after himself. He won't always have been like that. It's worth going back and having a look.

We could see things that he didn't remember, key pieces of information . . .'

Kyra was clutching at straws. She didn't even know if Ray was still alive. He hadn't been in great shape after the last time they had seen him and that had been some time ago. Even his son, Marcus, hadn't been certain of Ray's whereabouts after that disastrous interview. Marcus had been furious about the way the police had treated his father and put in an official complaint.

'I don't want you putting too much pressure on yourself. You look exhausted after the Lomax trip. I think this is too much for you. You need to take it easy now.' But Tom's tone wasn't one of empathy.

'I slept badly last night.' She sounded almost insulted. 'Ray Clarke could be the key to the whole case, Tom! Don't you see? He's the only witness that we have any chance of getting anywhere with—'

'Jimmy said no more, Kyra.'

'It's not Jimmy's decision!' she almost yelled. 'It's my kit!'

He pursed his lips and looked at her for a moment too long. 'I think Ray Clarke told us everything he could at the time. God knows, with the state he was in, that was useless. Imagine what he would be like now? Seriously? Why don't you pull out the old footage of the interview, and see if we missed anything? Transfer the file to your own computer, I'll tell the desk sergeant you have my permission. Take it home, look over it in your own time.'

Was he getting rid of her? Getting her out of the way?

'There's no point in trying to find Ray Clarke,' Tom insisted.

But Kyra had already decided.

ISABEL

The light hurts her eyes. Whatever he injected her with is starting to wear off. She feels as though she is lying on a shoreline, waves occasionally washing over her as a tide of fear comes in. Her brain anticipates a moment coming soon in which she will suddenly remember how afraid she is, and terror will hold her veins taut, like the strings of a puppet.

'You're a good girl.' She can see his mouth moving beneath the semi-opaque plastic, but the moulded curves shroud his real features.

'I know you're a good girl. You tried to help that man. It was a test.'

'Man?' Her voice is croaky. 'Test?' she says in a haze.

'Yes, the man on the ground outside the pub.'

Things start to come back to her slowly. Ruby, her mouth wide and red as she laughed a little too hard at a joke Liv had made. What had that been? A heaviness comes down on her brain, she wants to sleep again.

He prods her hard on her cheek. Her eyes spring open, her breathing is laboured.

'Remember?'

She does remember. She can see him now in her mind's eye – a young man lying face down on the pavement right next to the brick wall of the pub, one leg bent, one arm outstretched, his dark hair matted with blood.

'You see, I knew you were a good girl when I saw you were at the hospital. Kindness, compassion . . .'

'Who are you . . .' she begins to say, but the words melt in her mouth. She can't focus her eyes.

Her arms are underneath the sheet, beneath a buckled strap. She wriggles her fingers and toes, trying to bring back some feeling. The fug is starting to lift slightly from her brain.

She can see a smile behind the mask but she doesn't understand. Her survival instinct tries to decipher it.

He reaches out a hand and strokes her hair. He smells of lemon and soap.

'I was so right about my choice, Isabel.'

'How do you know my name?' She can feel tears pricking her eyes.

'I've been following you.'

She tries to get her mind to focus, thinking back to normal life, back to home, her dad, the hospital, walking around the shops, going to visit her friends. A chasm of grief and longing opens up and she feels as though she is falling.

'I picked you because you care about people, you know how to look after them. You have a good heart. I saw you with that man outside the pub. You didn't have to help him. But you did.'

'Was he okay?' Isabel has seen drugs used on patients many times. She knows that drugs can make you sleepy, or talkative. She knows drugs can make you feel no pain, or drugs can kill you. Maybe if she didn't have drugs in her system now she would scream and scream. Instead, she feels as though she is having a chat with someone on a park bench on a sunny day.

'Did you leave him there?' she asked. 'He was hurt . . .'

'I know. I put him there. How else was I going to get to you?'

You hurt him?' The thought are you going to hurt me? comes into her mind, but she is too afraid to ask. It seems easier to ask about someone else. 'But how? How did you know we were there? This doesn't make any sense. None at all.

'I've been watching you, Isabel. Waiting until you came to me. It's all meant to be.'

'But the man in the street – you couldn't have known he would be there, that I would help him, that Liv would be sick . . .'

'I'd like to say it was my scheme, my skills, my timing. But really it wasn't me at all. I mean, yes, I put all those plans together, I even managed to put a little of what you had yesterday in your friend's drink, remember, the stuff that made you vomit? But it wasn't luck, or chance. I think Elise must have been watching over me, making everything work out so well. She must want you, Isabel. She knows you will look after her properly.'

She lies for a moment in her haze, trying to understand what he meant. 'Elise? I don't understand—'

'You were going to call for an ambulance, that's when I had to step in. Your poor little face when you saw me! You smiled!' She sees the hint of a smile behind the mask again. 'You thought I was going to help. They always think that.'

'They?'

He turns away for a moment, and when he faces her again he is holding a syringe.

'But that's when I injected you. And then you ended up here.' She winces as the needle punctures her skin, but it doesn't really hurt.

'Don't worry now, Isabel. It will all be over soon enough.' And with that, she closes her eyes.

Chapter Twenty-Five

MONDAY 5 FEBRUARY 2035

8.23 p.m.

Kyra looked over the footage of Ray Clarke for the fourth time that afternoon. She still felt expectant as if somehow the man on screen, his frayed blue checked shirt, his shoulders slumped and his red, craggy face, would give her some clue as to what had really happened on the night of Jennifer Bosanquet's abduction in 2020.

He had been confused and disoriented at the time of the crime, under the tyranny of alcoholism. When he had come into the station to offer information about a newspop he had seen about a murder Tom had been cynical, but Ray was the only witness, however muddled.

Kyra rewound the data and listened again.

'Booze helps keep the cold out this time of year. I sleep in the garages to stay warm and keep away from the young ones, the druggies.'

Ray spat the last word as though the alcoholics were a better class of addict. Even on the screen Kyra could see his hooded eyelids, the slow movements of a man who had let something get the better of him.

She knew his statement read that the row of empty garages he had been sleeping in was behind the shops off Ullswater

Street, but then he changed his mind and said it was by an empty nightclub on the industrial estate behind the carpet factory. Both areas had been thoroughly searched back in the day, but no evidence had been found. Kyra remembered the disappointment when they realised that Ray's story was a mangled mess of clashing memories, confused and indecipherable. There had been no train line by Ullswater Street, so he couldn't have heard a train. They couldn't find the garages Ray had described. The most confusing of all – Ray had said a woman had been taken, but the police knew that the victim was still at home on the day Ray said he had seen her. Then, when they wanted to clarify some of the information, Ray was nowhere to be found.

'I saw a man there. He wasn't a street-dweller. He had a car, red one with a bash in the side,' Ray said quietly.

'Do you know which make of car?' Tom jotted down a note as Ray shook his head. 'The noises woke me up from a deep sleep.'

Asleep or drunk? thought Kyra.

'What sort of noises?' Tom asked.

'Scraping, banging, screaming, but then it all went quiet. I've seen the working girls go there sometimes, but it wasn't like that. That's why I came. I don't normally talk to coppers.'

'What was he doing?'

Kyra had rewound this clip so many times during the original case she knew it by heart – Ray, agitated and distressed, Tom, leaning across the table, the muscles in his shoulders taut as they strained against his shirt. He reminded her of a sniffer dog; *on to something* as he said sometimes.

'I saw him drag her to the car. He came out of the garage opposite, must have been about eleven-thirty as the train went past.' Ray scratched his head slowly, the unlit cigarette in his hand trembling. 'She'd stopped screaming. He put her in the car boot. I don't know if she was drunk or if he had knocked her out. But she wasn't moving.'

'Could you describe the man, Mr Clarke?' Tom's voice was steady, but he pulled at his earlobe. Kyra knew him too well.

'Didn't see much. He was wearing dark clothes, a hood.'

'Is there anything else you can tell us, Mr Clarke?'

He took his time thinking about this. 'Later, when I came out of the garage, I found a necklace.' He pointed to the floor. 'It was silver.'

'What did the necklace look like?'

'A little silver heart.' He held up his fingers as though he was still holding it.

'A whole heart?'

Ray shrugged.

'Was there an inscription on it, writing, anything?'

Ray shook his head. 'I don't remember.'

'Have you still got it?' asked Tom.

'No, I sold it for a few quid. Like I said, it was silver.'

Tom put his pen down for a moment. 'And you're sure this was February the eighth?'

'Yes. Saturday. Saturday,' Ray repeated, but then shook his head. 'I'm not a hundred per cent sure what day it was.' He considered this for a moment, then held up his index finger. 'No, I've made a mistake. It was Saturday the first.'

'What makes you say that?' Tom's voice was unable to hide his exasperation.

'Yes, because I had a newspaper. The story about the politician who smacked his girlfriend at the restaurant, so it must have been the first.'

'You don't remember exactly where this incident took place, Mr Clarke?'

'Not exactly.'

'But you think it was Saturday the first?'

'Yes, definitely Saturday the first. That was the date on the newspaper.'

'Mr Clarke, our victim was at home safe and sound on that date.'

Ray's eyes swivelled slowly in their sockets. He focused on Tom.

'But I saw her! I saw the woman. It was the first. The paper said,' he insisted.

'Mr Clark, had you drunk much alcohol that night?'

And then that was it. Ray clammed up as though he didn't understand the questions anymore.

Interview terminated.

Frustrated with the lack of information on the data and still sore at Tom for sending her home for the day, Kyra took a walk to buy some wine. On the main street she was bombarded, as usual, by targeted salespops. The advertising projectors stood bright in the darkness of the street. As she walked past, they scanned her and immediately reacted to her.

Kyra, when was the last time you had a check-up? Our private healthcare offers the very best in . . .

Don't you think you deserve a reviving health spa, Kyra? With vitamin drip, detox and total rest and relaxation, we'll make you feel like the best version of yourself . . .

'News,' she commanded, a little too loudly, and one or two people looked around.

A newspop immediately appeared.

There has been another attack by People Against Poverty, who claim the government has targeted the long-term unemployed by deliberately cutting all forms of discounted healthcare unless they find a job. Five private clinics were firebombed across the city . . .

'Lomax,' Kyra said to the screen.

There are questions about the security of Rockwell prison and their security firm Tartarus Security after notorious killer David Lomax, escaped on the night of Caylee Carmichael's death. To hear the whole story, scan your bank details . . .

Further along the road, Kyra passed a building that had once been known as Our Lady of Mercy Roman Catholic church but was now a homeless shelter, as so many disused churches were. Outside, between the gothic arches and stained-glass windows, many of which had been smashed and replaced with hardboard, a large screen projected life-sized images of missing people in the hope that someone might recognise them – name, age, last seen, what they might look like now. She thought back to what Marcus, Ray's son, had said fifteen years ago about his father's last-known whereabouts.

She stepped into the porch and stood wondering if she should ask around, knowing the chances of Ray even being alive were slim. If he was, he could be in any one of the shelters around London. Would the street-dwellers give information to a stranger? She doubted it.

She looked up to a painted plaster statue of the suffering Christ that hung above the sanctuary, gazing down on the crowd of despondent men and women sleeping on roll mats, or eating brown sludge scooped out from an enormous pot into small cardboard dishes. The smell turned her stomach.

As she was leaving, a street dweller was coming into the porch and she caught a glimpse of his face.

She could hardly breathe with shock.

Her father peered out at her from under a dark woolly hat, a great weeping sore on his lower lip and chin.

'Oh my God!' she whispered. 'Dad?'

The man suddenly lunged at her and grabbed her arms with his claw-like, filthy hands. His grip was tight, painful. He locked eyes with her.

'Kyra, love, you've got to stop this.'

'Dad?' she said, distraught.

'You're going to make yourself ill, Kyra. You'll never catch him, love. Go home. Molly needs you now. Your mum needs you.'

He let go of her and shuffled into the church.

'Dad! Dad!' screamed Kyra. A few of the residents gawped at her.

The man turned back to see what was going on, confusion on his face.

He looked nothing like her father.

She moved into the street, unable to breathe easily, using her inhaler, wondering what the hell was going on. Her father had been dead for nearly five years. Was this a phantom? Or was it because she wanted him back so much that somehow her brain had confused her? What had she been thinking? The street dweller was nothing like her dad. Her brain was traumatised with the technology. She had done this to herself. Jimmy was right – this had to stop.

But even then, she knew that she wasn't going to stop. Not now.

9.45 p.m.

'What's going on?' Not wanting to be alone, Kyra had driven to her mother's straight from the shelter.

Her mother, dressed for bed, shut the front door behind them and winced as there was a crashing sound coming from upstairs.

'Molly's having a hard time adjusting . . .' She shook her head, tears in her eyes.

'She's got to start acting her age.'

There was another thump coming from Molly's room as something hit a wall.

'She's young and upset,' her mother began.

'No, Mum! This is ridiculous! She's nearly an adult. She needs to grow up and stop being a burden on you.' She felt a surge of annoyance towards her niece.

'She's always been like that, Kyra. Always full-on, all or nothing. With your dad gone, she's been a lifesaver really. What would I have done with myself? Moped around the house? She's good company, mostly. She's having a hard time.'

'Don't be playing it down. If she's being a pain, then she needs telling.' Kyra was surprised at the aggression in her own voice.

'She always plays up at this time of year. She'll settle down when Emma's anniversary has passed,' her mother said gently.

'She needs to grow up. Emma was pregnant with her at that age.' A horrible phrase popped into Kyra's head, *stupid little whore getting caught . . .* She shook herself. Where had that come from?

There was a flicker of pain on her mum's face. 'I can't believe she'll never get to know her own mother.'

'I'll stay tonight. I'll go and have a word with her.'

As she moved to go upstairs, her mother caught her arm. 'Be kind, Kyra. Please. Just be kind.'

'She hasn't exactly been kind to you,' she replied, pulling away roughly. 'I'll put her straight.'

'This isn't like you.' Her mother appeared confused. 'What's wrong?'

But she ignored the question and stomped up to Molly's room.

'Molly, what the hell?' she said as she opened the bedroom door.

Part of her knew that a teenager who trashed her room was someone in despair, someone who needed help, but she felt a deep irritation bordering on anger.

'Get up!' she shouted at her niece who was lying on the bed amidst the chaos, clothes everywhere, the wardrobe doors open, pictures torn off the walls, possessions flung around, a long crack down her mirror.

Molly half sat up, her long dark hair tangled over her still-wet face.

Kyra bent down, grabbed her by the shoulders and roared, 'You can't behave like this!'

Molly winced.

'You're upsetting your nan. We all lost your mum. We all feel it. Stop being selfish!'

Molly looked at her with surprise and then shouted, 'You don't know what it feels like! I was there!' She seemed almost relieved to have someone to take her tantrum out on. She raised her hands to hit out.

'You don't remember any of it! You were only a kid!' Kyra yelled back at her, grabbing her by the wrists.

Molly opened her mouth in shock and then her expression morphed into a scowl. 'I don't care what you say, it still hurts. I know it's in my head but I don't remember.' She tried to wrestle away from Kyra.

'Stop being so dramatic!'

'Get off me, you bitch!' Molly burst out.

Kyra released one of her wrists and slapped her niece across the face, brief and hard.

There was a moment of stillness, both of them shocked.

Kyra let go of her altogether and put her hand to her mouth.

Molly's hands flew up to cheeks, her eyes welling up with tears, turning from anger to distress.

'Oh God, I'm sorry, I didn't mean to . . .' Kyra began. What the hell had she just done? She had never lifted her hand against anyone, never mind her niece.

'Get out of my room! Leave me alone!' Molly threw herself back on her bed, face down.

As Kyra left, she caught a glimpse of herself in the broken mirror, the crack dissecting her face, her heart also feeling fractured. She made her way to the spare room, in a daze, tears brimming in her eyes. What was happening to her? She lay on the bed, exhausted, feeling as though she was coming apart at the seams. How could she have treated Molly like that? She lay, unable to sleep, thoughts about the recent days' events tumbling through her mind, listening to her niece sobbing in the next room.

Finally, after Molly had cried herself out and was asleep, and her mother had long gone to bed, sounds suddenly burst in Kyra's ears, as though the screen downstairs had come on automatically at full volume. She sat up, disoriented and afraid, to the sound of two people arguing in her mother's kitchen, shouting, screaming, and smashing crockery.

It wasn't Molly and her mum arguing, it was too aggressive – they wouldn't behave like that, would they? She was certain that they were asleep. But then she heard the roar of a man's voice.

'How many times do I have to tell you, stupid bitch?'

There was a crash as something flew against the kitchen wall, shattering Kyra's nerves. She jumped off the bed, pulled on her sweater and made her way tentatively to the bottom of the stairs. This must be a dream, surely?

But when she got halfway down, she heard a woman's plaintive cries, 'Please, please, I'm sorry, I'm sor—' Followed by a sickening 'urrgh' which rendered the woman silent.

This wasn't a dream – it must be happening. This was too real. What the hell was going on?

'You stupid little whore! I . . . don't . . . have . . . to . . . tell . . . you . . . again!' came the man's voice, the effort of his violence punctuating his speech.

The door of the kitchen was ajar, and Kyra saw someone move on the other side. In a panic, she slipped on the last stair, twisting her foot. She winced in pain, stifling a cry, and crawled up a few stairs, horrified, but desperate to know what was happening.

Then came the woman's howls from the kitchen, 'No, no, please, let go, Dave!'

Dave?

'Why do you make me do this?' he yelled and then a horrible thudding sound.

Kyra lay sprawled on the stairs, not knowing whether to

go up or down, petrified, but desperate to stop whatever it was that was happening. Should she go into the kitchen? Would everything disappear in the light, as it had done at her flat the other night?

She pushed herself up straight, her foot aching, and took a deep breath.

It's not real! It's not real! she told herself, moving towards the door, ready to shed light on her own imagination, but this was the most vivid phantom she had experienced. She went to reach for the handle, breathless.

Terror stabbed at her heart as the door to the kitchen was flung open. There stood the large silhouette of a man who, even from this view, she recognised immediately.

David Lomax.

Her logical mind was telling her: *This is a phantom. He is not here. He's in Rockwell!*

But she was utterly petrified. Her legs quivered as though they were going to give way beneath her.

Her foot throbbing with pain, she clambered back up the stairs, using her hands to claw her way up, to the spare bedroom. She could hear the thudding of his feet as he made his way up behind her. He was gaining on her. Her heart and head pounded. Her mouth was dry. The woman in the kitchen was silent now.

Was he going to silence her too?

She flung herself into the bedroom and shut the door behind her, out of her mind with fear, desperate to find somewhere to hide. She ducked down onto the floor, ready to scramble underneath the bed when she saw a sight that almost stopped her heart.

Two children, a young boy and a very young girl, hid under her bed, their huge terrified eyes staring right at Kyra. The boy had his arm wrapped around the little girl.

They looked at each other, fear etched onto their little faces, and then turned back to Kyra, put their fingers to their lips and whispered *Shhhh!*

Chapter Twenty-Six

TUESDAY 5 FEBRUARY 2035

7.50 a.m.

Kyra sipped at the coffee in the reinforced paper cup that she held tightly, as though it contained liquid gold. She had bought it from a proper barista bar after smelling the aroma pumped out by the 3D salespop near the lab. It was the real thing; expensive and irresistible. She stood in the street nearby the lab and glanced at her Commset. Jimmy would be there in another ten minutes or so. He was usually on time for work. The main street was quieter at this time of day, but the ever-shining lights from the shops and salespops lit the gloomy early morning, straining her eyes.

Those children she had seen last night . . . What the hell was happening to her? The phantoms were getting worse. Was she going mad? Jimmy would be able to reassure her, wouldn't he?

Where was Jimmy? She tried to distract herself by giving in to the ubiquitous screens throwing out all sorts of images which vied for her attention.

The Well-Being Centre caught her eye.

Are you concerned about your health and fitness . . . you only have one body, Kyra, and we can help you to reach optimum . . .

Our latest computer programme to reduce stress has been rated by the Health Ministry as one of the best available . . .

Kyra swiped it away, only for it to be replaced with a more irritating salespop:

Having a partner can add so much to your life. We can match you based on your values, ideals and . . .

Tom immediately came to mind. There had been a point fifteen years ago when they should have made more of it, but that was in the past now. She lived with enough regret, she had to let it go.

She dropped her coffee in shock as Lomax's face appeared in front of her, staring out from the hologram, straight at Kyra, the eyes following her wherever she went. A newsreader's face replaced him.

And in breaking news, a secret source from the Met has divulged that police are now looking for more than one suspect in the Mizpah Murders. This surprise revelation comes as information was leaked that David Lomax, convicted of the horrific attacks on six women fourteen years ago, may not have acted alone. Reports that Lomax was not at the scene of the . . .

Looking down at the pool of coffee around her feet, Kyra groaned. No doubt the press were going to start digging around every tiny detail of the case and accusations of police incompetency would be flying. Tom would be furious. Where had the information come from? Was there a mole on the team? How would it affect her mother, or Molly, all the other families of the victims who would hear this and realise that they had been let down, that there might still be someone out there to fear – who might kill again.

Isabel Marsden appeared next, a full-body hologram much shorter than Kyra, her hair blonde and shoulder-length, her face pleading. She reached out her hands to Kyra, her voice echoing: 'Have you seen me?' She disappeared and reappeared, stretching out her hands again and again and repeating, 'Have you seen me?' on a loop. Then, Tom appeared in a face-to-camera interview. Kyra halted and passers-by moved around her as she stood still to watch.

'We are very concerned for the welfare of Isabel Patricia Marsden, twenty-one, who has been missing since Friday night.' Tom's voice was clear and deep, his gaze steady. 'She was last seen at approximately 10.40 outside the Farmers' Arms pub on Marlborough Street. Isabel is a student nurse and she was tending to an injured man outside the pub. We strongly urge that person to please come forward so that we can eliminate him from our enquiries. Isabel knows staff from the Royal University Hospital and there is a possibility she may have gone there with the injured man or been picked up by a non-registered taxi. Her bank card has not been used and there has been no activity on her social media accounts. If you have any information, even if you think it is trivial, please do not hesitate to call, text or email on the number on the screen. It is essential that we find Isabel as soon as possible.'

Kyra moved down the street and the press-conference newspop continued on another screen where Isabel's father, face white and strained, his voice trembling, begged for information.

'Isabel, I love you and . . .' He choked. *'Isabel, I love you and I want you home. If you are having problems, we can face them together and work through this. Please, if you are watching this, either get in touch and let me know you are okay or be assured that we are doing everything we can to bring you home.'*

She looked up to see Jimmy sauntering along the street, moving in time to music only he could hear. When she dived in front of him, his face fell.

'Jimmy! I need to talk to you.' Did he just roll his eyes?

'Stop music,' he commanded his Commset. 'I'm on my way to the lab.'

'I know. I know.' She grabbed his arm. She could feel the muscle tense. 'Please, Jim. I need to talk to you.'

He studied her face. 'You look like shit.'

She released her grip. 'Thanks. Please, come for a coffee with me?'

She saw the reluctance in his face.

Finally he said, 'You're paying.'

Relief washed over her but she couldn't manage a smile. 'Sure.'

They went into a nearby cafe, ordered coffee, synthetic this time, and sat observing each other.

'Are you well?' He was guarded but he was here, wasn't he?

'Just tired.'

'You know what I mean. How are you after the transference?' He said the last word quietly, even though there wasn't anyone sitting near to them, only a man in work overalls in the corner, engrossed in his food.

The two little children under the bed had been on her mind all night. She tried to focus on Jimmy's face to distract herself from thinking of the terror in their eyes. Lomax had seemed to disappear as soon as she had closed the bedroom door, but the children . . . they had been different. She had lain on the floor of the bedroom for some time, staring at them as they soundlessly stared back at her. She had managed to get rid of the phantom eventually. She was on top of this – wasn't she? Why the hell was she seeing children? Whose children were they?

'The actual transference went well. I don't know if I'm getting better at it, or if it depends on the person that I'm reading, but I feel like I'm seeing things clearer, getting to the memory faster.'

'That's good then?' he said, uncertainly.

'I couldn't see anything in Lomax's memories that suggested he was in any way involved in the murders. Doesn't mean he didn't do it. I'm still not sure to what degree people can block their memories in a transference. I don't know if it's possible.'

'We could set up some kind of control test for that,' he said and then grimaced again. Didn't he want to help?

'The only thing is, I saw some pretty horrible things in his head.'

Jimmy folded his arms and knitted his brow. 'What sort of things?'

'Hardcore porn, violence against women . . .'

'Surely that means he can't control what he shows you in his memories? I mean, wouldn't he block those memories from you if it was possible?'

'He's an animal, Jim. I think he enjoyed letting me see those things. If there was a memory in his mind that he wanted to hide, he might have tried to cover them with shocking images deliberately to put me off.'

'Did you see anything else? Residual memories, I mean. Phantoms.'

She hadn't intended to tell him, to tell anyone. Jimmy had warned her that it was going to be bad. How could it not have been, the sort of mind she had gone into? She hadn't planned on putting herself in Jimmy's 'I told you so' firing line. But who else could she tell? Not Tom, not Carter, not her mum, not Molly. But Jimmy was her lab partner. These were legitimate concerns that she had about this technology. These things were going to have to be faced. The phantoms were scary, but she could control them.

Couldn't she?

'What is it?' he asked.

223

'Nothing, it was only a side effect, you know . . . what we expected really.' She couldn't face him.

'Kyra, I can tell that there's something else.' He leaned over to her, his dark blue eyes full of concern.

She had been trying to muster all her mental strength, as difficult as that was after the depletion of going into Lomax's mind, and tell herself this was all imaginary.

But the faces of those children . . .

'The images from the transference are getting stronger, but the phantoms are also getting stronger.'

'Go on.' He was clearly deeply concerned now.

'Last night, I think I saw Lomax.'

Immediately, Kyra saw his expression change and she hated herself for being so weak, putting herself under scrutiny.

'At yours?'

'I was staying at my mum's.'

Exhaustion swept over her and she found herself crumbling, head in hands.

'Jesus,' said Jimmy.

'I saw him . . . but this time . . . he knew I was there . . .'

'This time?' Jimmy said, appalled. 'You mean you've seen him before?'

'It was as though he was *aware* of me . . . and I ran upstairs to get away from him.' Her face was burning. 'I know he wasn't real, but it felt real and I tried to hide . . . And under the bed . . .' Her mouth dried up. She sipped at her cup, her hands shaking.

'Go on,' Jim said, his face deadly serious, his eyes wide.

She could hardly bring herself to speak the words. 'Under the bed, I saw two little children. Hiding.' She held her breath, terrified of his reaction – of what it might mean.

'Children?' asked Jimmy, incredulous.

'A boy and a girl. The boy was maybe seven years old. The girl was two or three.'

'Who were they?'

'I don't know.'

She could see he was struggling to make sense out of what she was saying, was disturbed by her words.

'When I shut the door, it was as though Lomax just disappeared.' The heavy footfall getting closer up the stairs had stopped abruptly. 'But the children . . . they stayed there . . .'

'What happened then?' Jimmy spoke quietly, but was that horror in his eyes? 'What did you do?'

'I said loudly: *This is not real!* and then they vanished.'

There was a bubble of stillness between them, the clashing of crockery and chatter from gathering breakfast customers not able to break through.

'Does your mum know you're having—'

'No,' Kyra said quickly. 'She doesn't know I'm involved with the case again.'

'Unless the receptors haven't left your bloodstream. I mean, it's highly unlikely they would work without the kit—'

'Or without the subject being nearby . . .' added Kyra. 'I've thought of that. Maybe they are residuals and I'm seeing Lomax's other memories somehow, things that I'm not picking up on the headset? Things that happened at another time.'

'What if the receptors pick up much more information than we realised, more memories, but we can't read it all at the same time? Then your brain might show you those things at a different time. That might cause it.' He ran his hand through his dark curls. 'It still doesn't explain . . .' He stood up. 'We should scan you. We'll go to the lab before Carter gets in.'

'No,' she said, making a swiping movement with her hand. 'I'm fine. It's only side effects. Or else the tech is stimulating my imagination . . .'

This is only a psychological reaction to everything I've been through, she tried to persuade herself. *I'm not mad! I'm suffering from stress. That's all, isn't it?* But she knew there was more to it than that.

Distress suddenly overwhelmed her. 'I don't know what's happening to me.' Tears spilled from her eyes. 'I heard him beating a woman in the kitchen. I could hear her screaming and then he came out and followed me up the stairs . . .'

'Kyra, this isn't right. This isn't right at all. I mean to some degree, I would expect the psychosomatic asthma, going into someone else's memory would leave you feeling close to that person, would bring an empathetic response, but . . . this isn't good. When you saw the soldier – Brownrigg – that made some sense. You met him, you saw his experience and then you dreamed about the soldiers he fought with. You were still seeing his memories from his perspective. What you experienced last night goes beyond reaction to stimulus. Do you even know if Lomax battered a woman?'

'I heard it at the police station. There were complaints against him for domestic violence.'

Jimmy's shoulders relaxed a little but his face was still strained. 'That might explain it. If you heard about it then it might be the power of suggestion.' His eyes travelled to the floor for a moment and then back to her. 'What I don't understand is why you are *seeing* Lomax. You should be able to see things that you have experienced within Lomax's memories, from his point of view. I would expect that. But you shouldn't be able to *see* Lomax himself. We couldn't have predicted this. You should be seeing out of his eyes, from his perspective, not seeing *him*.'

'What if they are Lomax's kids – and I'm picking up a residual memory, one that my conscious brain wasn't aware of in the transference, but it's in here somehow?' She tapped the side of her head.

'Does Lomax have kids?' Jimmy asked.

She shook her head. 'Not that I know of. Maybe I'm picking up on stuff in his subconscious. This could really take our tech up to the next level.' Even she knew now that she was clutching at straws, trying to find a silver lining in this mess.

'Jesus, Kyra,' his voice was louder now, with anxiety, 'What do you think you are? Some kind of oracle? We called the machine CASNDRA to be ironic, not because we're psychic!'

'You should tell Carter – so he doesn't sell it to the MOD! Imagine what could happen to a soldier who performed a transference with a terrorist.'

'It's too late,' Jimmy said, then put his hand to his mouth. 'I'm sorry. I didn't want to tell you when you were upset, but the deal's been done.'

'That's my kit! My tech! We built that.' A sudden rush of anger. 'Has the machine gone already?'

'No, not yet, why?'

Two elderly women came into the cafe and made a big deal of where they were sitting and taking their coats off. Kyra immediately resented them. They made loud, cheerful conversation with the waitress and she had to resist the strong impulse to tell them to shut up.

'Jimmy, please, listen. I need to do one more transference. Please help me to do it just one more—'

'Jesus, you've only just finished telling me how this has been messing with your head! And now you're asking me . . .'

'Please, this will be the last time, I promise.'

'No, there's no way.' He folded his arms.

Why was he being so stubborn?

'It's my fucking tech!' Kyra said loudly and the women stopped their chatter and gawped at her. She scowled back. 'There's one more witness,' she told Jimmy, more quietly. 'Ray Clarke. He can't tell us what he saw because he can't remember . . . he was drinking . . . and . . .'

'No chance,' said Jimmy. 'You're my friend, Kyra. I don't really understand what you've got yourself into, but I'm not going to let you destroy yourself.'

'It's going to destroy me if I don't find out the truth!' Kyra yelled, banging her fist against the table, some of the coffee sloshing out of her mug onto the table top.

The other customers gawped at her now.

'What?' she said, scowling at them.

Jimmy stood up. 'I'm sorry. But enough's enough.'

Kyra watched him leave the cafe and thought: *I don't need you anyway.*

Chapter Twenty-Seven

TUESDAY 6 FEBRUARY 2035

9.32 a.m.

There was less than forty hours to go before the killer completed his pattern and the mood in the Hub was grim. It was compounded by a cloud of suspicion – who had betrayed the team and blabbed to the press? Kyra was the outsider, the obvious choice, and Harry and a few of the other officers had made their feelings clear.

'Alex, do you know if we can get in touch with Ray Clarke somehow?' Kyra had approached Alex when she was on her own, not wanting the others to overhear.

Alex regarded her quizzically. 'I think his son's contact details are on the system. Although he might not want to talk to us. He made a complaint back at the time about the way his father was treated.'

Kyra remembered. But it was worth a shot.

'Why do you want to talk to him again? He told us everything he knew back then. I can't imagine his memory has got any better.'

'We've got to try every avenue, right?' Kyra knew that wouldn't convince her. Alex was smart, intuitive, trained up, and determined. She would see what Kyra was trying to achieve. If anyone could understand the importance of her tech, it would be Alex. What if one day the police even bought the tech? She was exactly the sort of officer that would make the most of it.

Should she tell Alex? They had a bond, didn't they?

Alex called up the number on a nearby screen and raised her eyebrows as Kyra typed it into her Commset.

'Listen . . . don't tell Tom about this . . .' Kyra began.

'Jesus, Kyra!' Alex hissed, her blue eyes wide. 'Are you trying to get me into trouble with the boss?'

But then there was a hint of a conspiratorial smile.

Kyra smiled back.

Ray Clarke's son, Marcus, wore an expression of irritation, as though he had been interrupted in the middle of something very important. He appeared to be of a similar age to Kyra and might have been attractive if his face hadn't been twisted in fury. Kyra and Alex had gone to one of the viewing rooms for some privacy when they called him, hoping Tom didn't find out.

'Look, I told you lot fifteen years ago to leave him alone.' He peered down at Alex and Kyra from the screen on the wall. 'I knew this would come up when I saw that bloody news report about the Mizpah killer!' he exploded, no less belligerent than he had been back during the original case. 'No, you can't speak to him. You upset the whole family last time. He went on a bender after all that, just made everything worse. We don't want to talk to you. Dad's very upset again.'

'Your dad's still around?' Kyra didn't manage to keep the surprise out of her voice. He must have been lying about not knowing Ray's whereabouts. Had he been trying to protect his father? It was understandable.

Marcus's eyes narrowed. 'Why are you bothering us? You weren't interested in what he had to say back then.'

Out of the corner of her eye, Kyra saw Alex turn towards her.

'I'm not a police officer. I'm a neuropsychologist and I'm consulting on this case. I understand that your father was confused, but I think I might be able to help.'

Marcus studied her face for a moment. 'I don't think my father needs your help, miss . . .'

'Doctor Sullivan. Marcus, please listen to me,' Kyra could hear the desperation in her own voice. 'As a psychologist, I know that being unable to help can make a person feel frustrated, guilty, even.' She wished she could tell Marcus that she knew this from personal experience. Alex's eyes bored into her. 'I think I can help him move past that. Do you think I could talk to him, ask him if he might talk to us?'

'No, I don't.' Kyra steeled herself for another barrage of angry complaints. Tom was going to kill her.

But then Ray appeared on the screen.

Kyra was momentarily lost for words.

'I'm decrepit, but I'm not dead,' he told Kyra with a smile that lit up his startling blue eyes. She was surprised how warm she felt towards him immediately. Had he been listening to the whole conversation?

'The drink took its toll, but I can make my own decisions,' he said seriously, 'I just don't like to advertise that fact in front of my son. He can be very . . .' he searched for the word, 'over-protective.'

'Ray, you look well,' Kyra said, hardly able to keep the surprise and excitement out of her voice.

'A lot better than the last time you saw me, I'll bet. I could have gone either way but I decided to get help, dry out . . . I've been sober for over ten years. I stopped drinking because, after I saw what happened to that poor woman, I realised how precious life was. I couldn't turn back the clock. I couldn't undo all the damage I'd done through alcohol.

My poor son had been through enough.' She watched as he turned his wedding ring round on his finger. 'But I decided I could change. It wasn't easy, of course. The Chemaddict treatment was rough, but effective. I guess it's all a matter of how much you want it.'

'I guess it must be,' Kyra said.

'I must admit, it's shaken me up seeing the news. Brought it all back.' He moved his lower jaw up and down, lips closed, as if chewing. 'After the woman at the garage I didn't want to go on.' He paused. 'I wish I could go back and try harder to save her, told the police more. I don't think many people think about what it must be like to be a witness to a crime. Do you?'

'I suppose many people don't, no.'

Poor Molly seeing her mother taken.

'It stays with you. I still have flashbacks, sort of, only the vaguest images, nothing that could help to solve it. I often think if I could go back I would do this, or that, but then the realisation is that it is what it is, and I can't do anything. I'll have to live with the fact that I saw such terrible things and there's nothing I can do to change it.' His voice broke. 'That poor girl. I often think about her.'

She studied the craggy face.

'But you say I might be able to help somehow?'

Kyra felt a growing excitement. 'Please, yes. I've developed a technology that allows us to access memories, straight from the brain. It's painless, accurate and might help to find out exactly what you saw that night.'

Out of the corner of her eye, she saw Alex's gaze locked in her direction. She kept her focus on the screen.

'Well, I didn't expect to hear that.' Ray smiled, bemused.

'You're the only witness that we have. And I think, deep down, somewhere in that brain of yours, there is a memory, a clue, that's going to help us to get to the truth of the matter.'

She watched as he mulled this over for a moment. Then he reached into his pocket, pulled out an old photograph and held it up to the screen. Kyra studied the image of the young woman in her wedding dress, holding a small posy of hydrangeas, her red curly hair covered in a veil of gypsophila. A brilliant smile. 'My beautiful girl, Annette. She was the only woman for me,' he said, turning the photograph back and gazing at the image. 'I was lost without her, totally lost for a while.' He looked up. 'She would be disappointed in me if I didn't try to help.'

'Ray, I can't begin to thank you,' said Kyra.

But he shook his head. 'No, I should be thanking you. I feel like a man who's had a second chance. If there is something I can do to get that information out . . .' He closed his eyes tight for a moment. 'Then I will do it.'

'Ray, I'm going to be honest with you. This isn't going to be easy,' Kyra said. 'We'll have to revisit a very difficult experience that you have had. It will be traumatic. I can't promise that this technology won't have its effects. We'll have to look at those memories.' What sort of phantoms and physical symptoms might she have to deal with after she had been in Ray's mind?

'Whatever it takes,' Ray said.

Kyra took courage from the old man. 'Yes,' she agreed, 'whatever it takes.'

After they arranged a meeting, the screen went black and Alex stood looking at Kyra.

'So, are you going to explain that to me?' she asked, her arms crossed.

Kyra took a deep breath. She could trust Alex, couldn't she? She would have to now she no longer had Jimmy's support. She couldn't do this on her own.

'We've got until tomorrow midnight, judging by the pattern, to save Isabel. We have no witnesses and no leads. Neither the pub nor the hospital has anything we can work with. The house search has turned up nothing so far. Head Injury Man was really our last option and there seems to be no one else coming forward.'

'Head Injury came in to the station late last night,' Alex said but her expression was one of disappointment. 'Saw news reports and realised it was him. Came in with his dad and his dad's lawyer. He was terrified we were going to think he was Lomax's accomplice.'

A rush of dizziness overwhelmed her. 'Who was he? Anyone to worry about? Did he tell you anything useful?'

'No, not really. Matthew Halsall, a second-year university student. Doesn't recall anything. His flatmate came to look for him when he hadn't returned home an hour after calling to say he was on his way with their tea from the takeaway. He said he found him half a mile away from the Farmers' Arms slumped against a wall.'

'But no one called an ambulance?'

'Doesn't look like it.' Alex bit her lip and said, 'Going back to Ray – his testimony was confused and inaccurate at best. We were looking for information about Jennifer Bosanquet who had been abducted on the eighth of February, but Ray was convinced he had seen the woman on the first of February, so it didn't make sense what he was saying. Surely Ray Clarke can't tell us anything?'

'No, that's the point, he can't tell us anything,' agreed Kyra, 'but we can find out, if we go into his memories.' She wasn't surprised Alex looked confused. 'I've been developing a new technology designed to read memories from the brain directly. Recently, it has become obvious that this would be highly valuable in police investigations.'

'But how can we access those memories if he can't?'

'The human brain can see and remember things, even if the person is not conscious of what they have seen. Trauma, in particular, can mess up the memory to the extent that we can start to imagine things we saw, making stuff up, if you like. We are hardwired for narrative.' Alex's expression changed into one of disbelief, but she pressed on. 'The human brain needs to see a pattern, a story, so it tries to explain what it saw, even if what it saw was disjointed, incomplete – it puts ideas together to try to make logic of things that are often illogical. On the other hand, instead of adding things that aren't there, the brain also filters things out. But those things that were seen and logged by the brain are still there in the memory. We just have to access them.'

'People see and remember things, even though they don't know they've remembered those things?'

'Yes, and we can see what they saw, see what they have *forgotten* they saw. We can access Ray Clarke's memories and get a more accurate picture. It might give us some more leads.'

'You know of course that this won't be admissible in court? He'll be no more a useful witness to us in court than he was fifteen years ago.'

'We don't need him to be a credible witness in court,' Kyra replied. 'It's intelligence, not evidence. No more than a secret informant. Ray can't tell us even if he wanted to. He's lost the pathway to that memory. But this technology, it could get us right into those memories, we'd be able to see what he saw. Sixteen years since the first victims died and where the hell are we? This could help us solve this case and get him, once and for all. You never know, you might get a promotion off the back of it.'

Alex's eyes were wide. The corners of her mouth turned up.

'And you'll find out for sure who killed your sister,' Alex replied.

They were locked in a conspiracy now. There was no way they could tell Tom, he would be furious they had gone against his orders.

'Ray is more than willing to go through with the procedure,' Kyra added. 'It's not only about a face, seeing who did the crime, it's about the other things, the details that will lead to the criminal. There are things in Ray's mind that will have remained untouched for fifteen years. '

Alex said excitedly, 'It's the perfect crime scene.'

Chapter Twenty-Eight

TUESDAY 6 FEBRUARY 2035

4.37 p.m.

Kyra hated the expression *Time is a great healer*. It was never any easier, Emma's anniversary. It was just different. Different because Molly was so grown up now, because her own father was no longer there, because she herself was getting older. Nothing seemed healed at all, only more fragmented.

Cremation was compulsory, although particularly religious and wealthy Londoners would have their loved ones remains shipped out overseas – mainly Jerusalem and Mecca – if they wanted a burial. Land was too precious and too expensive here now and the government had ended the protests against interments only for those who could afford it with a blanket ban.

Kyra liked the minimalism of the Necroplex; the columns of small, shiny, grey engraved boxes that lined the white walls, four rows high, gave a calm, pleasing symmetry. There was room for a small candle and a posy of flowers next to each plot. Delicate strands of light from the abstract stained-glass windows hit the white in spots of colour, echoing the flowers of the orangery through the glass doors at the far end of the hall.

The orangery was a beautiful verdant garden replete with images of the deceased, memorial benches, water features and 'in memoriam' plants. Families passed each other in quiet sadness with brief, empathetic nods. Kyra watched her mother borrow secateurs from a basket by the door, make her way to Emma's rose bush and clip a few curling leaves.

Molly reached out and touched the photograph of her mother next to her plot. Emma eternally youthful, that heart-breaking smile, the dimples. Kyra couldn't help but smile back, albeit briefly.

Molly leaned her head onto her aunt's shoulder. Kyra remembered the promises she had made at Emma's funeral to do everything she could to protect Molly, to nurture her and steer her onto a stable grounding. She wasn't sure how successful she had been so far.

'I know I don't really remember having her around, but I miss her,' said Molly. 'Does that sound weird?'

'Not at all.'

After a few moments, Molly lifted her head and asked, 'Why did you argue with Mum last time you saw her? What did you row about?'

Kyra had never made a secret of the fact that her mother had left the cafe angry after they had had words, dragging Molly with her. She had played it down, of course, but her niece had always known. Kyra had always avoided answering this question honestly, brushing it off, saying it had been trivial.

Molly's golden eyes locked onto hers.

Kyra shrugged, 'Nothing important, something stupid . . . I can't remember.'

'Please tell me. I know there's more to it than that. You can tell me now I'm an adult.'

How could she tell her niece that the argument with her mother had been about the most important thing in the world – about Molly herself?

Kyra was distracted by a man who came in through the orangery door and stood there motionless for a moment. He was too far away for her to be able to see his face, and the hood of his jacket pulled up. There was something odd about him, out of place.

'Tell me,' insisted Molly. She wasn't going to let it go. Kyra would have to give her something to satisfy her curiosity.

'We'd been sitting in the cafe for over an hour . . .' Kyra began. 'It was not long after your third birthday. You kept looking for your mum out of the cafe window and asking for her. You drew shapes on the misty glass.'

Kyra remembered how furious she'd been. They'd been there for nearly an hour. She'd had more important things to do than sit around waiting for Emma to show up whenever. She had a proper job to get on with, not some ridiculous eco-mission with a bunch of misfits.

'Why was Mum late?'

'She'd been on an eco-protest, a high-profile one.'

The man with the hooded jacket began to walk slowly up the hall. He stopped at one of the memorial plaques and reached out to touch a flower in the nearby vase. There was something oddly stilted about the way he moved.

'You were playing teacups with your dolly.' She remembered Molly with a cake-smeared face, kneeling up on the chair, chattering away to herself, rearranging the cups and spoons, pouring her doll a pretend cup of tea, smiling up at a man who walked past her and patted her head as her mother arrived. 'You've always loved cake.'

Molly smiled, but sadness washed over Kyra. She had been angry with Emma and, when she finally arrived, she had let it get the better of her: *If you think going on eco-protests with people with stupid nicknames like Mick Tree and Rivergirl is more important than spending time with your daughter . . . Oh, by the way, living in the shithole is affecting Molly's health, she's been coughing all day and . . . have you been drinking alcohol? You smell like . . .*

'Your mum was a bit late meeting us. She was never much good at time-keeping . . . she was late because . . .'

The man moved slowly closer along the hall. He seemed to be going to each of the memorials. What was he looking for? He stood next to a couple who were comforting each other, disturbing their grief. They looked over at him, confused, until he moved away.

'What was she talking about the last time you saw her?'

I only had one or two beers on the train on the way back . . . I know how to look after my kid . . . I didn't take her on the protest, did I? I thought you two would enjoy spending time together . . . Do you know how hard it is to be a single parent and be on duty all the time . . . never having any fun . . . give me a break . . . you have no idea what it's like to be a parent.

Oh right, because I don't have kids I don't understand!

At least I didn't leave Mols with the other squatters, at least I left her with someone I could trust . . . Don't worry, Molly, Mummy and Aunty Kyra are just chatting.

When are you going to grow up and take some responsibility?

At least I'm fighting for a decent world for my kid to grow up in!

'You, always you. You were the centre of her world.' Kyra bit her lip.

She remembered many of the customers had observed the debacle, and the man who had patted Molly had shot the two sisters a glance moments before he had left the cafe, his expression . . . disappointed.

And Kyra's final parting shot: *You shouldn't have gotten pregnant so young! Are you even sober enough to look after that child . . . You're a terrible mother!*

How could she tell Molly any of this? She had always tried so hard to protect Emma's memory. But also, she didn't want to show her niece what a terrible person she herself was; how irritable, stubborn, judgemental. So different from the usual memories she told Molly about – when she would put Emma to bed and stroke her hair until she fell asleep.

She watched the biggest regret, the biggest sorrow, of her life unfold on the screen of her mind's eye – Emma standing up, knocking the table, crockery clattering, Kyra's body glued with stubbornness and resentment to the rickety wooden chair beneath her. Emma wrestling with her bag strap as it caught over the backrest. Molly's pet lip as she was torn away from her cake and her cups of pretend tea.

Her last vision of her beloved Emma had been her hand, holding Molly's much smaller one, disappearing out of the cafe door, back out into the cold night air.

And then, worse still – the thing she wished more than anything that she could change – she had sat there, at the table, stirring her cold coffee, feeling anger and resentment until she had suddenly come to her senses and rushed out of the door, the word 'sorry' on her lips.

But Emma and Molly had disappeared.

Kyra had run to the nearest corner, and found Molly standing alone in a side street, crying on the pavement, and at the far end of the Tarmac, hardly visible – the tail lights of a car.

A little chubby hand pointing, a tear-stained face, 'Mummy in car.'

Kyra never saw Emma alive again.

She came back from her memories, Molly's eyes urging her.
'Go on, Ky. Was she saying nice things about me?'

The man had come closer to them, was only a few metres away now. He stood looking at one of the memorials, hands in his pockets. Kyra could only see the side of his hood from here. He was probably someone in grief – was that why his behaviour seemed somehow strange? Bereavement affected people differently. He didn't look particularly big or threatening, but the bees begin to buzz again in her chest-hive, tiny stings all along her nerves. Molly, on the other hand, didn't seem to notice him, too interested in the information she was trying to glean.

Was he just another mourner? Or another phantom? Or was he more sinister than that? Had the MOD been following her after all? Were they a threat to her family? Hadn't she promised Emma, so many times, in this very place, that she would protect Molly?

'You okay, Ky?' Molly asked, following her eyeline.

'Yes, fine,' she smiled, putting her hand around her niece's shoulder. She looked back to see where the man was. He reached over to a candle and snuffed it out between his finger and thumb. The hairs on her neck stood up.

'Come on, let's go and find your nan.'

'But, Ky, you were telling me about—'

'I'll tell you more later.' There was a brief resistance in Molly, and then she gave in. Kyra ignored her insistence to continue the story and turned to see the man step forward and run his finger down the photograph of Emma. She felt a rush of nausea and hurried to the orangery door, leaving the man looming next to her sister's remains.

6.32 p.m.

When they got home, the three women followed the annual memorial ritual of settling down on the sofa in front of the screen to watch an old film, one of the classics that Emma had loved. Molly had chosen *The Breakfast Club*.

By the time the bottle of wine was half empty, the takeaway had been delivered and dished out. Even though Kyra had only drunk one glass, the alcohol took the edge off her nerves. She would have to leave eventually to meet Ray at the Lab as they had agreed. She wouldn't be too long, then she would come back here and finish the wine. It was comforting to be at her mum's, away from all the stress of the investigation. After she had eaten, she lay across the armchair, legs over one arm, watching the screen. She tried to fight it, but weariness overcame her and she began drifting off; her eyelids became heavy, her breath slowed. Even with her eyes closed, she could hear the dialogue from the screen and feel the presence of the two women she loved the most in the world nearby. She briefly jolted awake and saw her mother and niece, leaning against each other on the sofa, engrossed in the film. She needed to stay awake, but the exhaustion, wine and cosiness were too strong a cocktail.

Sometime later, Kyra slowly opened her eyes. The film

was still on, and, at first, she could not see clearly, her vision blurry with sleep. Was that Molly leaning over her?

She rubbed her face. 'What's wrong?'

But as her sight cleared, her mind could not begin to take in what was in front of her – Emma, her face white-grey, her eyes staring, the duct tape pulled down, but still covering her mouth, naked, except for her lower half covered in black plastic and, where her heart should have been, there was a gaping, glistening wound.

Kyra jumped up, clawing her way backwards over the armchair, startling her mum and niece.

'Jesus, no!' she cried as her sister's dead eyes followed her every move.

'What is it, love?' asked her mother, standing up, alarmed.

'Can't you see?' Kyra cried out, horrified, clambering off the chair and grabbing onto her mother, pointing to where the ghostly figure stood.

'See what, Kyra?'

Molly drew back, hugging herself in fear on the sofa like a little girl.

Emma stood silent, a harrowing spectre. She slowly lifted her arm and at the end of her wrist. A bloody stump pointed towards Molly, a bone shard jutting out like a misplaced finger.

'Mum! Mum!' cried Kyra, unable to tear her eyes away from her sister.

And then Emma was gone.

Kyra collapsed onto the sofa, her heart thumping against her ribcage, cold sweat on her brow. What had it meant? A warning? A judgement?

'Ky, what just happened?' Molly asked, her voice trembling.

When she saw her niece's face, Kyra tried to pull herself together, be strong like she always had been for these women.

'Molly, get my inhaler . . . in my bag . . .'

Kyra knew why it was happening and, although she kept telling herself that it was all in her imagination, she felt a deep sense of unease. It was the first vision that she had seen when others had been present. Was she losing control over the phantoms? Did this mean she was going to have to live with these things? Should she ring Jimmy?

No, she was on her own with this.

Molly hurried into the hall and brought her bag in.

Kyra dumped the contents on the sofa, found the inhaler and pumped the canister into her mouth. She waited until her breathing had calmed. Her niece and mother stood watching, panicked.

'I'm sorry. I'm sorry. I had a waking dream . . . that's all.'

'What did you see, Ky? What was it?' Molly asked, still distressed. 'Did you think there was someone in the room with us?'

'We've been doing experiments at the lab and it's spooked me. That's all. I'm fine. I woke up in the middle of a dream.' Her breathing was becoming much less laboured now, her buzzing nerves had begun to settle. 'I'm sorry I scared you . . . it was . . .' She shook her head, unable to explain further.

'What sort of experiments are you doing that could freak you out like that?' Molly asked with tears in her eyes.

She had to give them some explanation, didn't she? They were both gawping at her, bewildered. She was too exhausted to deceive them.

'I was with the family of a murder victim yesterday. My friend, Tom, had to tell them we'd found her body, that she wasn't coming home. She had a little boy. He reminded me so much of you, when you were little, and we lost your mum.' It all came tumbling out.

245

'Why were you visiting the family of a murder victim?' her mum asked anxiously, and then her voice hardened. 'Is that Tom Morgan? What on earth are you in touch with him for?'

'He asked me to do some consultancy work on a case. I'm sorry, Mum, I should have told you.'

'Yes, you should have told me! I thought all that was over a long time ago?'

Kyra ignored this and said, 'There's been a bit of confusion over just exactly who is responsible for . . . the death of . . .' She suddenly didn't know how to finish the sentence. Should she say the Mizpah murder victims, or should she say Emma's name? She couldn't bear to see her mother's face, so she left the sentence unfinished. 'The police think that he might have had an accomplice.' She couldn't tell them her own theory, that Lomax hadn't done it and the real killer had been out and about for the last fourteen years while Lomax paid the price. 'They want me to help using my technology to look into . . . certain people's memories to see who might have killed the victim, clarify what exactly is going on.' She hated lying to her mum.

'It's the Mizpah Murders you're working on, isn't it?' Her mother drew away from her, leaving Kyra unmoored. 'You're working on Emma's case? And you said nothing?'

'Mum. I . . .' She closed her mouth again. There was nothing she could say to make this situation any better.

'And it's making you see things that aren't there?' her mother said, horrified.

Why hadn't she kept her mouth shut? God only knows what her mother would have said if she knew exactly who Kyra had seen. Molly was sitting still, face aghast.

'Mols, I'm so sorry if I gave you a scare. It was a waking dream, nothing to be worried about.'

'You can look into memories to see who killed someone?' Molly said slowly, her face white.

'Yes, but don't worry, it isn't dangerous,' Kyra tried to reassure her. 'These are only side effects, but . . .'

Molly's face grew crimson. She jumped up and screamed at her aunt, 'And you didn't think to use this technology to find out who took my mum for certain? I've seen the news. I know there's doubt about who the real killer is.'

Her words were like a smack in Kyra's face.

'No, Mols! I don't mean—'

'You had some way of finding out who killed my mum and you didn't do it?' she shouted.

The question knocked the breath out of Kyra. It took a few seconds to gather herself.

'No, Molly, it's not like that,' insisted Kyra. 'There weren't any witnesses to your mum's abduction, so I couldn't—'

'Yes there is!' Molly screamed, 'Me! I witnessed it! I saw it!'

Kyra stood and squared up to her niece. 'It's not like that. You'd have to see it all over again, relive it. *I'd* have to relive it.'

'I want to if it means I can find out who killed Mum!'

'You were no more than a baby! I can't let you go through that again!'

Molly took a step towards her, jabbing a finger towards Kyra.

'Do you know what it's like always wondering who ruined my life? Who took my lovely mum away from me?' She was screaming in Kyra's face now. 'There's some asshole out there, living their life, laughing, having fun, even having kids of their own while my mum's in a fucking box!'

'You were only a toddler!' Kyra snarled. 'What the hell could you have remembered? I don't know if your brain would even have been able to understand what you saw.' Why was she being so angry? Why couldn't she take her

247

niece in her arms and hold her and tell her that they would use CASNDRA, that they would find out who took Emma from them?

Because it would mean that she would have to see her sister abducted, that she would have to accept that, if they hadn't argued that night, Molly would still have a mother. Is that why the idea of using the tech like that had never even occurred to her? Had she deliberately blocked the idea from her brain because she couldn't face it?

'I'm an adult now!' Molly yelled. 'You should let me make that decision! I can make fucking decisions! Do you know what it's been like for me without her? Knowing I saw someone take her but not being able to get it out? All those nightmares I had about Mum being dragged away in a red car. Do you know how much guilt I feel?'

'You haven't got the right to feel any guilt!' Kyra yelled, thinking of her own part in Emma's death.

'I saw the killer and I can't remember!' Molly's face was wet with tears, her nose streaming, her cheeks red. 'I must know something, anything, that could lead us to catch the bastard who did this to mum, to me, to my life!' She threw herself on the sofa and sobbed.

'Stop it!' Kyra shouted angrily, yanking Molly up. 'Stop being so dramatic! You don't even know the damage you will do to yourself if you see those traumatic memories as an adult. Think about how your behaviour is affecting your nan, you selfish little cow!'

Molly pulled away from Kyra and huddled into the sofa, weeping.

Her mother, who had stood by stunned, grabbed Kyra by the shoulders.

'Kyra, what has gotten into you? Why are you being like this? Why are you talking to Molly like that?'

Even her mother's desperation did nothing to quell Kyra's rage. Some part of Kyra knew that this behaviour didn't belong to her . . . that it had seeped into her . . . from Lomax during the transference.

'What are you doing to Molly? Don't you want to find who killed your sister? You owe it to me! If you can do this, then I need to know. Don't you think it would be better to go through those memories than live with not knowing?'

'No!' Kyra shrieked. She needed to get away. She scraped all her belongings up from where she had dumped them on the sofa and threw everything back into her bag. She went into the hall and grabbed her shoes and her coat in a daze.

Her mother came out after her. 'Where are you going? I thought you were staying here tonight.'

But Kyra had opened the front door and was sitting on the front step putting her shoes on. A fine misty rain covered her face like a veil. Her heart was thundering in her chest. She had already lost her sister, she didn't want to lose Molly too, but Lomax's violence and anger, like a virus, had invaded her system and was changing her beyond recognition, beyond her control.

'Kyra!' her mother pleaded but she ignored her, stood up and moved to the car. Molly came out into the hall. When she saw her, Kyra put her hand on the car door handle. 'I've got another witness! I'm going to see him tonight! I'm going to find whoever killed your mum, Molly. I swear to you!'

'If it wasn't for you rowing with her,' Molly screamed back, 'I'd still have a mum!'

And she slammed the door, leaving Kyra in the street in the rain.

Chapter Twenty-Nine

TUESDAY 6 FEBRUARY 2035

8.08 p.m.

It was the first time that Kyra had done a transference without Jimmy. She had given Ray the injection of the transmitters even though her hands had been trembling. What if she messed this up? It was the last chance she had to find anything that would solve this case and find Isabel Marsden alive.

There was no going back now.

She focused her mind on Isabel, alone and frightened, and pushed any thoughts of the argument she had had with her mum and Molly so that she could focus on the task in hand. She was doing this for them, too, wasn't she?

Ray lay on the bed looking small and vulnerable, like a child in the dentist's chair for the first time. Marcus stood on the other side of the glass, reluctant and protective.

Cosmo's screen flashed up the security camera image from the front door. It showed Alex's face. Kyra sighed, relieved. At least she wasn't on her own now. She pushed the door release and Alex hurried into the building, making sure the door was closed tightly behind her.

'I'm sorry I'm late,' she breathed. 'I couldn't get away from the Hub.'

She put a hand up to Marcus and Ray, who nodded in reply. Kyra saw her marvelling at the kit, confusion and admiration on her face.

'I haven't missed anything?'

'Will you wait with Marcus on the other side of the glass, Alex?'

Alex's eyebrows twitched.

'Keep him out there,' Kyra whispered. 'No one can stop the process once it's started. It's not safe.'

Alex nodded and left.

Kyra leaned over to Ray.

'Just you and me now. Half an hour, and this will all be over. We'll be having a cup of tea and we'll all feel a lot better,' she said with a wink, swallowing her fear about the phantoms she might pick up. What would she have to face after this? 'Don't worry, settle back and relax. I want you to think about the night you saw . . . whatever you saw. Don't force it, imagine yourself back there and I'll do the rest. Okay?'

Ray gave her the thumbs up.

She smiled, but her stomach was churning.

Kyra took a few deep breaths. *You're going into a memory, a crime scene, that's all. You've been to plenty of crime scenes. You can do this!* Ray was facing slightly towards her, his eyes closed, deep in his sockets, his jaw starting to slacken, his breathing steady.

She nearly jumped out of her skin as his eyes flicked open and he grabbed her hand with his own gnarly one. He was surprisingly strong.

'Thank you for doing this for me.' His voice was clear and earnest. 'I can't do this on my own. I've had my problems, but I know I saw something that will help.'

She believed him.

'Cosmo, prepare for transference. Dim lights twenty per cent,' she commanded.

There was a shift in atmosphere as the lights gradually faded and the bed on which Ray lay moved into CASNDRA's centre smoothly. Alex and Marcus stood in the shadows, but she could feel their gaze. Kyra's heart was beating fast. She settled back into her recliner and braced herself, trying to keep her breathing calm.

It was difficult to prepare a blank canvas of her mind for what was to come. Random thoughts and ideas popped up thick and fast, but she kept parrying. Her nerves and excitement settled a little as her determination took over and she let herself grow heavy.

There was darkness and perfume, sweet and strong, then a blur of blue, the colour of hydrangeas in her mother's garden. She could hear a buzzing sound, the overlapping of two voices. She tried to tune in, to make sense of the words.

Then she could see Ray's memories as the visuals kicked in: a bride walking down the aisle, coming closer, not smoothly and step-by-step, but instead in staggered movements, ten metres away, suddenly five metres, then right next to him – red hair, her smile reaching her eyes. One hand held a bouquet of blue flowers, the other hand reached out and a ring was placed on her finger.

Everything went black and then there was an overwhelming smell, wetness and dust, alcohol and filth, all filtering through her brain. It was dark at first, like awakening early on a December morning. The odour of oil and petrol came through strongly, so different from the clean fuels they used now.

The rain pounded down on a metal roof above her head, the sound vibrating through her brain. She saw through Ray's eyes as he lay on the ground of what seemed to be an old shed or garage. A streak of yellow light cut into the darkness and highlighted a newspaper near her, his, head. She could see the headline: POLITICIAN'S ASSAULT, and she remembered that had been the news on 1st February 2020. However, the newspaper was already dog-eared and dirty. Is this where the confusion lay? That Ray had said it was the first of February just because of a week-old newspaper? Had that been why the police had discounted his testimony? There was a torch nearby; she tried to reach out for it but found her hand paralysed and then reminded herself she was only an observer.

From the darkness, she heard muffled voices coming from outside, the banging of one of the large old wooden doors in the wind.

A man shouted, 'I've paid you for sex. I own you now!'

Then a scream.

Ray sat up, a misty vapour escaping from his lips in the cold air. Upright, Kyra's head swam with the effects of alcohol. An acidic gurgling in her stomach told her Ray hadn't eaten in some time and he had drunk something much stronger than she was used to. A woozy warmth travelled through her veins, moving up towards her head.

She was desperately willing him to move, turn on the torch, do anything, so she could get a look at what was going on. She shifted her body in the recliner in the lab, her muscles tense as she strained against the confines of Ray's consciousness, but then she crumpled, frustrated.

Behind that weather-beaten wooden door was the man who had killed again and again, and who was going to kill very soon, the man who had Isabel Marsden held captive in real time. The surge of intoxication in her bloodstream reached her brain just as Ray put his head to the floor.

There was a delay of two or three minutes before a shrill scream followed by what sounded like a woman crying and begging. Ray looked up again, vision heavy and blurred. Then the screaming again.

Kyra's body was rocking in fear and frustration in the recliner, but she could still feel the cold concrete beneath her. The noises stopped. She watched as Ray's hands scratched along the grimy floor of the garage, nails filthy and ragged, as he crawled closer to the door. He peered out from the cracks and gaps below the rotted wood.

From this angle, Kyra could see a car to her left, and ahead across a courtyard, another row of garages with wooden doors. The car was red, as Ray had said in the interview, although the only light was coming from a weak, yellowy wall lamp on the last garage in the row, so the exact shade of red was uncertain.

If she could only get a look at the number plate! Was that the piece of information that Ray had? Was she about to get this bastard? She thrilled at the idea of it, even with the overwhelming inebriation coming from Ray which threatened to dull her brain and her excitement, she willed him: *Go on! Go on! Get a look at the plate!*

As if he had heard her, Ray moved forward, shuffling along the ground, and pushed the door open slightly. Kyra held her breath, ready to remember the numbers and letters, but at that moment the door to the garage opposite flew open and banged against a wall. Her vision, Ray's vision, immediately transferred from the car to a small woman dressed in white. She was stumbling barefoot, disoriented, wailing in fear.

Kyra immediately recognised her – it was Jennifer Bosanquet.

Ray had been telling the truth after all – he had seen one of the victims of the Mizpah Murderer.

A shout startled her: 'Get away, get away!'

It was another woman's voice!

Ray peered into the darkness, but Kyra could see nothing. Jennifer appeared too frightened to flee, unable somehow. *Drugged?* She crumpled on the ground behind the car, cowering.

She was so close now that Kyra could hear her whimper in fear. She had to remind herself that Jennifer was dead already. This was in the past, untouchable. But her blood was itching, the bees in her throat stinging as she screamed in her mind: *Run! Run! Run!* All her instincts were urging her to burst out of the door and save the poor girl.

But there was nothing that could be done for her now.

Moments later, a man stumbled out of the garage and made his way to the back of the car. She could see he had dark hair but couldn't make out any of his features in the poor light. He pulled Jennifer roughly up by her arms. She pleaded, 'I'm Jenny, please, I'm Jenny,' over and over as she struggled feebly against him. He grabbed her around the throat and hit her once, really hard, and she mewled, a heart-wrenching sound.

As he let her go Kyra saw a glint, as though a silver moth had fluttered to the ground.

The man stood still for a moment, catching his breath, and then opened the car boot.

He knelt down and gently took the woman in his arms and lifted her. 'Don't worry, Elise. I'll be back for you very soon. I need to keep you safe in here for a while. You won't be alone anymore.'

Elise?

She groaned as he put her in the boot, as carefully as a mother putting a child down to sleep in a cot, and closed the lid softly as if not to wake her. He leaned against the car for a moment exhausted, but then regained himself and stood up straight, shoulders squared. He faced the garage opposite.

'Right, you fucking bitch! I'm coming for you!' he yelled into the darkness, and terror gripped Kyra as if he knew she was watching. Her body stiffened in fear, but he moved away into the opposite direction.

For a moment, she could see nothing as Ray put his forehead against the rough, cold stony floor. Then, he pushed the door open a fraction and peered out. From this perspective, Kyra could see that it was a red Ford Focus. She couldn't see the plate, only that rust had eaten away at the bottom of the car.

Ray's adrenaline flooded Kyra's blood as something banged loudly against the wooden door in front of him and a half-brick came rolling over and stopped. She heard a dull metallic thud as another brick hit the car and then the sound of the hooded man crying out.

A woman ran out from the garage and flung the door shut with a bang that reverberated around the yard.

She hurried towards the rusted car.

'Jenny! Jenny!' she shouted desperately.

The woman had dark skin, and long black wavy hair. Her black and white striped dress was ripped down the back and hung off one of her shoulders. Her mascara had run, giving her dark panda eyes. Blood dripped from one of her arms in a steady stream and part of her torn dress was wrapped around her hand. She scrambled around the car, slipping on stones, calling, 'Jenny! Jenny!'

But then the garage door flew open again and the man staggered out, a hand to his head, and screamed, 'Fucking bitch!'

The woman ran off into the darkness.

A split second later, he was in pursuit.

Kyra lay back on the recliner in the lab, drained, despondent. She had not been able to see the abductor's face, nor the registration. Ray's eyes, poorly sighted and fuzzy with alcohol, only captured the letter B, or was it an R? And who was Elise?

However, once the man had gone, Ray grabbed his torch and tentatively clambered up and made his way into the yard. Her body, Ray's body, tensed as he heard a noise coming from a nearby clump of bushes.

Kyra felt a rush of expectancy, but it was only a fox, its eyes flashing as they reflected the beam from the torch. She could see the swirls of light as Ray moved around; the concrete floor, blood spots against the grey, rubble and bricks strewn across the ground in the tight circle of white light. There was no sign of the other woman.

Ray began to shuffle back to his usual sleeping place, but stopped when his eyes caught something lying on the ground and he bent down to pick it up. A train rushed by, whipping up the nearby trees with a crashing sound and then everything went quiet again as the wind died.

The garage went dark briefly as though the torch had failed. Kyra became acutely aware of Ray snoring gently at her side and she tried desperately to tune back in to him. For the briefest of moments, before it disappeared for good, Kyra saw Ray's grubby palm and on it a broken chain with a silver pendant, half a heart shape, cut with a zigzag.

A Mizpah pendant.

And then all she could hear was a loud screeching noise that went on and on, as white lights ripped through her eyes and she thought her skull would be cracked apart.

Chapter Thirty

TUESDAY 6 FEBRUARY

8.44 p.m.

Kyra came up out of the transference gasping for breath, her head spinning, her heart pounding. She felt like Dorothy who had been deposited in Oz by the twister, everything suddenly in bright Technicolor, startling and overwhelming. All around her there were screeching noises, flashing lights and images of faces – Molly, her dad, Lomax and Caylee Carmichael – swirling in her vision.

Right in front of her stood Tom, the headset in his hand. Behind him, Jimmy, his face pale.

'What the hell are you doing?' Tom asked.

Kyra vomited violently and it splattered on the floor at his feet, covering Tom's shoes. His eyes narrowed and he clenched his jaw.

The room was still spinning, her ears filled with white noise. Another surge of nausea overcame her. She put her hand to her mouth. When she was able to speak again, she pointed at the headset and muttered, 'What the fuck, Tom?'

'What are you doing here?' Tom indicated Ray, who was snoring gently, slack-mouthed, peaceful as though unburdened. Maybe Jimmy was right and more than just memories had been transferred. There was accusation in Tom's eyes.

Marcus, obviously agitated by the intrusion, watched from the other side of the glass wall. Alex held him back.

Emma immediately appeared, standing next to Alex and Marcus, her face grey, her milky pupils staring blindly at Kyra above the tight silver duct tape. She held her arms up as if to put her hands on the wall, instead her bleeding stumps streaked the glass.

'Jimmy, what the hell are you doing letting him take me out of a transference like that? Do you know the damage he could have done?'

Her stomach roiled again and she swallowed hard. Emma appeared on this side of the wall and then took a few steps closer towards her, splashes of blood marked her trajectory across the lab floor.

'How did you know I was here?' Kyra glared at Alex, feeling betrayed. 'You back-stabber! I thought you were on my side! You said you wanted to help me find my sister's killer when all the time you were spying on me for Tom!'

'Kyra, it's not like that!' Her voice was muffled by the glass between them.

'Save it!' Was there no one Kyra could trust? She wanted to get away from them all. She tried to get up from the recliner, her legs new-lamb-weak, her head heavy as though she was still under alcoholic influence. Despair started to build up in her, the weepy self-pity of a drunk. This was coming from Ray, not her.

Jimmy pushed her down gently. 'Lie back, I need to check you over.' As she complied, Emma loomed closer. Kyra tried to look away, but the familiar smell of her sister's perfume wafted over her and with it came a cloud of memories that rendered her momentarily mute.

Jimmy snapped at Tom, 'You shouldn't have done that. It's dangerous to take someone out of a transference!'

Tom ignored him and ordered Marcus to come and collect his father.

Still feeling the effects of the alcohol Ray had drunk, Kyra rubbed her hand briskly over her face and noticed there was a ring on the third finger of her left hand. She examined the plain gold band. What had she seen in his memory again? She closed her eyes for a few minutes and listened to Marcus's gentle reassurances as Ray took his time to come around and Jimmy helped Marcus take his father into the foyer to recover.

When Kyra raised her head again, she saw Emma standing right next to Tom. She looked back at her hand and the wedding ring had disappeared. Her sister was still there, but Tom seemed to have no awareness of her.

'Alex, get in here!' Tom bellowed.

Reluctantly, Alex pushed open the glass door and stood in front of Tom.

'Alex, what the hell are you doing? What were you thinking?' Tom asked.

'I'm sorry, sir. Damage limitation. I thought Kyra was going to cause embarrassment and get herself into trouble.'

Her eyes were downcast.

No wonder she won't look at me.

'And you didn't think to tell me?' Tom barked.

Alex hadn't told him after all.

But Kyra knew that the ambition Alex had displayed when trying to find the real killer was going to work against her now. Alex wasn't going to risk her job. She would probably tell Tom everything, wouldn't she, to keep on the right side of the boss?

'I was going to, sir, but the opportunity hadn't arisen.'

'Go home. See me in my office at eight tomorrow morning.'

So how had Tom known?

Kyra couldn't focus her eyes on anything – was it a hangover or a migraine? – but she knew Emma was still nearby. That overpowering perfume.

Jimmy came back into the lab.

'Marcus has taken Ray home.'

Tom shook his head. 'I'll have to go and see them about this tomorrow.' He scratched his chin. 'This is an absolute mess, Kyra. I can't believe you've done this.'

'How did you get in?' Jimmy asked her.

'I took my keys back when we did the transfer with Lomax.'

Jimmy shook his head. 'Jesus, if Carter finds out . . . What the hell are you playing at? He'll take legal action. God knows what the MOD would do if they knew! I warned you about the side effects.'

'You don't get it!' she groaned.

'What have you done to yourself?' He tried to look into her eyes with the transilluminator, but she pushed him away angrily. 'You're going to kill yourself if you go on like this.'

'What do you care, Jimmy? I asked you if you'd help me and you wouldn't! That's why I asked Alex and now Tom knows, so that's the end of it now, I'll never be able to solve . . .'

'She didn't tell me,' Tom said.

Kyra swivelled round to face him.

'I did,' Jimmy said solemnly.

Cosmo, Jimmy's computer, of course. Kyra should have known. It hadn't even occurred to her to disable it. She probably couldn't have gotten past the security anyway.

'I've got a screen at my place, for security,' Jimmy said sheepishly. 'I saw you come in and . . . I panicked.'

'He rang me at the station, had a right bloody go at me.' Tom jabbed his finger towards Jimmy but kept his eyes on Kyra. 'Asked me what the hell I was doing putting you through this . . . especially after he had told me about how dangerous it is . . . blaming me for you being here—'

'What the hell did you do that for, Jimmy?' she yelled. Her arm shot out and grabbed a mug sitting on the work surface next to her recliner, her mug, the one he had bought her, and she threw it at him. He ducked and it missed, smashing against a piece of equipment, the fragments raining down quietly on the rubber floor. Kyra didn't know who was more shocked. Anger and shame made her turn away from him. What was happening to her?

But then she began to feel a giggle building up inside her. Where the hell was that coming from? Her mind was bobbing in a drunken haze and everything seemed ridiculous. She'd been trying to fight it, to stay sober, but it was easier to give in to it now. The feeling that this was the funniest thing ever swelled up and the next moment she was roaring with laughter.

The two men stared at her, horrified.

'Why are you two *so serious*? Look at you both, standing there like angry dads catching your kid out doing something they shouldn't be! Chill out!' She tried to look at her reflection in the glass wall. 'Am I slurring my words? Don't worry, it's just that Ray was drunk. It's got to me.'

She giggled as they looked on, at a loss. Jimmy moved away into a corner of the lab.

So what? She thought. *Bloody grass!*

Then just as soon as the giddy, silly feeling had come over her, it rolled away again and a black mood crashed over her. Shit, how could she make them believe her if she was acting crazy?

Sober now, she sat up with some difficulty and rubbed her eyes.

'I saw the whole thing, Tom. Ray saw Jennifer Bosanquet and—'

'I've had enough of this now!' he snapped angrily. 'I don't believe you're seeing anything other than what you want to see.'

Her mind now sharp again, it became urgent that he believed her. 'Tom, there were two women at the garage. I saw them both. It was Jennifer Bosanquet. I saw her, clearly.'

'And I suppose you saw Madelyn Cooper too.' Was that sarcasm?

'I don't know who it was, but she threw a brick. It hit the killer's car. She got away. This woman, she was dark-skinned. I've never seen her before. It certainly wasn't Madelyn. But she saw the killer and she escaped. Don't you realise what this means? That there's another witness somewhere!'

An expression of distaste crossed Tom's face. 'No, you're wrong. This machine – it's all bullshit. Madelyn's hands were found with Jennifer's body. There was no other woman. It's not his MO, you said so yourself, to take two women at once.'

'Killers adapt, Tom. He might have tried it and it didn't work. She got away!'

He turned to leave.

'Jennifer Bosanquet was there, I'm telling you. Ray definitely saw her. There was another woman with her before she died. I think Madelyn was the Mizpah killer's second attempt that year.' That poor girl huddling against the car. 'Jennifer wasn't so lucky.'

He spun around. 'There certainly were no victims who had dark skin. Jesus, Kyra, you're the profiler! You told us back then that serial killers go for their own ethnic group. They were *your* words.'

'There's always exceptions, and until we know the reason he is killing his victims then we don't know who he would go for. He could go for anyone! That's why this is so confusing! He has two types. For two very different reasons, neither of which we know!'

He moved back closer to her.

'If there had been another witness, she would have come forward back then. You've got to let this go . . .'

'I can't let it go, Tom, it's the only thing we've got. There're lots of reasons why witnesses don't come forward. You know that! She must have been terrified. If we can find this woman, then we have a new witness. Someone who was up close and personal with the killer. She could tell us where this garage is, give us more detail about the man, the car. It might lead us to him.'

He scratched the side of his jaw. She could hear his nails scraping against his five o'clock shadow. She knew him too well. The full hangover was kicking in now. She wanted to lie down and block out the light, but it was paramount Tom believed her.

'I'm telling you, I saw her!' she roared. Jimmy stayed back in the shadows.

A look passed between the two men. Tom patted her hand. 'Don't worry, you're bound to feel a little emotional after that.'

'Don't bloody patronise me,' she snapped, pulling her hand away and rubbing it where he had touched her. 'You think I'm mad.'

'It's not that.'

'You clearly fucking don't believe me!'

'Take it easy, Kyra.' There was an edge of threat in his voice.

'Don't tell me to take it easy! Do you know what I've just seen? And I couldn't do a damned thing to help. And now you're not even bloody listening to me!'

'What if it's not Ray's memories that you saw at all? Only things you want to see?' he said. 'We're all desperate to catch him. We don't need any wrong leads that will waste time. We've only got until tomorrow before . . . We don't have the luxury of time to follow false leads or to be running down blind alleys.'

She knew it was his frustration talking, but it stung.

'Why would my brain make that up? She was there. She was a mess, her clothes torn, her arm was bleeding, her make-up was all over her face . . .'

But his doubts made her question herself.

'Could you tell where the garage was?'

'No. It was too dark to see much detail. But a train went past, as Ray said.'

'It could be anywhere in London!'

'I'm telling you, I saw the necklace just as he said. It was a Mizpah. Can't we look into it?'

'Kyra, listen to yourself! Ray says stuff, it's been in your mind for over a decade, you forget some of it and then it pops up in your brain, but you think you're reading his mind.' His voice trailed off. 'You're the psychologist.'

'But we've done all the experiments, this works!' She looked over to Jimmy, but he wouldn't return her gaze. 'Tom, why are you being like this now?'

'I wanted something more concrete, that's all.'

Her head was throbbing. She wanted to go home to bed, log off for the next twelve hours or so. But tomorrow night was the night Isabel was due to die. She had to keep fighting, for Isabel's sake. She clambered off the recliner, legs still weak, feeling dizzy. She staggered towards the door.

'Let me help you,' Tom said, swiftly coming to her side.

'I think you'd better go,' Kyra snapped. '*You* asked for *my* help, remember, but now it looks as though you don't want it.'

He called after her, but she went into the toilet, shut the door and leaned against it, tears springing from her eyes. She went to the sink to rinse her mouth out. Her face was pale in the mirror, her eyes bloodshot. She thought of all the things that she had sacrificed so far – she had lost her job and her tech, Molly hated her, Jimmy didn't want to know and Tom didn't believe her.

She wasn't giving up now. With or without Tom, she would find out who this woman was.

At that moment, her Commset rang.

Alex.

'Kyra, please, I'm sorry. I didn't tell Tom anything, but when he was there I had to make up an excuse. I said the first thing that came into my head, pretended I was keeping an eye on you, but it isn't true, honestly.'

'I know, Alex. Jimmy told me.'

She could hear Alex sigh on the other end.

Screw Tom, she thought. *In for a penny, in for a pound,* her dad used to say. She wasn't going to give up now, not when she might have the only lead and just over twenty-four hours to save Isabel. At least she felt sober now, although her head was still throbbing.

'You know when you were looking through case files, did you come across any activity that might be our suspect, before the killing started – reports of violence, kidnap, maybe young women, someone working illegally in the sex trade?'

'I could have a look.' Alex sounded curious now. 'I'm at the Hub.'

'Great. Check out an incident at a garage, February, near the time Jennifer Bosanquet was murdered.'

'You think it might lead to our man?'

'I think there might be something that we've missed. But listen to me, Alex. Tom can know nothing about this. If you don't want to, if you think it's not worth the risk of getting into more trouble . . .'

'No, no, I want to. I'll be in touch as soon as I find anything.'

'Great, speak later.'

Kyra examined her reflection in the mirror and tucked a few strands of hair behind her ear. Standing right behind her, almost close enough to touch, Jennifer Bosanquet smiled.

8.59 p.m.

She is a beautiful girl.

Seventeen, eighteen with striking golden eyes.

Eyes that will see Elise.

It's warmer than usual tonight but she is shivering as she leans against the wall opposite CarterTech, holding a denim jacket which she wrings in her hands.

I ask if she is okay, ask her why she is standing in a dark side road at this time of night. Does she need any help?

She is polite but uncertain at first.

I tell her I was answering a job nearby, but it was a false alarm, we get them a lot.

She takes one look at what I am wearing and she quite candidly tells me that she is waiting for her aunt who is working late. She's begun to trust me. They all do.

She starts to cry. She has long, dark curly hair, a lovely face, made even lovelier somehow by her huge tears. Elise would think she was very pretty.

I ask her if she wants to talk.

She says it is a long story. She'll be fine.

At what point will she realise that she won't be fine?

I tell her it's too dangerous to be out on her own at night. I offer her a lift home, wondering if she will take it.

She refuses.

Instead, I bend down to the pavement, dangle the chain between my fingers and pretend I have found a necklace.

I ask if it's hers, but she shakes her head.

I hold it out to her to take it: whoever lost it isn't going to find it now, I say.

She pauses for a moment and I wonder if I've misjudged the situation.

But then she reaches out, with a half-smile, and that's when I grab her arm.

Elise will love her.

An angel with golden eyes.

She refused my offer of a lift.

But I take her anyway.

Chapter Thirty-One

TUESDAY 6 FEBRUARY

9.26 p.m.

Less than an hour later, Kyra was in Alex's car.

'Did you call ahead?'

'No, I thought a surprise visit might catch her off guard,' said Alex.

'How did you find her?'

'After your call I was looking at earlier possible attacks that might be linked to our killer. I think you might be on to something. A woman reported that she'd been kidnapped by a man fifteen years ago, early February. She didn't give a lot of details, but she said she'd been taken to some garages and held there for a few hours. It's not clear what the location was and she seemed very cagey about the attack.'

'Why has this only come to light now?' Kyra asked, sitting back in the car seat and holding on to the dashboard. Alex drove like a demon.

'She was vague on the details. Look at the notes.' She picked up a mini-screen from the side-pocket in the car door and pushed it onto Kyra's lap. 'It seems as though the officers who took the report suspected she was on Chinese Lè. They put it down to a trick and a punter turned nasty.'

Kyra scrolled down the reports. 'They thought she was a pro or an addict so they didn't bother to investigate?'

'Looks that way,' said Alex. They were heading into the suburbs now, the light dimming noticeably as they left the bright city behind.

'Damn it!' What a wasted opportunity. 'Maybe if those bloody officers had put aside their prejudices and investigated that report properly, then we mightn't have a pile of bodies and no one to blame.'

'I know, I know.' Alex took her hand off the steering wheel momentarily and waved it in the air. 'We've come a long way from then.'

Kyra was relieved when Alex had both hands back on the wheel again. 'How did you get her address?'

'She has an unusual name, Rosetta. That helped me to trace her. Rosetta Maguire.'

'This is brilliant.' Kyra was genuinely impressed. 'It sounds like she wasn't treated particularly well by the force back then. We'll have to go softly, softly.'

'Are you going to tell Tom?' Alex asked.

'After what happened at the lab? Let's keep it between us for now, until we can go to him with something . . .' She thought back to his words, '. . . concrete. Then, if we're wrong, we won't have upset him unnecessarily. You can tell him later. What do you think?'

Kyra held her breath.

'I might tell him afterwards, if we get somewhere,' Alex smiled. 'No point in upsetting the boss if we don't need to.'

Kyra exhaled.

9.52 p.m.

Rosetta was an attractive woman. Even now, in her mid-forties, there was not a sign of grey in her shiny black hair and her beautiful cocoa skin glowed. She wore a pink cashmere jumper and pale grey woollen trousers. Kyra didn't know how Alex had managed to find her, but she certainly hadn't expected such a wealthy home, given what had been suggested about her previous lifestyle.

Kyra saw a wariness in Rosetta's eyes when they showed their ID cards, but her demeanour was polite and welcoming. She invited them into a lounge with cream carpets and huge gilt-framed mirrors. Wide French windows with golden damask curtains on either side looked out onto a landscaped garden, lit briefly by the security light as a cat crossed the lawn. Kyra imagined the plants would be glorious when they bloomed in the coming months.

Rosetta indicated for them to sit on the cream and gold striped sofa whilst she perched delicately on the arm of one of the chairs.

'What's this about?' Her tone was light, and yet Kyra could sense a heaviness behind the words.

Alex began. 'We believe you reported an attack, fifteen years ago.'

Rosetta's face tightened. 'Fifteen years. That seems like an awfully long time ago. Why are you here now?'

'Because we believe that the information you could give us could be of some use to an ongoing investigation,' said Alex.

At that moment, a handsome, tanned man in his mid-fifties came into the room, holding two crystal tumblers.

'Sorry, darling, I didn't know you had company.' His eyes widened. 'I'll leave this until later.' He left the room to the sound of ice clinking.

There was a flicker of anxiety on Rosetta's face. 'There must be some kind of mistake,' she said, looking from Alex to Kyra and back again, her lips pursed. 'I have no idea what you are talking about.'

'Mrs . . .?' Kyra began.

'King.'

'Mrs King, we believe that your complaint wasn't investigated as thoroughly as it should have been, and we would like to make amends. We're so sorry it has taken this long.' She paused. 'We think you could be key to saving a woman's life.'

Rosetta stiffened and crossed her arms over at the wrists, the expensive wool of her jumper riding up her arms. She glanced over to the door that her husband had left slightly ajar.

'I have never reported anything to the police, never mind an attack.' There was an edge to her voice now, defensiveness and something darker.

Alex reddened and glanced at Kyra.

'Oh no, I tell a lie,' Rosetta said, the faintest of smiles showing on her lips.

Alex perked up.

'My Mercedes was stolen. Two years ago. Do you think you might have gotten me mixed up somehow?'

Alex went to speak, but Kyra stood up.

'I am so sorry we disturbed you, Mrs King. There's obviously been some confusion at the station. Sorry for wasting your time. If you would like to make a complaint, please say that it was me, Doctor Kyra Sullivan, who made the mistake, not my colleague. I can't apologise enough.'

When they had pulled away from the house, Alex said, 'Thanks for covering me there. I'm so sorry. I was convinced I had the right woman.' Her face was a picture of confusion and embarrassment.

'Don't worry. I'm just glad we didn't tell Tom,' Kyra smiled, feeling the relief coming from Alex.

She was secretly pleased. If Alex thought she had the wrong woman then she wouldn't be willing to offer any information up to Tom, whom she was always keen to impress.

'Really, don't worry about it. If there's any hassle, they won't be too hard on me. I'm not even an officer.'

'Thanks, Kyra. Shall I drop you off?' she asked gratefully.

'Yes please.'

All the way home, Kyra couldn't help thinking about Rosetta's hand poking out of the soft pink wool. It was very realistic, no doubt the best money could buy, but it had definitely been prosthetic.

11.03 p.m.

Before she went to sleep, Kyra had tried to call Molly, but she wasn't answering. She dumped her phone on the bed, padded into the kitchen to get a vitamin pod and washed it down with a drink of water straight from the tap. Minutes later, she rushed to the toilet and brought it back up again. Looking in the mirror, she saw her face was drawn and pale. Her skin was papery and her eyes dark underneath. Out of the corner of her eye, she saw a shadow, a figure, standing behind her, but she wouldn't look at it.

She would have to live with these things now.

Molly wasn't picking up. Kyra couldn't blame her. But she'd come around, wouldn't she?

She went back into the bedroom and curled up under the cover, thinking about everything that had happened over the last few days. So much had changed in such a short space of time. Her relationships, like her mind, seemed to be fracturing.

She reversed the pillow and lay back down on the cool cotton. It was pitch black in her bedroom, the black-out roller-blinds blocking even the streetlights.

She closed her eyes and eventually drifted off, but it was fitful sleep, interspersed with dreams and images; the bride she had seen in Ray's memories coming closer and closer, tiny gypsophila flowers interwoven in her beautiful red curly hair; Skylar Lowndry's body, frozen in the water, her face like a china doll, the Mizpah necklace visible below the ice – untouchable, the photograph of Isabel from the screens at the station, the burn on Riley's arm. She saw the emergency services, and the drones at the Eco-Centre, the peri-med at the gate, the police cars; the blue snake from Madelyn's tattoo turning into a real snake and slithering up her own body, from her thigh, across her stomach, up to her throat, where it coiled around her neck, strangling her.

And then she saw Emma being driven away in a red car, screaming.

She awoke and sat up, saying, 'Emma, I'm so sorry, I'm so sorry!' Words that often broke the silence after sleep.

She lay back down, soaked with regret.

Nothing could be done now.

In the darkness she could see her own hand resting on the pillow next to her – the gold gleam of a wedding band. She closed her eyes briefly, hoping it would disappear, and when she re-opened them she saw a worse sight – her own hand severed, the wrist stump pumping blood all over the pillow.

She squeezed her eyes shut and, when she opened them again, her hand was back to normal, but then her eyes were immediately drawn to the foot of her bed where there was an unfamiliar shape. Her clothes over the bedroom chair? In the darkness, her brain tried to decipher what it was, attempting to match the outline to something benign, ordinary.

The black shape lurched suddenly and made a snuffling sound.

Kyra immediately sat up and reached out for the lamp with trembling hands.

There was a click, but no light.

The mound began to move towards her. Her heart pounding, Kyra pulled the bedclothes tightly around her.

She clicked the light switch twice more. She must have switched it off at the wall. She reached down to the socket behind the bedside cabinet, the shape coming closer all the time.

In the darkness, right next to her ear, sudden screaming, so loud it appeared like lights in her brain.

Then Molly's desperate howls, 'Ky, Ky! Help me! Help me!'

She managed to push the switch and light flooded the room and blinded her momentarily.

When she regained her vision, the room was empty.

Chapter Thirty-Two

WEDNESDAY 7 FEBRUARY

11.19 a.m.

ISABEL

When she awakes, Isabel is lying between crisp white cotton sheets. Her head is on a soft white pillow and she can see the broderie anglaise edges to the bedding. She has no idea where she is, or what day it is. A child's night light casts a gentle glow on the walls. A synthetic calmness keeps her lying still – she suspects diamorphine. Her mouth is dry, her nose tingles unbearably. She is desperate to scratch, but her arms are so heavy. Her eyes travel down to the cannula in her hand and her heart sinks. Part of her wants to fall into a deep sleep. But then she thinks of her dad, her gran. She forces herself to fight it. She tries to move her arms again. How is she going to survive if she can't move her body?

From the corner of her eye she sees him sitting on the white rocking chair, motionless. She wonders if he is asleep. He doesn't wear his mask now and she knows this is a bad sign.

He is going to kill her.

His eyes open slowly, and he turns to her.

'You're awake.'

Her vision drifts to the white lace curtains and she wonders what lies beyond. Could she climb out of the window? She doesn't know how high it is from the ground. She tries to move her legs, but it is as though the messages from her brain aren't reaching the muscles. What if she shouted to the street below? Unless they are miles from anywhere, in the countryside?

'Are you okay?' For a moment he sounds like a normal person. 'Do you want a drink?' He holds a glass of water with a straw in it near her mouth and she sucks until the slurping noises from the straw tell her the glass is empty.

She isn't enclosed up here, not physically, not like in the metal coffin. If she could just move, she might have a chance. But he is in total control. She can see the button on the tube going from her hand into the drip and she knows he intends for her to be continually dosed up. She is trapped in her own body. Unless she can somehow get the drip out? She's used to this type of kit.

Isabel thinks of the cancer ward and the deaths of the patients that she has observed. The pain which had distressed them had finally been overcome by the powerful medication and they had drifted off. It had been a relief in the end. She knows about diamorphine, that the balance between pain relief and killing the patient is such a fine line. But she isn't ready to let go. She will wait until the meds have worn off a little. Pretend it's affecting her more. Wait until he goes out again . . .

He sits back down again and says, 'Look at me.'

She looks away from him, towards the window, the only act of defiance she can muster.

'This is my sister Elise's room. I need you to see who she was. Who she is. You need to know her so that you recognise her when you get there.' He held out a photograph — but she refused to look at it.

Get where? What does he mean?

He comes closer and checks her over with a handheld scanner like the ones they use in the hospital. She wonders briefly where he got this kit. Has she seen him somewhere before?

She doesn't want to show him that she is afraid, so she rolls her eyes, pretends she is stoned.

'Do you wonder where people go when they die?' he asks.

Her eyes flick to his face. *Oh God, is this it? Is he going to kill her now? All the things she has never done . . . the people she loves . . . Dad . . . Gran . . . Liv.*

'Don't be afraid. I've given you something to help you feel calm. I won't let you suffer, Isabel.'

She has a memory of her dad telling her to hit back when she was picked on by a bully at school. *She is small, but she has fight, doesn't she?*

'Do you believe in Heaven?' he asks. He kneels down next to her, his face close, his breath smelling of mint. 'Do you think it's real? I hope so. I hope there's a place free from all suffering, all pain. One where we can be with our loved ones again.' He frowns and sighs heavily. 'They won't have me now. I'm not good enough. I did bad things, the worst things, but I only did it to help her. I only did it for my little sister. Do you think God will understand?' He pauses, as though he expects her to answer. When she doesn't, he continues, 'The first women, well, they were bad anyway. But the others, the ones like you, I didn't want to kill them. But how else could I let Elise know that she wasn't on her own? I sent her angels because I love her so much. I did it out of love.'

He is staring intently at her but then he begins to weep.

'Elise was so good. She should have gone straight to Heaven. She never did a thing wrong. But I'm afraid she got lost some-where along the way . . .' He sniffs and wipes his face with his hands. '. . . because of the way she died. I think she wanted our mother's love so much that she couldn't let go. She couldn't find her way . . . and now she's lost. She's in the darkness.' He makes a soft grunting sound like a sob. 'I don't want to think of her alone and afraid. That's why I do this. I want to make sure that Elise isn't afraid. That she knows she's not on her own. Do you understand?'

'If you're so sure Elise is alone,' Isabel hisses groggily, 'then why don't you kill yourself so you can be with her, you fucking coward?'

She braces herself, but he smiles at this.

'Only innocents can be with Elise. She was pure, you see. She didn't deserve any of it. She was pure, innocent.'

'So, you're going to let another innocent woman die?' Isabel asks.

'I have to,' he says, as though it is the most obvious thing in the world. A strange smile appears on his lips. 'She would look up at me with her big blue eyes and say, "I love you, Stephen. You are the best big brother in the world!"' he says in a childish, sing-songy voice.

Isabel cringes. God, if she could only get up enough energy to move. She feels her eyes roll in her head.

'When she was gone, I didn't have anyone.' His face falls.

What the hell is he talking about? The door is shut. Is it locked? Where is her Commset?

'She's afraid. She's in the dark,' he weeps. 'She's a good girl. She shouldn't have died like that. Such a short, brutal life. I would have done anything to save her. But I was only a child myself. I wasn't strong enough . . .' He howls. 'I couldn't lift her body, she was wet, slippery. I couldn't lift her. I couldn't get her out.'

He begins to wail loudly, leaning over her body as he sheds his grief and his keening echoes the feeling she has inside.

She wants to live! She rotates her hand and she is sure she feels her cannula shifting, if she could just . . .

He lifts his head and she realises he is watching her so she rolls her eyes as she has seen the patients at the hospital do. He wipes his face on his sleeve and composes himself.

'But tonight, I am going to sit with you, I am going to protect your spirit. Tonight is your wake, your vigil, before you leave this world for good, before I send you to be with Elise.'

Isabel tells herself to focus on staying alive, not to listen to his words. She thinks about her grandmother's fob watch, the time ticking away. Nothing ever lasts for ever, her grandmother had often said: the suffering, the joy – nothing lasts.

'It won't be long now. All this will be gone and you'll be free.' He almost sang the last word. 'I wish I could come too, but I need to stay here. I will be a witness to his suffering as he witnessed ours. I have to stay here, make sure he suffers. Then I can be with Elise.'

He leans over her with a silver necklace in his hands. He puts the pendant in front of her eyes as if to show her. 'It won't be long now. Tell my sister how much I love her. Give her this. Tell her all the things that I have done, I have done for her. Tell her not to be afraid.' He reaches behind the back of her neck and clips the necklace on, then places the pendant at the base of her throat.

'May God watch between thee and me, Elise, whilst we are absent, one from another.'

Chapter Thirty-Three

WEDNESDAY 7 FEBRUARY

5.47 p.m.

Rosetta had dressed down for the occasion – jeans, a large brown sweater and sheepskin boots. Her hair was up in a bun and she was wearing glasses. She sat nursing a black tea in a basement cafe-bar not far from the police station. Kyra joined her and ordered a coffee for herself.

It was nearly evening. Kyra had slept heavily until the early afternoon, and then woke feeling hungover to the depressing thought that this was the day, on which Isabel was going to die – and there was nothing she could do about it.

In one last attempt to help Isabel, she had rooted out the mini-screen that Tom had left at hers. God, had that only been a few days ago? The images of Caylee were so horrendous that she had hidden it in a cupboard, out of sight. She had scoured her files again from the original case. She tried to eat and found she couldn't keep anything down. Then her day had taken an unexpected turn when Rosetta had contacted her.

And now here she was, hoping Rosetta would help her to crack the case.

Kyra had brought the police mini-screen in the hope that she might be able to corroborate some of Rosetta's information but, before she got out of her car, she realised that it might be too official and put Rosetta off, so she stuffed it into the glove compartment.

'I wasn't sure if I'd see you again,' said Kyra. She had hoped, but not expected. She had made it deliberately clear what her name was when she had left Rosetta's house; all it would have taken was a little research on the hypernet.

'Neither was I.' She swilled her cup but didn't drink it. 'This wasn't easy.'

'I'm sure it wasn't.'

'But probably not for the reasons you might think.'

'I'm here to listen.'

The waiter brought over the coffee and Kyra was impatient for him to leave.

'I couldn't talk in front of David. He's a good man, but he doesn't know about my past. I didn't want to talk to the police. I know you're not one of them. I looked you up. You're a scientist, a psychologist.'

'Yes, but I want you to know that I was working with the police at the time of your—'

'I know, but maybe you'll understand.' She took a sip of her drink, waiting until another customer made her way past to the bathroom before talking again.

'But before we start, I need you to make me a promise.' She grabbed Kyra's hand. Promise me that you'll keep my identity a secret. I'll tell you everything I know, but I cannot, cannot,' she stressed, 'lose the life that I have built up because of this case. What I went through . . . nearly killed me. My husband is a good man. We are respected now in the community. I have a lovely life, one that I could never have imagined . . . back then. I want to help you get him, but please promise me this.'

What choice did Kyra have? Rosetta — the key to cracking the case — Kyra's witness X.

284

'Of course, I promise.' She meant it.

Rosetta looked relieved, let go of her hand and began to talk. 'I was really angry, hurt, I suppose, when the police didn't take me seriously. I told them about Jenny. Obviously I was distressed. They used the word "hysterical". Why wouldn't I be? It was the worst thing I had ever been through and, believe me, I've been through some bad stuff.' She took another mouthful of tea. 'It never goes away. I wish I could block it out altogether. I was so freaked out that – I hate to say this but – I took some Lè to help me to cope, I suppose, and to give me the courage to face the police. We weren't exactly on friendly terms, back then.'

Kyra gave an encouraging 'hmm' and sipped her coffee. An excitement had risen inside her to find some new information, but she knew she had to take this easy.

'I had a problem. I don't mind admitting it now. You beat yourself up and get into a downward spiral of self-revulsion and using, but I understand now. Addiction – it's an illness. Who the hell would choose that sort of life?'

'Looks like you've turned it around.' Kyra remembered the cream and gold sofa and Rosetta's handsome husband. She also thought about Ray Clarke's transformation. Somehow good had come from bad.

Rosetta shrugged. 'I never knew what happened to Jenny. I was so off my face for a while after, and then, when I was lucid, I couldn't face looking at the news.'

'You never looked it up on screen?'

Rosetta shook her head. 'I didn't even know her second name. Strange how circumstance throws you together with someone and then you bond.' She put her hands up in front of her, palms up. Kyra couldn't help comparing them. 'However short a time . . . and then you can never forget them.'

Tom popped into Kyra's mind.

Rosetta's shoulders dropped. 'She died, didn't she?'

'I'm so sorry, I'm afraid she did. We found her a week later.'

Rosetta's expression was pained. 'She was so young, so innocent.' She put an elbow on the table, her hand to her head. 'I had a bloody good go, you know. I tried to help her get away.' She sounded defeated but there was a hint of strength in her eyes.

Kyra nearly blurted out: *I know I saw you*, but how could she have explained that? Instead she said, 'Tell me how you came to be there – where exactly was it?'

'I'd been making money, on the game. We didn't have anywhere like the Scrambles back then, nor the legal houses. We took our chances, me and the other girls. Jenny wasn't one of us, by the way. I'd never seen her before. God, it was such a cold night, freezing, not like you get now. A punter approached me, said his name was Stephen. I don't know if that was his real name or not. He seemed . . . ordinary.' She shrugged.

Kyra shook her head, desperate to ask for a description, but she held back *time and space*.

Rosetta continued. 'He said, let's go somewhere quiet and warm. He knew a good place and he was willing to pay more. I was glad to get out of the bitter chill. I usually worked with my friend, but her kid was sick, so she wasn't out that night. You start taking things for granted. I'd had a pretty easy ride up to that point, a few punters roughed me up, but I got over it. I had to, as how else was I going to make my money?

'I was reckless back then. I'd had a good job in the city. I was a party girl, got in with a crowd of people who had fun, and I mean fun. Got myself addicted to Lè. It wasn't as widely available back then as it is now. It was a status symbol. They were all big earners, I couldn't keep up. It was as simple as that.'

Kyra had thought Rosetta pristine in her beautiful home, but now the cracks were beginning to show. From this distance, fine lines were visible beneath her eyes, the hints of grey at the roots, a fragility Kyra had not noticed the first time they had met.

'In the end I was willing to take stupid risks. We went off, in his car, to some derelict set of garages up past the Townsend Factory, up by the Goreham train station.'

Kyra made a mental note.

'It seemed like it was going to be the usual, straight sex for a handful of cash. But when we got there, he offered me more, a lot more, if I let him tie me up. I wanted the money, needed the money, so he secured my hands with tie-wraps. Looking back, well, it rang an alarm bell. Then I wanted to get it over, get back to my turf.'

She gave off an air of weariness.

'Do you want a hot one?' Kyra said, indicating the cup. She was eager to hear the story, but this was probably the first time Rosetta had told anyone about that night, apart from the police officers who hadn't believed her. This needed careful handling.

'Yes, thanks.'

Kyra called the waiter over and ordered another. Rosetta disappeared into her memories for a moment. Would Rosetta be willing to use CASNDRA? Would that enable Kyra to access the sort of information needed to catch this killer?

She waited until the waiter brought the tea and they sat for a while drinking in silence. To Kyra's relief, Rosetta began to speak again.

'He tied me up and then he sat down on the ground and started talking to me. I thought he was just one of those lonely wankers who wanted to chat and, to be honest, I didn't mind as I can listen with the best of them. It's better than having to . . . you know. I was happy at first, but then I started thinking: if he only wants to talk then why has he tied me up?'

'Can you remember what he was talking about?'

'He told me that he had to do this. He said she deserved better.'

'Who did he mean?'

'I don't know.'

'Then he said,' she stopped speaking for a moment, swallowed hard. 'He said . . .' She stopped again.

'It's okay,' Kyra put her hand on Rosetta's.

'He said I was a terrible mother.'

Kyra drew back, surprised.

'I didn't know you had kids.'

Rosetta's face was like stone. 'I did, once. A daughter, Gabriella. They took her from me: Child Welfare,' she said, her face like stone.

'I am so sorry, that's awful,' Kyra said.

'No, it was the right thing to do at the time. I see that now. I was living in a house with three other people. We were high most of the time. One day, I found Gabriella in her cot. She wouldn't wake up. The medical team reported me to the authorities. When she was well enough to leave hospital, they took her to live somewhere else.'

'But you never got her back?'

She shook her head, a split second of pain in her eyes, and then she took a deep breath and straightened up.

'I thought about it. But I decided against it for two reasons. One is very selfish – I don't want anyone knowing about my past. My husband doesn't know I had a child. How could I bring her home with me when it would mean I would have to answer all sorts of questions? About a year after . . . I was in rehab, trying to get myself cleaned up. I started working for a charity to help women who had been . . . in my situation and that was when I met my husband – at a fundraiser. I lied about where I had come from, what my life had been like before I'd met him. Which is why I lied to you when you came to my house. I'm terrified he will find out. When we first got together I sort of hinted that I'd been wild in my youth, but I didn't tell him exactly how wild. He said it didn't matter, we were together now and we needed to forget about the past. I was grateful that I could make a new start, and grateful to meet someone who loved and respected me as a person.'

'You love each other?'

Rosetta smiled and her face changed altogether.

'You're lucky.' And, for a moment, Kyra had a tiny insight into what she could have had with Tom, and it hurt.

At this point, she abandoned the idea of using CASNDRA with Rosetta. Some things were best left buried.

'You don't have any other children?'

She shook her head. 'I told my husband before we married that I couldn't have children. It's not really a lie. I can't have them because I don't deserve them. That man, he was right about me being a terrible mother. I didn't want to ruin another child's life.'

'What was the other reason you didn't get her back?'

'Gabriella would be settled now. She didn't need me coming along and messing it up again. I couldn't face my daughter if she ever found out who, what, I used to be. She would hate me. I found out that she is with a lovely family, she has brothers and sisters, her adoptive mum is a teacher, they even have a pet dog. I don't want to spoil that.'

Kyra thought how much that made her a good mother, sacrificing her own feelings for those of her child's.

'But how did he, Stephen, know you were a terrible mother?'

Rosetta's expression became perplexed.

'I've thought about that so often, but I don't know. Maybe he knew about Gabriella somehow?'

'You didn't tell him about her, or give anything away by accident?'

She shook her head.

'He did all the talking. Probably because he knew he had planned to kill me, so he could say what he wanted.' Her eyes flared with strength again. 'But I wasn't ready to die.

'He talked about his own mother. He said his mother never protected them from the bastard. That's the word he used. He said she left the bastard to beat him and his sister. He said mothers who didn't protect their children were the worst. He said I didn't protect my child.'

'Did he say anything else?'

'No, because at that point, I heard a noise at the back of the garage. It sounded like an injured animal, but then I saw Jenny tied up against some pipes. That's when I really freaked out. I mean, what sort of person would have two women tied up in a garage? She was in a right state and she begged me to help her, but what could I do? Stephen started to get agitated, walking up and down between the two of us, ranting. He spoke kindly to her. He said he didn't want to lose her, said she was so important to him. He kept calling her another name, Ellis? Elise? *A good girl*, he said, *should be loved and feel loved. A good girl*, he said, *deserved her mother's heart*. I don't know what he meant by that. Do you?'

Kyra shivered.

'How did you get away?'

'He'd injected me with something to keep me quiet, but I'd taken so much shit over the years, I don't think he realised how immune I was to it.' She started to breathe heavily and pull at her hair. 'I can't believe he did this to me!' A few people glanced over at her distress.

'You're safe now,' Kyra tried to soothe her.

Rosetta glanced around self-consciously and then quietly hissed, 'He said he was going to give her my hands!' She briefly lifted her prosthetic hand from her lap. 'He came at me with some kind of saw and started to hack at my wrists. That was why he'd tied me up. He was really close and even though the pain was excruciating, the drugs took the edge off. I managed to headbutt him, right on the bridge of his nose. I was bleeding all over the place, but he was stunned and I managed to get free. He'd cut the ties when he was trying to cut me.

'I ran over to Jenny and freed her with the saw. She ran out while I struggled with him. He hit me then, and I fell backwards, and he ran out after Jenny. There were bricks lying around, I picked some up and threw them at him, to try to help her get away. I made a run for it. I thought she'd got away too. I thought she'd got away.' Her voice trailed off.

'I'm so sorry, Rosetta. You tried your best, under those circumstances, no one could have done more.'

She seemed comforted a little by these words.

'I came back a bit later, once I was sure he had gone. What if Jenny was still alive and I could help her? But by the time I got there, the ambulance was driving away.'

'Ambulance?'

'Yes, someone must have heard the screaming and called it in.'

A seed of doubt blossomed in Kyra's gut. Jennifer Bosanquet had been found floating in an outdoor lido by an early morning swimmer who had called the emergency services. If she had been found at the garage Tom would have known where Ray claimed to have seen something. There would have been photographs in the digital files she had studied that morning. There would have been a police search at the garage, forensic evidence . . .

What Rosetta was telling her didn't fit the picture.

'I went to the hospital myself afterwards but they couldn't save my hand.' She lifted her arm again. The colour of her prosthetic matched her skin perfectly, the fingers bent at natural angles, the nails painted the same golden-pearly colour as the nails on her other hand.

Unless Rosetta was mixed up about where she had seen the ambulance. Maybe it hadn't been at the garage, but at the hospital? She had been traumatised and confused; she had been a Lè user after all.

'Does anyone ever ask how it happened?'

'Most people don't mention it, but I see them staring sometimes. I say it was a car accident.'

'Rosetta, I can't thank you enough for coming to talk to me. You've given me more information than we've ever had. I am so sorry that no one listened to you back then.'

'I couldn't bear this happening to someone else.'

'You're taking a big risk. I appreciate that.'

Rosetta nodded gravely. 'He needs to be caught but, please, let the old me stay hidden.'

'Of course.'

She suddenly gripped Kyra's hand, her eyes pleading. 'Catch him! For Jenny's sake.'

Something almost electrical passed between them as Rosetta's hand rested on hers.

Kyra left the cafe-bar with one destination in mind.

The garage.

Chapter Thirty-Four

WEDNESDAY 7 FEBRUARY

7.19 p.m.

Kyra stood in the dark yard, in front of an old black wooden door, the one that she had already seen once through Ray's eyes. She knew for sure this was the garage where she had seen Rosetta, Jennifer, and the killer in the transference with Ray and now she was looking at it in real time. Unlike the transference, however, she was able to move around at will and walk freely between the two sets of garages which stood facing each other. The scientist in her knew that all the forensic evidence would be gone after so many years, but she wasn't going to give up. Not now.

Before she had set off in the car, clutching the serviette on which Rosetta had drawn a crude map, she had momentarily wobbled and called Alex, thinking she would prefer not to go alone, but she cut the call before there was any answer, in case word got back to Tom. She would rather risk being alone than have to deal with his incredulity. The last light was fading from the sky and the garage, set away from the main road down a rough, narrow path, was quiet and remote. It felt almost like a trap.

She made her way past the clump of trees, grown much bigger now, where Ray had seen the fox, careful of her footing on the rubbly ground. She was going to find a lead, she was sure of it. Then Tom would see how good the technology was. The police would be impressed, maybe even offer to buy the tech and then Carter would forgive her. But most importantly, she would have helped to find Isabel and catch the Mizpah Murderer.

Justice for Emma at last.

The yellowy glow from the yard lamp had long since gone. She flicked the light on her Commset, which gave out a bright white beam and, with some difficulty, yanked open the door into the garage that Ray had used for shelter. She lay down, too eager for information to worry about her coat on the grimy ground. The smell of oil was much stronger than she had caught in Ray's memories.

Peering out from beneath the cracked wood, she angled her head down so that she could shine her light across the yard and look out at the same time.

But she did not see what she had expected.

Her sight became refracted, as if she had a migraine halo, and split her vision into two, as if the past and the present were converging and both happening simultaneously. She saw the yard as it was when she had arrived and then she saw the yard as it had been the night Rosetta had been there. Then, the present day faded away and there was only the past.

Right in front of her eyes, just beyond the garage door, she could see the tyre of a car. She craned her neck to see more. The paintwork was a bright, cherry red, radiant in the white light of her Commset. The next moment, a half brick banged the garage door, making her heart burst into speed, the adrenaline flushing through her system.

She glanced over to the far side of the yard and, as she did so, Jennifer Bosanquet came running out, her feet bare, stumbling on the rubble in the yard, her tiny frame swathed in white fabric like an old-fashioned nightdress. She ran up to the door, right in front of Kyra, half a metre away, separated by only a few centimetres of rotten wood, and then cowered down behind the car, hiding. She was in Kyra's beam but she didn't seem to see the light.

Kyra's chest grew tight. The bees, ever present these days, made every nerve in her body hurt as the anxiety travelled through her body like electricity. She briefly closed her eyes, but when she opened them again, the car and the woman were still there. Her mind was reeling, her instincts were urging her to rescue the woman, her psychology training telling her this wasn't what it seemed.

Next moment, the garage door opposite burst open.

A hooded man appeared and honed in on the terrified woman. She whimpered. 'I'm not her! I'm Jenny! I'm Jenny!'

Kyra knew what would happen next. She had already seen it. This would be the last time anyone saw Jennifer Bosanquet alive.

'But I'm Jenny!' the woman cried more desperately.

The killer came really close and punched Jennifer once, hard.

Kyra, in her stunned confusion, could no longer stop herself from remaining still. She thought of Rosetta's courage, and grabbed a half-brick, the only weapon available. She knew in a matter of seconds he would be bending over Jennifer's body, picking her up and putting her in the boot of his car. She burst out of the door, brick raised above her head, ready to strike, ready to fight for Jennifer's life.

But the yard was empty.

There was no car, no woman, no killer.

Kyra ran over to the garage opposite and wrestled the rusty hinged door open. Shining her Commset torch in, she could see no one. The garage seemed to swirl around her and she staggered back into the yard and slumped down to the rough ground, sweating, heart pounding, limbs weak, wondering what the hell she was thinking.

This had all happened fifteen years ago.

But it had all seemed so real.

Her chest was heaving now, a hive full of honey, unable to let any oxygen in.

Why the hell hadn't she brought Alex with her? She tried her number, but there was no reply. They were probably in the thick of it now in the Hub – last-minute leads, desperate to make the next few hours count.

Midnight was beckoning – the hour of Isabel Marsden's death.

For a split second she considered ringing Tom.

'Dial Jimmy.' Her words shattered the eerie silence. 'Jimmy, pick up, pick up!' she urged. It went straight to automessage. He wasn't speaking to her. She couldn't blame him.

'Jim, please, I'm freaking out here, something weird's going on. I saw something but it happened years ago. I don't feel so good. Jimmy, I need you! I'm sorry. You were right, this tech is making me . . . just call me back.'

She wished she could have said, *Come and get me.*

She was on her own.

The light from the call went out and she was surrounded by stifling darkness. She moved to get up, her chest still tight, and pulled herself up to her feet, wheezing. Her head exploded into a sharp ache and dizziness which caught her off balance. She needed to get back to her car which she had left on the main road.

But to get there, she would have to walk down to the entrance of the yard, a tapering alleyway with tumble-down brick walls riven with buddleia on either side. The plants had been left to grow wild and now formed a tunnel of dead brown spear-shaped heads and branches wavering in the cool breeze. Kyra stumbled to the alley, desperate to get out of the yard. Up ahead, at a distance, she saw the bright lights of intermittent cars driving past, but they were suddenly blacked out by a solid shadowy mass beyond the thin branches which waved violently as the wind began to increase.

She stopped still, straining to see what it was. As her eyes grew used to the dark, her heart nearly stopped.

A figure stood motionless, silhouetted against the distant street lights, blocking the path. In his hand, she could see a hacksaw, the angular trapezoid shape visible in outline. Was it Lomax, escaped again? Was he going to make good on his promise to her? Who was it?

'Jesus, no,' she cried, frantically looking for an escape route. She switched her light off to make her position less obvious.

Adrenaline made her legs feel useless. Her mind flailed and in her panic, to get away from him, she retreated a few metres back down the alley towards the garages, and then realised her mistake as he moved towards her, maintaining the distance between them.

Could she run into one of the garages to hide, wait until he came further into the yard and then make a break for it? At least that way she might have a chance to escape.

But she knew he would move the second she did. He would be faster, on her before she even had a chance to hide. She eyed the hacksaw again and willed her body to do what she needed it to do, urging her legs to function, her eyes to guide her.

The second she moved her body, he burst into action and darted towards her like a lion on a gazelle. She scrambled her way to one of the rotten wooden doors, sliding on rocks and tripping over rubble. She heard him getting closer, the sound of his feet pounding the concrete. Darting into one of the garages, she caught her hand against the rusted lock, the pain shooting up her arm. Crouching down in a dark corner, she tried hard to stifle her laboured breathing, desperate to suck in the air as she shuddered in fear.

There was an almighty crash as he slammed his body against the wooden door.

She got up on to her haunches, like an animal ready to launch herself, to fight whatever it was that she was about to face.

Nothing happened.

She waited for another minute, the adrenaline burning her muscles, a growling fear in the pit of her stomach.

There was no movement.

She slowly stood up, her body tensed, and listened, scanning the air for any sound or smell that would tell her danger was near.

Then she moved towards the door in the pitch black, one footstep at a time, hearing nothing, seeing nothing. She reached out for the door, gearing herself up to going back out to the courtyard. Her fingers made contact with the splintered wood and she pushed it open in trepidation and peeked out.

She could see no one and launched into a run.

A loud animal roar burst into her ears and he came from behind, hurtling after her.

She caught her foot on a brick and fell, tumbling over and over, banging her hip and elbow, cracking her wrist, and grazing her face, until she righted herself and stood, and moved off again, in one swift motion.

Where was he? Who was he? She hurried towards the alleyway and the lights of the main road beyond the branches. She hit her car at speed and grabbed the handle but for some reason, the door wouldn't open. A shooting pain electrified her damaged wrist as she struggled with it. She heard him then, gaining on her. She tugged at the handle again, frantically pulling with short snappy looks back and forth, to see how close he was. There was no reassuring 'clunk' as the central locking responded to her hand print. Her face burned from the contact with the ground, her wrist throbbed.

He stopped two metres away, smaller than she had imagined. *It's not Lomax* but nonetheless terrifying – waving the hacksaw at her. His face was a dark space, a grim reaper's aspect.

Of course, the oil and grime from the floor of the garage.

He started moving slowly towards her, nothing between them, nowhere to hide.

She wiped her hand furiously on her jeans, spitting on them and rubbing again, then grabbed the handle.

He dived towards her, but the door opened halfway. She quickly tried to force her body into the narrow gap but he was too fast and he was upon her. He slammed against the car door, banging it against her head as she tried to climb in. Lights burst around her vision. Somehow, she managed to push him off.

His hands hit the window between them and the hacksaw cracked against the glass. Her foot was still on the ground outside the car. She was stunned, her head throbbing. His face was so close to hers now that she could hear his grunts as he forced the car door against her, the pain in her leg excruciating. He gritted his teeth together, spittle at the corner of his mouth. One of his eyes was closed over, the skin around it ruched.

Her body trapped, she did the only thing possible and pressed her heel down as hard as she could on his foot. It was not particularly forceful, she hadn't been able to get much momentum, but he yelped and released the pressure on the door briefly.

It was enough to give Kyra space to get herself into the car. Once in the seat, she went to pull the door closed, but his hand darted in and he grabbed her by a fistful of hair, pulling her head out of the car and slamming the door on it.

'I'm going to take your hands!' he whispered.

As she lost consciousness, the last thing she saw was the hacksaw.

Chapter Thirty-Five

WEDNESDAY 7 FEBRUARY

8.36 p.m.

Kyra screamed when she heard the thumping on the window of the car. It was still dark. How long had she been out? She brought her arms up to protect herself.

Her hands.

She examined them, trembling before her eyes, relieved.

'Kyra!' Jimmy stood on the grass verge outside, lit by the headlights of his own car. His curly hair was poking out from under a cap, his palms pressed against the glass. 'You okay? Open the door!'

With a shaking voice she ordered the car to unlock the doors and half-climbed, half-fell, out on to the grass. She grabbed Jimmy's arms and pulled herself up and held onto him.

'Has he gone? Has he gone?' She glanced around in the darkness, eyes wide.

He patted her back, uncertainly. 'You're okay. There's no one here.'

Jimmy had come for her. He cared about her. They were friends, for heaven's sake. He hadn't meant to reject her. He'd only been concerned about her, hadn't he?

'I'm sorry . . . about everything . . . about work . . . about pushing too hard . . .' she began.

'It doesn't matter now,' he reassured her.

She loosened her grip on him. 'What are you doing here? How did you find me?'

'You mean what are *you* doing here? I got your message and I was worried. I used the tracker I put on your car.'

'I'd forgotten about that.' It seemed like such a basic experiment now. So much had changed since then.

She finally let go and sat back down on the car seat, door wide open, feet on the grass beneath.

'You sure you're okay?' Jimmy asked.

'I'm alright now.' She ran her hand across her forehead. 'I'm glad you're here.'

'What on earth were you doing out here on your own at this time of night?'

She examined her hands again, relieved. She thought about Riley, the little boy with no mother. She steeled herself for his reaction. 'This is where Ray Clarke saw the killer.'

'What makes you think that?' he asked quietly.

'Rosetta Maguire called me. She was a witness to Jennifer Bosanquet's murder. The police overlooked her, took her for a junkie, but she told me everything.'

'About this place?'

Kyra nodded.

'Does Tom know you were here?'

She shook her head. 'He doesn't believe anything I say. He thinks I've lost it.'

Jimmy came around the other side of the car and got in and closed the door. Kyra immediately shut her door too and locked the car.

'Let's wait here until you feel a bit better and then I'll follow you back to yours, make sure you get home safe.'

'Do you think I'm mad, Jim?' She kept her eyes on the dashboard, the soft blue glow of the lights familiar and comforting.

'It's been a tough time. Don't worry about Tom Morgan.'

Tears of relief prickled her eyes.

'But I think you have let this get the better of you.'

She didn't want to hear it, and opened her mouth to speak, a sob escaping. 'Jimmy, I'm so sorry, about . . . everything. I didn't want to fall out with you.'

'It's fine, don't worry.'

She looked up at him now. 'Thanks for coming for me. I didn't . . .' she began, but she was interrupted when her Commset rang.

Why was her mother ringing this late? She sniffed and wiped her nose with the back of her hand.

'Hi, Mum, everything alright?' she said, trying to sound more cheerful than she felt.

'Molly's not back. I don't know what to do. She's not answering.'

Kyra sighed heavily and put her hand on the dashboard in front of her. How much more pressure could she take?

'You know what she's like, Mum. She'll come back once she's got over . . .' Her eyes flicked to Jimmy and back. '. . . the row last night.'

'No, Kyra, this is different. That was a lot for her to take in yesterday. I don't know . . .'

'Mum!' She hadn't meant to snap at her. Jimmy directed his gaze out of the window.

'Mum,' she said more calmly. 'She'll be back in the morning. She will. Try not to let it get to you.'

She ended the conversation, her mother still anxious, but Kyra was too exhausted to give her more comfort. She should be worried about herself right now, the things she was seeing, the man at the garage, not her niece's tantrums or her mother's worries.

'What happened here?' Jimmy pointed to the graze on her face, concerned. 'Do you know your face is bleeding?'

She flicked down the mirror behind the visor and checked her reflection. 'I fell over.' Was that a shadow on the back seat? She looked around and then back again to the mirror. She must have imagined it. She touched her face, it stung, the blood was gritty on her fingers. She flipped the visor back up.

'What were you thinking coming out here in the middle of nowhere on your own? Why didn't you ask me to come with you?'

'I saw him here,' she blurted.

'Who did you see?' She couldn't look at him, but she could hear the anxiety in his voice.

'A man . . . he tried to attack me.' She looked out of the car window. 'I don't know where he went.' Jimmy was silent. 'What if it was him? The Mizpah Murderer?'

'He was here? Jesus! Tell Tom!' he urged. 'There might be some evidence.'

'I said I saw him. I don't know if he was here . . . not really.' Her voice shook with nerves. She turned to face him now. 'Jimmy, I'm seeing things . . . all sorts of things. I don't know what's real.'

'It might have been the killer. How do you know he wasn't there? Would he have come back – after all this time? I mean, he killed someone the other day, it could have been him, right?'

Did he believe her? 'I saw Jennifer Bosanquet, one of the victims.' She searched his face for a reaction. 'She's been dead fifteen years.' She groaned and covered her face with her hands. 'I saw the man who took her. But I don't think he was there. I'm losing it, Jim. I am going mad, Tom's right.' She reached up and put her hands on the wheel.

'Kyra, this has got to stop,' he said gently. She knew he was looking at her, but she kept her eyes fixed on the windscreen.

'But I'm so close, Jim. Isabel . . . she'll die tonight if I don't find some way of . . .'

He reached his hand over and put it on hers. 'You're making yourself ill. This is the furthest we have ever come with CASNDRA. You've proved it works. You've proved yourself.' Feeling his touch broke her down, and she let out a wail.

'I couldn't save her, Jimmy. I couldn't save Jennifer.'

'You should be thinking about saving yourself. If the real killer was here – and he might have been – then he could have killed you.'

She stopped crying then and looked at him.

'Why didn't he kill me?' she asked, her face streaked with tears, turning the question over in her mind. 'Why didn't he kill me? He had the chance, but he didn't . . .'

Somehow she didn't fit the profile.

He went for young, petite innocent girls – Type B. They already knew that.

And . . . who else? What did the Type A all have in common?

Something that she wasn't. Something she didn't have or didn't do.

She thought back to what Rosetta had told her.

A good girl deserves her mother's heart.

Mothers.

That was it.

He was killing mothers.

I need to clear my mind. I want to forget about mothers, those who are supposed to protect you, take care of you. I wouldn't be in this position now if she had done what she was supposed to do. But I have never been able to get my mother out of my mind.

Even after she took her own life, unable to live without Elise, unable to live with the guilt of the fact that she had let the bastard into our lives, that she had brought the Devil to our door.

She hadn't been able to cope and so my little sister had drowned, but it was his fault, even though she should have protected us, protected Elise.

I wasn't there that day. I wasn't there to save my little sister.

I remember coming home from school. It was a freezing cold February day and the sky was already darkening. One of the mechanics, Martin, asked me what I'd learned about, if I liked my teacher. But then the bastard roared at me to get in the house – I wasn't to cause trouble in the yard. I remember clearly Martin frowned and when the bastard had faced the other way, he winked at me.

It wasn't until later that I heard that the bastard should have been in the house, looking after Elise. He was meant to be taking care of her but, instead, he was out in the yard, with the other men, playing with his cars, bantering with the lads.

He cared so little about us that he forgot.

Forgot about the little girl that he should have been keeping safe.

I shouted for Elise as I went through the door, she always used to come running to see me. One time, because my mother had been so out of it for the day, and mustn't have fed her, I found her eating the dog's food from the bowl on the floor of the kitchen. That man always treated his dogs better than us.

But this day, there was silence.

I looked around the door of the room my mother shared with him. That day, she was flat out on the bed, the doctor had given her some tablets to take to help her cope. Sometimes she took too many. Or she drank too much. Stuck her head in the sand. She should have been on her guard, but instead, she spent days in bed. All because of the way he treated her. I think she wanted to escape from him, any way she could. Some days, she would sleep for hours on end and Elise would curl up next to her while she was out of it. My little sister would sing or chat to herself, lying against my mother's semi-conscious body. Other days, Elise and I would hide from him, afraid that without anyone to witness he would do what he liked to us.

I checked my mother was breathing.

Elise wasn't there.

I went into my room and searched in the wardrobe, under the bed, anywhere a small child might hide from an angry, violent man. She liked to wrap herself up in a blanket, to feel comfort, I suppose.

But when I approached the bathroom, a growing dread began to fill me.

The door squeaked on its hinge and then stopped as it banged softly on the radiator behind it. The house was silent except for a rhythmic drip, drip, drip that seemed to grow louder and fill my skull. I remember looking down at my feet as I slowly placed one in front of the other on the black and white tiles. I had to force my eyes to travel up the bath panel, over the rim.

Elise's tiny body lay suspended in the water, her pale, flaw-less skin whiter than ever, her blue eyes open. The surface was smooth like glass. Her hair floated outwards like rays of light from the sun.

At first, I didn't understand what I was seeing.

I said, Elise! Elise stop messing! Get up now! You can't hold your breath like that for much longer. But when she didn't respond, I climbed into the bath with her. I remember the splashing and struggling as I tried to grasp hold of her, so difficult as the water made her slippy and she was heavier than I realised.

I wasn't strong enough to pull you out of the water, Elise, even though you were so small. Instead, I climbed into the bath with you and held your little body until the water was freezing. One last embrace before they took you from me for ever.

I tried, Elise, I tried to come with you that day, but somehow I couldn't stay beneath the surface.

My mother woke eventually.

The look in her eyes when she realised you were dead . . .

She blamed me.

She thought that I had drowned my own sister, my own beloved Elise.

But it was only because she couldn't bear to recognise the truth.

But I wasn't a killer.

Not back then.

He wasn't even in the house the day that Elise died. But he caused it.

He made my mother's life so bad that she put her own feel-ings above ours and zoned out. She never hurt us, but she left us. Maybe not physically, but she was absent. She wasn't there when it mattered.

A good girl should have her mother's heart, have all the love that a mother can give. A child should be loved, shouldn't they?

A mother's hands should be used for the good. For protecting a child, holding them, brushing their hair, picking them up when they fall, lifting them from the bath, wrapping a big towel around them and hugging them. That's what a mother's hands should do.

I am going to give Isabel the box now.

It is time she took it to Elise.

Chapter Thirty-Six

WEDNESDAY 7 FEBRUARY

9.45 p.m.

Kyra burst into Tom's office. He was studying his screen and rolled his eyes when he saw her. She didn't care. Her priority was Isabel.

She had convinced Jimmy that she was fine by the time they had arrived at her apartment block, and even gone inside and waited until he had driven away. But then she had got back into her car and driven straight to the station.

'Tom, I've got information,' Kyra began, excited and breathless.

He didn't move for a moment. His hair was ruffled and he had a five o'clock shadow. When had he last slept? He got up slowly and closed the door behind her.

'I think I know . . .' she began.

'Kyra, sit down,' he ordered. She did as she was told. There was no time to argue.

'You look exhausted.' He perched on the edge of his desk in front of her. She put her hand to her hair self-consciously. 'You should go home and get some rest.'

'We're getting too close to the deadline – if he hasn't killed her already.' She checked her Commswatch. 'It isn't ten o'clock yet. There's still two hours . . .'

He blew out a lungful of air.

'Listen to me,' she stood up and he leaned back away from her slightly. 'I think the murderer . . . he's killing women he perceives to be good girls, but also, he's killing mothers.'

What was his expression? Sadness? Pity?

'Most of the victims didn't have children.' He moved back behind his desk and slumped into his chair.

'No, I mean the first set of victims. Type A. The unknown woman, Madelyn, Amelia, Caylee . . . Emma.'

Tiredness washed over his face. 'Madelyn Cooper didn't have any children.' His voice was flat. Had he given up already?

Kyra placed two hands flat on his desk and leaned over towards him. 'Her mother told us back at the time that Madelyn had had a child when she was young and given it up for adoption at six weeks' old. Madelyn had a serious addiction and didn't feel as though she could parent a child. Her mother said in hindsight she was devastated that she hadn't adopted the baby herself because she had nothing left of her daughter once she was dead. It's on the files.'

'Kyra, this is desperation talking. What about the first victim, the unknown one?' Why wasn't he looking at her?

'The post mortem report says she showed signs of having given birth. We don't know what happened to that child. Caylee Carmichael had a young son, Riley.'

'So what? they're all mothers . . .' Tom said, hands out in front of him. 'Plenty of the female adult population of their age are likely to be mothers . . .'

'Why are you being like this? Why aren't you listening to me?'

'Look,' he snapped, leaning forwards over his desk pointing a finger towards her, 'I am in the middle of an investigation. I don't need you coming in and . . .' He stopped, his expression now confused, or irritated, she couldn't decide. 'Anyway, where the hell are you getting all this information from?'

'After the transference with Ray Clarke . . . it led me to another witness, Rosetta Maguire . . .' She remembered her promise. 'But, Tom, you can't use her name. She'll have to be a witness X. We need to keep her identity—'

'Jesus Christ, Kyra! You're not a police officer! It's not your job to solve crimes! Have you not had enough side effects to tell you that enough is enough! What are you doing to yourself?'

'Alex came with me . . . to see Rosetta. She's a police officer.'

'What?' He remained still for a moment and she wondered if he'd heard what she had said. But then he spoke into his Commset. 'Alex, get up here now.'

'I've got to get to the truth, Tom!'

'And you call this the truth? You think rummaging around in someone's brain for memories – which might, or might not, be real – is going to help to find out the truth?' He was shouting at her now. 'Let me tell you, Kyra, no one person holds the truth! We all see things differently, from our own perspective, for our own ends. We convince ourselves of what we see to back up what we believe. Even if this technology that you designed worked, we could never trust it! Even if we could access people's memories accurately, how do I know that the brain hasn't misinterpreted it? How do I know that you're not just telling me what you want to tell me, what you want to see? There is no objective truth, Kyra!' He collapsed back into his seat. 'I'm sorry I ever called you – I feel responsible that you're in the state you're in now—'

'This tech works, Tom! Rosetta doesn't want to be identified. Promise me you'll keep her identity secret.'

'This is bullshit, Kyra!'

Her Commswatch beeped.

Please, love, will you try Molly again? Have a look for her. I'm really worried now.'

Kyra felt a rush of anxiety for her niece, but she had two hours left to try to save Isabel. After that, she would find Molly and try to make things right, once she had a chance to rid her system of all the alien thoughts and feelings that were invading her from the transferences.

Alex appeared, pink in the face, and Tom stood up and squared up to her.

'What the hell do you think you're doing? Going behind my back? Taking orders from someone else?' Alex looked like a child being told off by the headteacher, hands joined together, head down. 'Going to some woman's house without my say-so? I told you yesterday you were in trouble. What the hell is the DCI going to say?'

Alex turned to Kyra, furious, 'Are you trying to ruin my career? You said to keep this to ourselves, and now you're telling my boss?'

'The pair of you should have told me if there was another witness,' Tom snapped.

'You invited me into this, Tom,' Kyra retaliated. 'You asked me, remember! If you feel guilty because you missed a crucial witness . . .'

'Don't try to . . .' but he stopped. Her comment had hit home.

'How many women could we have saved if someone had taken Rosetta seriously fifteen years ago?'

'And this Maguire woman?' Tom barked at Alex. 'Did she seem like a viable witness?'

Kyra held her breath. Was he going to take the lead and run with it? Was he going to interview Rosetta and use all the information that she had to catch him? Would they be able to find Isabel in time?

'She had absolutely no idea what Kyra was talking about.' Alex shot her a glance.

'No, but her husband was there, she didn't want to speak.' Kyra told Tom, desperately. 'She doesn't want anyone to know that she was there. I told you, she contacted me today and told me the whole story.'

'I don't want to hear any more!' Tom sat back in his seat.

'If he sticks to the pattern then tonight is the night she dies!' Kyra said. 'You've got nothing! Nothing besides what I'm telling you!'

'Yes, we have.' He spoke calmly now. 'We're investigating a man called Martin Coombes, who worked as an apprentice for Lomax back in the early noughties. The DCI is on to the fact that you might be related to one of the victims and there's no money left now in the pot for your fee . . .' He paused. 'We don't need you anymore.'

Don't need you anymore . . .

'I don't care about the money! We need to find Isabel and now!' Kyra cried. 'We've got until midnight and then it will be too late! He'll kill her!'

'We all want to find Isabel!' Tom bellowed. 'You can't destroy yourself in the process! Get her out of my office,' he commanded Alex, and then, 'Kyra, you need to go home and have a rest or I'm going to call an ambulance for you and get them to deal with you.' He spoke firmly, pointing at her. 'I got you involved and I'm sorry. I really am. I didn't realise it would have such an effect on you. But you have to leave it to us now.'

'But, Tom, I—'

'Or I can arrest you! Get her out!' Tom told Alex. His eyes were fixed firmly back on his screen.

Exhausted, Kyra let herself be led.

When they got to the main entrance, Alex paused.

'You don't look well. Please don't cause any more fuss. Go home.'

Another message came through on Kyra's Commset.

I'm worried sick. Please call me as soon as you can.

Kyra groaned. There was nothing she could do to help Isabel now. She needed to focus on her family. She turned to Alex. 'Please, do one last thing for me? My mum has messaged to say Molly's run off again . . . please, trace her phone . . .'

Alex locked eyes with her for a moment.

'I promise, if you do this for me I won't call you again.'

There was a pause, and then Alex said, 'I thought we had an understanding. I helped you, but you showed me up in front of the boss. I can't trust you, Kyra.' She looked down at Kyra's Commswatch. 'I'll do it for your mum, not you. But after this, I don't want to hear from you again.' She turned and went back into the station.

Kyra waited, agitated, in the main entrance, on the other side of the security door.

After ten minutes, Alex returned.

'I've found her phone. It's on Byrom Street.'

That was where the lab was. What was Molly doing there? Had she gone to see if Kyra was working late? She didn't know she had lost her job, so it was possible.

Kyra ran to her car after mumbling a thanks to Alex. Moments later, she was driving towards the lab, hoping Molly would still be there where she arrived. She would give her a good talking to on the way back home.

A group of armed police officers were rounding up the Lè addicts and the street supervisors were scrubbing up the refuse of the day as she turned off the main road and onto Byrom Street. Screeching to a halt outside the lab, Kyra felt herself gearing up to a confrontation with Molly.

But there was no one to be seen.

She got out of the car and checked the door to CarterTech, but it was locked. Graffiti on the walls opposite took on strange forms and shapes in the shadows and a creeping dread filled her.

'Call Molly.' Her Commset immediately lit up.

There was a brief moment of silence and out of the corner of her eye a small light appeared, partially hidden by a rubbish bag, a couple of metres away from where she was standing. A split second later came the buzz and ringing. She moved the bag out of the way with her boot and looked down to the bright screen displaying the word KY.

Her mouth dried up.

Molly had been here. Oh God, I told her I was going to do an experiment to find out who killed her mum! I led her here . . .

Her fingers fumbled as she scrabbled to pick it up, and her eyes caught a silver glint beneath it. Kyra knew immediately what it was.

A Mizpah.

The killer had taken Molly!

Hadn't she seen someone in the street by the lab, watching her? But how had he known where she worked? How had he found Molly?

'Call Alex.'

Alex answered after what seemed like ages, 'What, Kyra?' she said, her voice flat. 'You weren't going to call—'

'Please, Alex, he's got Molly.'

'What?' her reply was muffled. Kyra could hear the sound of Alex starting her car. 'I don't want to talk to you. You've got me into enough shit.'

Kyra's throat was closing up. Her lungs were suddenly restricted, her voice small, she whispered, 'The Mizpah Murderer. He's got my niece.'

In Kyra's eyeline Madelyn Cooper, wrapped in eco-plastic,

a black wound where her heart should have been, stood against the graffitied wall, her snake tattoo uncoiling, slithering from her thigh, up her torso and through the hole in her chest. It squirmed out of her back across the bricks and blended in with the sprayed artwork.

Had Alex even heard what she had said?

'He's taken Molly. I found her Commset, with a Mizpah pendant.'

She reached out to her car door, the lock automatically reacting to her. She sat in the driver's seat, light-headed, chest heaving.

'She's only run off again,' said Alex, sounding bored. 'You said yourself – she often goes off on her own. Go and have a sleep, Kyra. You're losing it.'

She could hear Alex make a muffled comment to someone else, and the sound of her engine.

'Please, Alex . . .'

'Look, Kyra, we've got to get Coombes, he's the most likely suspect. The armed response team are already there. We're on our way now, so I've got more important things to worry about.' There was brief pause. 'Molly will come home when she's ready.'

The call was disconnected.

Kyra started the engine and took the car to the junction, trying to decide whether to turn left or right. What was she to do? Where was she to go? Was there no one who would help her now? How was she going to find Molly? She rolled the car out slowly but slammed on the brakes as an ambulance appeared from along the main road, lights but no sirens, and came towards the car at speed. As he drove past her, the peri-med glanced in her direction.

It was then that Kyra remembered where she had seen the killer's face before.

Chapter Thirty-Seven

10.35 p.m.

ISABEL

Candles, there are so many candles, gentle lights flickering on the ceiling which seem to stretch high, reaching up, up, up. That's where she can see them, their wings wide and welcoming – the wings that will soon curl around her and lift her up. She wonders if it is an angel carrying her now, but then she sees his eyes and remembers.

She hears a sound like feathers fluttering, a rhythmic, swishing sound. Maybe she is already leaving her body, travelling through time and space, no longer held back by anything – no longer bound by the fear of what he will do to her, or the attachment she once felt to the world.

She can hear the angels singing, or maybe it is water flowing. For a fleeting moment, she thinks of her mother – she can feel her presence, somewhere in the world, as though they are connected, even though her mother is long gone. The hidden is becoming visible to her, her mind going beyond the physical.

'We're coming to the end now,' he tells her gently. 'You mustn't worry, everything is in place, everything will be peaceful. The pure and innocent should not suffer. It will be painless, beautiful.'

And something in his voice convinces her that it will be beautiful.

It made sense now, what Rosetta had said.

Rosetta – witness X – the whole key to unlocking this case.

When Rosetta had told her that an ambulance had come for Jenny's body, for a moment, Kyra had teetered on the edge of disbelief. But it had been precisely the fact that her gut instinct told her loud and clear that Rosetta was truthful, that forced Kyra to find an explanation.

The ambulance was driving away, Rosetta had said.

The T-shirt with two snakes and a winged staff she had seen in Lomax's memory; the access to medical opiates and a sternal saw; a peri-med pulling over to let her car into the eco-recycling centre fifteen years before.

She was sure of it now, the killer was a peri-med.

It was how he had chosen his victims: the burn on Riley's arm – Chloe had said his mother had had it checked over – and Rosetta said a peri-med was called when her daughter was found unresponsive in her cot. Did he think these mothers didn't take enough care of their children, like his own mother, maybe? Was that why he was punishing them?

Even the second set of victims, the B Type 'good girls' – Jessica Smith, a school teacher, ambulances sometimes went to school when children hurt themselves or got sick, didn't they? Jennifer Bosanquet – a church youth worker – she'd be out visiting the people in her parish who were ill. Perhaps she had encountered him there. Amelia Brigham – a social worker – they dealt with peri-meds regularly, she was certain.

But, more importantly, he had the ideal form of transport. Kyra imagined him bringing Madelyn's body with him in the ambulance, after brutally killing her elsewhere. He must have driven to the eco-recycling centre, placed her body at the foot of the slagheap of plastic and then *called it in himself.*

She knew from experience that, more often than not, ambulances arrived at the crime scene before the police got there. He could have called 999 for all of his kills and when the control room radioed, guess who would be nearby?

A ghost, Will had said.

She imagined him sitting in the vehicle, watching the unfolding drama of his own creation.

Best seat in the house.

It was the perfect method. Hiding in plain sight – someone who the victims would trust, someone who could transport bodies, someone the police wouldn't suspect – one of their emergency service brethren who had access to different vehicles, who had medical knowledge to drug his victims, who could get his hands on a sternal saw at the hospital.

The more she thought about it, the more it made sense to her.

'Dial Alex,' she told her Commset and moments later she answered.

'Alex, it's me.'

'Christ, Kyra! I'm in the middle of a crime scene,' she said as soon as she picked up. 'Have you not got the message . . .'

'Tell me one thing . . . Is Martin Coombes a peri-med?'

'What?' Kyra could hear people talking on the other end of the line.

'Martin Coombes – is he a peri-med? I think our killer drives an ambulance . . .'

But Alex cut her off. 'Martin Coombes is dead. CSIs did a forensic light source, a blue-light, and there's blood all over the place. Coombes is wrapped in plastic in the fucking loft, so I'm a bit too busy for your bull—'

'So why don't you listen to me? I've got a new lead. The killer – he's a peri-med. He drives an ambulance. I think his first name is—'

'Kyra, I'm really not interested. You told Tom I went with you to see Rosetta when you promised you wouldn't! It's your fault I'm on a warning. I'll never get a bloody promotion now.'

'Listen to me!'

'No! We've got a few hours to save Isabel, and I've got another dead body on my hands. Let us get on with it. Bye, Kyra.'

'But he's got Molly!' Kyra begged. 'We've got to get to him before—'

'Tom's right about you. You're fucking mental.'

Kyra opened her mouth to speak, but Alex had already cut the call.

There was a split second when it could have gone either way, when everything that had happened seemed to rush at her all at once and she might have been crushed under the weight of it. She might have crumbled in despair, fallen down a black hole of grief and helplessness, abandoned hope for a safe return for Molly and Isabel, given up.

But then she thought of her niece, her golden eyes, her gorgeous smile, her mother's spirit still alive in her, of the promises she had made to Emma in the Necroplex to look after Molly.

There was another way.

She scrabbled for Tom's police mini-screen that was still in her glove compartment and flicked it on, more determined than ever to show them that her tech worked, more determined than ever to get justice for Emma, but more importantly now to find Molly.

Less than three minutes later, she had located the statement of the first officer attending the crime scene at the eco-recycling centre in 2020. She scrolled through, looking for the name of the person who had called in Madelyn Cooper's body. UNKNOWN.

Then she looked for first response details.

She knew these reports didn't always have the name of the attending peri-med.

But, in this case, it did.

Stephen Fennig.

Stephen.

He had told Rosetta his real name because he hadn't expected her to live and tell anyone.

He would have given his real name in the police report because *he didn't think he would be caught.*

She commanded her Commset to call April Butler, the Human Resources manager at the hospital, deliberately using her vidscreen. She had been with Tom when they had gone to find Andrew Harper's information just days ago. The Human Resources officer would recognise her face, assume she was a police officer. Tom hadn't told her any differently. Kyra would ask for the details of Stephen Fennig, just as they had done with Andrew Harper. It was late, but April Butler answered.

Minutes later, Kyra had all the information that she needed.

Tom did not have faith in her tech. Alex doubted her sanity. Jimmy thought she was weak and couldn't handle the side effects.

But she knew where Stephen Fennig was.
She would save Molly, whatever it took.
She would get justice for Emma.
She would find Isabel.
She would show Alex, Jimmy and Tom.
She would show them all.

ISABEL

He lays her down carefully. The cold shocks her back into feeling her body, the surface hard and smooth beneath her. For a moment, she is alone with the lights, the angels, the voices. It is the most peaceful she had felt for a long time.

When he reappears he is carrying a red metallic gift box with a golden bow. It shines in the candlelight and makes her think of Christmas. She wishes he would go away. She wants to be alone, just her and the angels, but the second he speaks, the angels begin disappearing like bubbles popping.

As a child she read about near-death experiences; how there was a tunnel, a beautiful light at the end. She wants to fly away, be free from all pain, from Andrew, from time itself, time that her grandmother had given her, marked out in the silver casing of a fob watch. She giggles. It seems so pointless now, a watch! Why count the time when she can be free from it altogether?

'This is what you must do. Give these to Elise. Tell her I love her. Tell her I will be there, one day. Look after her for me.'

'Where is she?' asks Isabel. Her voice sounds soft, slow. It is a buzz inside her own skull.

'In the water, of course. You'll be with her soon.'

'What is this?' she asks sleepily as he places the box on her chest. She takes it awkwardly, the contents slide heavily inside. 'Open it and see.'

She thinks she might be smiling, like a child on her birthday, as she pulls the golden ribbon, feeling its silky softness until it pops open. Her arms are weak and heavy, her fingers fumble with the lid until she manages to remove it and drop it to one side.

From her prone position, she can't see what is in the box and so she tips it towards her face.

At first, her muddled brain can't recognise what she is seeing, can't make sense of it, possibly some kind of huge red spider with a grotesque viscous body? Her eyes narrow, trying to decipher it, but then, not able to hold the box steady, the bony, slimy mass slips onto her neck, the spider's legs wrap around her throat.

She tries to shrug it off, reaching up to pull it away, but her fingers are numb, and she struggles to grasp it. When she manages to take hold, it comes away in pieces, the bloody mass slipping back on to her body, the spider's legs in her hands. She inspects them, trying to focus – the spider's legs have silver rings and fingernails, painted black.

'Ah, ah, ah,' the sound coming from her lips.

'A mother's hands should be used for good,' he says, crouching down next to her, smiling, his eyes bright, as though she now understands. She lies trembling, the pair of severed hands grasping at her neck and shoulders. He removes the box and places the heart gently on her chest. Underneath it, her own heart beats furiously, pulsating through her ribcage, making the bloody mound appear to beat in time with her own.

'Give this to my sister,' he says smiling. 'A good girl deserves her mother's heart.'

And then the water comes.

325

Chapter Thirty-Eight

WEDNESDAY 7 FEBRUARY

11.17 p.m.

Kyra drove fast along the rain-washed city streets, shadows and images taunting her at the periphery of her vision. A homeless man shuffled along with his horde of plastic bags. He was real, surely? Or was it a memory she had picked up from Ray? As she moved through the tall grey buildings, travelling alongside her was an army jeep covered in desert camouflage; the driver saluted her. She quickly focused on the road ahead, ignoring the phantom, gripping the steering wheel tightly. She couldn't lose it now, not when she was so close to finding Isabel. She swerved to avoid two little children who stepped off the pavement and into the path of her car. She could see their small, pale faces staring after her in the rear-view mirror as she drove on.

'They're not real,' she said, out loud. 'I'm going to find Isabel. I am going to find her.'

She checked her mirror to see if the children were still there and was met by the gruesome sight of Emma, battered and bloodied, sitting on the back seat peering back at her, her white face marked with the striations of removed duct tape like sand ripples on a beach.

Kyra jolted the steering wheel in shock and the car mounted the pavement, juddering with the impact. She righted the vehicle, her heart fluttering in her chest. Her eyes flicked to the mirror again.

Emma was gone.

Releasing the pressure on the accelerator slightly, she focused on the road. It had taken less than three minutes to find his name, *when you know, you know,* her dad used to say, then literally seconds on the mini-screen for the directions for the address that April from the hospital had given her. Immediately, an estate agency website had come up, showing photos from some years back, a tumbledown house and a garage on a few acres of land out in the suburbs. For some reason it had been almost immediately taken off the market again. Kyra told her Commset to guide her and, within minutes, she was heading to Dreyton Lane. Stephen's home.

I'm coming for you, Mols. I'll be there as soon as I can.

Soon, this would all be over. She would no longer be host to all these memories that were haunting her, tormenting her. The dark, shadowy figures of memories that were not her own, constantly distracting her now, would disappear for ever. It was this case, driving her mad, pushing her to her limits. But she was going to solve the case and defeat them for good.

Most importantly, she would have Molly back. And she would have justice for her sister. Then she would get on with her life, take her mum and Molly on holiday, have a break before finding a new job, one where she wasn't beholden to some ignorant businessman and his money.

She drove further out to the suburbs, away from the city lights, and out into darker, tree-lined roads which gave way to lanes with hedges running down both sides. A fine rain began and her windscreen wipers swiped intermittently.

'You have reached Dreyton Lane,' her Commset stated, startling her. She pulled up to the side of the road but couldn't see any buildings beyond the greenery. Her breath caught in her throat, and she cowered when she saw a figure behind her car. It was a soldier, standing to attention, his eyes locked straight ahead of him, gun slung across his body. She swore, angry with herself for being so timid – how could she face the killer if she was frightened by these projections of her own brain?

Overgrown bushes concealed whatever lay behind. One or two ancient lampposts emitted a weak light. She drove to the end of the lane, and then turned the car around and drove back, slower this time, window down, leaning forward in her seat, hoping that Linden House was still there, that it hadn't been demolished, the bricks and wood re-purposed.

Just as her frustration was becoming intolerable, a white figure appeared amidst the hedges, giving off a spectral glow which lit the greenery around her like a religious grotto. She took her foot off the accelerator in shock and the car rolled slowly forward towards the apparition.

It was Skylar Lowndry.

Kyra switched the engine off, got out of the car and slammed the door hard, but Skylar remained, motionless, eyes shut, white dress dripping with water, the form of her body visible beneath the wet material, her porcelain face a death mask.

Kyra moved closer to her. From this position, she could see a wrought-iron gate, covered by leaves. Was Skylar guiding her towards Isabel? She steeled herself, her hand trembling as she reached out to open it, centimetres from the ghostly woman, trying to reassure herself that it was all in her mind.

Skylar's eyes flicked open, her eyes ice blue, lashes encrusted with tiny ice crystals. Kyra jumped back in fright, and the glowing figure disappeared, only to reappear on the other side of the wrought iron. All Kyra's instincts were telling her to get back in her car and drive away, but Molly was close, she was sure of it. And it gave her the courage to go on, to force the stiff, rusted latch and push the gate – which would only open enough for her to slide in.

The moment she was through, Skylar disappeared and it was dark again.

Once on the other side, breathless with fear and anticipation, Kyra peered around in the gloom. She flicked on her Commset light. The driveway was a patchwork of bricks set unevenly into the earth, greasy underfoot with the misty rain. It was a mechanics yard, littered with carcasses of old motors and dismantled engines. A driveway stretched out in front of her to a set of double gates on the far side. There was a large workshop with wide doors that were open, showing space for three cars. She could imagine it back in the day, the purr of engines, the mechanics dark with oil, the banter. But now it was dark and silent, the only car a rusted old red Ford Focus, a dent in the bonnet.

Molly, where are you?

Skylar appeared again, standing at bushes at the far end of the yard.

Kyra made her way over, feeling less afraid of the apparition now. The moment she moved, Skylar disappeared. Kyra scrambled through the bushes, and there, on the other side of the overgrown foliage, was a house in total darkness, except for Skylar, who appeared as a glowing form at the front door.

Molly would be locked in a room here, afraid but unharmed. Kyra had to believe that so that she could keep going. She moved towards the house. What the hell was she going to see in there?

If I call Alex, will she come?

She remembered Alex's last words to her.

Mental.

She was on her own.

The front door was shut fast and so she made her way around the building – every window was pitch black. She reached the back of the house. The only lights she could see were the intermittent flashes from her own migraine. She reached the back door, listening for any signs of life. Not a single sound in the thick darkness.

The door gave way beneath her fingers. Did he know she was coming? Was he waiting for her in the silence? She stood back, bracing herself, as though she expected someone to come flying out of the darkness at her, but there was no movement, so she stepped into the house.

She was standing in a kitchen. She noticed a shuffling in the corner of her eye and she saw two little faces peeping out from under the table, a boy and a girl. She ignored them, and continued her search, her eyes skittering over the draining board – a single plate, one cup. A peri-med uniform hung on a coat-hanger on a cupboard door, an iron nearby, unplugged, cold. There was a single chair by the table. A few clean plates stood on the drainer by the sink and the tap was dripping; the water was still connected. There was an old-style gas hob cooker on which sat a small pan containing congealed beans. The light from the fridge dazzled her when she opened the door. There was a half-pint of milk, some cheese, children's yoghurts . . . still in date.

Someone had been here recently.

What if they were still here?

Come on, Kyra, pull yourself together. You can do this.

She moved through the kitchen into the hallway, and stood in the hall listening, her desperation to find Molly and Isabel rising and swelling along with her fear.

Maybe he's not here. He might have gone out, maybe I can find Molly and Isabel and get them somewhere safe. He's Tom's problem. If I can find them before he comes back . . .

The front room was sparse, containing only a sofa, a screen, a small table. There was an empty set of shelves gathering dust. The hairs on the back of her neck stood up as she heard a thud in the hall. She switched off her Commset light and stood in the darkness, listening.

Something was in the house with her.

Being unfamiliar with the layout, she was uncertain of her escape route. Even with the added flood of adrenaline, she didn't feel confident of her flight ability. Her legs already felt like jelly.

She heard a muffled sound. Was that someone crying? Was it Isabel, hurt and trapped somewhere? Where was Molly?

Molly's going to be fine. She doesn't fit the pattern . . . she's too tall . . . she's not a . . . nurse . . . or . . . She's going to be fine. Fine.

She just hoped she was in time for Isabel.

She crept back into the hallway and stood still for a few moments, listening, terrified.

The sound was coming from a cupboard in the hall.

She took a deep breath and flung the door open.

A large grey cat flew out of the cupboard, startling her. He looked her over, his yellow eyes glinting in the shadows, and then strolled away. She bent over, somewhat relieved, and when she stood up she noticed there was another door inside the cupboard.

The round knob rattled but the door didn't give. She felt along the top of the frame and her fingers hit a key which unlocked the door easily with a loud click. Kyra opened the door and shone her light down the steps, into a cellar, but she could only see as far as a brick wall at the bottom. She took a breath as though she was about to dive into a deep, dark pool.

Emma, please, please help me. Help me find Isabel. Help me get the bastard who took you away from us. Help me find Molly.

Chapter Thirty-Nine

WEDNESDAY 7 FEBRUARY

11.47 p.m.

Her fingertips hit the rough brick wall at the bottom and she went to her right, moving her feet out in front of her in circular motions, blindly feeling for the floor, her Commswatch throwing out a small beam of light which trembled. The cellar stretched out into darkness. In front of her she could see a red generator, and a pair of long metal drawers – long enough to hold a body.

She moved towards them, her heart pounding. Was Isabel already dead? Was she too late? A sudden scaring pain ripped through her as her hip caught a sharp corner, and there was an almighty metallic crash. She froze, the sound still ringing in her ears.

She waited, tense and alert in the darkness for an attack; blinding lights, explosive gunshot.

Nothing.

Looking down, she gasped in terror at the sight of a metal trolley lying on its side, and, in the pool of light at her feet, lay the shards and serrations of an assortment of metal surgical equipment: scalpels, clamps, bone-cutters and levers, forceps, cannulae, curettes. She retched twice and stood for a moment, trying to regain use of her body.

She moved towards the metal drawers again and stopped dead when she saw, on another metal trolley, a turquoise gift box, glittering in the light of her Commset, a lime green ribbon next to it.

Her guts cramped, cold and tight.

The lid lay at an angle across the top, leaving the box half open.

Kyra took a step closer, flinching as she poked the lid away, and quickly moved back as though the contents might jump out at her.

Slowly, she leaned over, at a distance, and shone her light in.

It was empty.

Was there still time?

Breathing heavily, she focused on the drawers.

Stretching her hand out, she pulled the handle of the bottom drawer, bracing herself. There was a metallic 'clunk' as it released and slid out easily.

The tray was empty, reflecting her light in a dull haze on the brushed steel.

Kyra dropped her hands to her sides and took a few deep breaths.

She reached for the handle of the top drawer and tugged, but it resisted.

Her heart sank.

I'm too late! Isabel, I'm so sorry.

She slid the drawer out and, on the tray, covered in a white cotton smock, lay a slim body, the face covered with a white pillowcase.

Tom had been right – she had messed up her career, risked her health and broken her relationships and for what? All of it had been for nothing.

Slowly, she peeled back the pillowcase.

For a moment, she couldn't make sense of what she was seeing.

It wasn't Isabel.

It wasn't Isabel at all.

Kyra gazed in horror at the face of her niece, Molly.

She reached out to touch her but stopped before she made contact.

It was only a phantom. She was so overwrought of late, upset with the way things had been going with Molly. This was only her brain's way of expressing her anxiety.

Wasn't it?

Kyra looked closer – the pale skin of her face surrounded by her dark hair, her eyes closed as if she was sleeping. Kyra was immediately thrown back to the moment at the mortuary when she had had to identify Emma's body, holding on to her dad's arm, willing it not to be Emma, but knowing it was.

She was taken back to when she would stroke Molly hair, Emma's hair, as they settled down to sleep, comforting them as they drifted off.

Her hand trembled as she reached out to touch the dark curls, hoping the awful vision in front of her would disappear.

But it didn't. She could feel the soft curls underneath her fingertips telling her something she didn't want to know, the worst possible thing . . .

. . . this was not a phantom.

She let out a howl, her legs collapsing under her, and she slumped to the floor, feeling as though her heart had been ripped from her body. She had not been there for her sister when she had died, and now Molly, too, had died alone.

He had taken them both from her.

She could hardly breathe with grief and guilt.

She had led the killer to her precious Molly.

How could she tell her mother this?

She stood up and took hold of the sheet, needing to know, but dreading finding out.

Had he taken her hands? Was that what the box was for?

She wanted to tell her how sorry she was, how she should have cared for her better, how if she was still alive, she would do things differently, she would listen more, be more loving . . . she pulled the sheet back.

Molly still had her hands, crossed over her chest, as though ready for burial.

Kyra broke down, huge sobs racking her chest, tears flowing, dripping onto shroud over her niece's body.

She took hold of Molly's hand . . .

. . . it was warm.

Hope and desperation flooded her veins as she put her ear to Molly's chest.

A heartbeat.

Slow but steady.

'Molly! Molly!' she cried, kissing her soft skin, her tears falling on to her niece's cheeks. 'Oh, thank God!'

Kyra shook her niece by the shoulders. Molly's eyes flickered.

'Mols, come on, it's me, its Ky!'

What had he done to her? Nearby she saw syringes in a kidney dish.

'Mols,' she tried again, shaking her.

Her niece moaned, opened her eyes a little and then shut them again.

How could she get Molly out of that awful cellar? There was a small window, high up on the wall, but there was no way she could get Molly to that, never mind push her through it. Could she manage to carry her up the stairs? But there was no way she could run with Molly in her arms.

If he came back . . . and then what about Isabel? She still didn't know if Isabel was still alive.

She looked down at her Commswatch: 11.53 p.m.

If Isabel was still alive somewhere in this house, then Kyra had less than ten minutes to get to her.

She didn't care what Tom thought of her now. She had to call him. For Molly's sake.

There was no reply.

'Call Alex.'

Alex wasn't answering either.

Mental.

She left a message. 'Alex, please, you have to help me. I'm at Dreyton Lane, there's an old garage. There's a house – it's hidden, behind the bushes, hard to see. Molly's here. He's drugged her. Please come now!'

She stood for a moment and then dialled 999 and begged for the police and the Peri-Med services to come and help.

The moment the light from her Commswatch call faded she panicked. What if Alex didn't get her message or, worse still, didn't believe her? What if the police and the ambulance couldn't find them? Had she told them they were in the house behind the garage? She couldn't remember now. How long would they take to get there?

And what about Isabel? Was she still here? She wasn't in the other drawer – did that mean she was still alive?

She looked to her Commswatch again.

Five minutes until midnight.

Kyra's eyes travelled back to Molly again. She was out of it and would probably be like that for some time. She could stay here and wait . . . or she could go and look for Isabel. She had sacrificed so much already to get here. She couldn't stop now.

All her instincts went against what she was about to do.

'Mols, baby, I am so sorry but I promise, *I promise*, I'll come back very soon.'

She stroked her hair and watched her sleeping for a moment. An image of three-year-old Molly standing at the side of the road came into her mind.

Kyra slowly pushed the mortuary drawer half-closed again, her heart breaking.

Moving towards the door, her foot kicked metallic objects. She bent down and felt along the dusty floor until her hand hit metal. She picked it up and pointed her Commset to see – it was a scalpel, the blade sharp and shiny in the light. She curled her fingers around it, stood up and took a deep breath.

Her footsteps slow and steady, she made her way back up the stairs to the main hall, shining her light into the dark rooms and peering in as she passed, the overwhelming smell of dust and damp filling her nose.

Standing at the bottom of the stairs, her hand on the newel post, she blinked up into the dark void above.

She was going to find Isabel.

Chapter Forty

WEDNESDAY 7 FEBRUARY 2035

11.58 p.m.

The creaking of the stairs as she climbed to the top floor was echoed by the unfamiliar bird cries in the darkness outside. There was no decoration, no photos, no mirrors, just empty frames hanging on the walls. Kyra shone her light up at the ceiling. There was a loft hatch, but it had been nailed shut, ancient paint sealing the wood. No one had been up there for a long time.

The main bedroom was simple, like a monk's cell, with muted, neutral colours, a single bed, a small wardrobe and a tall set of drawers. The only decoration was an old framed photograph of a boy and a girl, the same blue-grey eyes and mousey hair, his arm around her. It was the two children she had seen under the bed. She checked under the bed and, whilst she was down there, tapped around the floorboards, looking for any place where Isabel might be hidden.

Midnight would bring Isabel's death. She might be dead already.

The second bedroom was empty, with an ancient thin cord carpet, and a simple rolled-up blind. There was no bed in this room, only a wardrobe, the doors open, not even a single hanger inside.

The next room she came to, the key was in the lock – it twisted with ease and she pushed open the door, holding the scalpel out in front of her in her trembling hand.

The temperature rose noticeably when she entered. There was a single white bed with a duvet with a pink cotton cover and pretty floral curtains, a rocking chair, teddies . . . a night light still glowing.

What did it mean? Why was there one beautiful room in a house that hadn't been loved or cared for in years? She lifted the bedclothes, and the hairs on the back of her neck stood up. The floorboards creaked behind her. She swivelled around and saw, at the other end of the hall, a little girl, standing in front of a closed door. The same girl she had seen under her bed. How could she forget that face, the huge terrified eyes?

Kyra steeled herself.

The little girl stood in an eerie glow, the rest of the house silent and black. She lifted a hand and beckoned Kyra. Slowly, wondering how she was managing to put one foot in front of the other, she moved towards the girl. Was this phantom like Skylar, guiding her towards Isabel?

The child remained still and Kyra reached out a hand. Her fingers moved through the spectral vision which shimmered like disturbed water as she pushed the door open.

Inside was a bathroom. The soft glow of candlelight reflected off the glassy surface of the water in the bathtub, which was filled to the brim and surrounded by pink roses and candles, the wax dripping down the sides. There were more candles and roses on the basin and the window ledge. A red box floated on the water, glittering in the wavering light, the ribbon tied into a bow on top.

A row of chains hung from the rail which had once held a shower curtain. Suspended from each thread of silver was half a Mizpah pendant.

Four. One for each of the victims found in water.

One for Skylar, one for Jennifer, one for Amelia.

And one for Isabel.

Kyra moved closer to look, and from this angle, looking down, she saw that the box wasn't floating at all, but resting on something previously hidden beneath the refracted light bouncing off the surface.

Isabel.

Kyra dropped the scalpel, dumped the box on the floor and reached into the water. She put her hands underneath Isabel's armpits and managed to pull her up far enough to get her head out, but the angle at which she stood gave her no strength and Isabel slipped beneath the surface again. Kyra stepped into the shockingly cold water, feet either side of Isabel's slim body, pulled the plug and tried again to lift her, this time sitting Isabel up, her top half slumped forward. Kyra had no idea whether or not she was still alive.

She was struggling to hold Isabel's head above the water and the bath was draining too slowly. How long could she stand this cold? Nearby she saw three syringes, two of which were empty. Could Isabel still be alive? Was she drugged like Molly was? How long had she been in the water? If it hadn't been long, that meant that the killer could still be nearby.

Determined, she placed her hands underneath Isabel's armpits again and, with all her strength, she heaved. Her feet gave way on the smooth surface beneath her and she slipped, falling onto Isabel.

She pulled herself up again, soaked with freezing water.

'Isabel!' she yelled, 'Come on, wake up!' She struggled with her body, pulling and twisting until Isabel was hanging forward over the side of the bath, her hands touching the soaking wet bathroom floor. Kyra climbed out of the water, lifted Isabel's legs and swivelled them over the side of the bath. Isabel slumped to the floor like a newborn foal.

Panting heavily, Kyra pushed Isabel on to her back and listened for any signs of life.

Nothing.

'Come on, Isabel!' she shouted. She made a fist and banged on the girl's chest, which made a wet slapping noise. She began to shiver as the water on her body met the cold air.

Moving Isabel's head back, and pushing her chin down, Kyra breathed into her mouth five times and then started chest compressions. Her hands were so cold, she could hardly feel them as they pushed against Isabel's small ribcage.

She put her ear to Isabel's chest again.

No heartbeat.

Come on, Isabel! We can't let him win! Breathe, please, breathe!

She blew into Isabel's mouth again and gave another thirty chest compressions, continuing the cycle of breathing and pressing until she was sweating, even though her body was shaking with cold from being wet through. Finally, exhausted, she placed her ear to Isabel's chest and heard the faint *thump thump thump*.

Isabel started to cough up water. She was disoriented and moaning quietly, her arms flailing weakly when Kyra, wet and exhausted, leaned against the bath and pulled Isabel to her chest to hold her.

'You're okay. You're okay,' Kyra said over and over.

When she got her breath back, Kyra, still shivering violently through shock and cold, laid Isabel down gently and went to the bedroom for a blanket to keep her warm while they waited for the emergency services that she was sure would be there soon. The little night light had gone out and the room was creepy in the moonlight. She pulled out her Commset from her back pocket and tried to flick on the light but water had gotten into it and it was dead. Where was the ambulance? Why weren't they here by now? Had Alex got her message?

She grabbed the duvet and moved back towards the bathroom, stopping momentarily on the landing to see if she could hear anything. Now she had found Isabel, her concern was for Molly. What if the drugs had got the better of her and her heart had stopped? She would wrap Isabel up and then go down to check on Molly.

She hurried back to Isabel, whose teeth were chattering, her skin goose-fleshed. Her eyes were rolling and she was mumbling incoherently. Kyra bent over her and put the duvet around her, stroking her cheek as she said, 'Don't worry, I'm going to get you out of here as soon as I can.'

'I don't think so,' came a quiet, calm voice from behind her.

Startled, she fell backwards and looked up. The last time she had seen this face had been fifteen years ago at the eco-recycling centre as he had sat in the driver's seat of the ambulance.

'Stephen Fennig,' she exhaled.

His short brown hair was brushed neatly over to the right, clean-shaven, the hint of a cleft chin. His features were normal, except for a scar over one of his eyes which had turned his iris a cloudy pale blue, like an opal.

He looked serene and terrifying.

Isabel was pale and shivering, but still breathing. How could Kyra protect her now? Oh God, Molly downstairs, on her own! Was she still alive?

'What have you done to my niece?' She launched herself up towards him, but he had the advantage of being upright. There was a sudden forceful blow to her ribs, a cracking sound, as Stephen kicked her hard, winding her, and then he pulled her up by the hair and grabbed her in a chokehold.

She struggled against him for a moment, then brought her elbow backwards, digging into his ribs. He made an 'oof' sound and let go of her. She pulled away from him.

'I know all about you, Stephen!' she croaked, scrambling against the side of the bathtub. She needed answers, whatever was going to happen to her.

'What do you know?' he said quietly, standing upright now, his hands poised in front of him as though he was going to grab her again.

'Why did you become a peri-med, Stephen?' she asked, rubbing her throat, her ribs burning with pain. 'You weren't smart enough to be a doctor? Ah, the urban myth that serial killers are all geniuses. Is that what you think of yourself?'

He turned his face one way, then the other, all the time keeping his right eye locked on her.

'I became a paramedic to save people.' There was no hint of irony.

'No, you hide behind a façade of helping people. That's how you get your victims, isn't it?' Kyra asked, as she stood up and faced him. 'People who are in trouble, in pain, who need you. Do you like being needed, Stephen? If you like saving people, then why don't you save Isabel's life?'

He rolled his shoulders. 'Isabel has a job to do and she's going to do it,' he said with chilling calmness and control. 'No one's going to prevent that happening.'

'You're not the biggest guy in the world, Stephen,' she goaded, trying to catch her breath between the words. Could she wind him up, get him off balance? It was a risk, but the alternative was that he would kill them all, and soon. Could she keep him talking until help turned up? If he focused on her, then he might forget about Molly.

They're coming for us, aren't they?

'You always pick small women. Is that so you can over-come them easily?' When this didn't hit home, she added, 'Was your mother small, Stephen? I bet your dad could really get stuck into her.' She was guessing, but his expression changed.

He grabbed her and threw her up against the bathroom wall, hard, and roared at her, 'He's to blame! He might not have done it with his own hands, but he's to blame!' His face was ugly with anger.

She glanced at the floor, trying to locate the scalpel.

'But you're no better than him,' she provoked. 'You pick small women and overcome them, hurt them, degrade them. You learned a thing or two from your dad, eh?'

'It wasn't my dad!' Stephen screamed, pressing against her harder. 'It was my mother's boyfriend. David Lomax and I are nothing alike!' Stephen's face changed, as though the words had somehow burnt his mouth.

David Lomax!

'If I had my time over I would go back and kill the bastard!' He punched the wall behind her head and she trembled.

'Is that why you framed him, made it look like he did it?' she asked, trying to hide her fear. Could she keep him talking until help showed up?

Help's coming, isn't it?

Stephen straightened up, took a breath, as though he was trying to regain control of himself. 'He has to suffer for what he did to my family.'

'But you're making Isabel suffer too, and all those other women,' Kyra could hear herself begging.

He calmed down then and stood still for a moment before giving a sinister smile.

'I heard what you said to your sister, a long time ago, in the cafe. Another bad mother.' He shook his head at her and tutted. 'Your judgement, not mine.'

Kyra's heart jolted. How did he know about that? Had he been there, in the cafe, and then taken Emma? *Your judgement.* What had he meant by that?

'And yet, there is Molly, downstairs, young, beautiful, innocent,' he said, raising his eyebrows as he spoke.

Her stomach twisted into a knot.

'Don't you hurt her . . .' she began. *Jesus, please let her still be alive!*

He jumped forwards, grabbed her roughly by the neck and pushed her over to the bath and hissed into her ear. 'It's too late, for all of you.'

The bath hadn't drained, the plughole stoppered with melted wax.

He forced her face down into the ice-cold water.

She struggled against his strong grip, panic rising hot and quick. She tried to kick out with her legs but her feet kept slipping on the wet tiles. Her lungs were straining now with the need to inhale.

But his strong, determined hands held her steady. Weakened by pain and broken by the thought that she might have condemned her own sister by her words, Kyra already felt herself defeated. Her strength was gone.

A moment later, he pulled her up by the hair. As she started to regain her breath, he whispered, 'Don't worry, I know you love her. I'll make sure to give her your heart. I've got the box ready and waiting.'

And he pushed her head beneath the surface once more.

She flailed weakly against him, her arms wind-milling in desperation, the water in her ears making everything sound muted, other-worldly. As the lack of oxygen started to affect her brain, she panicked more, fighting as hard as she could, but it was pointless, he had won.

Then came a stillness in her mind where all the meaningless everyday tasks and events, the plans she had had once for her life, the worries of the future, the work and the pain disappeared, and all she could think about was those she loved, her mum, her dad, Emma, Molly.

She had failed them all.

The cold had crept throughout her body now, a darkness was settling in her mind.

She had tried. All the sacrifices, all the effort . . . it had come to nothing.

The cold became an aching pain in every part of her body.

She felt herself giving up, giving in to the darkness.

Letting go.

The hands around her neck released the pressure and then twitched. Stephen lurched forward, crushing her ribs against the side of the bath and then he let go.

Her survival instinct that seemed to have failed her moments before kicked in and she reared up out of the water.

She took time to get her breath back, desperately sucking in the air, wiping the water out of her eyes. She spun around, bracing herself.

Stephen was slumped to the floor.

Molly stood at the bathroom door holding a surgical hammer, her white gown and pale aspect making her appear spectral.

'Oh my God, Molly!' Kyra struggled up and went to move towards her.

Her niece was still drugged, but there was recognition in her eyes.

'Molly, we've got to get out of here . . .'

Kyra looked round to Isabel lying on the floor. Stephen looked out of it, but Kyra couldn't leave her there.

Stephen suddenly reared up and grabbed Kyra's arm, digging his fingers in painfully. He used her to lever himself up and, still grasping Kyra, knocked Molly to the floor with a hard punch.

He turned to Kyra, blood from the wound that Molly had inflicted pouring down his face, the whites of his eyes and his teeth showing through the crimson as he leered at her demonically. He swung her around to face the water again.

She ducked down to her knees so he couldn't push her over the side and, as she tried to wrestle her arm free from his clutches, patted her other hand around on the wet bathroom floor and finally found cold metal.

She took a swipe and missed, but the second time she felt the blade make contact, scraping along bone in his face; then came the snap of the blade. He yelled in pain and loosened his grip, then fell to the floor, motionless.

Exhausted and weak, Kyra slumped to the ground next to Molly who was groaning by the bathroom door. She put her arms around her niece and held her tightly. Kyra looked over at Isabel, still wrapped up in the duvet. She had opened her eyes and her expression was one of confusion.

Next to them Stephen Fennig lay motionless, a scalpel protruding from one eye socket, the other milky-blue eye staring blindly.

An unbroken circle of silent women surrounded them – Jennifer, Madelyn, Jessica, the unknown woman, Amelia, Skylar, Caylee and Emma. They gazed down lovingly at Kyra, no sadness now, no fear, only peace. She could feel that their pain and anguish had gone.

They smiled as she held Molly and cried her heart out.

Chapter Forty-One

THURSDAY 8 FEBRUARY 2035

9.16 a.m.

Even though her eyes were still closed, Kyra could tell it was a bright day. She felt the cotton sheets beneath her fingertips and the pillow soft underneath her aching head. There was an excruciating pain in her ribs when she inhaled deeply. Should she open her eyes? What if she were to see pink floral curtains . . . a rocking chair . . . a nightlight . . .?

She was relieved to see, instead, the white of the clinical sheets and the hospital monitoring equipment next to her bed. On the wall in front of her a screen was on silent, an antiques programme showing ugly ceramic figures with outrageous price tags.

She'd made it out of that hellhole, somehow.

Where was Molly? Had Isabel survived? Her memories of last night hadn't kicked in yet, as though her brain needed time to reboot.

'Kyra . . .' Jimmy sat in the chair next to her hospital bed. He pulled himself upright and shuffled the chair closer. 'You're awake,' he said softly.

She lifted a few fingers, waving a feeble hello.

'Molly?' was all she could manage to say.

349

'She's here . . . downstairs . . . in another ward. She's going to be fine.'

Kyra took a deep breath, winced and then smiled.

'He injected her . . .' she began, an image of the mortuary drawer burst into her mind, the syringes, the horror when she had seen Molly lying as though dead. The hairs on her arms stood up.

'We know. The doctors are taking good care of her. Your mum is with her. She's going to be okay.' He fiddled with his Commset. 'I promised your mum I'd message her when you woke up.'

'Isabel?'

He opened his mouth to speak, but the door was flung open and two children burst in, a young boy and a little girl.

Kyra's whole body stiffened, accentuating her pain. A swarm of anxiety overwhelmed her. *No, no, no! I thought all this would end, when he was caught . . .*

Why was she seeing them now, after it was all over?

'Are you . . . alright?'

But Jimmy wasn't talking to her.

The children stopped still and stared at Kyra. The little girl pointed at her and said something unintelligible.

'Are you in the wrong room?' Jimmy asked.

He could see them!

Kyra exhaled, relieved.

A woman bustled in carrying a balloon, a water bottle, a potted plant in gift-wrap paper, a child's rucksack and a handbag. 'Grandad's next door!' she chastised, juggling all the items she was carrying to free up her own hand so that she could take hold of the younger child. 'I'm sorry, all these doors look the same. So sorry.' She pulled the children towards the door, apologised again and they all shuffled out.

Kyra's heart was beating hard, the pain in her ribs throbbing in time.

'Isabel's going to be fine, too,' Jimmy said, 'thanks to you. She's in the ICU, but she's doing well.'

Kyra lay back on the cool cotton, a glimmer of relief breaking through, one that she knew she would relish once she was out of pain and the exhaustion had passed, when she'd had time to make sense of everything that had happened.

Finally, she dared to ask the question that she was afraid to. She needed to know.

'Did we get him?'

'You got him,' he said quietly, firmly, his eyes gleaming. She let that sink in for a moment.

'Is he . . . did he . . .'

'He's in the hospital wing of a secure prison for now, but he's going down for good.'

She closed her eyes again, content, and let herself relax into the mattress.

Safe now.

She opened her eyes and was met by his concerned expression. He looked away quickly.

'Jimmy, what's wrong?'

He shook his head in reply, 'Nothing, everything's fine.'

'He's not getting out, is he?

'No, no.' He patted her hand.

'I'm going to be okay, aren't I?'

But he took a little too long to answer.

'Jimmy?'

'We'll have to see how things go when you are out of here. Your brain has been through a trauma. We can't even scan you. The MOD confiscated CASNDRA.'

The very idea of the lab made her feel physically ill. But the thought of her tech, all her hard work, taken by people who couldn't even begin to understand its applications, its effects, its consequences, ignited a rage in her.

Without the kit, Fennig, the man who had killed her beloved Emma, murdered and mutilated all those women, and ruined so many lives, would never have been caught. Isabel Marsden wouldn't be alive. Justice would not have been served.

She couldn't allow herself the luxury of imagining what good the tech might have been able to do in the future in the right hands.

But what price had she herself paid? How long would it take her to recover? Not only from the fear and stress of being attacked by Fennig, but from the side effects of the technology?

'We could build a new one?'

'Come on, Kyra, don't you think the tech has done enough damage? We can't let this happen to someone else . . .'

'What do you mean, not let this happen to someone else?' she said alarmed. 'Jimmy, I am going to get better, aren't I?'

His eyes met hers.

'These phantoms, they'll go now he's been caught,' she said. Was she trying to convince herself or him? 'They're psychological projections, caused by trauma. That's all. Now the stress is off . . .'

'You're the neurologist . . . there might be more to it than that.'

'No. I'm going to be fine,' she insisted.

When he didn't say anything, she repeated, 'Jimmy, I'm going to be fine! We'll find somewhere new to work together, when I get out of here . . . start our own business . . .'

'Yes, yes.' He nodded. But she knew him too well.

There was a knock on the door.

'Jimmy, don't tell them . . . Please.'

He didn't answer.

Kyra's mother pushed Molly into the room in a wheel-chair. Jimmy stood up. 'I'll give you guys a bit of space,' he said and kissed the top of Kyra's head gently before leaving.

Once the wheelchair was close to the bed, Molly launched herself out and flung herself across Kyra.

'Oh my God, Ky, Ky!' she cried. Kyra put her arms around her and held her tightly. It made the pain in her ribs worse, but it was worth it.

The look on her mother's face reminded her of the time she was eight and had got lost in the park – simultaneously angry and relieved.

'Is she alright?' Kyra asked her mum, rubbing Molly's back.

'The doctor says it's out of her system now. We'll have to keep an eye on her, but she'll be fine. They've set up a counselling and support programme for her.' Her mother's voice rose half an octave. 'The pair of you have had me out of my mind!' she cried. 'Honestly, love, you've been acting so strangely lately. That bloody Tom Morgan! You're always upset when he's around.'

Tom . . . did he know what had happened last night? Had he checked his Commset, seen her missed call? She couldn't remember.

'Sorry, Mum.'

'I think you'd better come and stay with us for a while,' her mother insisted. 'The doctor says you're going to have to take it easy and you'll need someone to look after you . . .'

'Maybe, only for a while, though.' Kyra smiled.

'I lost Emma. I thought I was going to lose you two as well,' her mum whispered. Kyra took hold of her hand.

Molly sat up. She appeared more cheerful now, although her face was white with dark shadows under her eyes. 'Are you going to come and live with us, Ky? That'll be great! We can watch films, share clothes . . .'

'We'll talk about it when I'm out of here,' she said.

'Come on, that's enough for now. Let Kyra have a rest,' her mother added.

'We got him, didn't we, Ky?' Molly's face was serious and childlike at the same time.

'We did, Mols. Nice work with that hammer,' she said, the corners of her mouth turning up into a smile. Molly beamed.

Kyra turned serious then. 'He'll die in prison.'

'It's what he deserves,' Molly said flatly.

'We'll come and see you later,' her mother said, turning towards the door.

'You were great,' Kyra said as her mum wheeled Molly out.

Jimmy came back in and sat on the chair next to the bed.

The screen in front of them was showing a newspop of Fennig's arrest, footage of Linden House. It looked very different in the daylight, with police vehicles on the garage forecourt and officers swarming over it. Nowhere near as terrifying as it had been the previous night.

Memories began swimming in her mind like jetsam that she had deliberately discarded, but were now washing up on the shoreline of her consciousness – the banging sounds as the police broke down the door, people shouting her name, her own voice, screaming as she saw the peri-med – the uniform terrifying her, shouts of 'she's here!' as they unwrapped Isabel from the duvet, herself wrestling with a peri-med who was trying to help Molly.

Then Tom, his arms around her, holding her, his soothing words.

She remembered clinging to him as he helped her down the stairs, Molly being carried out on a stretcher and placed in the ambulance, but after that . . . she didn't recall.

'Tom came for me,' she said simply.

'He rang me, told me what had happened, that they'd brought you here.'

'Did he say anything else?'

Jimmy looked down and then up again. His eyes met hers. 'He said he was sorry.'

She nodded. 'It doesn't matter now, anyway.'

At that moment, Tom came onto the screen.

'Volume up,' Kyra said.

Yes, mistakes have been made, and we must take responsibility for some of that. Our department is fully committed to working with all witnesses without prejudice to bring about swift and safe convictions. David Lomax's appeal will be heard today and, depending on the outcome, we will accept burden of compensation, but that being said, we were up against a criminal who was determined to make it look as though Lomax had committed the crimes and, in that respect, this has been an unusual case . . .

'Screen off,' Kyra said wearily.

'You need your rest,' Jimmy said. 'Get some sleep. I won't be too far.'

Kyra watched him leave and then closed her eyes. It had been good to see him and her mother, but to hear that Isabel was doing well and to see her beloved Molly gave her a deep joy and satisfaction.

She was exhausted and her head throbbed, so when she heard the door open again, she kept her eyes closed in the hope that whoever it was might go away, leave her to drift off.

She felt the pressure on the bed as the person sat down next to her and then they began to stroke her hair.

'You used to stroke my hair and hold my hand when I was little and I couldn't sleep.'

That couldn't be Molly, could it? She had just seen her mother push the wheelchair out.

355

It was a woman's voice, only a whisper, familiar although somehow she couldn't put her finger on who exactly. She felt so weary. Her mind wasn't functioning the way it used to. She would have to accept that now.

'You always cared for me so well. Love like that goes on for ever.'

It couldn't be, surely? Kyra didn't want to open her eyes and break the spell.

Instead, she wanted to lie there, let everything wash away, forget about Fennig, Tom, CASNDRA. The rhythmic stroking of her hair gave her a deep sense of peace.

'Thank you for saving my Molly.'

Kyra felt tears of happiness brimming underneath her eyelids. She was finally free of all the guilt. Molly was safe. Fennig was behind bars where he couldn't hurt anyone ever again.

It had all been worth it.

Kyra felt herself falling, falling.

'You go to sleep,' Emma whispered. 'I'm going to look after you now.'

ACKNOWLEDGEMENTS

Writing a book takes a long time, longer than I realised, but it is a task I was prepared for long before I wrote the first sentence.

I owe gratitude to so many.

My mum, Norah, gave me a love of books and stories by reading to me every night as a small child, encouraging me to go to the library regularly, and giving me my very own bookshelves in my bedroom.

My dad, Terry, gave me the confidence to be myself, and my life motto, 'Reach for the stars and you might land on the rooftops.'

My elder brother, Damian, gave me a curiosity for serial killers and forensic science (the books he read and the films he watched, not his actual activities.)

My younger brother Justin gave me the support through the writing process as he was working on his PHD dissertation at the same time and I can think of no one better to have been my writer-support-partner.

The writers' groups I have belonged to gave an ear and constructive criticism to my work in its early stages; Rose Lane Writers, The Inklings and the Wordsmiths.

My friend Sarah Parry gave me encouragement, honest feedback and support when I was trying to emerge as a writer. I don't think I could have done it without her.

My brilliant agent, Nelle Andrew, gave me a chance (although she slept on it!) and then she put me through my paces and knocked me into shape so that even though with no formal training in creative writing I was ready for the challenge.

My wonderful editor, Sam Eades at Trapeze, saw potential and gave me the chance to pitch an idea. Sam encouraged me to keep learning and striving to write the best story I could.

My other wonderful editor at Trapeze, Phoebe Morgan, who gave me the confidence to get over the final hurdle.

I'm so lucky to be surrounded by my friends – beautiful, intelligent, funny, capable women who give me constant love and support - Poppet, Mary, Maz, Cath, Mags, Claire and Fran.

And last, but not least, my family, Seán, Paddy and Tadhg, for their support, love, understanding and patience – you're my world!

CREDITS

Trapeze would like to thank everyone at Orion who worked on the publication of *Witness X* in the UK.

Editor
Phoebe Morgan

Project editor
Shyam Kumar

Copy-editor
Nicky Jeanes

Proofreader
Anne O'Brien

Editorial Management
Alice Davies
Jo Whitford
Charlie Panayiotou
Jane Hughes
Jake Alderson

Production
Fiona McIntosh
Katie Horrocks
Claire Keep

Design
Lucie Stericker
Loulou Clark
Joanna Ridley
Nick May
Rabab Adams
Helen Ewing
Clare Sivell

Audio
Paul Stark
Amber Bates

Contracts
Anne Goddard
Paul Bulos

Marketing
Sarah Benton
Tom Noble
Anna Bowen

Publicity
Maura Wilding
Alainna Hadjigeorgiou

Sales
Jen Wilson
Victoria Laws
Esther Waters
Frances Doyle
Ben Goddard
Georgina Cutler
Jack Hallam
Ellie Kyrke-Smith
Inês Figuiera
Barbara Ronan
Andrew Hally
Dominic Smith
Deborah Deyong
Lauren Buck
Maggy Park
Linda McGregor
Sinead White
Jemimah James
Rachel Jones

Jack Dennison
Nigel Andrews
Ian Williamson
Julia Benson
Declan Kyle
Robert Mackenzie
Sinead White
Imogen Clarke
Megan Smith
Charlotte Clay
Rebecca Cobbold

Operations
Ben Groves-Raines
Jo Jacobs
Sharon Willis
Lisa Pryde
Lucy Brem

Rights
Susan Howe
Richard King
Krystyna Kujawinska
Jessica Purdue
Louise Henderson

Finance
Jennifer Muchan
Jasdip Nandra
Afeera Ahmed
Elizabeth Beaumont
Sue Baker
Tom Costello